THE
ELDRITCH
CONSPIRACY

CAT ADAMS

THE ELDRITCH CONSPIRACY

A Tom Doherty Associates Book New York

This is a work of fiction. All of the characters, organizations, and events portrayed in this novel are either products of the authors' imaginations or are used fictitiously.

THE ELDRITCH CONSPIRACY

A Tor Book
Published by Tom Doherty Associates, LLC
175 Fifth Avenue
New York, NY 10010

www.tor-forge.com

Tor® is a registered trademark of Tom Doherty Associates, LLC.

ISBN 978-0-7653-2874-8 (trade paperback)
ISBN 978-1-4299-4826-5 (e-book)

First Edition: January 2013

Printed in the United States of America

0 9 8 7 6 5 4 3 2 1

DEDICATION AND ACKNOWLEDGMENTS

As always, first and foremost, this book is dedicated to Cathy's loving husband, Don, and Cie's equally loving son, James. Also, to our family, friends, and readers, and to all those people who have made serious mistakes and have owned up to them and tried to make it right. It's not easy, and it deserves kudos.

Our thanks to all of the people who help a book like this make it to print. To our wonderful agents, Merrilee Heifetz of Writers House and Lucienne Diver of The Knight Agency, our brilliant (blindingly) editor, Melissa Singer, and all of the unsung heroes at Tor who work so hard on our behalf. There are too many to name, but we do appreciate everything you do.

Finally, a brief nod to Angie, who was kind enough to let us use her maiden name for Bruno's first love. We appreciate it.

AUTHORS' NOTE

The Guardians of the Faith do not exist. We made them up. They are of no particular religious conviction and aren't meant to depict any. We needed an extremist group who would use religion as an excuse for their actions, so we created one. Because of where we placed our fictional kingdom of Rusland in Celia's reality, King Dahlmar is a member of the Russian Orthodox church, but the Guardians of the Faith are not in any way meant to be connected with that or any other church in *our* reality. The ritual Akkan is also a product of our imagination. Too, while there is, sadly, serious turmoil along parts of the U.S./Mexico border in our reality, and actual drug tunnels exist, the drug lords in this book are not based on any actual people, living or dead. The names were made up at random based on common Latino names. Similarly, the tunnels are not based on any real locations.

Cathy is a big fan of comic books. Cie is a huge fan of comics-based movies. There are nods to both DC and Marvel in this book, should you care to find them.

Also, in case anyone was wondering, the cat poster in the GA office exists. Cie owns it. The sign about the end of the tunnel is directly copied from a sign posted on a student's locker at a law school where Cie worked over a decade ago. Alas, we can only credit it as "Anonymous," but we know that we are quoting.

THE
ELDRITCH
CONSPIRACY

1

We were running out of time.

We'd crawled into the tunnels two hours ago, planning to be underground for only an hour. We'd planned to use the drug lord's own ATVs—parked in the main tunnel—to haul ass across the border, arriving in the United States near Calexico. It wasn't a great plan, but better than waiting for the cartel to tear apart the village looking for us.

But things had changed. Roving groups of guards had forced us into the side tunnels. Luis had assured me they would lead us to the same place and that the trip would only take a little longer. But we'd gotten turned around twice and now there was only an hour left before sunset.

"I need to rest, Celia. Please, can't we stop and sit down for a second?"

Serena's whisper made me flinch and I stole a moment to look at her face. She was nearly as pale as the vampires I feared would rise when night fell, and I didn't doubt she was in a lot of pain. I eased some of my irritation by remembering what it had felt like to walk with a broken leg in a makeshift splint.

"We don't have much time, Serena. We have *got* to get you to safety." My voice was likewise a whisper. It wasn't just that she was a nice person who deserved to get home to her family in Milwaukee, which she was—but she was the last employee of MagnaChem's Mexico City plant and if she didn't make it out alive, I didn't get paid my full fee.

She let out a small noise that was part whimper and part swear. She stopped walking and I had to as well unless I planned to drag her. I couldn't carry her—the tunnel simply wasn't big enough. We had to crouch slightly to keep from banging our heads on the support beams, and two people barely fit, standing side by side. Raising a hand to push the sweaty hair from her face, Serena began to beg. "I know. I do. But just five minutes. *Please.* Don't we have a charm left?"

Maria turned and looked at me with concern. We did have one. But there was a problem. "Yes, but we *only* have one Blackout charm left and we need it to cancel the noise of opening the tunnel exit. We'll be vulnerable when we crawl out if anyone hears."

Serena nodded and bit at her lip, then took a deep breath of stale air and stepped forward, leaning heavily on me, trying not to drag her shoe through the hard-packed dirt because noise echoed down here. I could tell she was mulling over the situation. I'd carried her in the main tunnel, when I thought we were going to use the ATVs. The main tunnels were smooth and wide, with concrete floors and excellent lighting. But this branch was almost claustrophobically narrow, the chiseled stone broken only occasionally by hand-fitted support beams of raw wood. The dim lighting was from low-wattage bulbs strung on wires along the ceiling, about half of which actually worked. The ventilation wasn't great, either. I was sweating heavily enough that the blouse beneath my jacket was sticking to my body and my bra was soaked.

Going into the tunnels where local priests told us the vampires live had been crazy. But desperate people take insane risks. After six weeks in Mexico, "desperate" was definitely a word that described me.

Ahead of us, Luis raised his hand and stopped cold. I likewise stopped while he listened. If I weren't so tired, I could have amped up my hearing. One of the nice things about being partially a vampire was having enhanced senses. But I was just so damned *tired*. It was all I could do to keep trudging along. Even my adrenaline rushes only brought me back to near normal.

After a long moment, Luis eased backward and lowered his voice to where he could barely be heard. "We're nearing the main tunnel again, but there are guards. If we stay here for five minutes or so, they'll pass and then we can reenter the good tunnel."

Beside me, Serena let out a relieved breath. So, she would get her rest after all. I took a breath and helped her to a sitting position, making sure her leg remained as straight as possible. It was swelling badly but there wasn't anything we could do until we got to a doctor or healer. I'd long ago expended every charm in my medkit on the others

I'd already gotten to safety, ferrying them one at a time across the border.

Maria, Luis, and I took up perimeter positions in the near darkness. There would be no rest for us. At least I'd had the good sense to make sure a priest blessed not only me, but also my weapons and ammunition. Vampires laugh off regular bullets. They don't laugh at holy items. They don't find fire amusing, either, which was why Luis was wearing a homemade flamethrower.

I really, really, hoped he didn't have to use it. A blast from the flamethrower would use up oxygen better left for breathing, and I didn't relish the thought of a possible cave-in if one of the support beams got badly damaged.

I shuddered in the dark, painfully aware of the not-quite-corpses "sleeping" somewhere in the tunnels. "I'm afraid of vampires," Serena whispered. "Present company excluded, of course."

I turned from watching behind us to glance at her. "Any sane person is. I sure am." That seemed to surprise her enough that I elaborated. "I've killed my share. I wouldn't be alive otherwise." Even though that was only partially true. "And I *am* still alive. The master vampire who bit me didn't finish the job." I have prominent, pointed canines, death-pale skin, and some enhanced healing abilities, among other things. But I still have my soul and mind. Most bats don't. That was another one of the reasons I *really* wasn't liking these tunnels. It wasn't just that I was afraid of feral bats, I was afraid of *becoming* a feral bat.

I felt, rather than saw, something in the darkness. Maria

stirred next to me, just a little flutter of the rope that bound us to each other so we didn't wind up getting separated.

"What's the problem, Graves?" Maria's voice was the barest breath of sound in my ear, a surprise since she's under five foot one and I'm five foot ten in my bare feet. I guessed she was standing on her tiptoes. Luis likewise moved closer until we were a mass of bodies, like elephants circling the wounded and vulnerable members of the herd.

Maria Ruiz Ortega had started this adventure as my guide. She'd felt she owed me a favor after I saved her brother Lorenzo's life (and missed my own flight out of what amounted to a war zone because of it). Luis was her other brother. They were astonishingly good looking, charming when they wanted to be, and absolutely deadly. Luis seemed like he was probably full human, but unless I missed my guess, with the full moon, Maria shifted. Werewolves are tough. Very tough. Between me, her, and a good flamethrower, if there was a way of getting out of this alive, we would.

I didn't answer, just used my arm to hold her back. Someone was coming. They were moving very quietly, their footfalls nearly silent on the smooth concrete floor to our left. Sunset was close and my inner vampire was ready to come out to play. In the past year I've gotten much better at controlling my blood lust and other abilities. Stress makes it harder, but here and now, they were useful. I could smell the faint scent of Maria's soap, her brother's sweat, and the rubber inner tube we'd used to secure Serena's broken leg to the boards.

More important, I could hear the pounding of their hearts and the tiny, frightened gasps from the wounded woman on the floor. And another heartbeat, one that was slow and steady. And close.

Maria helped me get Serena to her feet without even a whisper of noise. I pulled one of my knives from its wrist sheath and cut the rope that connected us. If we had to fight, or run, we needed to be able to move independently. Then we waited quietly.

There was a muffled crackle of radio static from less than a foot away and then a burst of Spanish that my mind translated efficiently. "Garcia, do you see them?" Before I came down here, my Spanish had been minimal, but I learn quick. I now understood every word coming over the man's radio earpiece and every word he spoke.

"No. I'm only fifty yards from the exit and there's no sign of them. Either they got away or they're still back in the tunnels somewhere. It's almost dark. What are our orders?"

A pause while we each held our breath. "Two more minutes, then we evacuate and seal the tunnels. If they're in here, the bats will take care of them."

"What about the boss's whore?"

"If the Abomination hasn't already eaten her, leave her. Paulo said he's tired of her bitching anyway." There was a muffled snort of laughter in front of me. Maria stiffened beside me, her lips peeling back from her teeth in a silent snarl.

So, this had been a trap from the beginning. Only the fact that I refused to cooperate, hadn't allowed myself to be led where Maria had wanted to go, had kept us alive this long.

There was a soft gasp from Luis as he realized the truth. She had planned to lead him to slaughter. But his gasp wasn't soft enough. I felt the air shift as the man in front of me turned.

The moment he was in range, I leapt, bringing my knife up at an angle. If he was tall, it would catch him in the guts; if average height, it would hit under the ribs. I put my all of my weight behind the attack, because if he was wearing a spelled vest, the knife might not get through at all.

He wasn't tall, and the spells on his vest weren't a match for my strength, along with the magic of a knife that qualifies as a magical artifact all by itself. The knife slid in and I felt his weight start to sag as wetness poured out over my hand. He tried to shove his gun into me but I slammed my hand onto it and his shots went down, ricocheting off of the floor and into the alcove.

Luis swore in pain and startled anger, and I smelled that he'd been hit by a stray bullet. I was just glad none of the ricochets had hit the tank strapped to his back.

The scent of blood was everywhere. My vision sharpened, my canines elongated. Saliva filled my mouth. I wanted blood. I wanted it like I've never wanted anything in my life. I heard the rattling sound of the bat in a nearby alcove taking his first breath of the evening and I hissed at him on pure instinct. The vampire part of me wanted to bite down on the neck of the man I'd gutted while the last flicker of life left his body, to taste the warm, salt-sweet flavor that was like nothing else in this world.

But no. I was human, damn it. I would not feed from a human. Never.

There was a flash of blinding light, a whooshing noise, and flame roared out of Luis's homemade flamethrower, filling the alcove, setting the waking vampire ablaze as Maria and her brother stumbled past me.

The heat was horrendous, breath-stealing. I could only whisper a silent prayer of thanks that we were near enough to the main tunnel that we could still breathe after the blast. I gasped, the nauseating smell of burning hair and flesh filling my nose and lungs, making me cough till I gagged. As suddenly as the blood lust had come, it was now gone. My stomach lurched; I pulled my knife from the guard, flinging his body to the ground.

Distant screams echoed through the rocky tunnels. The vampires were rising and some of the human guards hadn't made it out.

Oh, fuck a duck.

I picked Serena up by her waist and tossed her over my shoulder like a sack of potatoes. She didn't complain. We ran. By the light of flickering flames I could see the fork in the passage that led to the open desert outside. I could smell the sand. Twenty yards to the fork, so maybe thirty past that to the outside. We were nearly there. But closing fast from the other direction were vampires, newly risen and hungry for blood.

Maria stumbled and Luis went down with her. Luis

struggled to his knees, trying to get off a blast from the flamethrower. Then a pair of vamps was on him. They rode him to the ground. Fast, they were so fast. Serena turned her head, saw him bleeding, and screamed. The bats looked up, eyes glowing. I didn't doubt mine were as well because everything was in hyperfocus. I managed to pull my gun, but I was having to aim carefully so as not to hit the tank, and with Serena kicking in panic, it was hard. Luis's scream of agony cut off abruptly as the larger male broke his neck with a single vicious twist.

Another pair of bats, two females, surged forward. Maria began firing wildly, not aiming—which was useless. Grabbing her arm, I flung her ahead of me.

"Run!" I screamed, as I fired blessed bullets into the vamps to slow them down. It wouldn't stop them entirely, but I needed to buy us enough time to get to the cave entrance. Once there, I'd shoot the gas tank with a tracer round. The explosion would take out the vamps and, if we were lucky, block the tunnel entrance behind us.

Just a few more steps. I twisted, firing over my shoulder, struggling to stay balanced while carrying Serena. I pulled the trigger again and again until the gun clicked empty. I was almost to the exit. I could see the stars above and smell cactus and sage. So tantalizingly close now—but they were gaining on us.

A bat grabbed at my leg, causing me to stumble and nearly drop Serena. I kicked the bat in the face until she let go but that gave the others time to get closer. There wasn't time to pull out the derringer in my ankle holster.

Thankfully, I didn't have to. Maria had reached the cave entrance ahead of me. She'd pulled herself together, and though there were tears streaming down her snarling face, she stood, gun drawn, feet solid. She wasn't aiming at me. "Go, Graves! Get Serena to safety. They won't follow. I swear."

She waved me past, giving me a shove in the back with preternatural strength that sent both me and Serena sprawling a dozen feet from the tunnel exit. I pushed to my feet and screamed, "Maria! Get out! You can still make it." Even as I yelled, the bats leapt toward her. Crap.

She didn't go down when they hit. They hung on her, fangs embedded in her snarling form. One hand braced over the other, she took careful aim and sent a tracer round back into the tunnel. I followed the blaze of fire as it flew straight and true, right into the tank of her brother's flame-thrower.

I threw myself over Serena to shield her from the blast, but I had to look back. The explosion was pretty spectacular, imprinting red onto my retinas and turning Maria, Luis, the guards, and a dozen bats into charcoal.

Yes, she'd betrayed us, but Maria Ruiz Ortega had found her path to redemption from Paulo and his cartel.

2

The explosion attracted the notice of the U.S. authorities. They arrived in record time: Border Patrol, DEA, CIA. The hole in the desert floor was a popular place for the next few hours. I didn't know any of the agents, but I had a few friends in high places I could call on to convince the guys on-site that I was trustworthy and on the side of the angels. It also helped that I had my current passport, concealed carry permit, and FBI consultant badge hidden in zippered pockets sewn into my pant legs. Modesty be damned. I was out of those jeans in two shakes to get to my IDs once I was in custody and in a clean, well-ventilated holding cell.

The paperwork helped more than the friends, I think.

"Just one more time, Ms. Graves. How were MagnaChem and the drug cartel connected?"

I sighed. "As I have said to the last four people who asked, they *weren't*. I was guarding new management who were sent to the MagnaChem plant after the CEO was arrested and her board was replaced. Paulo Ortega just happened to decide to use the same town as a base, so the arrival turned into an evacuation. Serena Sanchez was the last employee out. Paulo was *very* annoyed that I managed to keep him from getting his hands on rich Americans to use as hostages. He'll also likely be annoyed that I told the agents on the scene how to find the drugs and guns I spotted in the tunnel." The man questioning me nodded, just as the four other agency representatives had. Then he left, and I sat, waiting for the next interrogator.

Finally, a day later, after painfully thorough debriefings by each of the agencies, I was allowed to go home. The agent who escorted me out of holding let me know that Serena had been airlifted to a hospital and undergone surgery on her broken leg.

I nearly wept when I saw my beach house, I'd been gone so long. This was probably my longest out-of-town job to date and it had definitely been one of the most tiring.

My first call was to my attorney, Roberto Santos. When I'm traveling out of the country and have no idea when I'll be back, I have my mail forwarded to his offices. For a hefty fee, the nice secretaries and accountants attached to his firm pay my bills, respond to crank letters and fan mail, and deal with most other types of problems. Roberto was one of my friends in high places—he's a very well-known attorney in government circles, which is why he's *my* attorney.

"Anything to report, Roberto?" I couldn't help but smile as I sank into my favorite recliner with a tall glass of crystal-clear water. After weeks of drinking liquids that I tried not to think about too hard, I was thrilled to have water without things floating in it. I mean, really. Water shouldn't come with *chunks*.

"Nothing other than what you already know. You certainly caused a stir this time. Three different agencies are torn between giving you a medal and charging you with obstruction of a government operation."

The water took on a bitter taste. "I hope you convinced them a medal was more appropriate."

He chuckled. "What I convinced them is that with you involved, all of the agencies had both plausible deniability of the deaths at MagnaChem and access to a large cache of weapons and drugs to splash on the front pages. I also *suggested* that you wouldn't claim any credit in the press. I hope I can count on that."

A snorting noise came out of my nose and I nearly spit water across the floor. Instead, I swallowed and replied, "No problem. They're welcome to the credit. I'd rather nobody even knew I was there."

"I thought that might be the case." I heard a voice in the background and realized I might have interrupted him.

"If you have an appointment, we'll talk later. I need a few days' rest anyway."

"That sounds perfect, Celia. I'll get your mail service restored and include our bill in the first batch. Be warned, it'll be rather large."

That made me laugh. He's nothing if not honest. Another reason I like him. "Well worth it, in my opinion. I'll be adding your bill to *my* bill to MagnaChem. Charge what you will."

I drank my water slowly, savoring it, and turned on the television to catch the latest news. Big shock—there was no mention of a small town being overrun by drug cartels just over the Mexican border. No breaking-news alerts about the murderous bastard who intentionally herded people into tunnels to be slaughtered by vampires. There were stories about similar atrocities in Africa, Indonesia, and the Middle East. Just not too close to home. Heaven forbid.

I nearly turned off the set, but stopped when the next story came on: an update on the M. Necrose pandemic that had begun sweeping across the country a few months earlier. I'd been one of the first victims of a bacterium that turned people into zombies. I turned up the sound.

"Mortality rates have dropped for the first time since the outbreak started," the silver-haired anchor read from his prompter. "Los Angeles General reported only five new cases this month and all were in early stages, treatable with antibiotics. The crematorium here in Santa Maria de Luna had only one disposal this week." The anchor took a breath as a graphic appeared on the screen: a color-coded map of the United States, showing the heaviest concentrations of the disease. "Every U.S. state now has reported cases, with the exception of Alaska and Hawaii. Officials at the Center for Magical Disease Control speculate that extra security measures for flights into Anchorage and Honolulu might have stopped the mages who were hired to infiltrate the schools."

Wow. The CMDC had gone mainstream since I'd been gone. That's the problem with having no access to television for weeks. It used to be that the magical branch of the CDC in Atlanta operated in secret. I hadn't even heard of it until I was exposed to the disease. The general belief was that the public would panic if it learned there were magical diseases that could spread to the human population, so nobody had ever mentioned that the agency existed.

It was true that there had been mass panic when the first cases appeared and there was no cure. People died. Lots of people. But we'd adapted. It had taken months, but parents were sending their kids back to school. Church attendance was up and telecommuting was giving way to heavy traffic. Pity about that part. I had liked the lack of traffic jams.

"The M. Necrose pandemic has now become the fourth deadliest disease outbreak in history, surpassed only by the Black Plague, the Spanish Flu, and the Bird Flu. Next up, sports on News Center Eighteen."

I turned off the TV then and took another long drink of water. It was as though I'd never been gone. The world had gotten along just fine without me. I leaned back into the cushions and listened to the sounds of the ocean through the open screen door. I might have dozed off; I'm not sure. Suddenly I heard a bang, started, and looked out the picture window to see my neighbor, Inez, at my door. She was wrapped in a towel.

Inez used to be the housekeeper for my best friend, Vicki Cooper, who had owned both my beach house and Cooper Manor, the mansion at the top of the hill. When Vicki died, she left me the beach house and left the mansion to Inez and her husband, David, who had been the groundskeeper. I trusted them to keep an eye on my place and to water my plants in my absence.

I opened the door with a smile. I hadn't seen her since well before leaving for Mexico. "Hey, Inez. How have you been?" I opened my arms to give her a hug but she just motioned behind her with a thumb.

"I was pretty good until your *puppy* dumped seaweed in my pool. I was swimming at the time."

That was when I looked outside. "Crap!" One of the abilities of a siren, besides being able to mentally influence some people, is an affinity with the ocean. I'd been away from the water too long in the Mexican jungles; my control was fuzzy.

So thinking about the ocean just now had caused the water to move inland. My cousin, Adriana, the Pacific siren princess, told me this was a common problem when sirens come into their power. The sea follows us. The water was up to the bumper of my car and had indeed dumped seaweed into the lower swimming pool. There's an upper one as well, but Inez prefers the lower one because it's on the beach. I doubted that seaweed was all that had been dumped in it; there were probably a few buckets of sand and a variety of small sea creatures playing there now. "Oh, man. I'm so sorry, Inez. I'll clean it up."

I must have looked pretty stricken at the prospect of cleaning up after my mistake because she shook her head with a note of amusement. "It's okay. Go swimming. It'll follow you back." I tried to protest, but she was firm. They would change the water, and I should go swim. "Really.

David's been meaning to scrub down the bottom. We'll open the drains and let the water go back out to sea."

One of the things I like about David is that he never uses chemicals in the water, so he *could* let it drain back to the ocean with the blessing of the State of California's environmental offices. Vicki had installed a very expensive reverse osmosis filter for the pool, so the water going out would be perfectly safe for whatever creatures it encountered.

I vowed to add a thousand to the amount I'd offered them to watch the house. Refilling the pool isn't cheap and despite her protests, I knew David had changed the water right before I'd left.

After writing myself a reminder, I changed into my suit and went for a swim. The tide rolled out with me, following me into the water.

There really isn't any way to explain what it feels like to swim in the ocean. Once my body cooled to the temperature of the water, it was as if every wave was an extension of me. I dove through the breakers and swells until the surface was nearly flat. There wasn't much of a breeze and the sun warmed my hair. A porpoise appeared and chuckled at me—probably commenting on the waste of using my arms. Feeling playful and relaxed at last, I played with the porpoise, diving right alongside his sleek gray form. We came out of the water nearly simultaneously, then dropped back in again. We must have done this about ten times before he bobbed his head in approval, tittered, and swam away to join a group that was tail-walking in the distance.

I floated on my back for a time while the seagulls overhead swooped and dipped in approval. I'd been away from the ocean long enough to pine for the sea, and yes, to miss my noisy feathered friends. One of them flew down fast, as though dive bombing a ship, and I nearly dropped under the water to avoid being hit. But it slowed at the last second in a fluttering of snowy wings and delicately dropped a tiny pink conch shell onto my bare stomach. Then it flew back up to join its fellows overhead. How sweet. A gift from my admirers.

I have weird admirers.

I suppose I should have called some people to let them know I was back. But I really wanted peace and quiet for at least a day or two. So I put my new conch shell on the mantel with the others I'd collected over the years, called out for pizza since my fridge was bare, and opened a bottle of wine.

I thought a lot about the wine before selecting a simple California white, ignoring the magically enhanced red I'd come to relish. I couldn't drink that wine right now, not without conjuring up a whole lot of bad memories. I didn't want to think about the man who'd created that wine. Not today. Maybe not tomorrow, either.

It took two more days of swimming, sitting on my favorite rock overlooking the water, and just padding around the house before I felt ready to be part of the real world again. Finally I dressed and headed for the office one morning instead of the beach. I was looking forward to a nice, normal day dealing with a backlog of telephone calls and paperwork—and chatting with Dawna, my smart, savvy receptionist, who is also one of my best friends in the world.

I run a private security business out of an office on the third floor of one of the last historic buildings in downtown Santa Maria de Luna. It's an old, red-brick Victorian with gingerbread trim, a wide front porch, and a balcony on my floor that lets me get fresh air while offering partial protection from the California sunshine. Once upon a time it had been a stretch to afford the rent. Prices in Santa Maria aren't as bad as in Hollywood or L.A., but they're not cheap, either. After I inherited the building (and the headaches that go along with owning commercial property) that wasn't an issue. I hadn't even known Vicki had owned my office building until after her death.

Pulling into my reserved spot in the parking lot, I found myself smiling. God, it was good to be back. I couldn't wait to get back to normal, or as close to it as I could manage. Dawna's car was in its usual spot. I wasn't surprised. As receptionist, Dawna wasn't scheduled to start for another hour, but she gets into work early more often than not. Maybe we'd get a chance to talk before the day's craziness started.

Ron's car was not in his spot, for which I was grateful. One of my tenants, Ron is an attorney and an ass, but not in that order. I really wasn't in the mood to deal with the level of bullshit his attitude creates.

Gulls swooped and dived overhead as I climbed out of the car. They cawed and performed aerial acrobatics, trying to get my attention. I smiled and made a shooing gesture. "Go play. I'm going to be inside all day."

Anyone watching would be amused to hear me talking to them. They would be shocked to see the gulls obey, swooping one more time before flying off toward the shore.

Dawna must have heard them, or me, because the minute I opened the door, she raced toward me and pulled me into a hug.

"Thank God, you're *back!*" I grunted a little as she squeezed me tighter. Dawna is petite, but apparently she'd continued the workout schedule she'd started before I left because she was much stronger than she had been.

She held me at arm's length, long enough for her dark eyes to take in every inch of me from head to toe. "You look like hell, girlfriend. What *happened?*"

I tried for humor. "I look a lot better than I did two days ago. I even trimmed the singe off my hair and scrubbed off the blood." Her eyes widened but I didn't elaborate. I wasn't ready to talk about it, so I made a show of looking her over in turn. I might look like hell, but she looked great. Part of it was just good looks. She's part Vietnamese and has the kind of exotic features that attract a lot of attention. She also knows exactly how to make the most of her assets. Today she wore a black pinstripe skirt suit with a snow white blouse, accessorized with a delicate diamond necklace and matching earrings. And of course there was that big honking rock on her finger.

After a whirlwind romance I sort of instigated by realizing, while on a date with a certain guy, that Dawna would make a much better girlfriend for him, she was going to become Mrs. Christopher Gaetano. Being engaged definitely agreed with her. She was practically glowing with joy.

I was happy for her, but thinking about it made me all too aware of the absence of John Creede from my life. "There's too much to talk about without coffee. Besides, if you have a minute, there are a couple of things I'd like to discuss with you."

"Uh-oh. That sounds ominous." Releasing me, she gave me a wary look and turned away to shut the door.

"It's not bad." I gave her a smile. "I promise."

"Good. You head on upstairs. I'll forward the phones to the service and pour coffee." She gave me a gentle push toward the stairs, followed by a shooing motion that was almost identical to the one I'd given the gulls.

"Thanks, Dawna."

"No problema."

The familiar words brought back my smile—a smile I held on to clear up until the moment I was standing outside the open door of the empty office on the third floor where John Creede had created the magical wine currently sitting undrunk in my beach house. Though he'd had other offices, he'd rented this one to be close to me while we were dating. The room was empty now; the floor was damaged where someone had pulled up the temporary flooring that had been where he'd performed his magic.

He was really gone.

Shit.

I blinked back tears. I was *not* going to cry, damn it. Absolutely not. I'd done what I had to do. I really did believe that. I'd do it again. But it didn't make it hurt any less seeing that empty office, remembering when Mexico had started to really go wrong.

"What do you mean you reassigned him?" I kept my voice down. The office door was closed, but the walls of the building were none too thick and I didn't want anyone overhearing this argument.

"I decided I needed to have Jorge help with the spell work on the vans."

"*You* decided you needed? And you didn't see any reason to check with me first, even though I'm the one in charge? Humberto was depending on Jorge to watch his back, and I assigned Jorge to him precisely because he could cast a protection spell in case there were booby traps. Which there were, so now I've got an injured man. What the hell, John!"

John gave me "the look." It was an expression I'd seen far too much of over the past couple of weeks: superior to the point of condescending. The men had seen it, too. It was undermining my authority with them and with the clients. People had begun to run my orders past John before actually following them, and to obey his orders before mine. That was unacceptable.

He spoke carefully, as though addressing a

child . . . or at least that was how it felt. "You hired me for my expertise."

Really? When did I say that? "No, Creede, I hired you because you have good men and good equipment, and I thought you were capable of following orders. Apparently I was wrong about the last part." I spoke softly, but my voice was cold enough to frost the windows, despite the Mexican midday heat.

His face darkened, anger making his golden eyes, filled with magical flame, flash menacingly. "We both know you *needed* to hire me, Celia. You're not qualified to handle this kind of project. Bodyguard, sure. But a full-fledged evacuation with a multiperson crew? I can't believe you agreed to handle the evacuation without a soul to back you up. Remember, *you* called *me*. Hired me to cover your ass so you didn't embarrass yourself in front of the clients."

Embarrass myself? *Embarrass* myself? Oh, no. Oh, so fucking no. "I called you because you had people available. Maybe I didn't mention you weren't my first choice. I called because your business has sucked lately. Remember that part? That I said on the phone I wanted to do *you* the favor of a quick paycheck? But screw it. You're fired. Get your Miller & Creede people together and get your butts back to L.A."

"You wouldn't dare," he said in a dangerous,

venomous whisper. I could actually feel the power of his magic building in the room, rising like scalding water.

I met his eyes without flinching, without backing down. "I'll have Dawna cut you a check for the days you've actually been on the assignment."

In a fit of pique, he'd taken both vans and all the contractors except Maria, Luis, and Lorenzo. It had floored me that he would risk people's lives that way. Totally unprofessional.

And very likely unforgivable.

But I'd gotten them all out. By myself. The only person who would be embarrassed by that was John Creede. The tricky part was going to be figuring out how to get the word out that I'd succeeded without "taking the credit." That little bomb hit me as I stared at the empty room.

"Celia." Dawna's voice brought me back to the present. "Are you okay? You look . . . odd."

I didn't feel odd. I felt hurt, sad, humiliated, and *pissed*. John and I had been fairly serious. I'd really thought he respected me as a person and as a professional, and that we'd be able to work well together. Apparently I'd been wrong. It hurt. A lot.

She passed me over a cup of steaming coffee. "Do you want to talk about it?"

"Not yet." Again, maybe never.

The eyes that met mine were worried. "Okay." She sounded doubtful. "If you say so."

"I do."

I was spared further discussion by Ron's baritone bellow from downstairs. *"Dawna!"*

"Oh *hell*," she muttered. Ron may not be my favorite tenant, but Dawna loathes him. Of course, since she's the receptionist, she bears the brunt of most of his bad behavior. More than once he's driven her close to quitting or to violence. He thinks his law degree makes him superior to the rest of us mere mortals. He's an autocratic, demanding bully, but he pays his rent on time and ponies up for building maintenance without too much complaint, so I've put up with him.

I laughed. "Good to see some things haven't changed. Go. I'm all right."

"But we were going to talk." She cast a filthy look at the staircase.

I knew she didn't want to go down there. I couldn't even blame her. But it was her job. Like it or (obviously) not. "We will. Later. Go."

With a huge sigh, she flounced down the stairs and back to work.

Later was a lot later. Ron kept Dawna hopping all morning and I wound up having an unexpected visitor.

"I need you to find my daughter."

The sunlight streaming into my office through the balcony windows wasn't being kind to the woman seated across the desk from me. Laka is from the Isle of Serenity, home of the Pacific sirens, and usually she looks lovely, thanks to her Polynesian coloring and features and a wide, easy smile that can light up a room. But she wasn't smiling today and there were lines of worry on her face, which I'd never seen before. She was dressed simply and wore no makeup, her hair pulled back in a thick braid that hung down her back. She looked old and tired. Then again, she probably was. Sirens can live a long time, and if her teenage daughter, Okalani, was missing, Laka probably wasn't getting much sleep.

I weighed how to respond. I'd met Laka's daughter a couple of years earlier when I'd been on Serenity on business. Okalani had a remarkable talent—she was a strong enough teleporter to be able to transport groups of people. She'd saved my life, and the lives of a lot of other people, using that gift. And while she had an attitude problem— what teenager doesn't?—I'd kind of liked the kid.

I wasn't surprised she'd gone missing. From the first moment I'd met her, she'd made it very clear that she wanted to get off Serenity and find her long-lost father and brother.

"Have you talked to her father?"

Laka gave a frustrated snort. Granted, contacting Okalani's dad was an obvious thing to do. But you'd be surprised how often people don't actually *do* the obvious.

"He won't take my calls. I went to the address in the telephone directory. His ex-wife says he's gone, and good riddance. I thought she might be lying, but there are initial divorce papers filed at the courthouse."

"What about your son?"

Her expression saddened, growing haunted. "My son is dead. He was killed in a vampire attack after one of his high-school football games."

"I'm so sorry." I was, too. Few football games are held at night because of the risks, but with the days so short in the fall and winter, sometimes games end after dark. The police do the best they can, but accidents happen. Tragic.

"Thank you. Losing him to Ricky was hard. But his death . . . perhaps you can understand now why I tried so hard to keep Okalani from coming to the mainland."

I did, actually. The siren Isle of Serenity has never had a vampire, never known a werewolf attack. The mental control the queen has over the island residents would force them to leave. I could understand Laka's desperation, knowing her daughter was on her own in circumstances unlike anything she'd ever experienced. That didn't mean I could help her. "Laka, I'm a bodyguard, not a private investigator. But I know of a couple of reputable—"

"No," she interrupted me. "Please . . . Okalani likes you, she trusts you." I started to explain that I wasn't trained to find people, but she interrupted me again. "But you're very good at uncovering the truth, Princess." Okay, now she was interrupting thoughts I hadn't spoken. Was she was rummaging around in my head?

I intentionally let my thoughts about her daughter go blank, focusing instead on the room. The curtains at the balcony doors were open, letting in lots of bright sunlight that gleamed off the wide, white trim of the baseboards and made the pale peach walls look even paler than usual.

I loved my big desk, which had two visitor chairs facing it; there was a second seating area in one corner, with a couch, a side chair, and a low table. Behind me was a large gun safe. Painted a dark forest green, the safe was a new addition to the office décor, and one I wasn't entirely pleased about.

I saw Laka's face register confusion for a moment before she looked directly at the gun safe. *Got her.* Sirens are telepathic. The "siren call" people talk about is a psychic compulsion, not some sort of music in the air. While it's considered extremely bad manners to intrude into other people's heads willy-nilly, many of the sirens I've met do it a lot.

Most of them can carry on conversations both audibly and mentally with equal ease. I've had to work hard to get good at that, but I don't really like doing it unless it's an emergency. It creeps people out. Hell, it creeps *me* out. I still haven't mastered keeping others out of my thoughts. Then again, I'm only one-fourth siren and my abilities were brought out by the bite of a master vampire who was trying to turn me. I may technically be a siren—and the multi-grandniece of Queen Lopaka—but I hadn't had a clue about that part of my heritage until the bat bite.

Laka eavesdropping on my thoughts without permission ticked me off. A lot.

Stop it! I growled the words in my head. I was sorely tempted to show her the door, enough so that I started to rise from my seat.

Laka flushed, but kept talking, desperation forcing her

words out in a rush. "Hear me out, please, Princess. Ricky, Okalani's father, has always been clever and charismatic. Charming enough to win people over, to convince them of whatever he wants them to believe. He talks his way into good jobs, and people who meet him would swear he isn't capable of stealing or conning people out of their money. But he is."

Something swam through her dark eyes, some memory that she wasn't yet ready to reveal—and I wouldn't dive into her head to pry it out. I sat back down, inhaling the thick scent of flowers that surrounded her. "When he was with me, on Serenity, I used my powers to keep him in check. Too many of my fellow sirens would have been easy pickings for Ricky, since at that time money didn't have much value on Serenity. I didn't allow him to take advantage of people. He hated that. He said I was manipulating him, making him into someone he wasn't. In a way, he was correct. I could make him *do* what was right. But I couldn't make him *want* to do it. Perhaps I was wrong to try to make him become a more ethical person. He grew to hate me, and to hate all sirens, because of what I did."

"So you sent him away."

I tried not to put any particular emotion in my words, but my feelings probably showed in my mind. I don't like that the sirens have historically considered men nothing more than tools of procreation. Their female-centric culture throws away male partners and male children like so much trash.

Laka's chin came up, her expression conveying pride, stubbornness, and hurt. It was an old wound, but I could tell from her expression that it still ached. "I did. I let him take our son, but I kept Okalani away from him."

I thought back, remembering what she'd said to me the first night I'd met her, the night Okalani had teleported herself onto my friend Bubba's boat. I'd nearly killed the youngster, thinking she was an enemy intruder.

"You told me before that he was bitter about being sent away?" I made it a question.

She sighed. "Yes. He was . . . is. It makes no sense to me. He hated me for making him law-abiding, but he hated it even more when I rejected him."

"And you think he'll take it out on your daughter by rejecting her?"

She shook her head and her expression grew hard and grim. "Oh, no. He won't reject her. He'll *use* her."

The way she said that . . . an image appeared in my mind. A darkened building, figures in black, and a floor-to-ceiling vault door. Whether it was my own vision or projected into my head by Laka, I suddenly understood why she was so panicked.

"You think he would use Okalani's gift to steal things?"

Her jaw tightened, like it wasn't something she wanted said out loud. But I'm like that. If it can't be said out loud, it shouldn't be thought. "I would rather not think he is capable of outright theft."

A moment's thought provided all too many ways Okalani

could be of terrific use to a con man and thief—the possibilities were endless. A simple variation of the old shell game, where instead of being palmed and moved, the ball would simply disappear into Okalani's hand while she stood several feet away. An apartment full of priceless antiques one minute, the next . . . empty, the thief chatting with the owner throughout the robbery. A murder suspect seemingly in two places at once, with witnesses in both places. I hid all that in my mind as best I could, and erected what few barriers I knew to keep Laka out. She didn't need to know how dark my thoughts were.

The siren looked beseechingly at me. "Please, Princess . . . please help me find my daughter."

Scooting back my chair, I opened my center desk drawer and pulled out a leather case that held alphabetized business cards. Flipping to "P," I selected one from the mix of private investigators and handed it across the desk. "Call Harry Carson. He's one of the best I know. I'll do some looking around and I'll talk to Okalani if I find her, but he'll find her if I can't."

She took the card and stared at it with relief plain on her face. Dark eyes filled with gratitude raised to meet mine. "Thank you, Princess. If there's anything I can ever do—"

I flinched involuntarily for at least the third time since she arrived. "Actually, there is." I rose and stepped around the desk.

She raised her eyebrows and cocked her head as I walked past her to the door, turned the knob, and opened it. My meaning was obvious; Laka stood and headed for the exit, pausing when we were inches apart to repeat, "Anything."

I sighed and looked at her wearily. "Stop calling me *Princess.*"

3

It was my morning for siren trouble. After Laka left, I started sorting through my messages, trying to put them in order of priority. The most important, and worrisome, were the multiple messages from Lopaka and her daughter Adriana. I knew Adriana was in the process of planning her weddings, plural, to King Dahlmar of Rusland. Other than sending an RSVP—regrets for the daylight ceremony on Serenity, because of my vampish skin problems; a big yes to the church ceremony in Rusland because I've always wanted to see Europe—I had no connection to the wedding. Since Adriana and I aren't close, that was no surprise.

Still, they were calling. Eight or ten times each. That meant there was a crisis of some sort. Crap. I so didn't want to deal with whatever it was. I wanted to ease back into my life, try to make some decisions about my future when I wasn't caught up in the crisis of the moment. But there you go. I picked up the phone and dialed the number Hiwahiwa, the queen's assistant, had left, and got *her* assistant, who told me that the queen was unavailable, but would call me back at her convenience.

So I hung up and dialed Adriana.

Now my great-aunt and I get along well, despite the fact that she's royal, and I'm an American and pretty irreverent besides. But Adriana? That's a whole 'nother story. The princess can be very . . . princessy. A diva's diva. She has a crown and an attitude, and definitely knows how to use both. On top of that she was busy getting ready for the impending nuptials, so I figured I'd get shunted off to an even longer line of assistants. Instead, she answered herself and on the first ring.

"Hello?"

"This is Celia Graves—"

She interrupted me before I could finish. "Celia, thank God! Tell me you're back from Mexico." She spoke in a rush, her voice breathless. At a guess I'd have said she was desperate, but that was so out of character as to be completely unbelievable.

"I'm back."

"Oh good." The relief in her voice was palpable. What the hell was going on? "How soon can you make it down to the docks? We need to talk."

I glanced at the wall clock. Not even ten thirty, my first day back, and I was already hip deep in crises. Not a record for me, but close. "Give me an hour."

I grabbed my Bluetooth earpiece and headed for my car. I might as well make a couple of calls on the way. I had to leave a message on Bruno's voice mail, but got hold of

Emma. A clairvoyant, she wasn't exactly surprised that I'd made it back, but she did sound hugely relieved. She didn't admit it, but I was guessing she'd "peeked" in the mirror she sometimes used as a focus. If she'd been watching me in Mexico, she'd probably gotten quite the eyeful.

We didn't chat long. She had a class to teach and traffic was getting heavy enough that I needed to concentrate on my driving.

Despite the traffic, I made it to the marina with time to spare. I knew my way around from back when a good friend kept his fishing boat here, so it was easy to find Adriana's slip. Actually, it would have been easy for anyone who knew anything about sirens—all you had to do was follow the gulls. They led the way, soaring and swooping and cawing with excitement, to the nicest yacht in the place.

Calling Adriana's vessel a boat was like calling the Hope Diamond a pretty rock. Her ship was freaking *huge*, with hand-carved teak and brass fittings. The stairway was steep. Not a gangplank—actual *stairs*. Everything was elegant and perfect, very much like Adriana herself.

Though I had to admit she wasn't entirely perfect. As Queen Lopaka's only daughter, Adriana should have been heir to the throne. Unfortunately, she wasn't siren enough, because like Emma Landingham, she was a clairvoyant. "True" siren talent can't coexist with any other paranormal or magical abilities, so she would never take her mother's throne. Worse, she probably had already seen in a vision just who would.

Fate can be so cruel.

She would never rule the Isle of Serenity, but Adriana was every inch a princess. It's all about the attitude. Today she was wearing big movie-star sunglasses, a man's dress shirt in white, blue jeans, and boat shoes. On her, it all looked like the height of fashion. Her long red hair had been tied back in a loose tail that did not distract from the amazing bone structure of her face. She was stunning. On my best day I don't look that good. That bothers me more than it probably should.

Adriana met me at the gangplank and invited me on board.

"Thank you for coming on such short notice." She smiled, and dolphins began jumping and playing in the water next to the boat. Overhead, my seagull escort wheeled and cawed happily before settling down on various high spots to watch.

Ever the gracious hostess, Adriana led me to a pair of built-in benches around a small table near the entrance to the cabin area. "Would you like something to drink?" She signaled and a servant instantly appeared from somewhere. "We'll have brunch now."

"Of course, Princess." He bowed low, backing away.

She sat and drummed her manicured fingers restlessly on the tabletop.

I waited for a little bit, letting her squirm. But I'm not really all that patient, and at the rate she was going, it would be next week before she got past the pleasantries. "Why don't you just spit it out?"

"Excuse me?" She blinked, obviously shocked.

I smiled. I didn't get an advantage over her often. She's

been trained to be poised in almost any situation. But it was obvious she needed something and just as obvious that she was not used to having to ask. I realized that it was highly likely that people had been anticipating her needs and whims since she'd been old enough to walk, maybe before. That explained a lot. If that was the case, she really wasn't nearly as annoying as she could have been.

"You brought me here for a reason, and there are no assistants around, so you must need to speak with me alone. Just say whatever it is you need to say. You won't offend me. I promise." I smiled again to take any sting out of the words.

She laughed. "Don't be so sure. I seem to recall the first time we met, our conversation didn't go well at all."

She was right, of course. I'd accused her of being unpardonably rude and she had challenged me to a duel to the death. Then again, she'd disrupted my best friend's wake to sing a torch song. "No," I admitted, "but we've come a long way since then." I didn't exactly like Adriana, but I'd seen enough of her that I'd grown to respect and admire her. I think she felt the same about me.

"Yes, we have." She relaxed a bit, giving me an honest smile. "It's because of you that I met my fiancé. Because of you, I may become queen of Rusland."

"Will," I corrected. "You *will* become queen."

She met my gaze. "It's still *may.* Apparently, it depends entirely on you."

Oh, fuck a duck, I thought, but managed a much more appropriate, "Excuse me?"

Adriana laughed, hard. It occurred to me, belatedly, that like most sirens, she was a telepath. She'd heard exactly what I was thinking. *Oops.*

She laughed harder, until she had to wipe a tear from the corner of her eye. "Oh, my. All right, then. I guess you won't be offended after all. So I'll . . . spit it out."

Of course, that was when the servers appeared. Servers, plural. One carried a tray bearing a frosted pitcher. The other was toting a tray of foodstuffs, many of them blended and presented in tiny glasses or semiliquids served on individual plates.

Only when everything was just so and the servers had disappeared did Adriana communicate with me. And this time, rather than speak the words aloud where anyone might overhear, she spoke to me mind-to-mind, in the way of the sirens.

There are no assistants because I have none anymore. Both were killed two days ago when a bomb went off in the shop where they were making the final arrangements for my bridesmaids' dresses. The shop and the dresses were completely destroyed, but that is nothing compared to the loss of life.

The people claiming responsibility call themselves the Guardians of the Faith. They've made threats. I have asked my dearest friend to step aside as maid of honor, because I need you to be. I know it sounds ridiculous. And I realize it is on obscenely short notice. But my mother's prophet, as well as my own visions, have told me that I need you to be by my side—not just as a bodyguard, but as a part of the wedding—if I am to be safely wed.

There have been other disruptions besides the bombing. My jet was tampered with and crashed. Thankfully the crew survived. There have been plots to discredit me in the eyes of Dahlmar's people and to create a royal scandal involving him. There was even an attempt on my life with poison.

People had died. These fanatics were serious. But obscenely short notice was right. The ceremonies were taking place in . . .

Less than two weeks. As I said, it is ridiculous. And I will understand if you are offended that I did not ask you sooner. You are, after all, my kinswoman, and you have done both Rusland and the sirens honorable service in the past. I am embarrassed that it did not occur to me to ask before. You have every right to tell me to go to hell, or even challenge me to a duel.

She was flushed and the hand holding her drink was trembling just a little. She was embarrassed. But more than that, she was afraid. I'd seen her calm and composed in actual battle conditions. But she was well and truly rattled now. That was so not good.

I answered with my mind as well. I always hate to "hear" my mental voice because it's the sharp, bitter caw of gulls, rather than Adriana's sweet song of island birds or her mother's tinkle of crystal bells. *Of course I'll help. I'd be honored to serve as both your maid of honor and your bodyguard. I'll need everything your people have on the Guardians of the Faith.*"

"*I'll have Kar—*

She stopped abruptly in midthought. I felt a flash of pain

and sorrow when she continued. *I'll have someone send the information to your office this afternoon.*

She closed her eyes for a second and I watched as she fought not to sag in relief. She was royal. Royals are not supposed to show that level of any negative emotion, particularly fear. But she was afraid: angry, hurt, sad, and absolutely terrified. Then she looked at me and thought, *I am grateful for your help.*

When do you want me to start?

Is tomorrow too soon? The situation truly is urgent.

I took a brief second to wave good-bye to my plan to ease back into work, then answered. *Tomorrow will be fine.*

Thank you.

I let out a noisy sigh before I replied. *Thank me if it works.* Of course if it didn't, we'd both be dead.

4

I was halfway to the college before I realized I'd been an idiot. I'm a professional bodyguard. I get paid for putting my life on the line to protect people. Yet I'd just agreed to guard Adriana without so much as a word about charging a fee. Admittedly, there are families where everyone respects that the others are professionals and have to earn a living. My experience with my family just hasn't been that way. Mom uses everybody without the slightest compunction. I do all kinds of things for my gran and wouldn't accept payment even if she offered. So it seemed that I'd just volunteered myself for a dangerous and expensive freebie.

Crap. Apparently Mexico had taken more out of me than I thought.

Maybe I could pass it off as a wedding gift. I mean, it's not like she and Dahlmar need another toaster. What does one buy the happy royal couple anyway? I mean, talk about people who have everything! Adriana had her own jet— well, she'd *had* her own jet. Dahlmar had his own *country*.

Pondering royal gift-giving kept my mind occupied until I reached the USC Bayview campus. Once there, I had to keep a sharp eye out for a parking space.

No luck. If I'd gotten here closer to noon I'd have stood a chance of finding a spot someone had vacated on the way to lunch. But it was 1:15, so the lunch crowd was back in class. I wound up driving a few blocks away and parking the Miata in the lot of my favorite restaurant, La Cocina. The owners are friends of mine and they know my car. They might get annoyed at me for parking there, but they wouldn't have me towed.

Before going out into the sunlight I slathered myself with high SPF lotion and grabbed a big floppy hat from the backseat. I debated whether or not to take my umbrella, but decided against it. After all, the paranormal studies building was in easy walking distance. With fresh sunscreen and the hat on I should be able to make it to the building without burning, if I hurried. Which, of course, I did.

Despite the international prestige of the program, the paranormal studies building itself is nothing special. It's roughly U-shaped, with the opening facing the university quad. One wing is all classrooms; the other, the administrative and faculty offices. The part of the building that connects the arms houses the big auditorium. The building's magical perimeter is one of the toughest around—one of the benefits of having lots and lots of mages-in-training who need to practice recharging such things.

The first floor of the building has lots of windows. On nice days like today, the place is bright and sunny and has a great view of the manicured lawns and well-maintained landscaping of the quad. The public spaces had been re-decorated not long ago; they feature cheerful colors and welcoming seating areas. The second floor is a whole differ-ent ballgame. The carpet is charcoal gray and industrial. The pale gray walls are marred with chips and marks from years of heavy use. Metal lockers, built into some of the walls, have been dented and battered by generations of stu-dents. Some of the old-style fluorescent lights were flicker-ing. Maintenance would get around to fixing them . . . eventually. Probably a few weeks after they'd gone out to-tally; sooner if somebody fell down the stairs in the dark.

The graduate assistant offices were in room 212, at the top of said stairs, in what had at one point been the storage room for magical supplies. It was a good-sized room, but I found it hard to imagine that more than a couple of people could work effectively in the space. But there were six names on the door, which was completely covered with a variety of posters and stickers that appeared to be several layers deep. I paused to admire my favorite, one of a train tunnel with the caption, "Due to repeated complaints about it being too dim and too distant, until further notice the light at the end of the tunnel has been shut off. The Management."

The door was ajar, so I peeked into the room, which was beyond crowded with six desks, six chairs, and an assort-ment of personal paraphernalia and teaching materials. I spotted two men and a woman, all looking to be in their twenties, huddled around someone seated at a corner desk.

They were so absorbed in what was going on that they didn't notice that I was standing in the doorway. As I raised my hand to knock, a wave of magic poured out from the group, knocking me back a step as a light show of rainbows danced in the air.

One of the men said, "What the . . ." in a tone that made it clear he hadn't been expecting what he'd just seen.

"I've been working on this artifact for over a year now. Every time I feed it with my blood, it charges a bit more." Bruno's familiar voice was completely calm and patient, despite the fact that he'd just sliced himself open. Of course his magic had probably healed the cut almost instantly. The knives I use are his work. Every day for five years he'd bled himself to create a pair of knives, which my best friend Vicki had then given me as a gift. Five *years*. He'd made the weapons because Vicki was a level nine clairvoyant who assured him that having those knives was the only way to save my life. She'd been right. Still, the dedication, the sheer *love* it took to create something like that floored me every time I thought about it.

"It can be drained if it comes into contact with another, more powerful, artifact. Not likely, since this is a mirror. But the Isis Collar drained a pair of knives I'd worked on for five years, sucked them completely dry in a matter of minutes."

"The Isis Collar is just a myth." The big blond guy stepped back, putting his hands on his hips—an aggressive pose. I recognized the expression on his face. He wanted trouble and was looking for a fight.

"It is now." I smiled as I spoke, making my voice light, trying to defuse the tension in the room. "When Isis took it home to wherever it is goddesses live. But I assure you, it was real."

"Celia!" Bruno leapt to his feet and the others scattered out of his way. He was across the room in three bounding steps, sweeping me into his arms to give me a kiss that left me breathless and blushing, my heart pounding like a trip-hammer. "I have *missed* you." He swung me around so that we were facing the others, his arm protectively around my waist.

"Guys, this is Celia Graves. Celia, these are some of the GAs I work with." He pointed to the scowling blond. "Jan Mortensen," he said, giving the name the Nordic pronunciation, then continuing the introductions. "This lovely lady is Trudy Cook." Trudy was pretty and petite, a redhead with a round face and clouds of curly hair that probably drove her crazy, but looked really good. The smile she gave me was a little forced. I didn't need to be a telepath to figure out she wasn't happy about Bruno's reaction to me. It wasn't just the siren thing, either. No, I'd have bet a fair amount of money that Trudy had a real thing for Bruno DeLuca.

Well, I didn't blame her, not even a little. After all, Bruno's tall, dark, handsome, charming as hell, and a powerful mage. The cherry on top is that he has a real sense of joie de vivre. He sings show tunes and cabaret numbers in the shower. He can dance and he knows more dirty jokes than anyone else I know.

A lot of folks are misled by his lighthearted side and his

heavy New Jersey accent. They think he must be dim or a bit of a thug. In truth, he's very smart and absolutely dedicated to his craft. Which was why he'd been accepted into Bayview's doctoral program . . . and how he'd convinced Dr. Sloan to be his advisor.

"And this"—Bruno gestured to a smaller black man whose close-cropped hair was going prematurely gray—"is Gary Jefferson."

"Hi, Celia." Gary gave me a smile that was a lot warmer and more genuine than Trudy's. "Bruno's told us a lot about you. Glad to finally meet you."

Gary might be glad to meet me and Trudy might be reserving judgment, but Jan, very obviously, was not at all happy. He gave me a frigid look down his patrician nose. While the others were dressed very casually in worn T-shirts and cargo pants or faded jeans, Jan wore an untucked blue-and-white striped dress shirt with the sleeves rolled up to show just a hint of the tattoo decorating his left forearm. It was obvious that shirt had been pressed and starched and the cuffs adjusted just so. It was a look straight off of the runways, as were the jeans with both knees deliberately torn out. Of course I got the feeling everything about Jan was deliberate.

I decided to ignore Jan and to focus on the others. I turned to Gary. "Thanks. It's good to meet you, too."

Gary smiled, then his expression quickly grew serious. "So, I've gotta ask, did you really, seriously, face down a greater demon?"

I shuddered. I couldn't help it. That was one of my worst

memories. "Twice. Not by choice." Bruno's grip tightened a little, and I could easily guess that the look he was giving Gary was something less than friendly. "I don't recommend exorcisms. They hurt."

"Had to be scary," the GA continued.

"It's utterly terrifying, and not something anyone who's been through it wants to talk about," Emma said from the hallway, cold and hard.

"Right." Gary squirmed, then decided abruptly that there was someplace else he needed to be. "Look at the time. I've gotta run. Later, DeLuca. Guys." He brushed past Bruno and me, stepped around Emma, and was gone. As Emma edged into the office and made her way to the one desk in the place that wasn't littered with scattered junk, she spoke very softly, to Bruno. "Just so you know, Professor Sloan was less than a minute behind me."

"Crap." Bruno released my waist and stepped over to the nearest wall. Seconds later he'd vanished, replaced by a battered coat tree with a couple of jackets and an umbrella hanging from it.

It's not that he doesn't like Dr. Sloan. Bruno thinks he's great. But the professor had been running him absolutely ragged when I'd left for Mexico. Apparently, he still was.

"DeLuca!" Dr. Sloan's voice preceded him into the office. "I've had a thought about that table. I want you to—" The short, wiry, elderly man appeared in the doorway. Looking around through thick glasses, he found Trudy, Emma, and Jan working hard at their desks and no sign at all of Bruno.

"Hi, Dr. Sloan. How are you doing?" I said.

"Celia." He smiled broadly and cocked one bushy eyebrow at me. "I'm well. The question is, how are you? Has the curse mark faded?"

"I'm fine. And I can't tell on the mark. Maybe a little. I'm not sure." I held out my hand so he could look at my palm.

"Jan, Trudy, come here. You'll want to see this. It's not often you get to see a death curse of this quality on a living human being."

They obediently came over to examine my palm. Dr. Sloan gave them a brief, esoteric lecture about the nature of death curses in general and of mine in particular—the one that kept putting me face-to-face with said greater demon—before releasing my hand and gesturing them back to work with shooing movements of his hands. Then, winking at me, he turned directly to the coat rack. "De-Luca, you may take the rest of the afternoon off to visit with the lovely Ms. Graves. But I expect you in my office at ten o'clock tomorrow morning, *without fail*. Do I make myself clear?"

The illusion faded, revealing a sheepish-looking Bruno. "Absolutely."

"Good." He turned on his heel and left. But his parting shot could be heard from the hall. "Have fun, kids."

"All right." Bruno turned to the others. "What did I miss?"

"You're kidding, right?" Trudy gave a derisive snort. "The

illusion was perfect. Your work is always perfect. The doctor must be psychic."

I shook my head no. He'd missed something. The illusion was not perfect.

Bruno turned to me. "What?"

I gave him a little smile. "Your cologne. He could smell your cologne. It's very distinctive."

Jan laughed. "Of course."

Bruno's expression darkened. "Hmm. Smell . . . I'll have to work on that." He wandered over to his desk, where there was a hand mirror in a scrolled silver frame lying next to a razor-sharp knife. With a quick, deft movement, he picked up one of the blades and sliced shallowly into his forearm. There was a surge of power as his blood spilled onto the shining glass and was absorbed into it. The cut knit itself closed as I watched. Bruno hadn't even winced.

"That is just so cool." I hadn't meant to say it out loud. I should be used to it by now. I've seen Bruno working often enough. But every time, it just gets to me.

I realized that Jan was glaring at me an instant before he shifted his gaze to the knife and then Bruno's face. Both men looked stubborn, just short of angry, and I had the feeling I had walked into the middle of an ongoing argument. "I fail to understand why you would do this to yourself for her." The blond man made a sharp gesture at me. "You yourself said that she allowed one of the knives you created to be ruined."

"I *told* you"—Bruno's eyes locked with Jan's—"she used

the knife to kill the überbat that attacked my brother. It's not her fault that Lilith had been a spawn before she was turned."

"She was?" That was news to me, but it explained why her death had been so weird. Normally, to kill a vampire you stake it, cut off its head and take out its heart, then have the parts cremated separately and spread over separate bodies of running water. When I stabbed Lilith with the knife Bruno had made for me, she'd burned to ash, from the inside out. It had been *très* creepy and totally unexpected.

"I've done the research. It's the only possible explanation for Lilith's ability to call a priest on holy ground . . . and for the damage to the knife."

Um, wow. Okay. I didn't even know that it was possible for a spawn to be turned. I mean, Spawn are the offspring of a mating between a human and a demon, so they're already monsters. Wasn't turning one into a vampire sort of . . . well . . . redundant?

"So you've said." Jan obviously didn't believe him.

"Jan," Trudy said, sounding martyred, "just stop, will you? You just saw the curse mark, which you claimed couldn't possibly exist on a living human. You've heard the stories about Celia's fangs, read about her in the magazines. Now here she is . . . fangs, curse, *and* in daylight."

"It isn't possible for one person—"

"To be that unlucky?" Emma gave a derisive snort. "You don't know the half of it. If the woman who cursed her wasn't already dead, I'd kill her myself. *Nobody* should have to go through the kind of shit Celia puts up with." She stood and gathered her things. "Now if you'll excuse us, Celia and I have business." She looked from me to Bruno and back. "Unless you're planning on bailing on me?"

I gave a derisive snort. "Of course not." I turned to Bruno, who was still glaring daggers at Jan. "You coming with?"

Tearing his gaze away from the other man, he turned to me. "Nope. You go see the house. I've seen it. We'll meet at my place for dinner at . . . seven o'clock? I want to have plenty of time to get things ready."

"Sounds like a plan to me." I collected another kiss before I left.

5

I **wasn't** sorry to leave. I'd be seeing Bruno later and the tension in that little office had been intense. As we were on our way out of the building, I asked Emma, "What was that all about?"

"If by 'that' you mean my snarling at Gary—"

"No. That, I get. He pushed your buttons when he talked about demons. No surprise, considering your history."

She nodded, her lips pressed in a tight line. "He just won't leave it alone. Demons fascinate him."

"And every time he brings the subject up, it chips away at the magical barrier muting your memories. Have you talked to him about it?"

She sighed. "I have. He's trying to do better. It wasn't his fault I walked in right then." She pushed open the door to the outside and held it open for me.

"Just bad luck," I agreed, then added, "Are you even supposed to park here?"

We were in the faculty lot and Emma was leading me to her father's assigned spot, which was occupied by a big black SUV. "Normally, no. But since Dad's in Cairo this year, he isn't using it, and I needed to borrow his Suburban. I figured since you were coming to the house anyway, I'd get you to help me move Vicki's big mirror. I don't really trust the movers with it."

That made sense. It was a full-length mirror in a big wooden frame, both awkward and heavy. She didn't need to worry about breaking it, though. It had been spelled until it was pretty much impervious to anything. So the problem wasn't with the mirror; it was human nature. Like my knives, the mirror was a major magical artifact and thus valuable as hell. People have killed for that sort of thing and many more would be happy to steal it. Emma had inherited the mirror from Vicki because she had been the only other person in our circle with clairvoyant abilities. Emma's not that powerful, a level four I think, but the mirror has helped her focus, so she's getting more control and better results, which is, in effect, the same thing as moving up a level or two.

"Do you mind?" she asked.

"Of course not."

"Oh good." Emma smiled, pointed the little black keyless remote at the SUV, and pressed the button. Beeping ensued, as did the popping of the door locks. She gestured to the passenger side. "Get in before you start burning."

I waited until she'd maneuvered the SUV out of the tight parking space before I brought up Jan Mortensen. "What's with him? Did he, like, not believe I existed?"

She groaned, then answered. "Jan Mortensen is very

talented and is a complete and total ass. I don't have any proof, but I'm pretty sure he's sleeping with one of his undergrad students."

"Eww." I gave a low whistle. While not unheard of, that was completely unethical and a firing offense if he got caught. Which apparently he hadn't . . . yet. Since Emma's a by-the-books kind of gal, and her father's one of the program administrators, I could understand why she was upset about it. "It's one thing not to believe all the stories about me. But he actually seems to hate me. Why?"

"I've no clue, but you're right. He's practically irrational on the subject. He and Bruno don't get along well because of it."

I almost felt like I should apologize, which was just silly. Mortensen's attitude problem was his problem, not mine. I'd never met the guy before today.

We chatted amiably all the way to Emma's place. She caught me up on Dawna's wedding plans and I told her about becoming Adriana's maid of honor. Finally, I got around to bitching about my fight with John Creede.

Emma hadn't heard we were on the outs. She paused for a long moment after I'd told the whole sad tale—up to the firefight and our escape through the tunnels. "You know," she said, "I almost feel sorry for the guy."

"*Excuse* me?" I stared across the seat at her, eyes wide.

"I mean it. You call him for help. I bet he figured you wanted him to be your white knight, charging in to rescue the damsel in distress—when in fact, you only wanted an efficient subcontractor with excellent equipment. That had to be a blow to the ego of the top guy in the game."

I spluttered. I couldn't help it. *A white knight?* Seriously? So not me.

She shook her head, grinning. "A lot of other women would've been angling for the rescue. Probably more than one had done just that. Set up a situation where only he could fix the problem."

"I'm not like other women."

"Amen to that." She laughed, then continued, "But anyway, I can see how he got his signals crossed and wound up grumpy."

"He wound up more than grumpy."

"So did you," she pointed out. "And when you get grumpy, you occasionally overreact. Like . . . kicking him out of the country when you had people to get to safety?"

Well, that was true enough. We rode in silence for a few minutes. I finally said, "I am perfectly capable of running a large team."

"Well, *duh*. Of course you are. Nobody said you weren't."

I didn't answer. She's a bright girl. She connected the dots and turned to me with shock clear on her face. "Tell me he didn't! That *bastard*." Emma's face flushed and her eyes blazed. If John Creede had been here now, she'd have given him an earful, no doubt about it.

"He's not completely wrong, though." I started reciting the facts. "Glinda offered me the job to get me out of town, not because I was qualified. The company kept the offer on the table because nobody else would take the job—including Miller & Creede. In fact, there's a good chance MagnaChem hired me because they figured I'd drag Creede into this. It's not like our relationship's exactly been a secret."

Emma pulled the SUV into her father's long driveway. "Okay, I can buy that." She cast a glance my way. Her expression was thoughtful, almost stern. In that moment she was every bit her father's daughter: cold, logical, and brilliant. "But let's look at this logically. You got everyone out, right?"

"Yes." It had been damned close, and hard as hell. But we managed it.

"Even after you fired his ass and had no replacements?"

"Yes."

"And the only injury occurred when John disobeyed your orders?"

"Yes."

"Other than you being left behind because you saved that local, everything went smoothly once you had a team that did what you told them?"

"Yes."

She made a voilà-type gesture, then slammed the Suburban into park just outside of the garage door. "Then you're capable. And he's an ass."

We didn't talk much for a while after that. First, we were mirror wrangling. Second, she'd given me a lot to think about and was giving me time to digest it. Still, I could sense her excitement from the moment we pulled out of the driveway; it grew steadily as we got closer to her new place. Her eyes lit up. Her fingers started tapping against the steering wheel. Hell, she was practically bouncing in her seat.

We rounded one last corner, and there it was.

Wow. Just . . . wow. I live in the guest house of a mansion and I've been in and out of some pretty magnificent homes because of my work. But Emma's place . . . it wasn't a mansion. It was a church. Okay, it was a small church, but it still probably took up most of an acre. Located on the outskirts of town, it was a beautiful old stone building with a pair of bell towers and gorgeous architectural details. It probably wasn't old enough or important enough to qualify for the historical society mission trail, and it was too small and outdated for a modern congregation. The church and grounds were surrounded by a gated wall; as we drew up to the gate, I spotted a parking area on the east side and a small cemetery on the west. I wondered who had been buried there—perhaps the very first missionaries stationed there?

"Is it decommissioned?" I was wondering if the place still qualified as holy ground.

"It's in the process," she said with a smile. "But even after the paperwork's done, this place has seen years and years of daily masses and prayers of the faithful. I've been told by a church authority that the prayers have sunk into the stone itself."

Wow. I whistled as she slowed the SUV. "It'll probably take a hundred years for that kind of protection to wear down." Emma would be safe—safe from vampires and demons. It wouldn't be anathema to werewolves, but that was a good thing, since her brother, Kevin, turned into a wolf with the full moon.

"Welcome to my Fortress of Solitude," Emma quipped. Hitting the button on the garage-door opener she'd clipped to her sun visor rolled back a gate that looked like wrought iron, but was probably heavy-duty, spelled silver steel. There was barely enough time for her rear bumper to clear the perimeter before the gate began moving back into place. And that perimeter! As we crossed it, the magic hit my senses like a ripsaw, making me yelp in unexpected pain. I've been able to sense the magical perimeters around most buildings for a while now. Most barriers are no big deal. The better ones are a little uncomfortable. But this . . . wow . . . and OW.

"Damn, girl, who did your spell work?"

"Kevin had somebody do it. It's seriously over the top, right? The wards aren't lethal, but only because I insisted." She shook her head.

I paused, trying to come up with a tactful way to ask a very personal question. Kevin had been my friend. Maybe he still is. We've had our issues, but I still care about him. He's a tough SOB, but sometimes even tough isn't enough. Things happened to him that nobody should have to go through. It left him with a bad case of post-traumatic stress disorder. Paranoia was just one of his issues. "Is he getting therapy?"

"Yeah. But I'm not sure how much it's helping." She

stopped the car. I saw tears in her eyes as she turned to me. "I'm really worried about him, Celia, but I just don't know what to do. He's been through so much. Most of it he can't or won't talk about, even to a therapist. I want to help, but I have no clue how."

The unfortunate truth was that there probably wasn't a lot we could do other than be there for him and be as supportive of him as we knew how to be. Of course in my case, being supportive might actually be better accomplished by my absence. How much did that suck?

I opened my mouth to say as much, but she held up a hand to stop me. "Don't. Just . . . don't. It isn't your fault. None of it is."

Then why did it feel like it was?

"Celia, he was in black ops. No matter how bad the crap you're involved in gets, none of it is as bad as what he got into on his own. Remember, he was going on missions with Jones and the others for a decade before he even met you. He's seen things that would put the rest of us in the psycho ward. And you weren't the one that got him put in the zoo. You're the one who got him out."

"The zoo" was what most folks called the jail for werewolves and other preternatural types. It had been a really high-tech, highly spelled installation out in the desert. Had been, until it was taken over by demons. Now it was a layer of glass and blasted earth.

I didn't know what to say, so I changed the subject. "So, how did you find this place?"

She blushed and I just knew there was more to it than

she was willing to tell. Instead, she backed the SUV into the spot closest to the front walkway. "Wait till you see the inside. Kevin's been helping me renovate. Some of the stuff he's installed is just so *cool*."

"I don't doubt it." Kevin's background has given him access to all the best toys. Besides which, he works in IT when he isn't running around being a soldier of fortune. He's a serious geek with major skills in all sorts of areas.

We wrangled the slab of glass from the back with me holding most of the weight. Emma set down her end of the mirror and pressed her palm against a recessed reader. When a button flashed green, she typed a five-digit code onto the keypad. I heard the click of the locks opening.

She pushed the door open, and we carried the mirror inside and set it down in the entryway. I took another step, into Emma's new private domain.

It was gorgeous. The décor was the perfect marriage of tech and classic design. All but one of the stained-glass windows had been replaced with frosted, so the open main area shone with light. The remaining stained-glass pane sent patterns of color across planked wood floors that were beautifully rustic. It *felt* wonderful; peaceful, positive energy just seemed to emanate from the place.

"*Oh, Emma.*" The intonation of my words made her smile broaden.

"You like it?" she asked eagerly, practically hopping from foot to foot with excitement.

All I could do was make an incredulous noise and nod. I finally found my voice as my eyes danced over the detailed architecture around the top of the wall. "Are you kidding? I *love* it. Give me the tour."

The more she showed me around, the stranger something seemed. Everywhere she mentioned a wall had been repaired or damaged door frame had been replaced, I noticed a particular pattern to the placement of the nails. Finally, I couldn't contain my curiosity any longer. "Is Kevin the only person who's been helping you with the renovation?"

She blushed and turned away. It was a simple question and had she simply answered it, I wouldn't have thought any more about it. But her reaction made it clear to me that she was getting construction help from Matteo DeLuca, one of Bruno's brothers. He's a Catholic priest and my guess was that he'd helped her find the church in the first place. He's performed both of my exorcisms, so he would understand why it was important that Emma be on holy ground.

He had also helped Bruno and me work on my beach house after a spell went awry and damaged the floor. I'd noticed that he put in the nails in a slightly zigzag pattern that he swore he'd learned from an old book. He said that old houses stood so long because the nails weren't hammered in right in a row so they never split the planks. The pattern was very distinctive and easily recognizable.

But it was her reaction that I found even more interesting. It gave her away and was the reason why she couldn't answer me directly. If Matty was in regular orders, his helping her wouldn't be a problem. Regular priests are able to have relationships and get married. But the militant orders have always required vows of celibacy. ....

"You are *kidding*! You and Matty? O-M-G!"

Her red cheeks remained. "We haven't told anyone yet. They can't approve his transfer to regular duty until after he becomes Bishop. Until then . . ."

"He has to remain celibate," I finished for her. "Bummer."

"Actually, it's okay." She smiled and it lit up her face. Oh, she was so gone for this guy. It made me happy. Matty is a great guy. But oh Lord, Mama DeLuca would have a fit. Emma's no more her idea of the perfect daughter-in-law than I am, and Isabella DeLuca is a force to be reckoned with.

I raised my brows, not speaking my concerns. But she just continued to smile.

"Really. He's worth the wait. Besides, it's given us the chance to get to know each other better, to not rush into anything. Between him and Bruno, I've heard so much about the family that I feel like I'll be able to recognize everyone once we meet."

If she was happy, I was happy for her. But it felt a little weird that everyone was so happy when I was so . . . well, *miserable*. Why couldn't I be happy with what I had?

All told, my visit with Emma was exactly what I needed after the stress of the day. She was so content and the house gave off such good vibes that I felt completely relaxed and at peace with the world as we drove back to campus.

I should've known it wouldn't last.

6

ave fun tonight," Emma teased as I climbed out of the SUV near La Cocina. I was going to retrieve my car and head for Bruno's, and Emma was going back to the office. She hadn't bothered to pull into the restaurant's parking lot—it was practically bumper-to-bumper in there and there was no reason for her to waste time to get me a few feet closer to my car.

"Oh, I fully intend to." My answering grin was probably a little bit wicked. I was really looking forward to an evening with Bruno. And if that went well, I was looking forward to an excellent *night* with Bruno. "I'll call you tomorrow."

"Okay."

I opened my parasol as I got out of the car, then slammed the door and went around the front of the vehicle to cross the street. I had been well trained in my youth; now I looked both ways, then took advantage of a break in traffic to start across the busy street.

I heard an engine revving and the squeal of tires, and

smelled rubber burning against hot asphalt. Even though I couldn't see the car's grille past the parasol that kept the sun from scorching my skin, thankfully my vampire reflexes had kicked in at the first growl of the motor. I dove for the far curb with everything I had. Normally that would be enough, since I can jump really fast and far with my enhanced muscles and most drivers steer *away* from people in the middle of the street.

But this guy corrected, making it very clear it was intentional. My body was still airborne when the car hit me— probably the only reason I wasn't badly hurt. I landed on the hood and rolled off past the driver's side window, catching a glimpse of the man at the wheel before falling to the street. The vehicle sped off.

Ironically, I landed facedown on the white pedestrian stick figure in the crosswalk. Everything hurt. A lot. And I was pissed off.

Because I knew who had hit me.

"*Oh my God!* Celia, are you all right?" Emma jumped out of the SUV and rushed up as other cars swerved around me. No one stopped, of course.

"I'm okay," I assured her as I pulled myself slowly to my feet, surveying the damage. Thankfully, I didn't seem to have any broken bones. A quick tongue survey of my mouth revealed I'd managed not to lose any teeth, although one fang had cut the inside of my lip.

Blood brings out the vampire in me quicker than almost anything. The smell, unmistakable copper and salt; the taste. Both my rage and my newfound hunger made me want to ignore my human nature and rip into the woman standing beside me. I could hear the rapid beat of her heart, smell the sweat of her fear. *Emma is my friend. She is not food. And I am not a fucking bat.*

I clenched my fists so hard that my nails dug into flesh. My exposed skin was starting to singe—I could smell it burning. I embraced the pain, using it to home in on my humanity. My voice was still a little rough when I asked, "Did you get the plate number?"

I opened my eyes to see her blushing furiously. I guess not. "It was so *fast*." Digging the cell phone from her over-sized bag, she said, "I'll call nine-one-one."

I stopped her with a hand on her wrist. "Don't."

Overhead, seagulls were swooping and cawing, obviously upset. I tried to think calming vibes at them. It didn't work.

"What do you mean, 'don't'?" Emma stepped back, angry and offended. She looked a little like an avenging angel, given her air of righteous indignation and her cloud of dark golden hair blowing in the breeze. "It was a deliberate hit-and-run. Whoever that was tried to kill you. We have to call the police."

When I trusted myself to sound calm I answered her, lying smoothly so she didn't go ballistic. "Emma, it won't do any good. He's long gone. I can't describe the car or the driver. You don't have the plate number." I shrugged. "The last thing I need is more trouble with the police. Please, just let it go."

I could tell she didn't want to listen. But she put her

phone away, lips pressed into a thin line of disapproval, then strode over to where I'd dropped my purse, her sensible heels clicking sharply against the concrete sidewalk.

"You realize you're insane?" she said as she returned and handed me my bag.

"Emma—." My voice held a note of warning. I love Emma, I really do. But I was stressed, I was angry, and the last thing I needed was a lecture.

She gave me a long look through narrowed eyes before lifting a hand in a gesture of reluctant surrender. "Fine, but don't expect me to like it." She would like it less if she knew I was lying a little. I'd gotten a good look at the driver. Emma added, "Let's get inside. You need food. You're starting to glow."

Well, *hell*. That wasn't good. I've gotten a lot more control of my inner bat recently, but stress and physical exertion aren't helpful. I should probably eat something. Not too much; I didn't want to ruin my appetite for dinner. Maybe just one of the special Sunset Smoothies La Cocina makes just for me. "I thought you needed to get back to the office and grade papers?"

"Screw it. They can wait another day. This is important. Go see if you can get us a table while I park the car."

There weren't any tables. In fact, the press of people was such that I had to take refuge on the patio and order my Sunset Smoothie to go. Better to leave, before people started looking like bloodsicles. Besides, I wanted a long hot bath and plenty of time to primp for my date with Bruno. I texted

Emma and told her not to bother coming in. She replied,
"You okay?" I assured her I was, and wasn't staying long. A
minute or so later I saw her SUV pull away.

Thinking about Bruno while I waited for my smoothie
helped me relax a little. It had been a long time since we'd
had an actual date-date. He'd been busy with his studies;
I'd been on a job. And while they may work for other
people, I think long distance relationships *suck*. E-mails,
calls, and texts are just not the same as face-to-face, skin-to-
skin communication. Absence does not make the heart
grow fonder. It makes it grow lonely. At least in my case.

Juan paused as he crossed the patio, carrying a tray laden
with food that smelled like heaven, to hand me my drink,
already in a to-go cup. I forced myself to look away and
took a long pull of my Sunset Smoothie, a concoction
whipped up specifically for me and only available at La
Cocina, where I've been a regular since my first week of
college. When Barbara and her husband found out I'd
never again be able to eat solid food, they took it as a challenge and created something that I could actually drink,
digest, and enjoy. When I first heard what was in it, I was a
little freaked. I mean, cow's blood? Seriously? But it tastes
great and I always feel better after I've had one.

I can try to deny it, but the vampire part of me has different nutritional needs than the human and siren parts. It's a
bad idea to ignore them. Control is about knowing your
limits and working within them, not pretending they don't
exist.

I plunged back into the crowded restaurant, heading for the cash register line to pay the tab. It was a long line, so, rather than waste time being bored, I decided to call Dawna and check in.

"Are you coming back to the office?" She had to shout so that I could hear her over the restaurant noise.

"I hadn't planned on it."

"Crap."

"What's up?"

"There's an Agent Baker here from the Serenity Secret Service. She says she has the packet you requested and needs to brief you before you start your assignment tomorrow."

Shit. I looked at the clock. I didn't have time to go back to the office for a briefing and still get ready for my date tonight. I just didn't. And while most times I'm all about the work, today I wasn't. I *needed* a night off.

"See if she can meet me at the office tomorrow morning early, say eight o'clock? I doubt Adriana gets out of bed that early."

Dawna put me on hold; I'd moved up to the second spot in line by the time she got back to me. "She has another appointment at nine o'clock, so eight won't work. But she can do six thirty or seven."

Six thirty? Really? There must be a lot of information to cover. I did some quick calculations in my head, considering travel time from either my house or Bruno's, and made a decision. "Tell her seven o'clock is as early as I can do."

"I'll let her know."

We hung up without saying good-bye and I paid my tab,

then headed out the door, still sucking on my smoothie. But I was especially careful crossing the parking lot and I used the little button a friend in the FBI had given me to make sure nobody had tampered with my car.

It's not paranoia if they're actually trying to kill you.

7

After the hit-and-run, it took a little effort, but I succeeded in pumping myself up once more. I kept telling myself that tonight was going to be a good night. I was going to Bruno's for our long-awaited and (in my case) much-anticipated date. I'd be going back to the old neighborhood and seeing what Bruno had done with my grandmother's old house while I'd been gone.

Gran's working-class neighborhood had been on a downward slide for a while, but now the area seemed to be turning around. The most recent wave of newcomers had been yuppies with small children; they wanted to live close to the city without paying exorbitant prices.

Before Bruno moved in, the Murphys had briefly lived in the house. I really liked Molly and Mickey and their girls, Beverly and Julie. Beverly was going to be a true siren, the first Atlantic siren since the Magna Carta, and her family had spent about a year living in my grandmother's small house so Beverly could benefit from being near Serenity and Queen Lopaka.

But the whole family missed their old home in Arkansas, and when they decided to go back, Bruno bought the house from them. It's a pretty little place, gray with white trim and a big front porch. The old rocking chair where Gran had nursed my skinned knees is still there, joined now by a matching antique glider just big enough for Bruno and me to sit on comfortably enjoying the sunset and the distant sound of the ocean.

He's been tending Gran's flower beds religiously; the poppies and Shasta daisies gave the place plenty of color and brought bumblebees and butterflies calling.

By the time I got there, it was almost too late in the afternoon for butterflies. I'd taken my time getting ready. I wanted to look my best. At the risk of going too dressy, I'd pulled on a strapless little black dress that was cut to make the most of my natural assets, short enough to show off my long legs and the ivy tattoo that wrapped around one of them, and low cut enough to flaunt a bit of cleavage. I'd even put on high heels. I wouldn't be able to run worth a damn, but I wasn't planning on running. My only concession to safety was a little black bolero jacket that was spelled and tailored to hide a pair of knives, a stake, and a little One Shot brand squirt gun filled with holy water. I never go out without *some* weapons. Besides, the sun was setting. The monsters would soon be on the prowl.

Fortunately, the smoothie had taken the edge off of my hunger. I wasn't having the usual problem with sunset bloodlust. Nope, instead I was feeling another kind of lust entirely. I hoped that once he got a look at me in this outfit, Bruno would share the sentiment.

Just thinking about it made me want to stomp on the gas pedal of my little blue sports car. But these days, when I drive, I make sure to obey all traffic laws. I glanced in the rearview just to make sure and, yep, as usual, there was a cop car following me, staying a couple of cars behind. The guy at the wheel was way too big to be my old friend Officer Clarke. Of course, I'd already seen Clarke, earlier that day, when he'd tried to run me over. I wondered idly where he'd gotten the car, but figured a cop would have easy access to a stolen or towed vehicle.

Don't think about it, Graves. It'll make you grumpy. And tonight is no night to feel grumpy.

A wicked little smile tugged at the corners of my lips as I pulled the car into Bruno's driveway and parked. As the cop who had been tailing me drove past, I reached out the window and came *this close* to flipping him the bird. I settled for a cheery little wave that would probably irritate him almost as much. I got out of the car and went around to the passenger side to retrieve my purse and the bottle of wine I'd brought as my contribution to dinner.

I strolled happily onto the porch and rang the bell.

No response. I took a deep breath and smelled . . . food burning. Leaning closer, I peered through the window and saw Bruno lying limp and unmoving on the couch.

Oh, *shit.*

I grabbed the doorknob as the smoke detectors inside the house blared to life—and the protective wards on the house blew me off my feet, throwing me over the porch railing. I landed hard on my ass on the front lawn and skidded across the grass.

Bruno appeared in the doorway, yawning and half-befuddled by sleep, but radiating power. He took one look at me and said, "Oh *fuck*, Celie, are you all right?"

I was breathless. Lethal wards are illegal, but his had packed quite a punch. I managed to wheeze out "Peachy" and "Fire?" That got him swearing again, and he rushed back into the house, presumably to deal with whatever was going on in the kitchen.

I rose creakily to my feet as some of his neighbors appeared at windows and doorways. The new people didn't recognize me, but old Mrs. Evans gave me a wave. Her husband was sitting in a lawn chair on their porch and laughing so hard there were tears on his cheeks. I was pretty sure he was going to wet his pants.

"Ow." I limped carefully toward the house. One of my shoes was simply gone. The seat of my dress had mostly vanished from my little trip across the lawn on my bottom, exposing the expanse of pale, bruised flesh my thong didn't cover. My vampire vision and hearing had kicked in— looking through the front door, I could see Bruno in the smoky kitchen, flinging open the windows to air the place out. I could hear Mr. Evans gasp, "Ethel, that's one boy who won't be getting any tonight," before falling back into helpless laughter.

I found the wine bottle, miraculously unbroken, a few steps from the porch. And while true aficionados would throw twelve kinds of fit at how it had been shaken, screw 'em. I needed a drink.

Bruno met me at the door. His expression was a strange mix of sorrow, frustration, and embarrassment. "I fell asleep."

"I can see that."

He didn't touch me. Instead, he took the wine bottle from my hand and backed up enough to let me pass. The smoke alarm cut off abruptly. In the sudden silence I heard a car pulling to the curb in front. I could hear Bruno swallow before he headed down the steps. Glancing back, I saw that the new arrival was a police car.

Bruno began explaining even before he reached the cop, who was a woman. Evidently Clarke's buddy hadn't been the one to respond to the call—a small mercy, but I'd take it. Although Lord help me if the officer wasn't wearing one of the police force's anti-siren charms. I tended to bring out hostility in most women. That's never good, and worse when I'm dealing with the police. "It was just an accident, officer. I was cooking lasagna for dinner and fell asleep on the couch. I've got the wards set to activate automatically when I fall asleep. When my friend arrived, she saw me lying on the couch and smelled smoke . . ." Bruno let the sentence drift off unfinished. "We're both fine."

"I think I'd like to check that out for myself, if you don't mind." The policewoman stepped onto the porch and into the doorway.

I turned to face her from the entrance to the kitchen, giving her a rueful smile. "Hello, Officer . . . ?"

"Dade. Karla Dade. Are you all right?"

"I'm embarrassed more than anything. I'll probably have some bruises. Did you happen to see my shoe?"

"It's in the next yard." She returned my smile. "Do you want me to call the paramedics so you can get checked out?"

"No. Thankth." Crap. A lisp. I'd avoided it before, but sometimes those final ess sounds gave me trouble. And just like that, she saw the fangs she hadn't noticed before. Her eyes narrowed and she gave me a long, long look.

"What is your name, ma'am?"

"Celia Graves."

She gave a little nod of acknowledgment. The name was familiar. The face probably was, too. But she was smart enough to check. "Do you have any identification?"

"In my purse."

Bruno handed her my bag—he must have retrieved it from the lawn; I hadn't even thought to look for it—and she handed it to me. I opened it and shoved aside my travel toothbrush and comb to pull out my wallet, which I passed to Officer Dade. She checked out my driver's license and my concealed carry permit before flipping the wallet closed and returning it to me. "Everything appears to be in order, Ms. Graves. If you're sure you don't want medical attention . . ."

"Not nethethary." Damned fangs. It was harder to control my speech when I was rattled, which I was, a little, though I was trying not to be. I fought hard not to react when she flinched. "Thank you anyway."

"Sorry for the trouble, officer," Bruno mumbled.

She eyed the charred remains of the pan of lasagna in the sink. "No trouble," she assured him. "You two try to enjoy the rest of your evening."

He led her back through the house and closed the door behind her. I went back to looking for a corkscrew.

"I am so sorry." I turned to find Bruno standing in the kitchen doorway, looking frustrated and hurt. "I wanted everything to be perfect. Fucking Creede, with his winery, and his . . ." I stepped forward and put my finger to his lips, cutting off the flow of words. He looked down and discovered my cleavage. There was a long, silent moment. When he was able to speak, his voice was a little rough. "That is a really nice dress."

"You're just now noticing that?" I teased.

He lifted his head and I saw that his eyes had darkened with desire. "You wore heels"—he took a breath—"and a thong."

"Yup." I was smiling now.

"You hate thongs." He stepped into me, his body pushing mine against the kitchen cabinets.

"I didn't want to ruin the line of the dress."

He drew a ragged breath, his eyes locking with mine. "Is there any possible way for me to salvage this evening?"

"Tell you what. You fix me some broth and a stiff drink, and we'll find out."

It was his turn to smile. "I can do that."

8

The earthquake woke me at 3:00 A.M., even though it wasn't a particularly bad quake and didn't last long. It was just enough to rattle the windows and knock things off shelves. I'm pretty used to them; this *is* California, after all. But even little ones tended to wake me up since I changed, and I didn't know if that was the vampire, the siren, or just me.

Not surprisingly, Bruno was still out cold. He was so exhausted I think he could probably have slept through Armageddon.

He'd been pushing himself too hard. Again. He was finishing his doctoral thesis, teaching classes, and I was betting he was moonlighting, quietly helping his brother Matty. Matteo's job is to take down major demons, übervamps, and all kinds of big-bads. But he's only a level-four mage—average—though with Matty's training, it's enough to make him a force to be reckoned with. But Bruno is a level nine, and I knew he'd never forgive himself if anything happened to his brother that he could've prevented.

Bruno needed sleep, and he wasn't going to get it if I was fidgeting next to him. So I very carefully disentangled myself—from Bruno and the bedding—and climbed out of bed. Pulling on Bruno's discarded long-tail T-shirt, I padded down to the kitchen, straightening pictures and picking up fallen knickknacks along the way.

I started coffee brewing and downed a nutrition shake while I waited for my caffeine fix. A stack of mail had fallen off of the counter. When I picked it up, a photo fell out. A sticky note in Bruno's mom's handwriting covered most of the image. "Angelina Bonetti is back in town. Her annulment is final. She asked me to give you this."

I do not believe in snooping. I don't. It's wrong. People are entitled to their privacy.

But I had to know. *Had* to.

So I lifted the sticky note off the picture.

The image was a surprise. It was a group shot of teenagers standing on a boardwalk. The one in the middle was Bruno, younger and wearing a Metallica T-shirt, worn jeans, and a grin. He had a girl on each arm, but the one on the left was his girlfriend. I could just tell. The girl on the right had bigger hair, more makeup, and less clothing, but the girl on the left had *it*. Charisma, star quality— whatever you want to call it, she had it in spades. Clouds of dark curls had been pulled back from a face dominated by huge dark eyes and the kind of sultry lips that just beg to be kissed. She wore plain shorts and a T-shirt, but they didn't look plain on her.

Angelina Bonetti, I assumed. I found myself fighting down a wave of pure jealousy.

"Morning, sunshine." Bruno greeted me from the kitchen doorway.

"Good morning." I held out the photo to him. Taking it from me, he glanced at it and gave a gusty sigh, then leaned forward to give me a quick kiss and set the picture on the kitchen counter behind me.

"Your high-school sweetheart?" I supplied, guessing.

"Yup." He slid one arm around my waist and pulled me against him. Since he was only wearing a thin pair of pajama bottoms I could tell he was happy to have me there. But he didn't make a move on me. Instead, he righted the little metal cup tree on the counter, pulled off a mug, and put it down in front of the coffeemaker.

When he spoke, his voice was calm and matter-of-fact. "Angelina, and pretty much everyone else, assumed that we'd get married and that I'd take over Uncle Sal's business while she stayed home and raised babies."

Uncle Sal probably has some legitimate businesses. But that's not the kind of business Bruno was referring to. The fact that Sal isn't in jail with Gotti and the others says he's smart and dangerous. "I'll bet Joey didn't make the same assumptions." Joey was Bruno's cousin, Sal's son and heir. I like him . . . sort of. But he's a scary bastard. Not as scary as Sal, but impressive enough all on his own.

"No. Joey didn't." There was a long silence. Bruno was lost in thoughts of the past. I didn't rush him. He'd tell me in his own time and his own way. "Joey and I get along okay now. But back then it was . . . tense. One of the reasons I came to the West Coast for college in the first place was to get away from the family, from everybody's expectations, so I could figure out what *I* wanted. All my life, all my decisions had been made for me. I wanted to make my own choices."

I thought about that for a long moment. It made sense. It also explained why he has had a hard time sharing in the past and including me in the decision making. I didn't like the notion. But at least it made sense. I filed that thought away for thorough consideration later, because Bruno was talking again.

"Angie wasn't happy about my leaving. She wanted me to go to school in New York so we could see each other. We broke up right before I left." He shook his head ruefully. "Broke my heart."

The coffee was ready. I moved aside and he busied himself pouring us each a cup. I started to say something, but he continued.

"I hated it here at first. I didn't fit in at all. My roommate in the dorm was a total asshat. Sal told me to give it time. 'Finish out the year. You still don't like it, then we'll talk.'" He took a sip of coffee. His eyes met mine over the rim and started sparkling. "Second semester, the roommate dropped out, I met you, and I had my first class with El Jefe."

"You think Sal knew?"

"Maybe. He's got clairvoyants on staff. I know he was worried about me and Joey. He never said anything, but I could tell."

I took a sip of my own coffee, and some of the tension in my shoulders eased a bit. "Did I ever tell you about the vision Dottie showed me last Christmas?"

With his mouth full of coffee, he raised one eyebrow in inquiry.

"I was really depressed because of the whole thing with Gran. She showed me what would've happened if I'd been killed with Ivy. It was pretty scary—sort of *It's a Wonderful Life* as produced by Tim Burton."

He put down his cup and looked at me seriously. "I'm not the same person I would've been without you."

"No, you're not." I brought the cup to my nose with both hands, deeply inhaling the wonderful scent of liquid nirvana before taking another drink. It kept me from shuddering at the memory of what Bruno might have become.

He smiled. "I like this me better."

It was my turn to look quizzical. "But you haven't even heard—"

He held up one hand. "Don't need to. I know what I was like then and I have a pretty good idea of what kind of man I would've become." He set his cup down on the counter and pulled me close. I put my coffee down, too. We were standing face-to-face, bodies pressed together. "Sweetheart, you don't need to worry about Angelina Bonetti."

The photograph drew my gaze like a magnet. Damn,

she was beautiful. And she was the type who would only have gotten better with age. *And* Mama DeLuca liked her.

"Celia." Bruno's voice was gently chiding. I looked up and found I couldn't look away. His gaze was intense, the flames at the backs of his eyes flaring. "I love you. I want *you*. And even if we don't work out, I'm not going back. I'm not that person anymore. I bought this house for a reason. This is my home now." He continued, speaking softly and with amazing intensity. "I like teaching. I'm good at it. Once I finish my doctorate and my course work, I'm going to apply for a university staff position. I'll still make artifacts, but I'll choose what to create and who to make them for."

Wow. Part of me was shocked . . . and another part wasn't. No, he hadn't discussed any of this with me before. But I wasn't upset about that. We aren't engaged. We aren't planning a future together. Not yet; maybe not ever. I'd been dating both Bruno and John Creede for a while and I would have had no right to bitch if he dated Angelina Bonetti or anybody else—even though I had to admit to myself that I wouldn't like it.

Teaching at Bayview would be a really good fit for him. He'd hate the politics, but he'd be good at it. And if we did manage to work things out and become a "real couple," well, he'd be right here. No more long distance.

"I'm happy for you. I think it's a good idea."

"But?"

I smiled at him a little sadly. "I feel like too much happened while I was out of town. Everything's changed."

A quick shrug. "You're tough, Celia. And smart. You'll catch up."

I didn't answer. I wasn't sure what to say.

He smiled and took my hand. "Come back to bed. Who knows, maybe we'll even get some sleep."

9

I'm sorry," I said as I extended my hand to the woman who had stood upon my entering the conference room. Helen Baker is a member of the Serenity Secret Service. She is tall, with chiseled features and a seriously buff body underneath the conservative black suit she was wearing with a dove gray blouse. The last time I'd seen her she'd had a buzz cut. Apparently she'd decided to let her blond hair grow out a bit; though it was still short, it was not as short, and it had been styled to look more feminine. She looked good, I thought.

Baker rose from the slight bow she'd given me and accepted my handshake. "There's no need to apologize, Princess. You're not late, I arrived early." That was obvious. She'd had time to take over the conference room, setting up her computer and a projection screen. And I spotted several old-fashioned display boards leaning against the wall.

I realized Baker was still standing. Apparently she wouldn't sit until I did. She was probably following royal etiquette. That was something I definitely needed to brush up on for my new assignment. I'd done a bit of research a couple of years ago, but it had been awhile. I'd forgotten most of it.

"Actually, I'm apologizing because . . ."—I paused for a second, searching for the right phrasing—"bringing me in makes it seem that you guys aren't capable of doing your jobs. And that is *not* true." I'd worked with Baker and other members of the Siren Secret Service before. They were efficient, well trained, and scary good. "I can't imagine why I'd be needed." I pulled out the chair directly across from her, turning it so that I would have a good view of the projection screen.

Baker smiled and took her seat. "But you are needed." She reached into the padded laptop case on the table and withdrew a manila folder. "I'm a clairvoyant. I've seen it myself. There are no specifics. The people moving against us have used powerful black magic to shield their actions— demonic magics. You, Princess, have more experience fighting the demonic than anyone on our staff. You also have fought and executed at least ten vampires, even one übervamp. There has never been a vampire on Serenity, so none of our people has that experience. We've trained for it, but training and experience are two very different things. Don't presume we're insulted. I assure you, we're not. We're eager to learn your techniques."

It was weird, hearing my last few years summed up so neatly. Baker made everything sound so matter-of-fact, but every one of those incidents had been terrifying, dangerous, and damn near fatal to me and lots of other people.

"So there's no friction?"

Her expression grew rueful. "Not from me. But I can't say that everyone on staff is thrilled. Especially since it's been made clear that the queen wants us to protect you as well."

"No."

She raised her eyebrows but didn't say anything.

"Say it to her as respectfully as you can, but no. If I'm going to do Adriana any good at all, I have to be able to do what is necessary. That means I have to take risks. I may have to throw myself in front of a bullet. I can't do that if you guys are protecting me. It won't work. And it puts your team in an untenable position. So, tell the queen that I refuse."

"Refuse to be in the wedding party or refuse to be protected?"

I shrugged. "I'd prefer protected. But whichever is necessary."

"She won't like that."

Probably not. But— "Queen Lopaka is a sensible ruler. She'll see the logic." And while she liked me, she loved her daughter. Protecting Adriana would be her primary concern.

"Very well, if you insist." She gestured toward the screen. "Shall we get started?"

"Please."

Baker's briefing was fairly thorough, especially considering they didn't know much about the Guardians of the Faith. They were a terrorist group that had started up about two years earlier, beginning with some anti-siren chatter on the Web. They hadn't become really organized or vocal until King Dahlmar's engagement to Adriana went public. Since then, they'd mobilized, taking credit for a number of smaller events before the plane crash and bombing of the shop where Adriana had bought her bridesmaids' dresses. All of the Guardians' propaganda was virulently anti-siren, and there were specific threats against Adriana, Queen Lopaka, and me. Their stated goal was to prevent the royal wedding at any cost.

I didn't like the "any cost" part, because that put them on a fanatic list that only a few groups in the world could lay claim to. Worse, despite all of the Guardians' activity, the siren and Rusland intelligence organizations had no names or locations for any members, and any leads tended to quickly peter out.

Baker turned to her laptop and began her next prepared presentation, on the wedding itself, complete with Power-Point slides. Nice that the queen's staff had embraced technology.

The ceremony on Serenity would be short and casual . . . and a security nightmare. In the distant past, sirens didn't marry. They used the men they wanted for as long as they wanted and then compelled them to leave and never return. Girl children were kept and raised. Boys weren't. But while change came slowly among the sirens, it did come. Marriages now existed, mostly as a promise to keep and support all children of the union. For the average siren and her husband, that meant posting an intent to marry in the newspaper and signing official papers in front of a local judge.

Adriana's marriage on Serenity would be a bit more formal than that due to her rank, but not much. The day of the wedding had been declared a national holiday. Streets were being blocked off along the entire 2.3 mile route from the palace to the courthouse where the chief justice would be waiting. The route for the procession—by the bridal party, on *foot*, nice and slow. My head hurt just thinking about all the ways that could go wrong.

Afterward, there would be a private luau on the grounds of the royal compound, for which security would be a piece of cake by comparison. I'd already RSVP'd "no" because of the whole sunshine thing, but Baker informed me they'd changed the plans slightly to accommodate me by placing the wedding party under a canopy and keeping the entertainment and the cooking pit in the open. Baker and her superiors had decided not to discuss the change of plans in public, giving us an element of surprise.

The second ceremony, taking place two days later in Rusland, would be a traditional Orthodox Christian wedding ceremony. This would be a much more formal and elaborate affair, much like the royal wedding of the British prince a couple of years prior. The Siren Secret Service was cooperating with their Ruslandic counterparts on the details.

I glanced up at the wall clock. "I know there's more, and

I'll need to go over it with you later, but we're almost out of time. What's on tap for today?"

Baker scowled, but couldn't really argue. "Adriana flew the queen and the other two bridesmaids over from Serenity last night. They are guests at the Serenial Embassy. They're scheduled to have breakfast until 8:30 with the ambassador and his wife. At 8:33, they'll get in the limo and come here. They should arrive between 8:59 and 9:04 depending on traffic." She glanced down, checking her notes.

"At approximately 9:58, you will arrive at the shop of designer Amelie Annette Bertrand. The shop has been closed to everyone except the princess and our people have made a thorough security sweep of the shop and the area around it. We will have guards posted at every exit and patrolling the neighborhood. At 11:45, the car will pick you up at the shop and take the group to Simone's, where a private room has been reserved for lunch. The facilities have already been secured. At 1:15, the car will take you and the others to designer Angel Herrera's showroom. Security measures will be identical to those at the Bertrand shop."

I could tell from her narrative that security for the day was going to be tight. Good. I still didn't know exactly where I fit in the scheme of things, how well the team would react to having me included. But there was only one way to find out.

"Do you mind if I have Dawna make me a copy of the itinerary while I go arm up?"

"Not necessary." She reached into the laptop case and handed me a sheet of paper and a thumb drive. "I was afraid we wouldn't have time to cover everything, so I took the liberty of putting it all on a flash drive for you."

"Thanks. Hopefully we'll get a chance to talk later today."

She shook her head. "Not in person, at least not today. I have an errand to run, then I am flying back to Serenity."

Well, crap. That sucked. While I could probably talk to any of the secret service agents, I liked and trusted Baker. "Is there anybody specific I should talk to?"

Ever prepared, she reached into the case and pulled out a business card. "Saren Albright will be the agent in charge on this detail. Here's her card. I'll let her know that you may be consulting with her later."

"Thank you."

"Just doing my job."

10

It took me all of fifteen minutes to decide that I didn't like the other bridesmaids. Olga and Natasha were Ruslandic royalty. I was betting their addition to the wedding party was political rather than emotional, because neither showed any kind of sincere affection for the bride-to-be.

Natasha was the daughter of a prominent conservative clergyman with major political power. She had been briefly married to King Dahlmar's son before his death. Olga was the daughter of Dahlmar's younger brother. Both women were lovely, with dark hair and smooth fair skin, although Olga had a sly way about her that reminded me of the petty little bitches who'd tormented me back in high school.

She and Natasha spoke mostly to each other, and in Ruslandic, knowing nobody else could understand, which was just plain rude. When I decided to tell them so, mind to mind, I hit a solid barrier and guessed that both of them were wearing anti-siren charms. That was very interesting, since those types of charms are difficult to make and even more difficult to obtain. It was pretty much an insult for them to wear them under these circumstances. On the other hand, it should have made them immune to the anti-siren sentiments that most women feel, yet both radiated a low level of hostility. Either the charms weren't working or there was some sort of problem. Maybe I should—

Don't.

Adriana's birdlike voice in my head was calm and patient.

They're being obnoxious.

She didn't bother trying to deny it. *If my mother can ignore it, so can you.*

I looked over at Queen Lopaka. Her expression was serene. She turned to meet my gaze and smiled. She spoke out loud, to my surprise. "We are most fortunate that both of Adriana's possible choices for a wedding dress had already been delivered. It would be much harder to find a suitable bridal gown than attendant dresses on short notice. The previous dresses were pale gold, quite lovely, but all wrong for your complexion, Celia. I think perhaps we should consider jewel tones this time. What do you think, Adriana?"

"I agree that gold won't work. Perhaps Amelie will have some suggestions."

"But I liked the gold," Olga whined.

I kept a smile pasted on my face and gritted my teeth. If Adriana could put up with having those two in her wedding party and the queen could be pleasant to them, then I could and would shut up and smile, even if it was through gritted teeth.

I was so relieved when the limo stopped and I could at

least put a little more physical distance between me and the other bridesmaids.

Since Natasha and Olga were busy ignoring us in favor of chatting with each other, I didn't feel guilty speaking mind-to-mind to Adriana. *I'm surprised there aren't any sirens in the wedding party.* I framed the thought carefully, concentrating hard on Adriana.

Rusland is a land-locked country. Most sirens would not be comfortable there. My best friend was willing to try, but she stepped aside so that you could join the party. It's probably for the best, as it would have been very hard on her.

Okay, that made sense. But it sucked. A girl wants her best buddies at her side for her wedding, not a group of near strangers.

My friends will be with me for a party prior to the wedding, and at the reception following the ceremonies on Serenity. Although I will admit I find Olga and Natasha tiresome, I would put up with much more to please Dahlmar and make a good first impression on his people.

Fair enough.

Dawna has taught me a lot about shopping. One: clothes don't have to be expensive to look expensive. And two: expensive clothes can look just as tacky as cheap ones. I recognized Dawna's lessons at the first shop we visited.

Amelie Annette Bertrand was probably the hottest women's clothing designer around. She could ask whatever price she wanted and people would pay it. She made sure that she was in the store herself to show Queen Lopaka and Adriana her wares. She was beautiful and charming. Olga was particularly impressed.

I wasn't.

Maybe I just had plebian tastes. But it seemed really tacky to me for a bridesmaid in a royal wedding to wear a dress that would make a Vegas showgirl blush. Bertrand's dresses were all too *something* for me: too low cut, too short, too glittery, too tight, too *loud*. Whether Adriana and her mother heard my thoughts, or simply wanted to see what else was available, we left Amelie standing heartbroken at the door of her shop as we drove off to our scheduled luncheon.

Simone's was a very nice little Italian restaurant that smelled of fresh baked bread and garlic. The tablecloths and napkins in our private room were heavy, cream-colored linen; the silverware, actual silver. They'd had plenty of advance notice, so the chef had outdone himself coming up with a special liquified meal that I could eat. Somehow, Olga and Natasha got seated at opposite ends of the table and were forced to either sit mum or interact with the others in the party. I wound up next to Natasha and found that, minus Olga's influence, Natasha was a fairly nice girl with a wicked sense of humor. Of course that only lasted through the dessert course. Once we were back in the limo, the dynamic duo returned to their old tricks.

Sighing, I counted to ten again, and settled in for what promised to be a very difficult afternoon as we drove to the next designer's shop.

Angel Herrera had a very tiny, very exclusive bridal salon

where we were served champagne, wedding cake, and strawberries. The bridal consultant absolutely refused to rush and presented us with a selection of impressive gowns. To my surprise, when I saw myself in the mirror, wearing the dress they'd chosen for me, I felt pretty good about the way I looked. A lot of bridesmaids' dresses are hideous— after all, you can't have someone upstaging the bride on her big day. Adriana, being a siren, had nothing to worry about on that front, and didn't want to punish her bridesmaids by forcing them to wear unattractive outfits, and Herrera and her people had taken those instructions to heart.

My proposed maid-of-honor dress was royal purple, a color that looks really good on me. It was cut low enough to make the most of my figure and the slit up the side was high enough to give a glimpse of the ivy tattoo I'd gotten years ago, to honor my deceased sister, Ivy. The dress was much more conservative than the ones at the other shop, but I was still a little worried about showing all that skin. There's a big conservative contingent in Rusland. What would they think of the foreign bride's attendants looking so downright sexy?

Then I saw Adriana's reflection, smiling at me, and figured if she was happy, that was all that mattered. That, and the fact that I looked really *good* in that dress.

I figured we were good to go. Right up until the bridal consultant told me, "I've found the perfect beauty enhancement spell for you."

"*Excuse* me?" I tried to make it sound as if I wasn't insulted, and failed miserably.

"Well, *obviously*, for any wedding you want to look your best, and for a *royal* wedding, televised around the world, you'll definitely need to hide those scars and your *fangs*." She gave a delicate little shudder as she said the word.

Lopaka's eyes narrowed dangerously. Without another word, she rose, which sent everyone else scrambling to their feet. You do not sit when the queen is standing. "We are finished here. Thank you for your time."

Holy crap.

My cousin gave a brief nod of agreement and the other bridesmaids hustled into the dressing rooms to strip as if they'd been given a telepathic message. They probably had. The queen, after all, was the best telepath in the world. Even if Natasha and Olga had basic anti-siren charms, Lopaka's mental voice could easily overcome them. And it was highly unlikely that Adriana's bridesmaids had been given charms made from Lopaka's hair—I was betting that the queen was very, very careful about who got near her hairbrush.

The consultant flushed, and her face set in grim lines, but I could see the panic in her eyes. Not only was she about to see what was likely a six-figure sale, once shoes and accessories were figured in, walk out the door, the design house's reputation would be ruined—everyone would know that her faux pas cost her a royal wedding. Worse, we still wouldn't have dresses. I could only imagine how hard people had worked to set up the appointments with the two salons we'd visited that day and how difficult it would be to make room in Adriana's and Lopaka's schedules for any additional shopping, especially considering that the wedding was only weeks away and the dresses needed to be purchased, fitted, and finished as soon as possible. All because of a little insult to me. I looked at my aunt and concentrated. *I appreciate the thought, but . . .*

Lopaka didn't even look at me. Her eyes were only on the consultant and flashed with anger. *But nothing. Celia, I appreciate your humility, but you underestimate your position. Right now, you are the most famous siren on the planet. Your heroics have been splashed across the media worldwide and have given us much prestige. You have set right some of our worst sins and the public consider us honorable at last. To allow this insult to stand would be to allow our entire nation and culture to be insulted. And that I will not tolerate.*

That took me aback. I hadn't thought of it that way.

Seriously, I'm not all that humble. Yeah, I know that *technically* I'm a siren princess. My grandfather had been Lopaka's beloved brother, but we hadn't known that until after the vampire bit me and my siren powers started wreaking havoc. I'd grown up poor, with a pretty dysfunctional family. And right at this moment, my mom was in jail, my grandmother wasn't talking to me, and my sister was (still) dead—and I hadn't seen her ghost in a while, either. So I just don't think of myself as a princess. As I told one of my friends when I found out, "That's just so . . . *Disney.*"

Now, the queen had made up her mind, and while I was family, I was also a subject. I ducked into the nearest dressing room, got out of that lovely purple dress, and pulled on my street clothes, half listening as the clerk tried to talk her way out of the pit she'd dug for herself.

The others finished dressing long before I did; of course, none of them had to arm themselves. Most of the weaponry I was carrying, including the holster with my 1911 Colt, was concealed by the spells put on my tailored black blazer. Even with the armament, you couldn't have faulted my fashion statement. I wore a red silk shell and new black jeans under the jacket; the Colt's black leather holster perfectly matched my short black boots, one of which had a built-in holster for my derringer.

When I was finally ready, Queen Lopaka and her security detail led the bride and her bridesmaids out of the store, leaving the attendant spluttering in our wake. A black stretch limo pulled up to the curb as we flowed out of the building.

Adriana and I were the last to exit the shop, and I stopped abruptly when my boots hit the sidewalk. Something was wrong. I couldn't have said what exactly was bothering me, but it didn't matter.

"Down! Everybody down!" I screamed, swinging my arm out and snagging Adriana around the waist. I shoved her behind me, almost throwing her to the pavement, as I put myself between her and the roadway.

For a fraction of an instant, time seemed to slow drastically. More guards appeared, seeming to hover in midair as the queen's eyes went wide. The back windows of the limo rolled down. Rifle barrels appeared. Natasha and Olga froze as members of the security team reached for them. The bridesmaids looked like deer caught in the headlights of an oncoming car—stunned and blank. Guns roared. Men and women screamed, glass shattered, and car doors slammed.

I got all this in fragments; I was busy trying to wrestle Adriana into the limited safety of the bridal shop when what she wanted was to rush to her mother's side. I heard an engine roar and a squeal of tires as a second limo tore off into traffic. In the silence that fell I realized that Lopaka, Natasha, and Olga had been driven away, leaving me and my cousin alone with the gunmen. It's not the way I would have done it, but I suppose it made sense—I was a bodyguard, and Adriana was my responsibility. It was actually sort of flattering that the Siren Secret Service presumed I'd get her to safety.

I tried to get her to calm down, saying, "They're fine. I don't smell blood behind me." But Adriana kept struggling with me. I suspected she didn't believe me—and she was right not to, because I was lying.

Finally I lost all patience and just slugged her in the jaw, then picked her up bodily and dragged her into the store. More gunshots sounded as the guards fought the gunmen.

Lopaka's voice rang in my mind, telling me to do what I was already doing. *Celia, get her out of there. Keep her safe.*

I kept my body between Adriana and any open space. The two remaining bodyguards seemed to be giving me some cover with their Kevlar-covered bodies. We passed the bloody form of the dying bridal consultant, her body riddled with bullets and shards of glass.

My cousin began to come back to her senses, which meant she was no longer dead weight, but it was still hard to move her. "Damn it, Adriana, come *on*." I was shouting, but since my ears were ringing from the gunfire, I assumed Adriana was similarly affected. I didn't remember pulling a weapon, but there was a gun in my left hand. I dragged her past a pair of circular racks filled with a rainbow selection of floor-length gowns, toward the back door.

Then I saw movement and ducked, pulling her down with me, gesturing for her to hide in the dress racks and to stay absolutely silent. It was a bridal shop, so nearly all of the racks had floor-length gowns. Peeking around a gorgeous, slinky red silk I couldn't wear on my best day, I saw a pair of men in business suits moving quickly but nearly silently through the store, guns in hand. That must mean the two guards outside hadn't survived. Damn it.

The first covered the second, who pushed back the door of each dressing room in turn. The way they moved told me there were wearing bulletproof vests under their dress shirts. They switched positions for the second rank of changing rooms. They were definitely pros.

Adriana stayed silent, but only to those with no telepathy. In my head, she was terrified, indignant, and angry. *You expect me to* hide?

Hell, yes. You're the one they're after and you're unarmed. Let me do my damned job. Stress always made my telepathy work better and I knew Adriana could hear me clearly.

Fine. But give me one of your guns.

I risked a glance at her. *What? Are you nuts?*

My cousin gave me a scathing look. *I know how to shoot. And if something happens to you, I'd like to at least be able to defend myself.*

She had a good point and I didn't have time to argue. I handed her the derringer from my boot and slithered as quietly as I could to the next rack.

They'd reached the last dressing room and found it empty. Scowling, they started scanning the store. They knew we had to be in here. But they didn't see us and they were running out of time. Police sirens wailed in the distance, closing fast. If the attackers didn't go soon, there'd be no chance of escape.

They split up, each moving down an aisle of racks. I shifted position, getting ready. Switching off the safety, I braced my gun hand and waited until the first man leaned down to check under the counter. Then I stood. It only took a second, but I felt like I had all the time in the world. The second guy turned at my movement, his gun pointed straight at me. But he hesitated for just a fraction of a second. I didn't. I fired three rapid shots into the central mass of number two's neck before diving under a clothing rack, rolling as fast as I could through the tangling fabric. Even if the bad guys always seem to wear vests, they nearly always forget to protect their necks. A head or neck shot will kill you just as dead.

Number one fired at where he assumed I must be. Close, no cigar. I felt the sting of splintering white oak flooring entering my flesh through my jeans, but the bullets themselves missed.

The police sirens were close now. Swearing, the assassin bolted out the back door. I heard the roar of an engine and the squeal of tires, and he was gone.

I bolted out from under the rack and started to give CPR to Thug Two. I would be damned if he was going to die before he told me why they wanted Adriana dead. My cousin joined me a moment later, just before the police edged in cautiously, weapons drawn. I would have done just the same, considering the dead bodies and blood every-where. They found me keeping the guy's heart beating—a bit of a losing battle because Adriana was having a hard time keeping his blood in his carotid artery. I hadn't meant to sever it, but there you go. Adriana and I had tried to save him, and I knew the EMTs who'd come with the cops would do their best, but the odds weren't good.

11

One more time, if you would, Ms. Graves. I understand that you called out as the car was pulling up to the curb and shoved your cousin behind you. No one else had noticed anything wrong with the limo. How did you know there was a problem?"

I sighed and tried to stay calm. It had been a very long, stressful day. I needed to eat. I'd been at the police station for a number of hours by now and, while I can go longer between feedings than I used to, my control isn't perfect by a long shot. Especially when I've been busy trying to save lives.

My stomach growled impatiently. I tried to ignore it, forced myself not to look at the pulse beating so temptingly in the detective's throat.

Deep breath. The man's just doing his job. Stay calm. "Most of the others were probably at bad angles, and the windows were tinted. Adriana and I were the last to leave the store, so we had a different point of view, through the windshield."

"Ah. And what did you see that tipped you off?"

I'd had time to think about it and had finally realized what had been bugging me. "It wasn't the same driver we'd had earlier in the morning. The first guy's hair was really short; the second guy's hair brushed his ears and collar. It also seemed to me that the car was moving too fast. I mean, yeah, the driver might've been the kind to slam on the brakes at the curb, but most pros aren't like that, especially when they're driving royalty."

"Detective Rawlins," my attorney, Roberto Santos, said in his honey-smooth voice, "my client has been extremely cooperative. She has given a full statement." He was sitting next to me, which was the usual for me when I was being interviewed by the police, at least in this country—even when I was just a witness. He hadn't had a lot to do thus far, because there were all kinds of witnesses saying that I'd basically saved the day and helped foil an assassination attempt.

Self-defense and defense of the life of another notwithstanding, I'd put three bullets into a guy's neck. He was dead and I'd killed him. It was all clearly visible on the store's security feed.

Roberto continued, sounding perfectly reasonable, "Ms. Graves has worked with your sketch artist and given a description of the man who escaped. But she has a serious medical condition that is made worse by stress. I really must insist that we take a break at least long enough for her to use the facilities and to eat so that nothing . . . *unfortunate* happens."

Okay, maybe that was pushing it a little. Of course,

Roberto couldn't know how much progress I'd made in controlling my condition.

"Mr. Santos." The detective's lips moved up in a semblance of a smile, but his eyes were cold, hard pebbles set in an equally stony face. "A man is dead. Your client killed him. She shot him, deliberately and repeatedly. She will sit here answering questions for as long as I feel it's necessary."

I didn't sigh. I didn't fidget. I just closed my eyes and counted to twenty. Perhaps Detective Rawlins was just a good, old-fashioned, hard-headed detective. Then again, it was possible he was one of the members of my "fan club," the group of officers who've decided I'm a monster and are willing to go to almost any lengths to prove it. They want me locked behind bars or put down like a rabid dog. Either way, he was pushing my buttons. That was a very bad thing.

There was a tap at the door. Rawlins made a low, grumbling noise, then rose and left the room, closing the door behind him. I'm sure they didn't think I could hear them through a closed door, especially since they were speaking softly. But my vampire nature was very close to the surface now, and that made eavesdropping easy.

"You have to let her go," said a man's voice, not one I recognized.

"The hell you say! She's a freaking killer. She's admitted it." That was Detective Rawlins.

"Doesn't matter. It was a righteous shoot. Even if it wasn't, she's got diplomatic immunity from *two* countries. She's also a freaking celebrity, and she just foiled an assassination attempt on members of a royal family. We've got press screaming for blood, politicos riding our ass, and no good reason to keep her. We can bring her back in if we need to. For now, cut her loose."

"Have you *looked* at her? She has *fangs*. She should be staked or put in a fucking cage. Even her attorney admits that she could lose control if she doesn't eat."

"So let her eat, and let her *go*."

"Is that an order?"

A pause and then the voice lowered to a growl. "Does it need to be?"

There was a long silence. I could hear Rawlins breathing harshly. "We'll wind up regretting this. When that time comes . . ."

"*If* that time comes, there'll be a note in your file." The voice made it a threat.

"Good," Rawlins spat. "Glad to hear it."

When they cut me loose, the first thing I did was grab my cell phone and dial Adriana's number. The call went straight to voice mail. Annoying, but not unexpected. Roberto had told me that Lopaka and the others had been taken to the secure ward of a local hospital, but he didn't know which one. If Adriana was there with her mother, it was likely that no call could reach her. So I dug out the card Baker had given me and keyed the number into my phone. The line rang only once.

"Princess." Ah, caller ID, gotta love it.

"Special Agent Albright."

She sounded both amused and exhausted. "Am I to assume the police have finally tired of interrogating you?"

"They have. How is the queen? Where are Adriana and the others?"

"Her Royal Majesty is in intensive care at St. Anthony's Hospital. Princess Adriana is with her."

Intensive care? It was that bad? I couldn't help but worry. Despite only knowing her for a short time, I really liked Lopaka.

"What about Olga and Natasha?"

"They're secure at the Ruslandic Embassy."

"As soon as I can get some weapons, I'll head over to the hospital."

"Don't bother. We've got it covered for now. Get some rest. Check in again in the morning." She hung up before I could argue. No surprise. She had a lot on her plate.

My aunt, the queen of queens, the most powerful siren in the world, was in intensive care. Crap.

It took a minute for that to fully sink in, which told me just how distracted I was. Sirens are hard to kill. Very, very hard to kill. I'd seen one get shot to pieces and she had kept breathing, her damaged heart still beating. It isn't public knowledge, but I had it on good authority that the only things that can actually kill a pure-blooded siren are weapons wielded in jealousy—an emotion that is a poison to us—or certain specially made magical artifacts.

The shooters in the car hadn't been women, so jealousy wasn't a factor. That told me two things. First, someone in the know had leaked exactly where we were going and when we'd be there. Second, the attackers had arranged for literally dozens of bullets to be spelled—because that was the only way to try to kill royal sirens. Even a thousand standard rounds wouldn't be enough. The cost to prepare this attack, in both time and money, had to have been outrageous. So we were looking at a well-funded group with inside information and access to some of the top-tier mages in the world. Artifacts take a long time to produce, which meant that these had been created long before Adriana and Dahlmar's engagement was announced. The wedding was just an excuse.

That was *very* interesting.

I couldn't help Lopaka at the hospital. My job was to protect her daughter. I wouldn't be able to do that properly without rest. I wanted to do that someplace safe. I also wanted to go over the intel Baker had given me, and see if there was a clue that would tell me who the traitor was.

Because there was a traitor. Someone allowed that limo to get close enough to kill.

12

I really appreciate this, Emma."

"So you've said . . . repeatedly." She smiled to take the sting out of the words. "Seriously, it's all right." She handed me a nutrition shake. "Drink this. You're glowing."

She was right. I didn't feel vampy, exactly, but I wasn't myself, either. I'd been hungry back at the police station and while I was waiting for Emma to come pick me up. Now, back at her new home, not so much. Still, I twisted open the bottle and drank as Kevin shoved past me into the main living area.

I flinched. He was really pissed and not even trying to hide it. I hadn't expected him to show up, but he and Emma had arrived in his big truck and Emma had given me a this-wasn't-my-idea look as they pulled up to where I was sitting and watching cops and civilians flow in and out of the precinct house. The ride back to the old church had passed by in a silence cold enough to frost the windows of his truck. Emma might not mind my being here. Her brother obviously did.

The second I stepped into the living room Kevin turned to me, his expression granite. In a flat yet furious voice he said, "Computer, big screen, channel six."

At the far end of the room, the television came on. The perky brunette and her silver-haired coanchor wore grim expressions as film of the front of the destroyed bridal shop ran in the background, immediately followed by photos of King Dahlmar and Princess Adriana.

"A terrorist group calling itself the Guardians of the Faith has used various social networks to claim responsibility for the attack." A close-up of a screenshot appeared; the group's avatar was a blue-green S bisected diagonally by a bloody harpoon. I'd seen that symbol before, but couldn't remember where or when.

I pummeled my brain, searching for the answer as the anchorwoman droned on. "The group has vowed to continue the violence against all sirens unless King Dahlmar breaks off his engagement. Our sources say that the governments of all three nations are treating this as a credible threat." An image flashed onto the screen of a note written in a foreign language, accompanied by photocopied pictures of Lopaka's face, Adriana's, and mine, all marred by black "X" marks.

My stomach heaved and I locked my knees to keep from swaying on my feet. It's one thing to hear you've been targeted. It's quite another to see it in color on the big screen.

"Damn it, Kevin!" Emma was seriously pissed. Her eyes

were blazing and there were two spots of color on her cheeks. "Was that necessary?"

Her brother was perfectly calm. Smug, even. The bastard. "She wasn't taking it seriously enough. She never does. She brought you into it without a second thought."

Emma rounded on him in fury, hands balled into fists at her sides. "You didn't have to do it that way. You were deliberately brutal and callous and you know it."

"Celia's tougher than you give her credit for. Quit treating her like a fragile snowflake." Kevin made a disgusted noise and stomped over to fling himself into a recliner. Emma led me to a nearby chair, where I sat down hard and lowered my head into my hands. Above and around me, I heard Emma and her brother arguing and the television playing sound bites of statements released by the Ruslandic and Siren ambassadors, but nothing really sank in. Terrorists. I was being hunted by armed, organized, freaking *terrorists*.

"She needs to know what *you're* risking, having her here," Kevin said.

Emma glared at him. "It's my choice to make,"

He slammed a fist down on the armrest, causing his assistance dog, Paulie, to raise her head just a bit. "It's unnecessary. There are other places she can go. Places that won't endanger *you*."

Keeping Emma safe had always been Kevin's main priority. It was why he and his father had served me up as bait for the insane siren, Eirene, a serious misstep that had cost me my friendship with Warren and nearly cost me my life. But Emma had grown tired of being babied. She was a grown woman now, capable of striking back and of making her own decisions.

"Not tonight, she can't. The cops took her guns as evidence, remember?" Emma argued. "Bruno can't get into her office until morning."

He can't? Why not? I opened my mouth to ask, but she'd moved a step forward and was pointing a finger at her brother's nose. "Celia's staying here until the sun comes up, and that's final. This is my home and it's my choice, Kevin. Mine. Not Daddy's, not yours. Mine."

"I don't like it." He probably meant having me here. Then again, maybe not. Having Emma stand up to him probably wasn't a happy development in his life.

"You don't have to." Emma met his gaze without flinching. Points to Emma. Kevin was maybe a step and a half from going wolfy. His eyes were glowing amber and I swear his teeth looked sharper than normal. He was clenching and unclenching his fingers around the arms of the chair. It might have gone further if Paulie hadn't placed herself between the two of them and started barking.

Kevin glared at the dog and she sank into a sit. But she didn't move out of the way, just stared at him with those huge brown eyes: calm, trusting.

He sighed and closed his eyes.

"I'm going to go outside and calm down."

"Good idea." Emma's words were crisp. "Meanwhile, I'll fix us all something to eat."

"Come on, Paulie." Kevin strode through the living area to a side door, the dog at his heels. I couldn't help but heave a sigh of relief as the door closed behind them. Kevin was not himself. Not at all. Maybe being out in quiet and moonlight would help. I was betting he'd go to the little walled cemetery on the west side of the building. I'd wandered through it when I'd visited before and seen that it really was old, two hundred years at least. Where the stones could be read, they told of the missionaries who founded the church and of their very first converts. They'd probably been such true believers that there wasn't even a single ghost left to haunt the place. Hopefully the graveyard would be peaceful enough to soothe Kevin's troubled soul.

I stared at the door for a long moment. "Do you think you should call his Vaso?"

It was Emma's turn to sigh. "Wish I could. She had to go out of town for a few weeks. Her mom's dying of cancer."

Well, hell. "Can we send him to her?" I asked hopefully.

Emma shook her head. "He can't travel when he's like this. Certainly not this close to the full moon. Once that's passed, in a couple of days, he'll be better. He always is. Now, you settle in and watch the news. You really do need to know what's going on. I'll be in the kitchen if you need me."

I checked my watch, then said, "Computer, big screen, channel ten, please." Since Channel 10's nightly newscast starts at ten o'clock, I'd be able to catch the beginning of the report.

It didn't hit me as hard the second time. I sat in the recliner, watching the images on the screen and mentally going over everything I knew and suspected. Which wasn't much. I needed more information.

I called out to my hostess, who was cooking scrambled eggs in the kitchen. "Emma, do you think Kevin could set up a secure conference call for me?"

"Probably. The question is whether he *will*." She came in, carrying a plate that smelled like heaven. The eggs were runny, but there was cheese, and she'd brought along a couple of jars of baby food. "But it'll have to wait until morning in any event. We don't have all the equipment he'd need. How many people would be involved?" She handed me the plate. "Eat."

I ate. When I'd finished, I called Special Agent Albright and got not only the numbers I requested, but an update.

They'd put an aquarium in the queen's room at Adriana's suggestion. Her royal majesty was conscious and improving. She was still in intensive care, but the doctors were hopeful. The princess was already on her way back to Serenity. Apparently Chiyoko, the siren queen of the Japanese islands, had managed to scrape up a quorum and had called an emergency meeting of all of the siren queens. Adriana was going to attend on behalf of her mother.

I asked Albright about traveling to Serenity with the princess, but she rejected the idea.

"You have other things to do." Her voice was calm, but was rough around the edges. People who didn't know her might think none of this was bothering her. I guessed it was.

"Like what?"

"I need you to convince the other bridesmaids to remain in the wedding. Her majesty's assistant has scheduled a dinner for the three of you tomorrow evening after their afternoon television interviews have finished."

Oh goodie. I was going to get to spend time alone with Olga and Natasha. "My job is to protect the princess." I said it, but I knew I was fighting an uphill battle.

"It was an order, not a request."

Of course it was. The question was whether or not I was going to obey it. I might technically be a siren—and technically, under Lopaka's rule—but I was born and raised an American. I am not good at taking royal orders.

Please, Celia. I heard Queen Lopaka's voice very faintly in my mind. She sounded weak and very tired. I thought about her lying in the hospital bed, maybe still in the ICU, worrying about her daughter, her throne, and the public humiliation she'd face if the wedding didn't happen, or even if the bridesmaids bailed from fear of the terrorists.

She was my aunt, and she'd said please. "All right, I'll do it." And I would. But I wouldn't be happy about it.

13

woke to the light patter of rain against glass, the smells of breakfast, and the sounds of familiar voices. I lay in a pool of muted light in a rainbow of colors filtered through stained glass. It took me a few seconds to get my bearings. Emma's guest room, formerly the choir loft. To my right was the door to the stairs that led down to the bathroom and the old foyer. To my right were the floor-to-ceiling drapes that covered the half wall that looked down into the living room. A glance at the clock told me it was ten in the morning. I'd slept longer, and more deeply, than I had in weeks. Just like the night I'd slept at Bruno's, I hadn't had any nightmares, so I actually felt rested. It was a nice change. Some of those dreams. . .

I shuddered.

It felt good to actually get real rest. On the downside, sleeping in meant that it had been a lot of hours since my last meal. I was hungry, and the smell of coffee, bacon, and hash browns wasn't helping one bit. My stomach growled and my vision started to shift to vampire focus, even though it was morning, not night. *Crap.*

I wanted to go downstairs and find out what was going on. But I didn't dare, not like this. I'd gone too long between meals before and wound up having bloodlust. Most of my nightmares lately have been dreams of waking up after too little nutrition and too much exertion and stress, and slaughtering the people I'd been hired to protect. The worst part was, carving those paths of destruction had felt *good.*

Thing is, there's no Ensure in the jungle. No baby food in the cramped cellar of an old church or a drug-smuggler's tunnel. Sometimes I had to eat what I could find that could be squished into a paste and mixed with polluted water from improperly dug wells. I felt hungry almost all the time I was on the job. My nightmares too often felt like they were one tiny step away from my reality.

I recognized the ache in my stomach and the twitching of my muscles. Then I realized that the bands of light decorating my vision weren't just from the stained glass. I was seeing things as a predator. Crap.

I rose without really meaning to. Gliding with unnatural grace to the half wall, I pulled the curtain back a fraction and peeked out.

I know I was careful. The curtain barely twitched. But Kevin's voice rang out from downstairs only seconds later. He sounded more cheerful than he had the night before, almost actually welcoming. "Morning, Celia. 'Bout time you got up. Breakfast is at the foot of the stairs, along with a change of clothes. You need to hustle. We've almost got everything set up."

"Thankth." God, that lisp! And my voice was about an octave lower than normal. Kevin's head shot up at the sound, his eyes narrowing and seeming to glow. A fellow predator who knew what I was feeling.

"Eat. Now," he ordered, then called to someone I couldn't see. "Guys, we're delaying the video conference. Celia has to feed."

Feed. He'd used the word I refused to use. I fought through the rising fog of bloodlust. Food. I needed food. There were humans downstairs, filled to the brim with blood. I could hear their heartbeats, smell their sweat—patterns that hinted how each of them would taste. Glimpse the bands of color that spoke of their emotions: warmth, fear, worry. But I knew I'd have to get past the wolf to get to any of them. The wolf was a threat. I began trying to figure out how to get rid of him.

Kevin gave a low growl, blocking the stairway. He *knew.* The wolf could sense what I wanted.

I fought my inner bat for control and won, but it wasn't easy. "I need . . . food." The words sounded sort of strangled, my struggle reflected in my voice.

"There's a tray at the bottom of the stairs." Emma stepped into view and patiently repeated what her brother had already said. "Kevin didn't think it was a good idea for anyone to bring it up."

Kevin was so freaking right.

He pushed Emma back. "Get away, Em. She's right on the edge." He looked up at me with an expression that mixed anger and respect. "I'll be barricading the door."

I forced myself away from the half wall as he closed the door and locked it audibly—making it very clear that I would have to go through him to get to anyone in the room beyond. I flowed down the staircase to a tray that couldn't possibly hold anything that would compare to what my body really wanted . . . *needed* at that moment.

I guzzled the diet shake on the tray first, hoping it would take the edge off. It did, but not enough. My hands were still shaking hard enough that it was all I could do to get the lid off a jar of strained-beef baby food. I couldn't seem to get the spoon into the jar. In the next instant I wrapped my lips around the opening and poured it into my mouth, sucking at the goopy contents and swallowing as fast as I could. I stabbed and slashed at the glass, feeling my fangs slide uselessly against the sides of the jar. Only then could I make my fingers work right. The shakes finally stopped after the second serving of baby food. By the time I finished the third—peaches—I was actually able to think clearly.

I sat down on the bottom step, breathing hard, as if I'd been running. What the hell was wrong with me?

Slowly my brain started to focus. Had Kevin said video conference? I'd asked him to set one up, but hadn't really thought he would. He'd been so damned uncooperative last night.

I knocked gently at the door. I couldn't smell him anymore, but I bet the wolf in him could smell me. Hopefully he'd realize that it was safe—that *I* was safe, now. He opened the door a crack and peered in at me, estimating the threat, while I squinted past him at the living room. My plain human vision showed me that he'd set up video equipment in the center of the main room. All right then.

"I'm going to hit the bathroom and change so I look presentable for the camera."

He nodded, pleased that I didn't press to go to the others right away. Vampires are tricky, so my backing down hopefully helped him realize I was probably back to normal. At least I thought I was.

Bruno had brought the bag sitting at the bottom of the stairs. I could tell by what he'd packed—all things he could pick up at my office, including a change of clothes. He'd even brought my spare makeup kit, which I kept in my desk. Best of all, he'd brought weapons—not mine, he couldn't have gotten into the safe, but a sweet little Glock with an ankle holster. And people wonder why I love him.

Twenty minutes later, after a shower and makeup, I was fit to step in front of a camera. The front room was already buzzing, but I easily spotted Bruno, who looked like he'd been through the wringer. There were dark circles under his eyes, he had beard stubble, and his eyes had darkened to almost black, the way they do when he's really, seriously angry. He smiled when he saw me, which softened the harsh lines of his face a little. But only a little, and only for a minute. He was wearing black jeans and a black Bayview college sweatshirt that had the sleeves chopped short and had a vertical slit cut in the neckline.

"Morning, sunshine." Bruno tried to shake off his weariness for my benefit. He came over to give me a hug and a quick kiss. "Mnn. You taste like peaches." He licked his lips.

"Baby food," I admitted, giving him a quick squeeze. "Better than snacking on you guys. What's up?" I asked. He shook his head. Apparently he didn't want to talk about it, at least not in front of the others. Okay, we'll go with a safe topic. "What have I missed?"

He opened his mouth to respond, but didn't get the chance as Dom Rizzoli tapped me on the shoulder. He's the only FBI agent I know well enough to be friendly with. Short, dark, and as Italian as pasta, he was wearing his "fedley" suit: nice, dark gray suit coat and pants, white shirt, blue tie, and black shoes with a high gloss.

"We're on."

I didn't want to leave Bruno's side, but there was no arguing with Rizzoli when he used that tone. Besides, he was most likely in the thick of things, and I needed to know what was going on. So I gave my sweetie another hug and walked over to the video setup. Kevin pointed to a masking-tape X on the floor and I stood on it.

"Good morning, Princess." On the monitor in front of me, Hiwahiwa bowed at the waist. "It is good to see you well. Princess Adriana will be joining us in a moment."

I dipped my head and shoulders slightly in return. "And good morning to you."

"Hello, Celia." King Dahlmar's voice. The video screen in front of me now split into four sections. Hiwahiwa was in the upper left, Dahlmar in the lower right. I spotted Creede standing next to him. I hadn't expected him to be there, but should have. After all, John Creede has saved the king's tail more than once. It would make sense for the king to call on him for such a special occasion as his wedding.

John's a handsome man, with a strong jaw and good cheekbones. His eyes are the color of honey, his hair a warm light brown with golden highlights. He keeps it cut short, or it would fall in unmanageable and unmanly curls. His nose is sharp, not quite a beak, though there is something like a bird of prey about him.

"Your Majesty. You look well."

He made a small scoffing sound that most kings wouldn't be seen making. "My future wife was nearly killed. Her mother is in the hospital. My country is turmoil and terrorists are plotting. Hardly *well*, I'm afraid."

There wasn't much to say to that, so I didn't respond. Creede gave me a brief nod. His expression was odd. Part teeth-gritted anger; part sad, puppy-eye regret. He looked good, but like he'd already been through a long day. As usual, both he and the king were wearing splendid suits.

I wasn't thrilled at my own image, in the fourth segment of the screen. I didn't look great. Nobody had mentioned it yet, but only because they were all too polite. If it's true that television adds twenty pounds, I was in real trouble. I've been dropping weight for a while because of my nearly all-liquid diet and it was really starting to show. I'd gone from fashionable to gaunt in the last six weeks. But at least I was dressed in my own clothes, which mostly fit. For a moment I imagined what I'd look like in Emma's duds—we are so not the same size or body type—and my stomach turned over.

Before I could say anything, my image disappeared, replaced by Queen Lopaka's. That made sense.

She was propped up in the hospital bed. Standing on either side of her, out of the way of the medical equipment, was a pair of her personal guards, looking grim and determined. I understood the grim. I hope the full complement of four were in the room, two out of sight of the video camera. In the background, I caught a glimpse of the aquarium. A pair of angel fish floated next to a seahorse in the blue-tinted salt water, while a starfish crawled up the side wall.

"Greetings, niece, Dahlmar, Mage Creede." I noticed that she didn't address Rusland's ruler as "King." Well, they were about to become family. First-name terms for her future son-in-law seemed reasonable.

At least I'd finally learned enough protocol to know that when the siren queen addressed me as family, I was supposed to do the same. "Good morning, Aunt Lopaka, I'm glad to see you up and about." I was. She didn't look good, but she was alive and upright. And if she was online, she was out of ICU. Chances were good she'd recover fully given a bit of time.

"Thanks to you in great part. Without your warning I'd be dead. As it is, I believe I may actually wind up with scars to rival yours."

Hiwahiwa's image was replaced with that of the queen's daughter. As always, Adriana was a vision of auburn-haired beauty. Today she was wearing a raw-silk suit in forest green, a cream-colored blouse, and emerald jewelry. She made me feel like a toad. She looked directly into the camera and for some reason I was sure it was my image she was staring at. After a moment, her eyes went distant and I knew she was having a vision.

I'd been with Adriana once before in a vision. She seemed to work best when helped through the images. I wasn't sure anyone else had noticed her going out of focus, so I held up one hand to keep the others from speaking, leaned forward slightly, and said, "What do you see?"

"You have . . . fangs, and scars." Her voice was gentle and floaty.

"I do. Is that important?" Most of the worst scars were covered, but the tank top I wore under my blazer had a scoop neck that didn't completely conceal the claw marks where a demon had gone after my heart.

I motioned to Bruno for a paper and pen and waved at Hiwahiwa to come closer to the camera. I wrote down a message on the pad Bruno handed me and held it up for Hiwahiwa to see. *Put a cool, wet cloth against the back of her neck.*

It had worked before to help Adriana out of a vision. Because, realistically, we didn't have all day for her to get lost in her head. Hiwahiwa leapt to obey. She pulled the scarf from around her waist, quickly wet it with some water from a pitcher, then carefully placed the damp scarf against the neck of her princess.

Adriana laughed abruptly, coming back to herself in a

rush. "Oh! I'm such a fool." She was talking to herself, so I didn't answer.

"Adriana?" Lopaka's voice was both sharp and concerned. The queen warring with the mother.

"I'm sorry, Mother." Adriana turned slightly, addressing the image of her mother, I suppose. "I just realized it hasn't been Celia in my visions. So many visions since I met her, but not her. It's someone who looks like her, but without the scars or fangs." She was having a hard time containing her happiness, which was a little weird considering the circumstances of the meeting, but probably made perfect sense to her in terms of the vision.

She turned to Hiwahiwa and touched her shoulder. "The cloth helped."

The secretary looked startled that Adriana had touched her. She bowed her head and was modest. "It was Princess Celia's idea, Highness. I was only the instrument of her instruction."

Adriana looked at the camera and smiled. "My thanks once again, cousin." I just nodded. She could have thanked Hiwahiwa, too. But it wouldn't do any good to step into that mess. I'd learned long ago that Adriana considered her staff mere tools, whereas I thought of them as closer to friends. Of course, Adriana had touched her, which is something I'd never seen her do. Maybe I was rubbing off on her or maybe she was preparing for her new role as queen. Today's royalty have to be more hands-on than in the past. Princess Diana changed a lot of things.

"I see." Lopaka obviously didn't, but she wasn't about to

let a little thing like a vision derail this meeting. She spoke briskly, in a tone that made it clear she wasn't interested in anyone's reaction to what she was saying. "Celia, I know you are going to object, but as your queen and your aunt, I insist that you have a security detail, at least until after the wedding."

"No." My voice wasn't angry or insulted. It was just firm.

She tried reason again, maybe understanding she had no real way to make demands of me. "You have been specifically targeted by terrorists because you are a member of our family. They may also have seen, as our prophets have, that you are instrumental in keeping Adriana alive and seeing her safely wed. So, object if you must, but I'm going to insist that you have at least one agent with you at all times."

I opened my mouth but was preempted.

"I agree," Dahlmar said firmly. "The wedding must go forward as scheduled. We cannot show any sign of weakness. But Celia's life is too important to be risked needlessly. She should be guarded as well as the rest of our families."

Adriana was nodding wordlessly.

Maybe reason would work in reverse, too. "What you're asking simply isn't possible, Aunt. I appreciate the sentiment. I do. But the roles of protector and protectee are very fixed. Adriana saw me as part of her wedding party in the role of a protector. I'm happy to take that role because it's what I'm trained to do. But I cannot be watched and guided and followed at the same time, just as you could not be both queen and waitstaff at the same dinner. If I'm guarding Adriana, I cannot allow anyone else—including another guard—to be close to her. The risk might be *from* the guard—intentional or not. Can you see my concern?"

Lopaka entered my mind, and her voice was the angry sound of chimes caught in a hurricane. *Celia, don't be dense. This is another situation like the one at the shop. The eyes of the entire world are on us. It is necessary that you be publicly acknowledged as the valued member of the royal family you are. You must have the same kind of protection as any other member of the royal family. I will advise my head of security to assign someone you approve of to work with you and to help you select a team who will facilitate your work in protecting my daughter. I must insist on this.*

I didn't like that but there had to be a solution that would satisfy everyone. *Give me a moment to think.*

She turned so smoothly to address her daughter that I doubted anyone knew she and I had spoken privately. "Adriana, I know you did not want to leave my side in the hospital, but I appreciate you making that sacrifice. Queen Chiyoko . . ." She let the sentence go unfinished. Probably best. I'd met Queen Chiyoko, another of the siren royals, from the Pacific Rim siren clan. From what I'd seen, there wasn't any nice way to finish a sentence about her. Maybe she was a terrific ruler. I didn't know. I did know she was arrogant, ambitious, and wanted to see me dead.

"She and some of the other queens are already here and have requested the large conference room for later today." Adriana's eyes flashed dangerously. Chiyoko was definitely a tough customer, but I wouldn't want to cross Adriana with that look on her face. "Don't worry about a thing, Mother. I will take care of it. Concentrate on getting well. You will have your throne to come back to."

Apparently Lopaka had seen the same steel in her daughter that I had. She smiled, proud and pleased. "I don't doubt it. You will be a fine queen, daughter."

There was a flicker of warmth in the green eyes. Adriana spoke again, with a heavy sigh. "I don't worry about my safety for the moment, but I won't be able to leave Serenity for the duration of this impromptu queens' council. Celia, I must ask for your help. Someone must be responsible for obtaining the bridesmaids' dresses. And someone must guard Natasha and Olga as well."

I hated it, but she was right. If someone was whittling down the wedding party to disrupt the event, the bridesmaids were certain targets. But while Adriana was confident about her safety, I didn't know that I agreed. A lot of people live on Serenity, not to mention the many visitors arriving for the wedding. No doubt the queen's guard and security force was going to be pressed to the limit, running background checks on every guest and citizen. I certainly couldn't be at two places at once. Serenity. Who was on Seren—? Okay. I had a thought about a scenario I could accept. Lopaka must have been listening in to my thoughts because she lifted delicate blonde eyebrows just as I once again raised a hand to catch everyone's eyes. "Sorry to interrupt, but how about this—I've worked with Helen Baker of the Siren Guard. I trust her skill, and her loyalty is without question. If she's available, I'd be willing to work with her as a *partner* in protecting Adriana and the Rusland bridesmaids. Partners protect each other, which meets your desires, and I can trust her to guard Adriana while on Serenity, meeting my goals. Would that be satisfactory?"

Lopaka nodded. "That would be satisfactory. Her skill is renowned and I would trust her with my life . . . or that of my daughter. I will make her available."

Adriana mirrored her mother's dip of the head. "Baker is acceptable."

It didn't appear that Dahlmar had met her, even though he was once on the island when she was working with me. He deferred the issue about the protection of his future bride to Creede by looking up at him with a questioning expression. Creede said, "I've met her. She's qualified. Quick, a good shot, smart. No objection from me."

My cousin actually breathed a little visible sigh, as though a huge weight had been lifted from her shoulders. "Then it's settled. Celia, as for the dresses, at this point I honestly don't care what they look like or how much they cost. Just get the bridesmaids into a shop and find something suitable. Your taste in clothing seems to be similar to my own."

Wait. She wanted *me* to shop for the bridesmaids' dresses? With Olga and Natasha? I bit my tongue until I tasted blood. I wasn't going to say anything because anything I said would come out bitchy. I might think all kinds of things, and the telepaths might hear them, but my lips would be sealed.

Creede raised a single eyebrow, and I swear I saw the

hint of a smile twitch at the corner of his mouth. Surely he couldn't read my mind from such a long distance? Surely not.

Could he?

Another smile twitched at his lips. But when he spoke his voice was utterly bland and businesslike as he changed topics. "The authorities have spent the last several hours going over the magical signatures of the evidence. Both Mr. DeLuca's signature and mine were on some of the artifacts that had been shattered and worked into the bullets. So the authorities were very interested in what the two of us have been up to. I was detained and have been answering questions. As, I believe, has Mr. DeLuca. Fortunately for each of us, it was obvious that the items had been created some time ago."

Oh, crap. That explained why Bruno looked like hell. Frankly, I was a little surprised he'd gotten out as quickly as he did. It had to have been ugly. I was surprised neither of them was still in custody or being questioned. I looked from one to the other. They might have been friends if not for me. As it was, they respected each other as men, mages, and rivals.

Creede continued, "There was a more recent signature I didn't recognize. Bruno, had you seen it before?"

I stepped back so that Bruno could stand on the X. "It was vaguely familiar." He ran his hand through his hair in an unconscious gesture of frustration. "I know I've seen it somewhere, but I can't pin down where. I'd thought it might be from when we worked with so many people on the rift. But if you don't recognize it, that can't be it."

That got me thinking: Where had Bruno spent time with a bunch of magic users without Creede?

The answer was obvious, at least to me. "The college." Emma echoed me an instant later as Kevin nodded. Clearly I hadn't been the only one to figure it out.

Rizzoli looked from me to Bruno, to Creede, to Kevin and Emma. "All right, people. Somebody spill it. What college? What are we talking about?"

I didn't answer, just turned to Bruno. Rizzoli was quick. He'd catch on in a second without a blow-by-blow. "It's got to be. Who there has enough juice—"

Bruno's expression was thoughtful. I could tell he was going through everyone on staff in his mind. He turned to Emma. "Em? Who's tested the highest in the GAs?"

"Jan." She turned to Rizzoli. "No question. Jan Mortensen is one of the graduate assistants at the university. He's a powerful mage and the most secretive person I know. He always works magic by himself, and he always cleans up even the tiniest trace of his workings once he's done. I've never met a mage as careful as him."

"I've never worked with him," Bruno admitted. He sounded surprised, like it should have occurred to him that it was unusual, but it hadn't before.

"No," Em said. "And that's weird all by itself. Because Sloan's been having you work with everybody. You do amazing artifact work, better than even our tenured professors of magic." Wow. I do believe he actually blushed at the compliment. Admittedly, Emma is pretty stingy with praise.

She continued, musing almost to herself as she spoke. "But Jan's never even seemed interested in spending any time with you and keeps avoiding me when I try to schedule it. But there's a good chance something he worked on is in Dr. Sloan's office somewhere. Sloan was his advisor last year."

"We will need to *question* this Jan." Dahlmar spoke softly, but his voice sent chills up my spine. I'd had a chance to see some of Dahlmar's retainers in action. And while they'd never done anything untoward, I got the distinct impression they would, just as soon as the setting was a little more private.

"No, Your Majesty." Rizzoli stepped onto the X as Bruno vacated it. His voice was as hard as granite, and about as warm. "*We* will need to question him. The attack was on American soil. We will be happy to cooperate and share information, but we are the lead investigators and are in charge." He stepped off of the X, and in what was probably the most carefully planned "accident" of his career, stumbled and wound up stepping on the red button on the power strip, bringing the video conference to an abrupt end.

Just as well. Because while the king hadn't had a chance to say anything, his expression said more clearly than words that he'd do what he damned well pleased. Lopaka's face had looked much the same.

It seemed a lot of powerful people really wanted to talk to Jan. We'd just have to see who got there fastest.

14

I slathered myself with sunscreen—Emma kept extra bottles on hand for me—and checked my weapons while Rizzoli called for backup to meet him at the university. Rizzoli, Bruno, and I walked out toward the cars, leaving the others behind. We were halfway across the parking lot when the guys exchanged a look. Rizzoli turned to face me, pulling his hand out of his pocket; he was holding something that I couldn't see.

"What?" I looked from one man to the other, trying to figure out what was going on.

"Sorry, honey. You're not coming. Not this time." Bruno didn't sound sorry. He sounded smug. I'd barely opened my mouth to argue when I heard the crack of a spell disk breaking and found I couldn't say anything.

I'd been hit with a full body bind. I couldn't move a muscle. The *bastard*.

Once upon a time I'd suggested this exact spell to Creede. He'd worked out the kinks and started mass-producing different variations. The one favored by law enforcement froze all of the major muscles, but left the heart and lungs alone. Some people could even manage the occasional finger twitch. The binding lasted for ten minutes—long enough for the bad guy to be cuffed and put in the back of the squad car. From what I'd heard, John had been making a fortune off of them. They were certainly useful. I wasn't surprised Rizzoli stocked them. I was just surprised he'd use it on me.

"He's right, Graves," Rizzoli said. "You're sitting this one out. I respect you and you're capable as hell. But you've been named a target by these guys and you're a civilian. I can't risk it. I wouldn't be taking DeLuca here if I didn't need him for permission to search the office. I am sorry." At least he sounded like he meant it. Of course that didn't make me any less pissed when I watched him walk over to my Miata and let the air out of two of my tires.

"I can't believe you did that!" Emma stood in the doorway, glaring from Bruno to Rizzoli and back again. Kevin, a step or so behind her, was chortling.

"She'll be fine in ten minutes," Bruno assured her. "And you know how Mortensen feels about her, and even vampires can be killed by magic. Do you really think she should come along?"

Emma's lips tightened into a thin line. "No, but that's not the point."

Bruno didn't argue. Instead, he picked me up at the waist and carried me into the shade, where he leaned me against the trunk of a tree like a freaking surfboard. Leaning over, he gave me a quick peck on the lips.

I have never wanted to knee a man in the crotch so badly in my life. He had no idea how thankful he should have been for that full body bind. Not a clue.

"Gotta go. Love you."

Emma came out to stand beside me, looking grim, as Bruno and Rizzoli drove away in Rizzoli's car. She showed me the set of keys she was holding. "They didn't disable my car. When the spell breaks, you can take it. But you have to promise me you'll be careful. Jan is powerful, smart, and he really does hate you. I don't know why."

I would've promised . . . if I could've. As it was I just stood there like a freaking statue, my mouth partially open. I was so furious I wanted to cry, but I couldn't even do that. I was so completely helpless. Every second stretched into eternity. Emma, bless her heart, stood next to me, waiting, offering moral support.

Finally, finally, the binding spell wore off, releasing me so suddenly that I stumbled and would've fallen over if Emma hadn't caught me. It took probably five more minutes for the cramping to pass enough that I could have any hope of walking to the car.

"Bruno's going to be pissed if you let her go," Kevin said. The whole time Emma had stood beside me, he had been leaning casually against the doorjamb with Paulie sitting calmly at his feet. He didn't sound like he was going to interfere or like he was passing judgment. It was just an observation.

"Bruno DeLuca can kiss my lily-white ass," Emma snapped.

Kevin shook his head. "Whatever. I'm staying out of it."

"Good," Emma and I snarled in chorus. Raising his hands in surrender, Kevin backed into the house, pulling the door closed behind him and giving himself plausible deniability if Bruno tried to give him a hard time later.

I climbed awkwardly into Emma's little subcompact. My muscles still weren't behaving normally. Fortunately the car had an automatic transmission. I wouldn't have to try to handle the clutch or shift gears once I got it backed out of its parking spot.

Emma pressed her keychain into my hand after I strapped on my seatbelt. "Be careful."

"I will. I promise." I meant it, too. I'm not invincible. The events in Mexico showed me that all too clearly. But I wasn't going to sit back and let Bruno get away with pulling a stunt like this. No way. If I did that he'd feel free to do it again, or something else he considered "necessary" or "for my own good." Screw that—twice—with something sharp.

It was a long drive from Emma's to the university, long enough that I was able to calm down and think by the time I reached the edge of campus. Oh, I was still furious, but it wasn't the blind, unthinking rage that had overcome me when that spell disk cracked open.

They shouldn't have done it and they'd both be getting hell from me about it later.

But that didn't change the reality of the situation.

Dominic Rizzoli was a federal agent. He was smart, tough, and experienced. He was in charge of an investigation to capture a terrorist. He was entitled to give the orders.

More to the point, his talent—and greatest gift—was intuition. He knew where to be, when to be there, and who he needed with him.

If I went against that, I'd be doing to him exactly what Creede had done to me, and I'd be risking lives doing it.

It was a bitter realization. It hurt, and I hated it. But it was the truth. So, rather than pull up to the parking lot and flash my FBI consultant's badge at the security guard standing there, I drove past and parked in the first shady, curbside spot I found. It was a no-parking zone, but I didn't plan to stay long.

I had just started trying to figure out exactly what I was going to do next when Okalani stepped off the curb less than thirty feet ahead of me.

The last time I'd seen her, she'd been a pretty girl of fifteen or so with exotic features, dark brown skin, and hair that would've been kinky-curly if it hadn't been kept cropped close to her skull. She'd looked and acted like a kid. Now, even though not that much time had passed, she looked older, harder. The baby fat had left her cheeks and there were harsh lines at the corners of her mouth.

Holy crap.

I threw open the car door and started climbing out, calling her name.

She turned, and when she saw me, I had microseconds to recognize the expressions that flickered across her face. Recognition, guilt, and terror. She turned, as if to someone standing beside her, though there was no one there. As she did, I saw something flicker at the edge of my consciousness. It was something familiar, yet foreign. I started toward whatever I saw . . . and smelled something I'd smelled before.

Okalani's eyes went wide with horror. "*No!*" she screamed, and leapt toward me, blocking me from reaching past her.

Our fingers touched, the briefest of contacts, and I felt the world lurch sideways.

When everything was still again I found myself in a darkened room lit only by the little red dots from plugged-in surge protectors and a crack of light around each of four doors. Not much light to see by, but I don't need much. Besides, I knew where we were. I'd been in this room dozens of times while attending the college. We were in one of the auditorium classrooms.

Okalani was with me, her breathing harsh. Not from the effort, from tears.

"Were you the bait? To get me close enough to murder?" I kept my voice level even though I wanted to shout at her. I had a feeling I knew exactly what had just happened. It was that little turn that gave it away. If she hadn't done that I would never have noticed the man-shaped shadow that stretched along the ground beside hers. A shadow that seemed to have no source . . . and he'd made the same mistake Bruno had. I could smell his cologne, a very unique, European scent that wasn't often encountered in SoCal. Jan Mortensen. He'd been using magic to hide himself, but forgot those two telling details. Lucky for me. If he'd stuck around a little longer when I'd gone to visit Bruno in his office, I might be dead now.

Okalani sobbed. "I couldn't let him . . . they said you were evil and needed to die, but seeing you, I just couldn't. You're not evil. You're *not*." Her whole body was shaking with the violence of her emotions.

Who the hell was Jan Mortensen and what did he have against me?

Crap. Okalani might be an idiot for getting involved with him, but she'd saved my life. "Thank you." I'm not much of a hugger, but it was obvious she needed to be held, so I took her in my arms. It was awkward. I'm not really good at that sort of thing, and she was wearing this huge backpack besides. "Tell me."

"I . . . I can't. They'll kill me." It wasn't just an expression. It was the honest truth. She held out her arm and I saw the mark of a binding oath on her skin, throbbing an ugly red. She'd nearly already said too much. Binding oaths were serious business. I'd watched Creede's partner decay before my eyes after breaking one.

Suddenly she realized just how serious the situation was. She'd been too shocked before, acting on instinct. Now, looking at the mark, it really hit her. I could see it. She looked around in panic, her dark eyes so wide with fear that the whites showed all around the iris. But it wasn't just the throbbing red pattern on her arm that was bothering her. She'd finally realized where we were.

"Oh, *shit*. No, no, no! We have to get out of here!" I had to grab both of her shoulders and give her a light shake before her eyes would focus on me again.

"Okalani, talk to me. Why is it bad we're here?"

She reached up and ran fingers through her hair, not to smooth it, but as though she wanted to rip it out. "We are so screwed. Princess, I am soooo sorry. I've been taking classes since I moved here. This semester was Practical Matter Teleporation. Dr. Greene's assistant set up a spell so that everything teleported on the university campus for the next twenty-four hours would come here. It's for homework—she's going to review the final product after transit, to see if it survived the trip. And she's sealed the room so nobody can tamper with their results. I have to get us out of here. I told Jan about the assignment. He *knows* we're here. He'll come here looking for us any minute. Oh my God, oh my God. Where can we go? What'm I going to do?"

"Calm down!" I snapped it as an order. Amazingly enough, it worked. She stopped babbling. She was still trembling and terrified, but she seemed capable of listening. "You said the room's shielded—"

"I can teleport through shields. But where can we go? They're everywhere."

She could teleport through shields? Oh, I really wished I hadn't heard that. It was bad on so many levels. Nobody ethical would've taught her that particular trick. It would mean she'd be able to go anywhere at will. Paintings at the Louvre would be easy pickings. High-security prisons wouldn't hold her.

I forced the thoughts from my mind. I didn't have time to think about that right now. Soon, very soon, Okalani and I would be having a chat. But not now. "We need a plan. I promised your mom I'd find you and help you, and that's what I'm going to do. But you need to stay calm and listen."

"My mom sent you?" There was a hint of anger in her voice, but there was hope, too. The kid I'd known on Serenity wasn't completely lost.

I spoke to what was left of that kid, hoping there was enough of her still inside the young woman in front of me. "Your mom loves you, Okalani. She misses you. And she's worried. Terrified you're in trouble."

That proud chin rose, so much like her mother's. "I can take care of myself."

Yeah, right. She'd been doing a bang-up job of that. But sarcasm, while merited, wouldn't help. I sank onto the edge of the stage, narrowly avoiding an odd assortment of items on the floor. Apples, oranges, the mounted head of a bull moose, and even an old Henry repeating rifle. I had more to say to Okalani, but first, I needed to let Rizzoli know about Jan before he escaped completely.

Dominic, it's Celia. Can you hear me? If you can, think the word yes as hard as you can. Scream it in your mind.

Yes. The sound was distant, like a bad connection on a cell phone. But it was him. I've always found it fascinating that the words I hear in someone's mind have the same intonation as if they were actually talking. Dom's mental voice was *pissed.* I didn't have to ask why.

Yeah, yeah. I know. But you can't have believed I'd stay at Emma's house like a good girl, could you? Anyway, Jan Mortensen was using the same hiding spell Bruno uses— remember the potted plant when we first met? Mortensen

*was on the corner of Market and College less than five min-
utes ago. The kid he was with is a teleporter. She whisked me
away before he could do anything unfortunate.*

That got his attention. His voice strengthened in my
mind. *Whisked you* where *exactly?*

I wasn't positive I should say, but someone had to get us
out of here safely. *We're in one of the small auditoriums on
the first floor. The one where Dr. Greene is having the as-
signments sent. Ask someone in the Paranormal Studies class
where that is.* I paused, listening with my ears rather than
my mind. Yes, I'd definitely heard someone messing with
one of the auditorium doors. *And Dom, you might want to
hurry. I think Mortensen may be here.*

I heard the sound of a hand pressing hard against the
door's trip bar, but it didn't open. The door was locked.

Okalani whimpered. "We have to go." She grabbed at
my arm.

She had it halfway right. *She* needed to go. She might be
sixteen, but to me she was still just a kid, and she was a witness. Maybe the only witness who could help us unravel
what the hell was going on. But if I left with her, Jan would
just leave, disappear before Rizzoli and the others could get
him.

I stood up and grabbed hold of her, facing her and taking one of her arms in each hand. Staring into those frightened brown eyes, I willed her to do what I said. "Okalani, I
need you to listen to me. You need to go to your mother's,
have her hide you somewhere safe, and then call me. I've
got connections. People are on the way here now. I'll work

something out. Give me twenty-four hours; I'll get in touch with you. But you have to go to your mom's. *Now.*"

"But my father—"

I heard the sound of a key turning in the lock. Jan was a teaching assistant. Of course he had a key. Shit, shit, shit.

"*Go!*" I whispered harshly, giving her a hard shove. I felt the whiff of displaced air as Okalani vanished. She'd been telling the truth about the shields.

I took cover behind the lecturer's podium. Squatting down, I drew the Glock from its ankle holster as the door opened and the room was filled with blinding light.

Dom. He's here.

We're on our way.

Weapon drawn, I peeked around the edge of the podium. It was Jan, and he saw my movement. With a word and a gesture he threw a ball of fire the size of my head straight at me, like a sizzling comet. I dived and rolled out of the way as the podium was engulfed in flames that spread like napalm across the stage.

He didn't stop firing, either. I kept rolling, right off the edge of the stage, knocking miscellaneous crap to the floor with me. There was so much stuff on the floor by then that I stumbled trying to get my feet under me. Man, what I wouldn't give for one of those body binding charms.

Another blast hit the stadium seats beside me. I smelled burning paint, cloth, and hair. My hair was singed, but I wasn't hurt . . . yet. On the other hand, I hadn't been able to stop moving long enough to get off a single shot.

"*FBI! Freeze!*" Dom's bass bellow came from the doorway.

He had his weapon aimed at Mortensen. The mage screamed a single word in a language I didn't know, and an explosion rocked the room, moving outward from where he'd stood, sending chairs, chunks of concrete, and twisted metal speeding outward in a deadly storm.

I heard Bruno's voice shout a phrase in a tongue that might be early Latin. I was going to need a Rosetta course for ancient magical languages pretty soon. The fire disappeared but I still took what cover I could on the floor between the nearest two rows of seats and waited a moment that seemed an eternity for the wreckage to land.

When I felt it was safe enough to poke my head up I saw blood and destruction. Dom was alive but he and three other agents were injured. Bruno was curled in a fetal position near the wall, moaning. His counterspell hadn't been without consequence.

There was no sign of Jan Mortensen.

15

If i hadn't been friends with Rizzoli it would've been worse. If Dom Rizzoli was more of an ass and less of a professional, it would've taken longer. After all, there were injured agents, an injured civilian (Bruno had a cracked rib and needed some stitches where he'd been hit by a piece of flying debris), a missing witness, and an escaped villain—to say nothing of considerable property damage. Not a banner day for the feds or the agent in charge.

But it wasn't my fault, except for the small matter of showing up at the college. I specifically hadn't followed Rizzoli. I wasn't lying about that and he said he understood. So my questioning was friendly and relatively short, particularly when compared to what had happened at the police station the previous day. I was even able to clean up a little after the session so I didn't look quite so much like the sole survivor in a disaster movie.

I sat in the lobby of the federal building, waiting for my ride and thinking.

The lobby of the federal building is beautiful. The floors

are marble, the atrium area stretches up three stories. A mural stretches along two walls, depicting scenes from the beginning of the Bureau to the present. The entrance doors and reception desk take up the third wall. The fourth is unpolished black stone and nearly covered with two-inch brass plates with the name, rank, and date of death of agents who have died in the line of duty. It's a grim reminder of the price paid to keep the public safe.

No new plates would be put on the wall because of this morning's fiasco. I was glad. We'd been lucky. I was lucky they'd arrived in time. The feds were fortunate in that Bruno had managed a partial shield when the blast hit.

That had been one hell of a spell. It wasn't the work of a student. Not even a graduate student. It was the kind of spell used by trained combat mages in military operations. You do something like that without a team behind you, you're going to be wiped out for a week or more. Good news for the feds and all of the others out hunting Jan. They'd still have to contend with any traps he'd set for them. But he wouldn't be doing any new magic for a few days at least.

"Wow, that's grim." Dawna came up beside me. She stared up at row after row of little brass plates.

"It's supposed to be." I turned to her. "Thanks for coming to get me."

"No problema. Ron's in court all afternoon. It was just going to be me and the crickets." She tried to sound lighthearted, but her smile didn't light up her face the way it usually did. As always, she looked lovely enough to be garnering a fair number of stares, but she didn't even notice. That was so not Dawna. Her suit today was a deep crimson. The jacket had an embroidered collar and a little peplum that drew attention to her tiny waist. The knee-length pencil skirt was just long enough to be modest, showing off a terrific set of legs. Her dark hair was loose, hanging in a sleek, shining curtain down her back.

"What's wrong?"

"Nothing. It's not important."

I didn't believe her, but I also knew that pushing was pointless. She'd tell me when she was ready. But she would tell me. Dawna's the kind who needs to talk things through. Still, it might not be the kind of problem you'd want to discuss in a public place that had both video and audio surveillance.

We exited into bright sunshine and I immediately felt my skin starting to burn.

"I hope you're parked close. My sunscreen's worn off."

"Crap, they don't let anyone park within a block of the building. Get in the shade and wait," she ordered. "I'll come get you."

It made sense, so I was happy to agree. I ducked into the shadow of the building and felt the painful heat of my skin ease almost immediately. I closed my eyes for a second in blissful relief.

Most of the time I'm okay with the "new me." Some of the siren stuff is actually cool. The vampire healing is great. But if a genie gave me three wishes, my very first one would be to go back to being a normal human.

I waited, expecting Dawna to come around the corner in her little Chevy hybrid. Instead I saw das Humvee pull to the curb.

I say "das Humvee" because this wasn't any old Hummer. No, this was a macho man's wet dream—the full military-sized model, completely customized. It was huge, glossy black, and ostentatious, with lots and lots of chrome that glared blindingly in the afternoon sunlight.

"Holy crap."

The passenger door swung open. "Get in."

"What the hell?"

She gave an impatient gesture. I dashed across the sidewalk and hefted myself inside.

It wasn't easy. I'm a tall woman, but this thing was *big*. I couldn't imagine how Dawna had managed it, especially in a skirt and heels. I especially couldn't figure out how she reached the pedals or how she'd managed to lean across the length of the front seat to open my door.

As soon as I had my seatbelt fastened, she pulled away from the curb, traffic parting in her path like the Red Sea parting for Moses.

Sitting there, I couldn't *quite* see to the next county but I could certainly see over all the other cars into the next block. I drive an old Miata, an itty-bitty sports car that's slung low to the ground. Riding in the Humvee was a totally different experience.

"I hate this damned thing," Dawna muttered. "It's so freaking *huge*. It's impossible to find a place to park."

Yeah, that would be a problem—assuming you weren't

willing to crush the lesser vehicles that dared get in your way. But damn, the interior was nice. Unlike military models used in the field, this had real leather, real wood, lots of gadgets. It even had the after-market button with shielding spells. How cool was that?

"Then why are you driving it?"

"Chris insisted." She said it bitterly, not a good sign. "He said that if I was going to be spending the day with you, this was the closest thing we had to a tank. And I shouldn't hesitate to use the shielding spell, either. And see that blue button over there?" She pointed to a button that, like the shielding spell trigger, was after-market, but—also like the shielding spell trigger—very well installed. "That's a panic button. We press that and the Company descends on us for a rescue."

"Really? No kidding?" Okay, that was freaking cool. John Creede had a disk like that, which he carried around in case of emergency. But to have it built into a car? *Awesome.* No, I don't like the Company. They're one of those private mercenary and magical contractors that do all sorts of Soldier-of-Fortuney things that countries don't want to get their hands dirty handling. But a panic button to save one of their people? That appealed to the gadget geek in me in a big way. It was cool. It just was. The moment I got "people," I was going to have one.

"No kidding." She smiled in spite of herself. "Chris isn't just a medic, he's got an actual healing gift. That's really rare. And last year he bought into the Company. He's a junior partner now."

I didn't know what to think about that, let alone what to say. "Um, wow. How do you feel about that?"

We were at a stop light, so she gave me a long, level look. "About as happy as he feels about my working for you. I mean, he likes you and everything. But he says being around you is like riding out a hurricane, a coup, and a bomb attack simultaneously."

Uh-oh. Not good. "Crap."

The light changed, and we surged forward. "Don't worry. I'm not quitting."

I let out the breath I'd been holding. "Oh good. Because I've been thinking about doing something, and I was kind of counting on your help."

"What?" She didn't say "what now" but her tone of voice implied it.

I winced but plowed on. "I've become too high profile to get many bodyguarding jobs as an individual." There was no escaping the fact that business has been down. I hadn't taken the Mexico job just as a courtesy.

She nodded in agreement, but kept her eyes on the road. Apparently driving something this much bigger than she was used to took quite a bit of attention.

"And subcontracting the help I needed for a bigger job didn't work." Understatement of the decade. I started drumming my fingers on the armrest nervously. Why was talking to Dawna making me nervous? Because what I was about to say was big, and I wanted her to agree. It should have occurred to me before now that she might say no, but it hadn't. Just like it hadn't occurred to me that Chris, who was my friend, damn it, wouldn't want his bride-to-be hanging out with me.

"So what are you going to do?"

"I'm expanding the business. I'll hire my own people, send them out on individual jobs, work with them running the bigger ones." I took a deep breath. "I was hoping you'd want to go in with me. I can't meet with female clients because of the whole siren thing." Sirens make normal, fertile women irrationally angry and jealous. It's biological. "You're better with people than anyone else I know."

"So, a glorified receptionist."

"No. A *partner.* Seventy-thirty. You handle the office end and the computer research. I handle the staffing and action."

She was so startled she hit the brakes, hard. We were lucky not to be rear-ended. Amazingly, nobody hit us. Hell, nobody even laid on the horn. They just adjusted, driving around. Being behind a car that obviously costs six figures or more tends to make drivers more nimble. I know it does me.

"A partner?" She looked at me, wide-eyed. But when she spoke again, her voice was only a little bit higher pitched and breathy than usual. "Why not fifty-fifty?"

"Because I'm putting up the building and the money. This is going to take a lot of cash to pull off."

She started the vehicle moving forward again, keeping her eyes on the road. "Then it's probably a good thing I deposited the check from your aunt, for protecting Adriana. It'll make a good start. And hey, if she makes it up the aisle safely, you'll earn the bonus. That should give us more than enough to get started."

Us. She'd said us. I found myself grinning hugely. And a check from my aunt! I'd have to remind Dawna to send her a contract—though, knowing Dawna, she already had.

"But I'm not taking less than sixty-forty. You *need* me. Your people skills . . . well, they sort of suck." She pulled smoothly into the right turn lane, all shock gone, her expression growing almost smug, dark eyes sparkling with mischief.

I knew that look but wasn't sure where she was going with it. "What?"

Smugness grew into a grin. "I can't wait to tell Ron."

16

Dawna had brought me a printout of Olga and Natasha's schedule for the day, e-mailed to her by Helen Baker. While she drove to the tow lot, where we'd redeem Emma's car, I scanned the sheet of paper. Protected by several agents each, Adriana's bridesmaids were spending the day doing interviews. I hoped that would keep them safe and out of trouble until it was time for us to meet for dinner.

After returning Emma's car to her at school, getting my knives from the police station (they wouldn't release the gun, it was evidence), and checking my bank balance—Lopaka's check had caused it to rise quite nicely—we hit the drive-through at Arby's for a pair of French dip sandwiches. Dawna ate one sandwich, setting the second aside for later. I drank the au jus from both of them. We chatted about the new business plan, kicking ideas around. I'd call Roberto as soon as I had a chance, and get him started on the paperwork for our new partnership. Then it was on to my favorite store.

Isaac and Gilda Levy own a shop that carries high-end magical weapons, extremely high-end spelled clothing, and jewelry. The jewelry is Gilda's contribution. Isaac does the spell work and tailoring. It started out as a small place, tucked in beside a dry cleaner in a neighborhood that was just a bit off of the beaten path. But the store had grown over the years I'd known them. They hadn't moved, but they'd expanded into the spaces on either side, and the resulting emporium was now fairly large, bright, and airy.

Gilda Levy met me at the door and gave me a huge hug, squeezing me tight enough that the various gems on her many necklaces began digging uncomfortably into my chest. Gilda is not a beautiful woman in the traditional sense. She's short, standing all of four foot eight inches. She's nearly as wide as she is tall, with wiry salt-and-pepper curls that are moving more to salt as the years pass. But she's got a smile that could melt the polar ice caps and there are laugh lines at the corners of her bright, dark eyes. She practically buzzes with natural energy, zipping from here to there: always busy, always productive. She wears designer clothes in bright colors and enough bling to make the most overdecorated rapper jealous.

Today she was in a pale turquoise pantsuit with a cream, turquoise, and teal striped silk blouse left unbuttoned to show just the right amount of decolletage, which she had accessorized with about ten pounds of jewelry.

"I'm so glad you're safe. We've been worried sick about you." She gave a delicate shudder that made the bangle bracelets she wore jingle. "Terrorists. Our Celia targeted by terrorists. What is the world coming to?" She turned, looking over her shoulder, and called out. "Isaac, Celia's here. Do you have her new jacket ready? She's damaged this one."

She was right, of course. The explosion had done more than stain and rip the fabric. The spells Isaac had worked into the jacket had probably been destroyed. But they'd done their job. I didn't have so much as a bruise from the blast that had destroyed most of the auditorium. I wondered if the FBI would pick up the tab for the restoration.

Isaac came to stand in the doorway between the front of the shop and his workroom. "It's ready for the final fitting. And just in time, from what I hear. Come to the back and I'll finish it up. You're wearing your holster?"

I shook my head. "No. The police kept my gun as evidence."

"You're not unarmed?" He gave me a stern look.

"I have a Glock in an ankle holster, and I'm wearing my knives."

"Good. But that doesn't help us with the fitting. Gilda . . ."

"I'll take care of it, dear." She scurried off to the weapons department with Dawna following in her wake. I followed Isaac into the workroom.

The outer shop is bright, open, and designed to catch the eye of the customers. Every article is lit and displayed to its best advantage. Isaac's workroom is a much more personal space. There is a silver casting circle eight feet in diameter in the center of the room. Inside it are three platforms of various heights that always remind me of the medal stands at the Olympics, but which actually perform a much more prosaic function. Having the client stand on the low dais puts most of them at the perfect height for Isaac to hem and tailor a jacket. The "second place" dais is great for hemming skirts. The highest one is just right for hemming the legs of trousers and tailoring them to fit perfectly to disguise an ankle holster. I remember how excited Isaac was when he had them built. No more crawling around while he performed both mundane tailoring and complex spell work.

Along the walls, outside the circle, are cube-style shelves in unfinished oak that contain books in multiple languages, various spell components, and sewing equipment. In one corner, an old wooden roll-top desk sits next to a beautiful old sewing machine. A high-definition television hung from a mounting attached to the ceiling that could be rotated to face anywhere in the room; it is primarily used to keep clients from getting bored during long fittings.

At the moment it displayed a talk show. I recognized the guest—one of Adriana's bridesmaids, the lovely Princess Olga. I'd never seen the hosts before. Not a surprise really, since they were speaking Ruslandic.

"I really wish I was better at languages," I complained as, at Isaac's gesture, I climbed onto the appropriate platform.

"Ruslandic is not one of mine, but Gilda is fluent. She prefers to watch in the original language when she can, as translations are so often bungled." He held up a needle and pointed it up at me. "Did you know that American English has the most words of any language in the world? And yet, they never seem to be able to adequately translate a word that has only four or five meanings in a foreign language."

Gilda was fluent in *Ruslandic*. Really. How . . . awesomely useful. Oh, the wheels in my mind were free-spinning. "Isaac, do you carry audio equipment for surveillance?"

I looked hot. Men stared and women glared as I followed the maître d' through the trendiest of trendy L.A. restaurants to the private dining room where I'd be meeting the princesses. I wore a tight, bloodred dress with a sweetheart neckline. The hem came to my knees and there was a little slit so that I could walk. Three-inch heels in black matched the jacket I wore and the purse I carried. They also matched my shoulder holster as well as the hilts of my knives and my gun. But nobody would see those. Actually I thought the handbag kind of ruined the look, but I'd had to pick one large enough to hold a netbook.

I made up for the bag with my jewelry. It was perfect— understated and elegant. Each of the individual pieces was spelled: the bracelet was also a microphone so that Gilda could hear everything that went on. I just had to be careful not to bump things as I ate. My earrings were speakers so that she could translate the Ruslandic for me. The gear had set me back a fair amount of money, but, by God, tonight I'd know what Olga and Natasha were saying and whether or not I needed to be worried about them.

I felt like a spy in a 007 movie. I even had my very own thug. Agent Baker was on her way back from Serenity, so

my secret service escort tonight was Agent William Griffiths.
He was a big, imposing redhead, and looked almost as good
in his suit as I did in my dress. I'd take him to a premiere
anytime.

He didn't bother checking the room. It had already been
done. Instead, he waited until I was seated at the elegantly
appointed table before going to stand discreetly by the door.

I'm a casual-dining kind of a gal. I like old-fashioned
diners and places like La Cocina, which might be described
as dives—if you didn't mind risking your health saying it in
front of the owners. But I've been to high-end restaurants
on dates, and heaven knows the amount of time I'd stood
where Griffiths was now, on the edges, making sure the
beautiful people stayed that way. I know what to do with all
the various pieces of silver and crystal, and I can even manage my skirt when the maître d' pushes in my chair without looking awkward. But I still, secretly, feel more than a
little out of place when I eat in places like this. Everything
was so perfect: candlelight, fine linen, watered silk wall-
paper. I felt a little like a kid playing dress up.

Olga and Natasha, however, were born to this sort of
thing. They strolled in together. Olga's head was held high,
her posture almost angry, demanding attention. Natasha,
on the other hand, looked pensive. Her whole body language was off. She didn't seem afraid as much as worried
and distracted. They were an odd pair. Not friends. No, I
decided, they were more like acquaintances, thrown together by chance. But that wouldn't keep them from

teaming up on someone if they felt it was to their advantage. I'd seen that already.

I started with small talk, in English, while the staff filled our water glasses and set out fresh-baked bread that smelled like heaven on a plate. "How did the interviews go this afternoon?"

Natasha opened her mouth to answer, but Olga talked over her. "It is boring. Always the same questions. Very . . . what is the word? Tedious."

Bullshit. I'd seen most of Olga's interview while I was being fitted for my jacket and this dress. She'd loved every minute of the attention. With Gilda translating, I'd been able to watch and listen as she ever-so-carefully tried to make Adriana look bad. Olga never said anything directly insulting—she was far more subtle than that. But she managed to shade her answers in such a way that the public— particularly the Ruslandic people—would be watching my cousin very warily.

Natasha hadn't been much better. She'd expressed wide-eyed concern over attending the bachelorette party I would be throwing for my cousin. She'd heard scandalous things about such affairs. It was a perfect ploy, playing to the religious and conservative elements. Never mind that I hadn't scheduled any such party. Now I had to either give one or figure out a good reason not to—or the press would report that we'd caved to conservative pressure.

Dawna suggested that she might be sincere since, after all, a bachelorette party is a pretty standard custom. I didn't buy it. I'd been shopping with Natasha. Either she'd been doing a fine job of acting when she picked out the racy bridesmaid's dress, or she was lying now. I was betting the latter.

They were making trouble. But it wasn't the deadly kind. Just pettiness. I would've thought it was the result of the siren effect if I didn't know for a fact they both wore an anti-siren charm. Maybe it was just bitchiness, or regular old jealousy. Whatever the reason, the result was the same. If there was any time in the schedule where it could be shoe-horned in, I was going to be throwing a party. There'd be live tweeting by a planted reporter. And I was going to make damned sure it was sedate and boring enough that nobody could accuse anyone of misbehaving. If there wasn't, well, we'd just find another form of damage control.

"Well, maybe you won't have to do any more interviews," I suggested with saccharine sweetness.

"Most unlikely," Olga sneered. "This is the wedding of the century. The press are insatiable."

"Then you're still planning on being part of the wedding party? I'm so glad." I tried to sound both sincere and chirpy. I'm not sure how successful I was at it.

Olga gave me a very unfriendly look over the rim of her water glass. "My father has reminded me that it is a great honor and my *duty* to be part of the wedding." Ah, duty. But was it her duty to celebrate it, or destroy it?

"Natasha?" I made it a question.

"I will not let fear control me. We have skilled guards to protect us. These . . ."—she paused, searching for the right word in English—"villains will not succeed."

"Oh good. I'm so pleased. I was afraid I was going to have to talk the two of you into going through with it, but apparently you're already on board." I was smiling so hard my face was starting to hurt.

We were interrupted by the waiters bringing in the soup and salad course. For me, consommé and a bowl of apple-sauce. I waited until the waiters left before continuing. "The two of you probably know that my cousin has put me in charge of getting the bridesmaids' dresses."

They didn't answer, just stared at me. Natasha's face was expressionless. Olga's eyes narrowed with suspicion. She didn't like that news. Not a bit. I think she believed she could work her way around Adriana. I wasn't so sure about that, but I did know that *she* knew she wouldn't get around me.

"I've brought a computer with me. After we finish dinner, you can look at the dresses I'm considering and we can make a final decision."

After that, dinner was strained. There wasn't much in the way of conversation. Really, what was there to say? So I concentrated on enjoying my food, which really was excellent, and hoped Gilda Levy wasn't getting too bored, waiting for the other women to speak.

When the last of the dessert plates were cleared away, I pulled out my netbook and hit the keys to begin the holographic fashion show that Dawna, Gilda, and I had worked so hard on this afternoon.

There were a lot of dresses. Thirty in all, selected from the websites of various designers and high-end bridal shops. We'd arranged it so not one of the images showed where the gown came from. I wanted the selection to be made on merit, not name. Every dress was pretty, demure, and designed to look good with a jacket. I'd insisted on that, because even during the wedding I intended to be armed. A few of the dresses were knee length, most were floor length. There was silk and satin aplenty, beading and lace. Every one of them was available in purple, a color I was sticking with because (a) it looked good on all three of us; and (b) Adriana had approved it.

"No." Olga slammed her palm onto the table, making the remaining silverware clatter. She glared at me. "None of these will do. Absolutely not."

"I like the third one quite a bit," Natasha said with a quiet firmness that surprised me.

Olga didn't glare at the other woman; she was too shocked. She turned to her, wide-eyed, and spoke in rapid Ruslandic, which my hidden friend helpfully translated.

"*What are you doing? We agreed!*"

"*Perhaps I've changed my mind. Adriana has done nothing to harm us and we owe this one our lives. Are you not woman enough to admit that perhaps the men were wrong?*"

"*Idiot. Those men were not shooting at us. It was the sirens they were trying to kill. It's been all over the news.*"

"*A stray bullet can be as deadly as an aimed one. Think of the woman who waited on us in that shop. She was not a target, but she was killed just the same. Her only crime was having little taste.*"

"*Adriana is controlling our king with her siren abilities.*"

"*Perhaps my father believes that. I do not. The king wears a charm, just as we do.*" Natasha wasn't budging on this. Her eyes had begun to flash with real anger and her chin was thrust forward aggressively.

"*Your father . . .*" Olga was apparently trying to play her trump card. It didn't work.

"*Is wrong. He has not met the princess. Either of them.*"

Well, well, well. Wasn't that just fascinating? Still, if I didn't say something, and quickly, they might get suspicious. So I widened my eyes in mock innocence and said with a smile, "I liked the third one, too." It was even the truth. The dress was simple purple silk with a sweetheart neckline and ruching at the side. It flowed in a beautiful A-line down to a floor-length hem. It was simple, elegant, and would look good on all three of us. "Olga, you're outvoted. Dress number three it is."

"I refuse. I will *not* wear that." She didn't slam her palm on the table this time. Instead, she rose to her feet in a huff that I could tell was mostly hot air.

I merely shrugged at her display. "Fine. No problem. It's a shame you'll miss out on being part of the wedding of the century. But hey, I'm sure your father will understand you foregoing your *duty* when you explain that it's because you didn't like the dress."

She turned on me in real fury. "You wouldn't dare!"

My smile was more than a little bit predatory, but for the first time this evening I wasn't faking it at all. I'm pretty sure my teeth showed. "Oh, but I would. Now, are you in or out?"

"I will be speaking to the king about your insolence," she announced before turning on her heel and flouncing out with her guards hurrying to catch up.

"Go for it," I called. "He already knows I'm insolent." If she heard, she ignored me.

17

It was late. I was tired. Dealing with difficult people wears me out more than just about anything else. I also didn't want to go home until the secret service types had gone over the estate with a fine-toothed comb. Call me crazy, but staying somewhere nice and anonymous, where no one would know where to look for me, sounded like a really nice idea. So I told Gilda, Isaac, and Dawna, via my jewelry, thanks, have a good night and see you in the morning, said the words to end the spell, and rented myself a suite at a nearby hotel that I'd used for clients more than once. Griffiths contacted his superiors, who sent reinforcements to stand guard until morning. I made a couple of calls to let my friends know I was okay, sent an e-mail arranging for the dresses to be delivered to Isaac's shop, filled out my breakfast order and hung it on the door of the suite, stripped, and fell into bed.

I slept well, better than I had in quite a while. No nightmares, not the recent ones, not any of the old standbys that recur when I am stressed. Let's hear it for utter exhaustion!

I woke feeling rested, which was a nice change of pace. After a long, luxurious bath and a room-service breakfast, I brushed my teeth, put on more new clothes that were examples of Isaac's tailoring skills, and was actually looking forward to the new day.

My optimism lasted all of ten minutes—until I called the office. I had three messages from Laka. The first let me know first, that Okalani was with her and safe, and second, that she, Laka, was very grateful. The next two were increasingly frantic. Her daughter had bolted. Had I heard anything?

I swore long and hard. Damn it to hell. Couldn't the kid just stay *put* for twenty-four damned hours? I'd talked to Rizzoli. He was going through channels. I had no doubt that everybody on our side wanted the information Okalani had and would be more than willing to deal with the kid to get it. But damn it, we were dealing with multiple agencies from multiple countries. That takes time.

And now Okalani was gone. She wouldn't be safe, and I couldn't produce her.

The logical place to look for her was with her father. The best place to get his address, the university. I didn't have the pull to do it. Emma could probably get the information out of the university computers, but looking up that sort of thing could get her fired if anyone found out. Calling Rizzoli would get the feds looking for her, but even my handy-dandy consultant status didn't guarantee anyone would share information with me.

I was angry at Okalani, angry at myself. But mostly, I was afraid. These people were playing for keeps. If they found her before I did . . . "Don't think about it, Graves. Just find her."

I dialed the number Laka had left for me. She picked up on the first ring; her hello was breathless with hope and the raw edge of tears.

"It's Celia."

"Have you heard from her?"

"No. But I have an idea of where to look. I need you to call the university. Tell them you're her mother. Find out what she listed as her home address, or if she listed her father's numbers in case of emergency. Then call me back at this number. Can you do that?"

"She's a student at the university?"

"Yes. Paranormal studies."

"Oh, I . . . I didn't know." She sounded hurt and confused. I could understand, even sympathize, but we didn't have *time*.

"Can you call?"

"I'll do it now."

"Good. Call me back with the information at this number."

I hung up and made a quick call to Dom's direct line at FBI headquarters. It went to voice mail. I left a vague message for him to call me, that it was important, but didn't give any details. After all, there was a chance I would find Okalani before he called and save myself a lot of trouble.

I debated calling Queen Lopaka and decided that talking in person would work better. So I distracted myself
with packing my things while I was waiting for Laka's call,
taking special care with the previous night's outfit.

As a courtesy, I stuck my nose out the door. I was pleased
to see who was standing there.

"Hey there . . . *partner*. We need to leave in ten."

Baker let out a little laugh. "Good. I'll make sure the car
is ready." If I'd spent as much time in airports as she had
lately, I'd have looked a wreck. But Baker's hair and makeup
were perfect, her charcoal gray suit was crisply pressed and
beautifully tailored. There was no hint of all the weaponry
I knew she was wearing. She looked as fresh as a very professional daisy. "By the way," she assured me, "the estate is
clear. You can go home if you want. Our people are on the
way to check out your office now."

"Cool. You can stay in the guest room. Hope you packed
a bag, Agent Baker."

She smiled; apparently she'd expected the offer. Likely if
I hadn't made it, she would have found a reason to suggest
it. "I did." She stepped into the suite, closed the door, and
watched me gather the last of my things. "And please, Princess, if we are to be *partners*, you should call me Helen."

"Then I'm Celia, not Princess. Tell you what, Helen.
Let's go shopping in a great place I know. We'll get lots of
shiny things that go bang." She laughed and held the door
for me. I liked that she looked both ways, hand on her
weapon, when she did so. Yes, I wanted to go home, but

more than that I wanted to get to my office and stock up on weaponry. I'd picked up quite a few things at the Levys'. I mean, seriously, how could I not? But given what was going on, I wanted gear I was familiar with. It was a real pity about the Colt, but the police wouldn't be giving it back until they were damned good and ready. The derringer was with Adriana and probably needed to stay there. Until I got a chance to take it to the range and fire it, the Glock Bruno had given me was new and unfamiliar enough that I didn't quite trust it. Yeah, I know Bruno takes care of his weapons. That wasn't the point.

I didn't see myself having time to go to the range in the next couple of days. I had to find Okalani and get back to guarding Adriana.

I had drawn even with Baker when the phone rang. I sighed and Baker did as well. Then I answered. As I was calming Laka and getting information out of her, trying to convince her there was no need for her to come to the mainland, Baker . . . *Helen* was on her radio, making sure our car was being checked again for any possible threats and making changes to our travel plans that ensured that if Laka was phoning duress, nobody would be able to intercept us.

Wow. Even more paranoid than me. I really did like her.

But I doubted that Laka's breakdown could be faked. Waiting was eating her alive. She was terrified for her child and wanted, needed, to be doing something. Unfortunately, there really wasn't anything she could do. I told her the best thing she could do was stay right where she was, even though it's not what she wanted to do. She wanted to be out, pounding the pavement, knocking on doors, calling random houses to see if anyone had seen her daughter. I understood. I'd been there.

Checking out of the hotel didn't take long. A heavily armored luxury sedan waited at the curb with William Griffiths at the wheel. Baker got in front. I had the backseat to myself. I debated where to go first as Griffiths waited patiently for instruction. Finding Okalani and bringing her in for questioning was a priority. I was going to do my best to find her, but the fact is, the authorities all had better resources and more people to throw at that problem. She might hate me for it after, but we could both live with that. The question was, who to approach first? "Take me to the hospital, please. I need to speak to my aunt."

"What about the office?" Helen looked at me quizzically. No doubt she'd heard stories about my safe. She would be disappointed in the new one. My old safe was much cooler.

I tipped my head. "Can't take weapons in there anyway. Why load up my pockets, just to unload them?"

"Point." To her credit, she didn't say anything else.

"Right." Griffiths punched the address into the GPS system and pulled smoothly away from the curb.

A comfortable silence fell, broken only by the impatient tapping of my fingers against the leather armrest.

"Screw it," I muttered after a few minutes' thought. Maybe Okalani's father was a villain. But he was her dad.

She loved him. Maybe he loved her, too. This might be a bad idea, but I didn't have any really good ones. Pulling the note from my jacket pocket, I dialed the daytime emergency contact number Laka had given me. I nearly dropped the phone when a pleasant, recorded voice answered:

"This is the Santa Maria de Luna Police Department. If this is an emergency, please hang up and dial nine-one-one. If it is a nonemergency, please enter the extension number now. To reach our company directory, press seven."

Oh, shit.

Okalani Clark, Ricky and Okalani's daughter, was Okalani CLARKE. With an E. Laka's former husband was my hit-and-run driver and would-be killer, J. Clarke. Ricky was a nickname. Maybe his middle name was Richard. Not that it mattered.

I sat there, cursing myself inwardly for being so incredibly dense. How had I missed something so obvious?

The pleasant recording responded to my nonresponse. "I'm sorry, I didn't recognize your entry. If this is an emergency, please hang up and dial nine-one-one. If it is a nonemergency, please enter the extension number now. To reach our company directory . . ."

I pressed a series of numbers from memory. I needed to talk to Alex.

She picked up on the first ring. "Detective Alexander."

"Alex, it's me."

She gave a huge sigh. "Now what?"

"Gee, glad to know you're happy to hear from me."

"Celia, I like you. I really do. But every time you call, there's trouble, and not just little trouble, either. Your trouble usually comes with a body count. So don't be surprised if I'm not thrilled to hear from you."

"Well, crap." There was an uncomfortable pause.

She was the one to break it. "Well? What is it?"

"I have a problem."

She gave a bitter laugh. "Of course you do. Tell me."

I started with the hit-and-run attempt and kept right on going until I reached the present, with Okalani missing and Jan Mortensen wanting her dead. "I could be wrong. Hell, I hope I'm wrong. I like the kid. And I don't ever like to think about there being crooked cops in the department."

"Nobody does," Alex agreed. Her voice was serious. "Rick's not with the department anymore. He was asked to resign a couple of weeks ago."

That shocked me. The PD doesn't fire someone lightly. There are long, complicated processes involving internal affairs and board hearings. "He was asked to resign?"

For a long moment we sat in silence. I'd just come to the conclusion that she wasn't going to answer me when she sighed and started talking. "Several very valuable things went missing from evidence. Everybody from the Chief on down had to take a polygraph. Anyone who refused would be put on suspension, pending investigation."

"I take it the investigation went badly for him?"

"There wasn't enough proof to satisfy the DA. But, yeah. He did it. We don't know exactly how he did it. But we know it was him."

I had a pretty good idea how he'd done it. I didn't like getting Okalani in trouble with the cops, but this would give Alex a great excuse to bring the kid in for questioning if she found her. It might even save the girl's life. She'd be safer, harder to get to, in police custody. Assuming of course she'd *stay there*.

"Did you know Clarke has a kid?"

"Had. He *had* a son. Kid got drained by vamps after a football game a couple of years ago."

"*Has*," I corrected her in turn. "A daughter, who was raised by her siren mom on Serenity. She's the teleporter who helped us when we put Dahlmar back on his throne. She moved to the mainland to live with her father. She's admitted to me that she can take things through magical barriers. You might want to bring her in and talk to her about it, and while you're at it, you might ask her about her father's anti-siren sentiments and their connection to Jan Mortensen."

Alex's breath whooshed out in a low hiss. "Why are you bringing this to me? You know the feds are going to want to talk to her."

"So are King Dahlmar and Queen Lopaka's people. I thought I had her stashed safely away, but she bolted. I think she's trying to save her father. That's the first place Mortensen and the others will look for her. She's in trouble, a lot of trouble. You may be her best shot."

Alex paused. "So, find Ricky and we find the girl?"

"I think so."

The thumping I heard might be Alex's fingers drumming

on the desk. "I shouldn't be telling you this, but I heard he's gotten himself a job working security for one of the big movie studios outside of L.A. But *we'll* check it out. No civilians on this one."

"Thanks, Alex."

"Whatever." She hung up on me without saying goodbye. That hurt, but not enough to matter. Not today.

18

I went to see my aunt to ask her to be merciful. After all, the queen knew Okalani. The kid had been helpful during the whole situation with King Dahlmar a couple of years ago. Hiwahiwa, the queen's personal assistant, was close to Laka and Okalani as well. I hoped that Queen Lopaka would take all of that into consideration and be lenient. My mistake.

"High treason is a capital offense."

I was in my aunt's hospital room, sitting in the chair beside her bed. It was a small room filled with lots of equipment and I was feeling a little claustrophobic, especially since equipment was hardly the only thing in the room. Flowers covered nearly every flat surface, towering arrangements from heads of state around the world. A saltwater aquarium burbled beside me, colorful fish swimming in lazy circles. The sound and sight were soothing. I needed to be soothed. Her Royal Majesty was not feeling the love right now. There was no mercy in her for a subject who'd conspired with terrorists.

Normally I would've agreed, which made me less than effective at arguing on Okalani's behalf. But I was doing my best, playing up the young woman's past service. "She saved your life, if you remember, and kept Dahlmar on his throne. Adriana wouldn't have met him if not for Okalani. She ferried mages back and forth when the rift was chewing up the world. All while knowing she could die at any time. Really, she's done a lot of good for the sirens."

The queen sat rigidly straight—she would've been upright even if the bed hadn't been adjusted to the sitting position. She was wearing a lovely peignoir the shade of pink you find inside the bend of a conch shell. Her color was good. Apparently her recovery was progressing rapidly now that the doctors had consulted with physicians from Serenity who were, naturally, more familiar with siren biology. "You act as though Okalani is still a child. Perhaps in your world she is. But in our world, she is not. I, myself, had been on my throne for three years by the time I was her age."

"But you are . . . extraordinary. Most people are not."

"I admire your compassion." Her tone of voice contradicted her words. She heard that thought, or else she read my body language, because she said, more gently, "Truly. I do."

One of these days I was going to have to learn to shield.

Yes, you will. In truth, you have much to learn. I understand your feelings. I even admire them. But I am queen. I have been so for hundreds of years. My first duty is to my people. Okalani betrayed us. That betrayal cost lives—siren lives and human lives. She worked willingly with people whose goal is to exterminate us like vermin. Even sincere contrition is simply not enough. She must pay for her crimes, and the law established by my people is clear. The punishment is death. But if she cooperates, shares everything she knows, I will allow her an . . . honorable death.

What the heck was that? *I don't understand.*

Her actions have dishonored her entire family. Her mother, any siblings, the family for three generations in either direction will bear that shame in the eyes of my people. It is our tradition. But if she truly helps us to stop this madness, I will allow her to commit Akkana—ritual suicide. Nothing can save her, but it will at least spare her family the taint of her shame.

Ritual suicide? That was the *good* option?

I am sorry, Celia, truly.

I couldn't tell if she was or not. I was just hoping something would change to make any action unnecessary. *So am I.*

The queen spoke her next words aloud, giving me at least the illusion of mental privacy. "Go. Think about what we've discussed." She reached over, patting my hand. I'm not really the patting type, and neither is she. It seemed an odd gesture. Then again, she was in an odd mood—angry, regal, but also extremely tired and very worried. "Pack everything you will need for several days. My jets are busy today ferrying most of my sister queens home, but I will have

Hiwahiwa arrange a flight for you tomorrow. I would that it were sooner, but we will simply have to trust the Secret Service a bit longer."

"I could fly commercial."

She smiled more broadly, her eyes lighting up a bit. "That won't be necessary, but thank you for offering. Frankly, security would have a fit, and rightly so. No, tomorrow will be fine."

I surprised myself by saying, "I wish you were coming, too."

"As do I. I hate this more than you know. Chiyoko has kindly offered to stay and to advise Adriana." The bitterness in the queen's words was palpable.

"Oh, hell."

"Indeed. I had hoped that using the video conference idea you had given me, showing her that I am recovering, would dissuade her from this unseemly grab for power . . ." She let the sentence trail off unfinished.

There was nothing I could say. From what I'd seen nothing, ever, would dissuade Chiyoko from anything. I had never spent more than a few minutes with her, but they'd been memorable. Besides, power-hungry people are never satisfied. It's an addiction. Any addict always wants more.

I looked at my aunt. She was wearing out. Sirens might be tough, but they weren't invincible, and the terrorists had very nearly succeeded in killing her, thanks to the information Okalani had provided.

Perhaps the queen was right. Or not. I just didn't know. I did know there was nothing more for me to do here. "I'll let you get some rest. Try not to worry any more than you have to."

She gave a snort of amusement, then nodded, a silent gesture giving me permission to leave.

Taking my cue I rose, bowed, and walked away.

Baker led me down one of the back stairwells after notifying Griffiths that we were leaving and telling him where to meet us. I'd turned off my cell phone to meet with the queen and switched it back on as we went down the stairs. There were five missed calls, all from Laka.

I knew I should call her back. Maybe Okalani had come back. More likely, she hadn't and her mother just wanted updates. Whatever, I didn't want to deal with it. Not now, with my conversation with the queen so fresh in my mind. Later. I'd crush Laka's hopes for her daughter later.

The car pulled to the curb, Griffiths at the wheel. Baker led. She was cautious, spraying Griffiths with holy water from both a general purpose container bottle and from one that looked to be part of her own private stash, to make sure it was truly him and not a shape-shifted spawn, before letting me get into the backseat.

"Where to?" Griffiths half turned, looking at me over the top of the front seat as Baker climbed in on the passenger side.

"Home," I answered. "Take me home."

"Princ . . . Ms. Graves, we're here."

I blinked in surprise, waking. Griffiths seemed to be a

quick learner, or perhaps Baker had clued him in on the "no princess" policy. I reached into my bag and pulled out the remote that granted me entry to my home. It's not just one where you push a button, like a garage-door opener. I have to enter a code and press my fingerprint to a pad. Magical biometrics. Good stuff.

Cooper Manor is a large estate with elaborate security, for which I'm grateful every day. There's a long, winding drive through manicured lawns that leads to the mansion. A small branch off of that drive leads to my parking lot.

"How long was I asleep?" I was shocked. It wasn't even ten in the morning and I'd dozed off?

"You've had a rough couple of days," Baker said. "And there are more of them on the way. Rest when you can."

She was right, of course. My life had been rough, and for longer than a few days. But the fact that I'd fallen asleep was a good sign—I'd chosen well. With Helen Baker as my "partner," I felt secure. And Griffiths must have proven himself to my subconscious, too. Trust is a wonderful thing. As Griffiths pulled the car into the little parking lot near the guest cottage, I made up my mind. I needed more than rest. I needed peace. Until I got things straight in my head and my emotions under control, I was going to be useless. "I'm going to the beach."

They didn't say a word. Of course, they were sirens, so they'd know all about the call of the ocean. I pulled my house key from my pocket and tossed it to Baker. "My bedroom is the yellow one. Feel free to take either the blue or the white."

I climbed from the car, grabbed a beach umbrella from the storage box on the back deck, and went looking for peace. My private bit of beach is a little strip of sand and rocks that edge onto the ocean. It's too rough and rocky for good boating or surfing, but it's beautiful. I found a sandy spot next to my favorite rock, pitched my umbrella, and sat staring at the ocean and watching the gulls play.

Within ten minutes I reached an unpleasant conclusion. Two hours later, I hadn't changed my mind.

I couldn't help Okalani, no matter how much I wanted to.

I'd given my information to the police via Alex and to Rizzoli via voice mail. Alex was good at her job. If she found the kid, Okalani would be arrested and probably turned over to the feds. If the feds found her, or got her from the police, she might be able to make a deal—information in exchange for witness protection. I'd seen it happen before.

But if the sirens found her, she'd be killed. Honorably or dishonorably, she'd be just as dead.

The best thing I could do for Okalani was stay the hell away from her and pray that the good guys who didn't want her dead found her before the ones who did; and that either set found her before the villains.

It sucked.

Staring at the ocean didn't make it suck any less. I was hurt, sad, and angry. I wished . . . Not that it mattered what I wished. As my mom used to say, "If wishes were horses, we'd be up to our eyeballs in shit." In fact, I might be anyway.

19

My flight would leave at 2:00 P.M. from a private airstrip not far from town. It was probably an hour's drive from the office. Since it was private, I'd be able to pack whatever weaponry I cared to bring. I could strip the safe bare if I wanted. I was going to take spell disks, my guns, various ammunition, my knives, and some One Shot brand squirt guns filled with holy water. I probably wouldn't need the special loads on Serenity; there are no monsters on the islands. Well, there aren't *supposed* to be. But we'd be going straight from Serenity to Rusland, and I might need them there, so I needed to pack them now if I wanted them later.

I would also have time to meet with the client who'd been on the books since the day I got back in town.

I could hear Ron and Dawna arguing the moment I climbed from the car. So help me God, if I hadn't had to go to the bathroom so bad I would've climbed back in and have Griffiths drive us somewhere else. But the morning rush hour had offered up bumper-to-bumper traffic and I'd drunk two large mugs of coffee. So I steeled myself and entered the lion's den.

"I've *had* it!" Ron is not a small man. He towered over Dawna, even in her heels. But she stood toe-to-toe with him, not giving an inch. Years of putting up with his crap had finally come to a head. I could tell that from across the room. Ron was an idiot if he didn't recognize it. "That woman is a menace."

That woman? That would be me. It always is.

"All right, what's up?" I asked. Baker had entered ahead of me and Griffiths was behind. They both kept one hand close to their sidearms, ready to act as backup, but they didn't need to. On my worst day I could handle Ron without breaking a sweat. He's a big bully, but there's no substance to it.

He whirled around at the sound of my voice. "You!" He pointed a meaty finger at my face.

"Yep, me. Now, what's the problem?" There was an edge in my voice you could shave with. Like Dawna, I had pretty much reached the end of my ability to put up with Ron's abuse.

"I'm moving out! I can't take any more of this. Terrorists! There are actual terrorists after you, with bombs. You being here endangers all of us." He started to move forward, to try to use that big body to intimidate me, but Baker suddenly appeared just in front of him. She wasn't aggressive; she barely even seemed to move. But she stopped him cold.

"Okay," I said in a perfectly pleasant tone of voice. Because, truthfully, imagining Ron out of my hair really was just so incredibly pleasant.

He stood there, blinking a little as if we'd startled him. "Okay?"

I sighed. "Ron, actual terrorists have made viable threats. Any sane and rational person would get as far away from that as possible. I'm a little startled to find out you're rational, but hey, good on you." I heard a soft snort of what might have been suppressed laughter. Griffiths, I think. I didn't look. If I did, Ron would notice and we'd have more of a fuss on our hands than we already did. "You want out of your lease, I'll let you out. Hell, if you can get moved out by the end of the week and leave the place clean, I'll not only give you back your deposit, I'll refund this month's rent as a gesture of good will."

It took him a few seconds to take that in. He'd won. But he was Ron, and he was an attorney, he had to push for just that little bit more. "My moving expenses—"

"No."

He opened his mouth to argue, but I cut him off. "No."

I turned aside and moved around both him and Baker, to the reception desk where Dawna had resumed her usual seat. I was not going to argue. If he took the offer, fine. If he didn't, he was a fool. Either way, I was finished with it, and him. "When's my client due?"

Behind me, Griffiths gave a polite cough.

Apparently, I'd been too involved to notice a new arrival. Just great. Peachy. I pasted a smile on my face and turned to greet the newcomer. Points to me, I was even able to hold on to the smile when I saw who it was.

Angelina Bonetti.

Oh, hell. This was so not my day.

"Ms. Bonetti."

"You know my name." She wasn't happy about it. Her eyes had narrowed, her voice polite but chilly. She'd expected to surprise me, have the advantage.

"Bruno showed me your picture." Oh, she didn't like that, not a bit. It showed. Apparently he was supposed to keep her from me, like some deep dark secret. The woman he'd always hold a torch for, someone to be ashamed of still having feelings for. And maybe he would have kept her a secret—if I hadn't found the picture. Or not. Because he'd had the whole day to plan our date. To clean up. Why keep an incriminating photo around if he was embarrassed?

I forced myself to keep smiling. "I understand you were his high-school sweetheart. If you'll have a seat, I'll be with you in just a minute." I gestured toward the lobby. I didn't stay to see if or where she went. Whatever was going to happen next could wait. I was going to the bathroom. Now.

As I was washing up, I took stock of myself in the mirror. I was wearing a nice black suit with a white blouse. My hair was pulled back and my face was made up in my usual business-appropriate way. My bone structure has always been a little harsh, but that became more apparent after the bite—and even more so since I'd dropped weight in Mexico. I've learned to keep the fangs hidden most of the time. My skin doesn't glow green unless I'm vamping, which isn't often anymore. I could hold my head up at any business meeting in the city. Unfortunately, I couldn't hold a candle to Angelina Bonetti.

I've known some gorgeous people. Vicki Cooper, my best friend since college, was the daughter of a pair of A-list movie stars, and was so beautiful that when she went out in shorts and a tank top she could actually stop traffic. Seriously, I honest-to-God saw a guy almost wreck his car because he was staring at her.

Angelina left Vicki in the shade. She'd grown into the face I'd seen in the photo. She was still petite, tiny even, but with dangerous curves that were emphasized by the crossover cut of the sapphire-blue dress she was wearing. The jewels she wore at her throat, wrist, and ears were sapphires as well, with just enough diamonds to add a little sparkle. Her long, dark hair had been swept back and to one side in a casually messy braid, a style that emphasized a heart-shaped face dominated by huge, doelike eyes and full, red lips.

She was overdressed for a simple business meeting and I doubted it was accidental. How I reacted would determine if she got the upper hand.

"She's trying too hard. That means she's nervous." My reflection smiled at me. It wasn't a happy smile. But I stiffened my spine, dried my hands, put a quick, glossy shine on my already pink lips, and went back to the lobby by way of the kitchen, where I fetched coffee for myself and my guest.

Baker was coming down the stairs as I entered the room. She gave me a brisk nod to let me know the office was clear. I acknowledged the gesture and turned to my client. "Ms. Bonetti, if you'd like to come upstairs? I hope you like coffee." I extended the cup to her. "It's black, but I have cream and sugar available in my office if you'd prefer."

"Black is fine." She stood, smoothing her dress with an automatic gesture before taking the cup from my hand. God, she was tiny. I felt awkward and huge standing over her. Normally, this kind of thing doesn't bother me. Hell, Dawna had to be about this woman's size. So what was the problem?

Attitude. Which meant I needed to adjust mine. Stat.

Baker took the lead up the stairs; Angelina, Griffiths, and I followed. The stairs to the third-floor office are steep. I'm used to them, and I knew the agents worked out. And it seemed Ms. Bonetti did, too, because she made it to the top without getting breathless or spilling her coffee. Point to her.

As we climbed, I remembered the night I'd gone to the winery in the Napa Valley for the debut of the new wine John Creede had helped create. Before that evening, Dawna, Emma, and I had spent several days in a spa. I'd been pampered and patted, trimmed and manicured. Hair extensions, smoking dress, and perfect makeup.

It took me a few minutes to channel the Celia I'd been that night, but by the time we reached my office, I was the woman John's assistant had mistaken for a model. Point to me.

We took our seats, me at my desk, Angelina in one of the matching wing-backed visitor chairs. Baker and Griffiths waited outside the closed door.

"So." I smiled with saccharine sweetness and grabbed the bull by the proverbial horns. "Shall we sharpen our claws, or should we just cut to the chase? I'd prefer the latter. I've got a lot to do today."

She didn't even blink. "I want him back."

Wow, that was direct. I took a sip of my coffee before answering. "I'd say that's up to him."

"He wouldn't be with you at all if it weren't for you using your siren magic on him." Her words were crisp, her back rigid. It was obvious that she was furious, and I hadn't done a damned thing. I hadn't deliberately worked siren magic against Bruno and I'd taken measures to protect him, but I couldn't help having my siren abilities work against me with Angelina. It made me uneasy, since jealousy can be used to kill us.

I shook my head. "Nice try. But I gave him a charm that counteracts siren magic."

"He doesn't wear it."

She stated it as a fact. There was no doubt in her voice, none, which I found very interesting indeed. She knew about the charm. Bruno might have told her, but I doubted it. No, I'd lay my money that Bruno's mother was the source of her information. It made me wonder if talking was all Mama had done. The charm had been made with my hair—hair that could be used in all sorts of spells: tracking spells being first among them. Assuming, of course, someone was a witch or mage with a certain level of ability. Bruno's mother is such a witch. He comes by his talent naturally.

"Not my fault. Not my problem. We got involved and were engaged before the bite. I was no more siren than you when he gave me a ring." I took another sip, trying to look casual.

"You're not even faithful to him. You expect him to *share*, of all things." She was practically spitting out her words. Funny, now that she was getting angry, she wasn't nearly as attractive. She looked cold, hard, and capable of almost anything.

"Why did you come here?"

"I wanted to see what I was up against. Now that I have, I realize I shouldn't have worried." She rose to her feet, using rage and posture to make herself more imposing. "Good-bye, *Princess*," she hissed.

I stayed right where I was and kept my voice bland as butter. "Good-bye, Ms. Bonetti."

I watched her sashay out. She didn't slam the door because of the agents standing outside. But she would've. Bitch. A beautiful bitch, but a bitch nonetheless.

Meeting with her probably hadn't been smart, but hey, not my fault.

"Whatever." I shook my head. At some point I was going to have to really think about what had just happened— probably talk it over with Emma and Dawna. But right now I had an unexpected hour to myself and I had all sorts of uses for it.

I spent the time productively, going over the schedule of wedding events, looking for a spot to shoehorn in my party. It seemed that my best choice was the night of the rehearsal dinner on Serenity. The notice was so short it was practically breathtaking. There was no way was I going to get a venue. They'd all be booked up. I suppose there was probably a suitable room in the palace. It was a *palace*, after all. But what kind of party happened in the bride's home?

I looked around, trying to come up with some inspiration, and found it. The office. This building was secure. It was historic and elegantly furnished. There were multiple bathrooms and a kitchen. If Ron took me up on my offer (and he would—there was no way he'd miss a chance to save a buck), there was a good chance he'd be out of the way. We could put a bar in the lobby and the buffet in the conference room, and have a DJ and dancing in the empty offices.

It might just work.

Holy crap. It really might.

I called Baker and Griffiths in to review the plan with them. They immediately started poking holes in it.

"No caterers. There isn't enough time to do background checks on their staff and drivers," Baker stated.

She was right, of course. Small caterers wouldn't have the facilities to do something this quick. Big ones were, well, big. "Crap."

"You could use staff from the royal kitchens," Griffiths suggested.

"There are all sorts of laws about importing food," I pointed out.

"True," he agreed. "But if they come over today, they could buy and prepare the food here."

Baker grinned; her smile lit up her face, taking years off of her appearance.

"What?" Griffiths and I chorused.

"I am picturing Chef Antoine's reaction to working in an office kitchen."

The two of them laughed. Apparently it was an inside joke. Whatever. "Do you think it's workable?"

"Call the princess. She's in charge. If she agrees to it, we will *make* it work."

20

Adriana's answer (to my secret relief) was no. She already had plans with her gal pals from Serenity during that time slot. Even though they were no longer in the wedding party, they were her best friends, and she wanted some time with them before she moved to the other side of the planet. And, as she pointed out, there was no other room in the schedule, and security would be a nightmare. She thanked me for the thought, but insisted that it just wasn't workable. She added that her friends had asked her to invite me to come along. I told her I'd be happy to, but as her security. She didn't argue, just said, "I'll tell them you're coming."

I didn't dance out of the office after that call, but I wanted to. I'd have done my duty by Adriana the same way I would for Dawna and Emma when the time came. But Dawna and Emma, I *know*. I know who to invite, and that if I didn't have it at La Cocina my friends would be seriously disappointed, as would Barbara.

So with a smile and a clear conscience I told Dawna,

Baker, and Griffiths that the princess had declined. I promised Dawna I'd keep in touch by phone and e-mail over the next few days, and with quiet delight, grabbed my things and headed off to the islands.

The Isle of Serenity is actually the largest of a chain of small islands in the Pacific between the mainland and Hawaii. For centuries the Pacific branch of sirens have made it their home and, until recently, kept it and themselves shut off from the rest of the world. The islands hadn't appeared on maps. They weren't on flight paths. Magic had been used to keep people the sirens didn't want to see at bay.

That was all changing, and changing rapidly under my aunt's new "inclusion" rules, with mixed results. East Island has the royal compound, the queen's private docks, and the nature preserve. West Island is as modern as you could want, with a couple of actual cities and the international airport. I'd been worried that there'd be trouble since I was bringing in enough weapons to arm a developing nation. Although Baker and Griffiths had assured me that my permits, my rank, and the direct orders of the queen herself would smooth the way, I was fretting.

Turned out I shouldn't have worried. Adriana had decided to meet the plane, with Queen Chiyoko at her side, and with all the pomp and circumstance that a real princess would receive. It was so weird. But I'd wager it would be best not to get too used to it, because once the wedding was over, things would get back to normal with startling speed. The attention span of the public in general and the press in particular is exceptionally short.

What a relief that would be. Until then, however, the spotlight was on the sirens, particularly their royalty, including me. I knew full well that my appearance was a direct reflection on Adriana. So before we got ready to land I popped into the miniscule but well-appointed on-board bathroom and primped. I could, and would, look my absolute best.

So my hair was fluffed, my makeup in place, and my smile fang-free when I stepped out of the plane and onto television screens throughout the world.

Adriana embraced me with actual warmth. To my surprise, Chiyoko hugged me, too. Her posture was so stiff she might as well have been wearing a whale-bone corset under her pretty red suit. But while it was obvious she didn't like me any better than she had the last time we'd met, and hated having to touch me even the littlest bit, she smiled like a pro for the cameras and said all the right things.

I was expected to say a few words, so I told everyone how happy I was that King Dahlmar and Princess Adriana had found each other, and added that I was incredibly flattered to have been asked to be part of the bridal party.

One of the reporters in the back tried to ask probing questions about my mother and my childhood. I pretended not to hear, answering other, lighter questions instead. Then I posed for a few more photos, before we were whisked across the tarmac to the motorcade.

We drove swiftly through the city, our path cleared by

an advance team. Neither Chiyoko nor Adriana seemed to want to talk, which was fine by me. I contented myself looking out the car window.

Serenity City was a lot like L.A.—minus the movie stars and plus a lot more flowers. There were lots of boutiques and a handful of high-end department stores. There were few signs of the earthquake that had roused me from sleep that night at Bruno's, though I knew from news reports that it had been felt here, too. If there had been any damage, it had already been cleaned up thoroughly. Everything had been gussied up for the royal wedding. Banners of black and silver alternated with ones of purple and gold above all the main streets. Posters of Dahlmar and Adriana's engagement photograph hung in shop windows that also displayed commemorative plates, knickknacks, and anything else you could think of. Adriana looked stunning, nearly ethereal. Dahlmar looked regal and elegant. I think they'd added a little more black to his hair than he really has. But hey—artistic license and all that.

The place was pulsing with life, too. Gulls wheeled and cawed overhead, their voices competing with the sounds of the city. Baker commented that the roads were packed because so many people had come to witness the first half of the wedding festivities. It had to be a security nightmare, but an electric current of excitement ran through the town, and for the most part everyone from the mainland seemed happy in their ill-fitting lavalavas and Bermuda shorts. They lined the streets, shouting and waving wildly as we went past, cameras and cell phones clicking away, capturing fleeting images of royalty. Adriana and Chiyoko did the tipping-hand "royal wave" as we drove down the street. I couldn't bring myself to, so I just smiled a lot.

We'd reached the highway leading to the east half of the island before Adriana broke the silence. "What is the status of the bridesmaid dresses?"

"They should arrive at Levy's today." I smiled. "Isaac and Gilda have agreed to do the tailoring and the spell work. Agent Baker told me that they've cleared their background check, so no worries there." I hadn't been worried. I've known and loved Isaac and Gilda for years. But Adriana had wanted reassurance from her own security people. Her big days were coming up very quickly and things hadn't ex-actly been going smoothly. She needed to know that some-thing, at least, was going according to plan. Well, plan B. Or C, or whatever plan we were on by now.

"You should be using one of the royal tailors, not some stranger." Chiyoko didn't even bother to look at Adriana when she said it. It was a small slight, but a deliberate one. Since she outranked my cousin, she knew she could get away with it.

Still, Adriana isn't one to let things slide. She smiled ever-so-sweetly and answered, "Isaac has done all of Celia's tailoring for years. In fact, that's one of his outfits she's wear-ing right now. Cousin, how many weapons do you have on you at this moment?"

I took a quick mental inventory. "Two guns, a pair of knives, two One Shot guns with holy water, about a dozen various spell disks"—I paused, knowing I was forgetting something—"oh, and the garrote."

Chiyoko turned away from the window, her eyes just a little bit wider than usual. "Truly?" She stared at me, looking me up and down very carefully. "I can't see any of it." Her voice was more curious than disbelieving.

I don't like flashing my weapons, but I could tell that Adriana was up to something. So, sighing, I pushed up my left sleeve a bit to reveal the hilt of the sheathed knife. At Chiyoko's raised eyebrow I opened my blazer enough to let her see the holstered gun and the small loops that held my squirt guns.

"What are the empty loops for?" the queen asked.

"Stakes, usually. I'm not wearing any because there's never been a vampire on Serenity."

"Until you." She smiled like butter wouldn't melt in her mouth.

"I . . . am . . . not . . . a . . . bat." I spoke softly, almost gently, but enunciated every word past smiling teeth. She obviously wanted to provoke me, was counting on my getting angry and saying or doing something that would cause trouble. I wasn't going to oblige her.

"And yet obviously not fit for the throne."

"Very true. I made that clear the last time I was here. I don't want the throne."

She smiled again, and this time it was the cat that ate the canary. "Then your aunt, Queen Lopaka, has neither heir, nor any prospect of one."

Aha. There it was, out in the open. I smiled again, and this time I made sure my expression was every bit as predatory as hers had been. "Oh, I don't know." I looked at Adriana to confirm whether my suspicions about her vision of the other day were correct. "My cousin is a prophet, and I believe she's seen who the new heir will be. It isn't me."

The car turned and stopped; apparently we'd reached the gates to the queen's compound. Perfect timing. I couldn't wait to get out of this car, but Chiyoko needed to hear about the future High Queen of Serenity from the princess who had seen her.

"It's true, Aunt." Adriana used the familiar term that I suspected was more a tradition between the royal houses than a fact of biology. "You should check with your own prophet. My sister-to-be will someday look remarkably like Celia, but without the fangs, tattoo, or scarring."

"You lie." She spat out the words, glaring at each of us in turn.

"Be careful, Aunt. Do not assume I will not call for a duel. Or Celia, either. She's quite the fighter, as I'm sure you remember from watching the two of us duel." Adriana kept her tone light, but her green eyes were flashing dangerously and there were spots of color on her cheeks.

Oh, hell. I didn't say anything, but I thought at her, hard. *Don't drag me into this.* Yeah, I'd fought a duel with Adriana—I'd had to. But I did not want to fight another one, thank you very much. And against Chiyoko? Unh-unh. Nope. No way.

Adriana smiled without mirth. "You needn't worry, Aunt.

My mother will bear a suitable heir before I, myself, have children with Dahlmar. This I swear."

I wondered a moment at her wording. Was she preggers? Oh crap. I mean, no big deal to the sirens. But Rusland's ultra-religious types might have a fit.

I'm not pregnant yet, Adriana admitted in my mind. *We have abstained by our own choice. But I will be, soon enough after the wedding that they'll be counting on their fingers.*

The car had started up again, apparently we'd cleared security. Just another minute or two and we'd be pulling up to the main building.

Um. Congratulations?

This time the smile lit Adriana's face. *Thank you.*

I glanced over at Chiyoko, trying to see if she was listening in or not. She probably was. Most sirens do. They shouldn't; even they admit it's rude. But they do. The queen's visage might have been carved from granite. "We shall see."

The Secret Service agent opened the car door. I got out so fast it made him blink. Adriana announced that she was going to her office to take care of some business. She said that she'd be under guard and occupied until dinner, and suggested I go unpack.

That sounded like a great idea to me. I got as far as my old rooms in the guest house before Queen Lopaka's assistant, Hiwahiwa, appeared at my door. She wore a green lavalava and would've looked perfectly elegant if she hadn't been so obviously upset. While I didn't know exactly what her relationship was to Laka and Okalani, I was betting there was one and it was close.

"Princess, please, can we talk?"

I wanted to say no. I really did. Instead, I stepped aside, letting her walk past me into the living area.

My suite in the guest house is very, very nice. It takes up most of the top floor, and since the security was so good, I felt perfectly fine about opening the French doors to the balcony off of the living room so that I could listen to the waves and smell the ocean breeze. I could feel the sting of spelling at the edge of the balcony but it was so elegantly done that I wouldn't have noticed without my vampire blood.

The cabinets, dresser, and built-in desk were solid oak. The desk held a top-of-the-line computer. The curtains were dark gold, the color a perfect match for the carpet, and both had been color coordinated with the cream, gold, and brown checked comforter on the bed. There were half a dozen throw pillows in brown and gold, although at the moment most of them were piled in the far corner of the room rather than on the bed. I didn't like throw pillows much.

A conversational group was arranged at the other end of the room, all of the furniture equally expensive, comfortable, and color-coordinated. The final touch was a beautiful, abstract oil painting that used all of the colors in the room. It was huge, taking up most of one wall. But it was gorgeous, the kind of thing I could stare at for hours while noticing more and more details.

Hiwahiwa walked straight over to the conversational group, waiting expectantly for me to join her. I tried not to sigh as I took a seat, which gave her permission to sit down. The sooner we got through this, the better it would be.

"Laka sent you?"

"Yes, Princess, she did." Hiwahiwa looked at me with sad eyes. "Okalani hasn't returned. Not knowing what else to do, Laka sought the advice of a prophet." The tears that had been brimming in her eyes spilled over. "In the vision, her captors said they had to keep her alive for now, but she is terribly injured."

Captive? Was that even possible? I mean, Okalani was the strongest teleporter I'd ever even heard of. I knew she could teleport through shields. What could possibly hold her?

I should have known Hiwahiwa would be listening to my thoughts. I simply had to learn shielding if I was going to spend any time on this island.

"There was a demon."

I didn't know what to say. Demons. They are the worst of the monsters. Fully evil, frighteningly intelligent, and literally hell-bent on the absolute destruction of humanity. I've run into them before, even had one specifically targeting me for special attention. There is nothing in this world that is worse. Then again, they're not from this world—they have their own dimension. They can only come through here and wreak havoc when invited. And still, bad as they are, dangerous and evil as they are, there are idiots who will call them up. With the right protections, they can sometimes be trapped within a casting circle. But get one thing wrong . . . I shuddered, my flesh crawling with goose bumps.

Emma had been captured and abused with the aid of a demon. Her father and brother had betrayed me in order to save her. In the end, I'd helped them willingly. We saved her, got her out. But she'd had to have the memories magically wiped to stay sane.

"I'm so sorry." I was. More than I could say. Because Okalani wasn't just in physical jeopardy. She'd done things that could damn her soul. Unless something was done, she could be the demon's plaything for all eternity. I didn't know if hell was real, but souls most certainly were and demons could claim them, leaving the body an empty shell. I've been told by priests that it's worse than death.

"So am I." Hiwahiwa was actually wringing her hands. "Laka is . . . not right. It's as if she's lost her mind. The doctors have her sedated."

I could see that. How bad would it be, knowing the child that you loved was in such danger and that there was absolutely nothing you could do to save her? Worse, Laka probably blamed herself. Although there was no way she could've stopped this from happening.

"Princess, before she passed out, Laka gave me a message for you. In the vision the men controlling the demon were talking. They said that you had been captured, that they were going to use cameras to film them feeding you to that thing and broadcast it on the Internet."

I managed to make it to the bathroom before I threw up.

I took a few minutes to clean up, brush my teeth, and try to pull my thoughts together. It was hard to do. My emotions kept getting in the way—foremost among them panic. I forced myself to take deep, soothing breaths. I could do this. There were no demons here, now. I was fine. The future isn't set in stone. Every choice we make can cause changes, ripples in time and reality. Visions show probabilities, not facts. Even Vicki, who had been one of the most powerful clairvoyants born, had admitted that. This could change. I could change it. Sometimes, just the knowing of the future is the changing event.

When I managed to get myself under control, I went back into the living room. I found Hiwahiwa standing at the French doors, looking out at the ocean.

She spoke without turning around. "I'm sorry for my indiscretion, Princess. I shouldn't have upset you. You won't be able to save her. No one can. Her body is broken. She will . . . *die*." Her voice broke on the last word. She gave a harsh gasp. "But she repented what she did. She was trying to make it right. If you kill her . . . her soul . . ." Hiwahiwa couldn't finish the sentence.

Her soul might be saved? Maybe. I didn't know. I'm not religious. I've had exorcisms performed on me to remove demon taint. I've received last rites from a warrior priest, even though I'm not Catholic. I've had rabbis, imans, and monks pray over me. I didn't know for certain if Hiwahiwa was right. Redemption is a tricky thing. But I believe in God. I believe he/she forgives us if we truly regret our sins and try to make amends. I believe. But I don't know.

"Please, Princess. If you get the chance, *please*." I tried to stop her, but Hiwahiwa actually dropped to her knees, begging. "You have to kill Okalani."

How could I say this without insulting her? "Hiwahiwa, I wasn't raised here. I'm not a siren by birth. I was raised in

California, to American standards. Honor killings are still murder there. Suicide is a crime in many states, no matter the reason. Please understand that because of *my* beliefs, which are every bit as important to me as your beliefs are to you and Laka, I cannot . . . *will not* intentionally take a life unless I'm trying to save my own or someone else's."

She stared at me for a long time. I let my mind go blank, just feeling the pain I knew she was feeling, both at Okalani's situation and the choice I had to make. Finally, she stood, smoothed her lavalava, bowed her head as she'd been trained to do when in the presence of royalty, and backed away until she could turn and leave. Not a word was spoken, but I could hear heart-breaking sobs erupt from her on the other side of the door after it had closed.

Crap.

I sat and got more and more bummed the longer I was alone. After nearly an hour of wallowing, since I was already depressed, I tried calling my gran.

Don't get me wrong. I love my gran. She's good and kind—but hardheaded as hell. When my mom disappeared into the bottle and started sleeping around, Gran was the one who made sure there were groceries in the house, that Ivy and I made it to school. She's been a font of love and wisdom my whole life. But at the same time, she's always enabled my mother's drinking. It was her car my mother was driving the last two times she was picked up for drunk driving. Now my mom was in prison on Serenity, and she'd made it very clear she never wants to see me again. She cut me out of her life, and I'm all for it. But that destroyed my relationship with Gran, who blames me.

But Gran isn't the only one who is stubborn in the family. I keep trying, keep hoping that we can work something out. Besides, what with the press coverage of all the bullets and bombs, she had to be worried. Maybe this time she'd take my call.

"Hello?" The voice on the line sounded both older and feebler than I remembered. My grandmother had always been a ball of fire, with enough energy for two people twice her size. Not today. That, more than anything, frightened me.

"Gran, it's me."

"Celia! Oh thank God! Sweetie, are you all right? I've been watching the news. They said you were all right, but . . ."

"I'm fine, Gran." Tears stung my eyes at the sound of her voice, hearing the words that made it clear she really did still care. I tried to pull myself together as my grandmother said soothing things to me.

"I love you so much, Gran. I've missed you."

"I've missed you, too, sweetheart." There were tears in her voice now; I could hear the thickness in her words.

"I was wondering . . . would you maybe like to have dinner when I get back to the mainland? We can go wherever you want. My treat."

"On the mainland? Where are you?" Her voice was odd. It was the tone of voice she always used when she'd done something that she knew I wouldn't approve of, usually something for my mother. Hearing that was oddly reassuring in an "oh shit, here we go again" sort of way. It gave me something familiar to cling to.

I forced lightness into my voice that I didn't really feel. "I'm on Serenity for the wedding. I'm the maid of honor, if you can believe that."

"Serenity? Oh." Now she definitely sounded weird. And worried. "Well, I'm sure they're keeping you much too busy to see me. You're probably staying in the royal compound, too, what with security being so tight. Most of the restaurants are on the other side of the island."

Okay, that had me totally confused. Yeah, I was on Serenity. But Gran has a lovely apartment in an assisted living facility in Santa Maria. "Gran, what are you talking about?"

"Serenity, of course. Didn't Dawna tell you? I sublet my place on the mainland and moved here so that I could see your mother more often without having to make a long, expensive trip."

What the hell? No, Dawna hadn't told me. Of course, her grandmother might not have told her. Or Dawna might have lost track, what with all her own wedding stuff going on.

I made myself sound cheerful as I said, "Well, now we've just got to get together. After all, I'm already here. Have you been to the compound? It's amazing. You really should see the place. We can have a good, long visit."

"Oh, I'd like that. I really would." She sounded as if she meant it, but I could still hear a little thread of something fishy in her voice. Whatever it was, I'd find out when I saw her. Gran has never been able to keep a secret, and unlike my mother and me, she's dispositionally incapable of being sneaky. "I'll check to see when the shuttle runs out there."

Okay, that wasn't good. Normally she'd be having me drive her. Why didn't she want me to see where she lived? I opened my mouth to say something, but she was babbling, trying to make sure I didn't get the chance to ask any pointed questions.

"And honey, I want you to know how proud I am of you. My grandbaby, in a royal wedding! It's so exciting. You'll have to tell me all about it. I can't wait to see the dress you'll be wearing. I bet you'll look so pretty."

"Thanks. I'll see what I can do. In the meantime, it'll take me a little time to work out the details, but I'll get back to you as soon as I can. Okay?"

"You do that, honey, you do that. I love you, baby."

"Love you, too."

I hung up the phone with mixed emotions: Love, frustration, and worry mingled with happiness at having actually heard her voice for the first time in months. My gran is a good woman. She isn't perfect, but who is? But she was hiding something—probably something about my mother. I was going to find out what it was.

21

I'm supposed to be guarding you." I kept my tone light and pleasant, but inside I was seething as I sat in Queen Lopaka's office, having a "brief conversation" with my cousin. Adriana had begun using her mother's office when Queen Chiyoko arrived; I bet that had been a calculated move, to prevent Chiyoko from going through Lopaka's things and to keep people from getting used to seeing Chiyoko in Lopaka's place.

Adriana had practically begged for my help when we'd had lunch on her yacht. Now I kept getting shunted aside. First she'd left me behind to get the dresses. Then she'd said that I wouldn't be needed today as she'd be in meetings and a state dinner. Tomorrow, because she'd be in meetings all day, she suggested I go shopping. *Shopping,* for God's sake. What the hell? It was worse than annoying. It was insulting.

I know, and I am sorry. But none of the prophets, myself included, sees any threat to me this evening, and I would rather not have . . . tension between you and those previously assigned to guard me.

Tension? I hadn't been tense, but now I was getting that way. Was there some sort of political pissing matching going on among the security agents? Because that's the surest recipe for betrayal.

Celia, please? For me? I do understand how you feel. But it was hard enough convincing my regular bodyguards you were needed on the mainland. We used the excuse that you had actual experience with monsters. But we are on Serenity now. . . .

I saved your life on the mainland, and it wasn't from monsters.

She sighed. *Yes, you did. And it made the others look bad. They died and you survived.*

I suddenly put two and two together. *Which made things worse. There was only your word, and mine, that the gunmen killed the guards.*

I wouldn't have thought it possible, but yes.

That is so stupid. But typical. People don't rise to the level of bodyguarding members of a royal family without drive and ambition. Pride rides right along with those. No doubt some of the agents were just fine with me. And some of them weren't. Their skill was being called into question. How could it not be? Probably the same thing was happening with Dahlmar's people. Miller & Creede would definitely make all but the best look bad.

Adriana was trying to soothe the wounded pride of both

loyalists and detractors. I let out a slow breath. *So long as it doesn't actually put you at risk, who am I to argue? We need your people on their game and at their best, not distracted by petty bullshit. I guess I can be big about it. Fine. I'll* shop. *I'm going to need a couple more lavalavas anyway. And it'll give me a chance to check in on my gran.*

She nearly collapsed in relief. *I understand rock and hard place. Been there. Thank you. Truly.*

I shrugged. *Whatever. But you realize that this is making me totally useless.*

Her face actually showed surprise at this. *No! That's not true at all. You saved my life and that of my mother on the mainland. A couple of sentences from you in the back of the limousine has discomfited my mother's greatest rival more effectively than all of my reasoned arguments. You have been far more helpful than even I'd imagined you could be—and you don't know our culture all that well.*

I blinked at that. I had?

Adriana stood and walked to the window, keeping her back to me. Her hands were clasped lightly behind her back; for all appearances to anyone watching, she wasn't meeting with anyone at all. *Celia, I am not fond of Queen Chiyoko. I can admit that. But I am coming to believe that she actually is trying to do what she believes is right for our people. She believes you would be a disaster on the throne and that my mother needs a true heir, one steeped in our traditions and beliefs, who can rule our people.*

Well, she was right about that. Especially after hearing some of their "traditions and beliefs." *Well, I'm definitely*

*not your girl. I can't even get the support of your freaking
bodyguards.*

Adriana flinched at the bitterness in my words, hanging
in the air, but didn't argue the point. She walked back to
the desk, then picked up and put on a lovely pearl ring,
part of a suite of jewelry laid out for her. She continued to
speak with her mind, which was getting tiring for me. Not
tiring, as in I was annoyed, but tiring, as in exhausted.

*I understand her concern, and would be more forgiving,
were it not that she is so determined to use this situation to
take my mother's place as high queen.*

Adriana put on the last of her jewelry and stepped toward the couch where I was sitting. Now she spoke aloud—
she had shut me out of her mind as easily as closing a door.
Someday, I vowed, I was going to be able to do that. Pro-
jecting is all great and good, but I was sick to death of having sirens and other telepaths wander in and out of my
thoughts at will. If it took training and practice, I'd train
and practice. Some thoughts should not be available for
public consumption.

"Shall we? We don't want to be late." Adriana gestured
toward the door. I walked out ahead of her and was pleased
when Baker and Griffiths immediately fell in around us. I
forced myself to smile, smile, smile as we went to join King
Dahlmar and the others for a private dinner.

The dining room we were using tonight was elegant,
decorated in shades of sea green, turquoise, and gold.
There were two layers of linen covering the tables, a dark
teal underlayer covered by creamy white. The dishes were

fine china, and above each place setting was a small bowl made from half an abalone shell, cradling flowers floating in water. The effect was lovely, and the room smelled wonderful even before the food started to arrive.

I had fully intended to sit next to Adriana, but we were the last to arrive and there was only one place open at Dahlmar's side. Adriana smoothly crossed the room to greet Dahlmar, who rose . . . followed quickly by everybody else. My cousin's fiancé helped her into the seat between him and Natasha, then sat. I took the last remaining chair, between Olga and a man who didn't appear to be either Ruslandic or Siren.

The staff began moving about, pouring water, bringing in baskets of fresh baked bread that smelled like heaven. I wished, mightily, that I could eat bread, but that was not going to happen. So I turned my head away and distracted myself as best I could by checking out my dinner companions.

It turned out that the man I didn't know was the American ambassador, so at least we could talk about the weather and television we liked. Olga pretended not to know English, which suited me fine.

Dahlmar and Adriana only had eyes for each other. They were in love, pure and simple. He acted proud, protective, and possessive. She practically glowed every time she looked at him. I was very happy that they'd found each other.

Next to Adriana, Natasha looked . . . odd. There was a strangely vacant expression on her face, as if she weren't quite all there. The movement of her hand as she reached for her water glass was jerky and uncoordinated, so it was no surprise that she knocked it over. Everyone jumped, and in that instant of distraction I felt the flare of magic and saw a drop of golden fluid being slipped into Adriana's water glass out of the corner of my eye.

"Don't drink that," I ordered as Adriana lifted the glass while servants cleaned up the spill and cleared away the plates from the first course. I leapt to my feet so fast that my napkin and fork went flying. In the next heartbeat, I was at Adriana's side, reaching for the glass and her wrist.

She froze, giving me a wide-eyed look. King Dahlmar's expression darkened. He took the glass from her hand, turned to me and said, "Explain, please."

"There's something wrong with Natasha." I gestured toward her.

She was the only person who hadn't pulled away from the table, stood up, or otherwise reacted to my racing to the rescue. Even now, though her name had been spoken and people were looking at her, she just sat there, staring blankly into space, her expression empty and dazed.

"I'm guessing it's a compulsion spell of some sort. She slipped something into that glass while you were all distracted by the spilled water."

A man suddenly appeared beside me. As he stepped into view, I realized I had seen him sitting at the table when Adriana and I had entered the room and I had instinctively "cased" the joint. So, family, friend, or member of the wedding. But clearly, more than just that. He bowed slightly to King Dahlmar. "If I may?"

The king gave a curt nod. "Please do."

Who the hell is this? The way he spoke to Dahlmar made it obvious he was with the Rusland contingent. He reminded me a bit of the late, and sincerely lamented, Ivan, King Dahlmar's personal bodyguard. Ivan had been one scary SOB. A mage of considerable skill, Ivan had once gotten his king safely out of an attempted coup and out of Rusland without a scratch. This man was cut from the same cloth, only better-looking—tall, dark, and very handsome. His hair was cut close to his head; there was a touch of gray at each temple. He had a square jaw, penetrating hazel eyes, and the kind of aristocratic bearing that made me wonder if he was a royal cousin. I knew from Baker's briefing that the king's best man was a friend from his childhood. Perhaps this was that man.

Most people in Natasha's position would have moved or reacted by now—protesting the accusation, arguing her innocence—even if she was guilty. Instead, the bridesmaid was a prettily dressed-up doll with nobody home in her eyes.

Still holding the water glass, the man moved with liquid grace around the table until he was standing over Natasha. I felt power rise in a warm, liquid rush as he began murmuring. There was a sharp flare of heat and a sound like a gunshot. Natasha stiffened in her chair and shrieked something in her native language.

He spoke, his tone one of complete command. I didn't have a clue what he said, but I could tell he wasn't talking to Natasha. Somehow he'd trapped the person controlling her and was forcing him or her to answer questions using Natasha's mouth.

"Damn it. I have *got* to learn Ruslandic," I muttered softly. Dahlmar overheard and began translating, speaking so quietly I don't think anyone else could hear.

"Igor used Natasha to form a link to the witch who had taken use of her body. The witch swears she was not trying to kill Adriana, that she is not connected to the Guardians of the Faith."

I thought furiously. "What did she put in the glass?"

"Igor?" Dahlmar demanded.

The mage barked the question in Ruslandic. Natasha screamed again, twisting and turning in her seat as though pinned in place.

"Peanut oil," Igor answered.

Adriana paled a little.

I turned to her. "I take it you're allergic to peanuts?"

"Yes," she said, nodding. "But it wouldn't have killed me."

Natasha shouted something that I didn't understand, but suspected was along the lines of "See, told you."

"What would happen?" Igor asked.

"I'd break into hives. They are miserable, and last for days."

"And wouldn't you look just lovely in all your wedding photos?" I noted sarcastically.

It was a petty, catty, and very feminine thing to do. At that moment I believed what the witch had said. The Guardians of the Faith were into bombs and shoot-outs, maximum carnage, maximum press coverage: in short, terror. This was the exact opposite. It had all the signature markings of the usual siren bullshit. If this witch, whoever she was, was jealous of Adriana for any reason, and she'd touched that peanut oil, even one drop might be deadly to Adriana. I didn't say this out loud. The fewer people who knew, the better. After all, I'm siren enough to have to worry about it.

"King Dahlmar, is there a woman in your past, a witch, who would have reason to be jealous of Adriana?" I asked in an undertone.

Dahlmar was shaking his head, but Igor—how had he heard me?—answered. "Irina. Duchess Irina Turescheva."

"That was over long before I met Adriana," the king protested. Adriana remained silent, staring intently at Natasha.

"For you, perhaps. For her, not so much, I think." Igor turned to Natasha. "Irina Turescheva," he called, then spoke firmly in Ruslandic. King Dahlmar had stopped translating. Reaching into his pocket, he withdrew a cell phone, dialed a number from memory, and began barking orders into the phone. He'd had to raise his voice, Natasha was screaming herself hoarse and thrashing back and forth in the chair. She gave one last shriek, her eyes rolling back into her head, and collapsed.

Igor muttered something that was probably an obscenity as his hand shot out, checking for a pulse in Natasha's neck. Apparently he didn't find one, because he swiftly moved her to the floor and began CPR compressions. I went down on my knees next to her head to help.

The world narrowed to the three of us. CPR doesn't look like hard work, but it is: the physical labor of the compressions, the effort of breathing for two people. I was feeling light-headed by the time the EMTs arrived, and Igor looked beat. But when they hooked the machine up and gave her a shock, her heart started beating on its own and she took a deep, gasping breath.

"Oh thank God," I whispered. I sat on the floor, knees bent, not wanting to move. Igor used the table edge to haul himself upright, then extended a hand to me. I took it, grateful for the help.

"I will go to the hospital with her," King Dahlmar announced. "And we must call her father."

"Of course, Your Majesty." Igor bowed. Pulling himself together, he led his king out the door after the paramedics. With Dahlmar gone, I didn't have to wait to be seated. I fell into the nearest chair.

Adriana gave me a long, penetrating look. *So much for your being useless.*

22

By the time I went to bed that night, I knew that Natasha was going to be fine. She'd need to rest for a couple of days but the doctors swore there'd be no permanent damage even though she'd been used in a tug-of-war between a pair of powerful magic wielders. After Dahlmar, Igor, and Natasha left, the dinner party quickly broke up. I saw Adriana to her room and left her with trusted bodyguards, then returned to my rooms. A few minutes later, Helen Baker brought me a tray of delicious, nutritious liquids.

The next morning, after a blissfully uneventful breakfast, the bride and groom adjourned to a morning-long interview with the royal biographers, which was to be followed by an afternoon photo shoot. I was left to my own devices.

First, I called Alex. I doubted the police had had any luck tracking Okalani, but I wanted to be sure. If they needed a bio sample for a magical trace, I'd get one for them. Unfortunately, my call went straight to voice mail. I left a message, promising myself to try again later.

I was tense, so I decided to go for a run. With enough clothes and sunscreen I should be okay if I stuck to the shady trail that wound through the compound and adjacent nature preserve.

So I gave my security team a couple of minutes' warning, started out with a few stretches, then Griffiths, Baker, and I headed out.

It was so good to feel the wind in my face. I was wearing a silver-gray jogging suit with long sleeves and full-length pants, and a baseball cap with my ponytail pulled through the back. Coconut-scented sunscreen protected my face and hands. I felt the tightness in my body ease at the steady, rhythmic movement.

Griffiths and Baker kept pace with me easily. They were fully armed and alert. So was I. If we compared weaponry, I was betting it would be a close tie. I don't think any of us really expected any trouble but we didn't let down our guard. Natasha might not be the only person being controlled by someone on the outside.

The trails were absolutely stunning. Serenity is naturally lovely, with lush foliage in every shade of green and a rainbow-hued array of flowers and exotic birds. By the time we finished the run, I was relaxed yet fully alert, ready for whatever the day would bring.

After the run, I took a quick shower—so did Baker and Griffiths, who were briefly replaced by two other members of the Siren Secret Service—and the three of us headed to the far side of the island so I could find a dressy lavalava for the wedding.

It was early afternoon and I was on my third or fourth shop when Baker started acting uneasy. She kept tapping her fingers restlessly against her leg and checking her watch.

"Is something wrong?" I asked.

"I'm not sure. It's just this feeling I've got . . . not a vision, not even a premonition exactly."

"You're a prophet, right? Like your mother?" Baker's mother had been Pili, the queen's own prophet. Pili had sacrificed herself to close the demonic rift months back.

"Yes. And I know that we have to get to Ms. Peahi's apartment and get her out of there. Right now."

Gran? Why would Baker have a vision about my grandmother?

I hurriedly put the clothes I'd been gathering back on the rack. I'd already found a dress for the wedding and a spare for other events. I could get by without anything else. "Let's go. But you'll have to lead. I've never been there."

Baker hit a number on speed dial on her cell phone and advised her people where we were headed. Our driver took us through the commercial district, where the streets were crowded with tourists, then into more residential neighborhoods, which were quieter.

We soon left the prettier neighborhoods behind and drove into an area that looked like it was badly in need of renovation. When we pulled up in front of one building, I was shocked. *This* was where my gran was living? The place was worse than a dump. Baker opened the lobby door and the scents of old urine and rotting fruit, masked nauseatingly by room deodorizer, hit me like a punch to the gut.

We walked across matted brown carpet so filthy it was sticky. The sound of a squalling baby carried clearly through the paper-thin walls, as did the blaring of a television news program rehashing the investigation into the terrorist attacks.

There were no elevators. We climbed a steep, narrow staircase up to the second floor, where I saw my grandmother's name on the door of apartment 210, a bare three steps from the top of the stairwell. I stared at the dirty door with its shiny new deadbolt, my vision blurring with tears of anger and frustration—anger that my gran had been reduced to this, frustration that she'd kept it from me.

Strong emotions bring out the vampire in me, particularly when I haven't eaten. So while the smells squelched any hunger pangs I might have had, my inner beast was very close to the surface. My eyes shifted into vampire focus, so that I could see each tiny hair on the back and legs of the little gray spider lying in wait in a web attached to the far corner of the hall ceiling. I could clearly hear every sound and movement in the building.

So I was able to hear the front door opening on the floor below, the rapid breathing and pounding heart of someone in a hurry. I smelled my grandmother's distinctive perfume mixed with the heady scent of fear—fear that made my mouth water.

She started up the steps, her breath almost sobbing in her chest, as the door opened again, bringing with it the scent of an unwashed male.

"She's coming, and there's someone stalking her." My words were a sibilant hiss as my fangs extended, making speech more difficult. The derringer I'd tucked into my boot top was in my hand, though I didn't remember drawing it. I was edging toward the staircase when a strong arm grabbed hold of mine. I turned, hissing, but Griffiths didn't flinch. He jabbed his finger in a silent order for me to stand behind Baker, then moved smoothly down the stairs before I could argue. Baker stepped forward to block me.

There was a muffled scream and the sharp scent of chemicals and the temperature dropped like a rock. Ivy was here. Gran was in danger and my baby sister's ghost was here to help if she could. I pushed past Baker, but before I'd gone down more than two steps I heard the sounds of a brief struggle, then silence, except for the ambient noise of the building and harsh breathing.

"It's over." Griffiths's voice was calm and his breathing was steady. Apparently he'd been able to subdue the attacker without so much as breaking a sweat. Then again, he's a big guy. A big, tough, well-trained guy. When I reached the ground floor, I saw that he had bound the bad guy with spelled cuffs and was using his ever-trusty cell phone to dial for an ambulance and backup. My grandmother was lying at his feet.

I was kneeling next to my gran's unconscious body before the second word had left Griffiths's mouth. I pulled her against me, getting her off of that nasty, disgusting floor. The chill of Ivy's presence settled around me as I held Gran close and checked her for injuries. Her breathing was steady. Her heartbeat was slowing back to normal.

She was going to be all right. I sent up a silent prayer of thanks and twisted to look at her attacker.

"*You!*" he snarled, then spat at me. The wad of saliva missed my face, thanks to my excellent reflexes. The phlegm left a trail of slime as it slid down the wall behind me.

Only the fact that I had my grandmother in my arms kept me from lunging at the bastard and choking the snot out of him for what he'd done to her. Staring across at him, I realized that he looked familiar, but only vaguely, like someone I'd met once, briefly. Then again, maybe he just had one of those faces. Average height, dark blond hair, and ordinary features; built like he worked out, but not excessively. He wore ordinary jeans and a plain red T-shirt. The only thing out of the ordinary about him was the mark on his forearm—a tattoo in the shape of an elaborate, colorful cross in vivid green, red, and gold. I felt the magic from that mark and realized the tattoo was camouflage. He'd taken a binding oath.

I found myself snarling, rage coloring every syllable I uttered. "What did you swear, and who did you swear it to? Why were you trying to kidnap my grandmother?"

His eyes blazed with pure hatred. If looks could kill, I'd be dead in my boots. But they couldn't, and glaring was all he could do, bound as he was by both handcuffs and magic.

"I will tell you *nothing*, siren witch."

"Oh, you'll talk." Griffiths's smile was absolutely chilling. "You'll tell us everything we want to know."

If the man on the ground had any sense, he'd be terrified. Because he was dealing with sirens. When push comes to shove, they can use their magic to make a man do almost anything without hesitation. I, myself, had used my talent to save my life and that of my friends. The result still haunted my nightmares.

Why did he look so familiar? Damn it. I would swear I'd never met the guy, and yet— Nope. I couldn't remember, and the harder I chased the thought, the more elusive it became.

I was still trying to remember when the EMTs arrived a few minutes later.

"I'm going with the ambulance." It wasn't a question. He'd have to bind me tighter than he had the prisoner if he wanted to stop me.

Baker turned to Griffiths. "Go with the prisoner. I'll see to Ms. Peahi. When she's stable, I'll bring the princess to headquarters. She can help with the questioning."

I watched as the EMTs gently placed my unconscious grandmother on the gurney. The man on the ground had attacked a helpless little old woman, would have done God alone knew what to her before he was done. Hell, yes, I'd help with the questioning.

I was looking forward to it.

Even in an ambulance, the drive to the hospital took awhile. The streets were just that crowded. Less than twenty-four hours remained before the ceremonies on

Serenity were to take place, and excitement was building to a fever pitch.

My grandmother began stirring after a few minutes and soon she was asking what had happened and complaining that she was fine.

She didn't remember a thing after waking up that morning.

On the one hand, that was a relief. She'd been so terrified, it was a mercy for her not to have to remember.

On the other hand, she'd make a lousy witness when it came to trial. And I was more than a little worried by the amnesia. The chemical on the rag was simple chloroform; it shouldn't have caused memory problems.

I wanted to ask the EMTs, but I didn't want to alarm Gran. I concentrated hard and sent my question directly into the thoughts of the woman taking my grandmother's vital signs.

She glanced at me before returning her attention to the gauge on the blood pressure cuff. *We're wondering about her memory as well. It might be the bump on her head, but security took a sample of the cloth he held to her mouth to see if there's a curse involved, and we've swabbed her mouth and nasal passages. I'm sure the doctors will run more tests, but I'm betting there's magic involved. Try not to worry. She's old but she's stronger than she looks. Barring complications, I think she's going to be fine.*

I let out a breath I hadn't known I was holding. *Thank God.*

How are you? Any bloodlust?

When I thought about it, I was a little surprised that I

didn't feel any, considering the stress I was under. It would be really sad to think that this level of stress was my new normal. No. *But I should probably eat something, sooner rather than later. Is there a cafeteria at the hospital?*

Can you eat solids? Her mental voice managed to sound surprised.

Not really. Baby food, mostly, and stuff run through a blender. Broth or soup will do. I drink nutrition shakes in a pinch.

Then you should be able to get something. But take care of it quick. We don't want there to be any problems at the hospital.

No. We don't.

I silently relayed our conversation to Baker, who had pulled out her cell phone and begun sending text messages. She tilted the phone to show me that she was sending more security agents to the hospital. One of them met us as we arrived and handed me a nutrition shake and some broth. Not exactly high-class dining, but it was good enough to keep the monster at bay while we got Gran through the check-in process and into a private room.

The whole time, Gran alternated between insisting that she was fine and worrying aloud about the cost of hospitalization. Eventually they gave her something to help her calm down and rest—or maybe just to get her to shut up. When she was sleeping, deeply and peacefully, I sat beside her for a while, studying her. She looked fragile, old, and tired. Lines of care that hadn't been there six months ago had etched deep creases between her brows and at the corners of her mouth.

Oh, Gran, why didn't you tell me? I'd have helped. You know I would have.

Queen Lopaka's mental voice intruded on my thoughts, cold and imperious. *That is good to know. I was appalled when Helen advised me of your grandmother's situation. I wondered how you could let my brother's widow sink to such depths. It seemed like atypical behavior for you.*

I sighed both physically and mentally as tears filled my eyes. *We had a falling-out when I refused to keep dealing with my mother. The last I knew, Gran had banked the money from the house sale and was living in a nice assisted-living place on the mainland. I knew she was visiting Mom once a month. I'd hoped . . .*

What had I hoped? That Gran would stop being codependent, stop rescuing my mom? The habits of a lifetime are a bitch to break, even if you want to. Which Gran didn't. She was determined to save my mother from herself, would fight for her salvation to the last breath. But I just didn't have that in me. I felt my mother should pay for her crimes. She'd broken the law. Only prison could fix what was wrong.

I should've checked up on her. I should've stopped her somehow. I guess I expected . . . I don't know. She's always been the one to take care of me.

Lopaka's voice softened in my mind. *She probably hid it from you precisely for that reason. And she very well might have hidden it from your attendant spirit.*

The sirens mostly consider me a true siren because I happen to have friends who are clairvoyants and my sister hangs around me, even after death. Prophets and attendant spirits are royal attributes. I consider them mostly coincidence.

Probably. Hiding stuff from me is classic Gran. Yes, she'd hide her problems from Ivy and lie to my mother. And to me. Not to be a martyr, nor a hero. But just because she's Gran.

Indeed. I see now why my brother loved her. She might not have been siren royalty but she was worthy to be the mate of one. There was both frustration and admiration in her voice. Typical.

Lopaka's mental voice sounded exhausted. She'd contacted me mind-to-mind before, even over long distances, without strain. But this time was different. The queen might be recovering, but she wasn't herself yet by a long shot. I let out a little growl. *You need to rest.*

Yes. And I will. But now I need you to go with Agent Baker. The questioning of the prisoner is not going well. Our psychic believes something important will occur tomorrow, but cannot obtain details. While I am willing to use torture if necessary to save lives, Gunnar believes the man's hatred of you may enrage him enough that he will be unable to guard his thoughts from us if you are in the room.

I didn't know who Gunnar was and didn't much care. I didn't want to leave the hospital; I wanted to stay and make sure that nothing else happened to Gran.

There will be guards on the door at all times. She will be protected.

"Ivy, are you still here?" I spoke both in my head and out

loud. My sister's ghost hadn't done anything since letting me know she was with us in Gran's apartment building, so I wasn't sure I'd get an answer. She used to be with me almost always. Now, she spent her time guarding our mom in prison. It was hard work for the ghost of a grade-school kid, but I was betting she was doing a damned fine job of it. That didn't stop me from missing her.

The overhead light flashed once. That was our code. One flash meant yes, two no.

"They want me to go question the bad guy. Can you keep an eye on Gran for me?"

The light flashed once again.

"Thanks. Love you, Ivy." Tears stung my eyes as I looked first up at the light, then down at my grandmother on the bed. The lights flickered wildly for a few seconds. I took that to mean, *Me, too.*

I wanted to be there when Gran woke up. We needed to talk, about so many things. Today's little adventure had taught me not to take her for granted. I was going to work things out with her even if that meant dealing with my mother again.

The queen's voice tickled my mind again, the tinkling of crystal chimes. *The doctors have assured Adriana that your grandmother will sleep deeply for several hours. If you go now, you may be back before she wakes.*

You're sure?

Please, niece. I will ensure my sister-in-law is safe. But there are others who are not. Lives are at stake. You must go, and quickly.

Put like that, I really didn't have much choice. The queen was considering this a family matter.

Family. That meant a lot on this island. I've never had much of it. Most everyone I considered family was lying on that hospital bed. I bent down to kiss my grandmother's cheek. "I'll be back as soon as I can," I whispered.

The interrogation room was grim. The cinder-block walls were painted a funky pinkish-tan. Brick red trim surrounded the one-way mirror familiar to anyone who has ever seen a crime drama on television. A battered table was bolted to the floor. On it, untouched, rested two glasses and a sweating plastic pitcher of water.

Again, anyone who watches television knows why the water is there. But you'd be surprised how many people actually drink it. It's impossible to sit in a room like this and not be nervous. Nerves make a person thirsty. But a full bladder, when there's no possibility of emptying it, is damned uncomfortable, and pissing yourself is degrading, humiliating, and puts you at a disadvantage with the interviewers. The clock on the wall, with its big, easy-to-read numbers, is there so that the prisoner can't help but be aware of the seconds, minutes, and hours passing.

If any of this was having an effect on the prisoner, I couldn't see it. He sat calmly, his arms resting on the table, breathing slow and easy.

He'd obviously played this game before.

So it was time to change the rules.

A large man in a very high-end suit handed me an earpiece. Baker had introduced him as the secretary of Siren Security, Gunnar Thorsen. It was evidently a cabinet post, but with active duties. *Very* active lately.

He looked about as you'd expect from the name: big and Nordic. His long blond hair was pulled back into a braid, revealing chiseled features and eyes the ice blue of a winter sky. His expression was just that cold. "We have a psychic on duty," he explained.

As if on cue, the psychic began speaking in my ear. "Testing, one, two, three, testing." I heard her loud and clear.

"It works."

"Good. You've fed?"

I blinked a little at the directness of the question. "Yes."

"Right. We need him alive and talking."

Um, wow. Okay. I've come close to losing control a time or two, but I have never actually fed off of a human. Nor do I intend to. It would send me over the edge, make me fully a vampire. I am not, and will never be, a bat. Ever.

I looked through the glass at the prisoner and felt a fine burning rage fill me. He was a terrorist. He'd tried to kidnap my gran. I had no idea what he'd intended to do with her, but I assumed it would have been bad. As it was, she'd wound up in the hospital.

I wouldn't feed on the bastard, but that didn't mean I didn't want to hurt him.

I beat down my rage by force of will, calming myself with slow, deep, breaths. After a moment, I was back in full control. "I'm good. Let's do this."

The psychic nodded in approval, so Thorsen led me out into the interrogation room.

"*You!*" The prisoner leapt to his feet, sending the chair crashing to the floor behind him.

"Yup. Me." I gave him my sunniest, most saccharine smile.

He stood, snarling, breathing as heavily as if he'd been running. It was obviously all he could do not to leap across the room and attack me.

"*He wants to kill you.*" The psychic's voice came clearly through the ear bud. "*He's not striking because he knows he can't make it past Thorsen. But if he sees an opening, he'll take it. You will need to be very careful. He's hoping that if he kills you, we will kill him. It will keep him from revealing anything and having the curse take him. He wants to die a martyr to his cause.*"

Oh great, a cause. As if any religion justified murder, or the kidnapping of little old ladies. I stared at him and tried to put my finger on what it was about him that seemed so familiar. Who the hell *was* this guy?

"Why do you look so familiar?"

"You don't recognize me?" He spat the words.

"Should I?"

"*He's thinking about a brother. Something about a desert and a demon. Damn it, he's shutting it down. Keep him engaged.*"

A desert. And a demon.

Just like that, I knew. I had never seen him before, but I knew him all the same. The psychic was right. I'd met his

brother. His name was Barnes. He'd delivered me to Eirene shortly before she called up a greater demon to devour
me and my friends. To save us, I'd used my siren powers,
engaging Eirene in a battle to control the men working for
her. It had been too much for them. Their minds were destroyed, snuffed out like candles in a hurricane.

I shuddered, my stomach roiling at the memory. It had
been an accident. I hadn't meant to hurt anyone, much
less kill them. But I'd done it.

He must have seen my expression. The memory was still
raw in my mind. He nodded and sneered. "So, you do remember. You remember what you did to him. Good. I
want you to know that you and that other siren bitch are
the cause of this. You reminded us why sirens have no
place in this world. We will wipe you out like the vermin
you are."

He wasn't foaming at the mouth, he was *smiling*. That
was even more terrifying. Because while I'd done something hideous and evil by accident, his actions were absolutely deliberate.

The tattoo on his forearm was beginning to glow, the
colors shining like light through stained glass, like sparkling jewels. He was talking, and that was starting to activate the death curse that was part of the binding oath he'd
taken to keep their secrets. I could feel the magic coming
off of him in waves of heat. "The first real blow is tomorrow.
But it won't end until you're dead. Every last one of you."

Now he was foaming at the mouth, his eyes rolling back
in his head. He made thick, wet choking sounds, his body

spasming so strongly that he tripped over the chair. It was like a grand mal seizure, but magical, not physical, in cause. A strong smell of sulfur filled the room.

"*Medic!*" Thorsen's bass bellow was loud enough to hurt my ears. He rushed to the still form on the floor and began giving CPR. No artificial respiration. The smell of sulfur and bitter almonds hung too heavy on the body. But he kept working to keep the prisoner's heart pumping until the EMTs arrived and pronounced him dead.

23

I sat in Thorsen's large, airy office, shivering in reaction, huddled over a cup of steaming coffee. Thorsen had personally taken charge of my debriefing. Undoubtedly the psychic was being debriefed and writing a report somewhere else.

Emotions swept over me in waves. Guilt: I was the one who caused this. I personally had caused an entire terrorist organization to be formed. People were dying, and it was all my fault. No, not *all* mine. Eirene owned a share of the blame. Of course, she was already dead, and even half the blame was more than enough for me.

Anger and frustration: that man had been a terrorist and an asshole, but he shouldn't have had to die like that. The guys we were up against acted as if people were as disposable as used tissues. That was just so wrong. That they were heating it up and serving it as religion only made it worse.

"When he was dying, the psychic got the impression of a cross, and the tattoo on his arm was of a cross as well.

It's obviously a symbol with some importance to them. Do you have any idea, other than the obvious, of what it signifies?"

"Nope."

There was a tap on the door. A petite brunette with a crisp uniform and a no-nonsense attitude peeked in. "Sir. We ran his prints through the system. They came up for a minor infraction in Detroit, USA, under the name Jason Barnes. I'm running the name Barnes through our database. We're getting a ton of results, but none of them seems relevant."

"Stay on it."

"Yes, sir." She ducked back out.

"The clairvoyants kept saying that you were the key to what is going on, but they couldn't tell me why. The queen insisted that you were loyal and had saved her and Adriana at the bridal shop. I wanted to judge for myself."

"And?"

He answered my question with a question. "What happened in the desert? How did you know Jason Barnes's brother? What do you know about the Guardians of the Faith?"

I was being interrogated. Oh, we weren't in a cinderblock room with a one-way mirror, but this was an interrogation nonetheless.

Fair enough.

I straightened in my chair. "Are you taping this?"

He arched a single blond eyebrow.

"I'll tell you what little I know. Lives are at stake. But I don't want to risk some of what I'm saying to leave this room."

"I can't promise you that." He shook his head. "I have to pursue my investigations, to protect Queen Lopaka and the others."

I hadn't expected any less, but he was missing my point. "I know that. But I have enough problems with the press, and with law enforcement officials thinking I'm a monster. Use the information any way you need to, but be discreet. I don't want to see it on the news."

He nodded his approval. "You have my word." He gave the words weight and I felt magic building behind them. He made a quick gesture with his right hand and I heard a sound like the ringing of a bell, saw a flash of color as red runes flickered to life in the ceiling and walls.

"Now, talk."

I wasn't sure what was relevant, so I told him everything that had anything to do with the sirens. I started with the curse Stefania had laid on my sister and me—when I showed him the mark in my palm, he said "Hmm" in a quiet voice. I went through the incident in the desert, my encounters with Okalani, and everything else, including what Hiwa-hiwa had told me regarding the clairvoyant's vision.

He asked many questions.

Most, I answered. Some, I couldn't—because I flat out didn't know. He didn't seem upset or disappointed, just accepted my lack of knowledge and moved on.

Finally he leaned back in his chair, fingers steepled to tap against his lips. His expression was serious and thoughtful.

"Well? What do you think?"

"I think," he said, leaning forward and setting his hands, palm down, on the desk, "that this is a fucking mess."

Well, that was honest.

"And while I don't think you should be held responsible for it, your actions were one of the root causes of recent events. Still, I can't see what else you could've done under the circumstances, and you can't be held responsible for your enemies' terrorist actions." He sighed. "Your aunt wants me to keep you safe, but you're caught right in the middle of this mess. I don't see that there's anything that can be done about that, either. The death curse has something to do with that, no doubt. If Queen Stefania wasn't already dead . . ." He let the sentence dangle. He didn't need to finish it. I knew exactly what he meant. I felt pretty much the same way.

We had a moment of silent accord. Then I said, "So, now what?"

"Now you go back to the hospital to stay with your grandmother and I get to work. But please, if you can, *try* to stay out of trouble, at least for the next few hours. My agents are stretched thin enough as it is." He gave me a real smile. His eyes sparkled and a pair of deep dimples creased his cheeks. He rose. With a gesture of his hand, the runes disappeared, the magic dissipating like mist before the sun.

"I'll do my best," I promised as I rose to my feet. When I extended my hand to Thorsen, he shook it.

It was late by the time we got back to the hospital; my

conversation with Thorsen had taken quite some time, and then I had my driver stop at an all-night pharmacy. I picked up some toiletries and clothes for Gran plus baby food and nutrition shakes for me. I downed two of the shakes in the car, so I was reasonably well fed by the time we got to the hospital. The guards at Gran's door checked my identification and squirted me with holy water. Once they were sure I was really me, I was able to enter the room.

She was still out cold. Lying on the hospital bed, she looked so *tiny*. Her slight body barely raised a lump beneath the thin green hospital blanket. She was snoring a little, a sound familiar from the many times I'd slept at her house. Hearing it made me smile. As I stood next to the bed, looking down at her, I promised myself that I'd keep her safe somehow; that we'd work out our differences, whatever it took.

But it wasn't going to be easy.

Still, that was a problem for later. For now, I just needed to be here with her. So I stacked my packages in the corner and settled into the recliner next to the bed.

The chair wasn't too uncomfortable and I was freaking exhausted. This had been an incredibly long day. I needed rest. There were guards on the door. So I closed my eyes and soon dozed off.

Previous experience had taught me that I wouldn't get a lot of sleep in a hospital. Every few minutes, one staff member or another would come check on my grandmother. Still, I did get some rest, but it was just dawn when I woke for the first time in years to the sound of her voice.

"Celie? What are you doing here?" She didn't sound happy to see me.

I used the lever to shift the chair to its upright position and tried to shake the cobwebs from my head. Gran was sitting on the edge of the bed, feet dangling.

She scooted off of the bed, steadying herself with one hand on the mattress as her feet reached the floor.

I rose, intending to help her, but she waved me aside.

"No. I can get myself to the bathroom without your assistance, thank you." The words were as bitter as acid, and I stepped back, stung.

She was steady enough to make it the few steps to the bathroom and use the facilities. That seemed like such a good idea that I followed her example as soon as she was done.

When I came out, she was back in bed, tucking in to the breakfast I'd heard arrive while I was in the bathroom. She had the wheeled tray pulled close and the bed adjusted to allow her to sit up straight.

"Before you say anything," Gran said, setting down her spoon and looking me straight in the eyes, "I remember now why I'm here. I was just sleepy and disoriented. So you don't need to worry about that."

I opened my mouth to respond but she kept talking.

"And I don't want any lectures from you about where I've been living. It's my choice and my money. I've been making my own decisions since before you were born. . . ." She was starting to work up a good head of steam. If this kept up, we'd have a fight, which I didn't want, but she apparently did. Most likely she thought the best defense was a good offense. But she didn't need to defend herself from me. Why didn't she realize that?

"Gran, stop. Just *stop*. All right? I get it. You wanted to be close to Mom so you could visit every day and you wanted to make sure she had everything she needed at the prison. Money just doesn't ever go as far as you think it's going to."

She subsided a little, but her expression remained wary. She stared at me, chin down, eyes narrow with suspicion. That look, more than anything, told me just how hard times had been for her lately.

"I wish you'd talked to me. I could've helped, could've visited."

"Why would you bother? You don't visit your own mother." Wow, the amount of bitterness she fit into that sentence was enough to choke on.

I took a deep breath, fighting to maintain my self-control. "I love Mom. I will always love Mom." God help me, that was the absolute truth. "But I won't let myself in for more abuse. I'm not that much of a masochist."

"Celia Kalino Graves! Your mother *never*—"

I cut her off. "Bullshit. You don't believe me, hire a clairvoyant. Have them take a look back for you. Hell, I'll even pay for it. But I'm warning you—you won't like what you see."

Gran's jaw set in a hard line and we glared at each other. This probably wasn't a good time to have this particular argument. She was in the hospital for a reason. But this confrontation had been brewing for months, years even.

God help me, I was tired of trying so damned hard to do everything right, to make everything work, only to watch my mother destroy my efforts . . . and then have to listen to my gran make excuses for her.

To my own surprise, I wasn't shouting when I responded. "You want to know why I act the way I do? Go find out. Then we'll talk. But until you know the facts, don't you dare judge me. Don't you *dare* tell me that Ivy and I lived some idyllic childhood with a mother who cared about us. Because we *didn't*."

"Get out." She didn't yell, but there was a cold fury in her voice.

"Gladly," I snapped back.

I picked up most of the packages I'd stacked by my chair, leaving only the ones with the clothing and toiletries I'd bought for her. Then I left, without saying good-bye, without so much as a backward glance. But not without regret.

None of the guards said a word as I left the room—not the two by the door, and not Baker or Griffiths, who were seated beside a small table on the far side of the hall. They had to have heard. I'd kept my voice down, but Gran hadn't, and the walls were paper thin. But all four were tactful enough to at least pretend they didn't know what had happened on the other side of that closed door.

Baker offered me a box of tissues, which is when I realized that I was crying. Damn it! I took a few tissues and tried to pull myself together. It took a few ragged breaths, and blowing my nose several times, but eventually I calmed down.

"Not that I'm objecting, but why are you two still on duty? Don't they ever let you sleep?"

Baker gave a delicate snort, which pulled a small smile from me. "Please, this close to the ceremony, with as many tourists and strangers as we have on the islands, it's all hands on deck."

"Besides"—Griffiths gave me a grin that didn't seem the least bit weary despite the long hours—"you're where the action is."

Wasn't that the damned truth?

24

We were on our way back to the compound. I
wanted a shower, coffee, and breakfast. I knew that
I had a lot to do. But I couldn't think what. I couldn't
seem to think at all. I was on emotional overload. So I rode
in the back of the limo in silence through streets that
weren't yet crowded because it was barely dawn. Oh, there
were a few die-hards, their dome tents pitched along the
parade route, fans waiting for the best seats to the show of a
lifetime. But mostly the thin, watery light of a new day revealed empty streets and darkened shops.

It suited my mood.

Adriana might be perfectly happy with how I'd handled
things thus far. I wasn't. Gran could have been killed. Queen
Lopaka nearly had been. Natasha had certainly had a close
call. We all kept scurrying around, putting out fires, but we
were just reacting and getting nowhere in terms of finding
out who was behind it all. I had no doubt there were all
kinds of agencies working on this, but so far their results
had been less than stellar.

But I was expected to slap on a smile and keep marching blindly forward to the wedding.

I hated it.

Right now I hated my whole freaking life.

I knew I was feeling sorry for myself. But I couldn't seem to help it.

I needed comfort, a friendly voice, somebody to lie through their teeth if necessary and tell me that it *wasn't* all my fault, and that eventually everything would be fine.

I checked my watch, figured out the time difference, and called Dawna. After all, what are friends for?

Dawna sounded bright, perky, and cheerful enough to make my teeth ache. "Good morning! 'Bout time you called in. You would not believe the stack of messages I have for you!"

"Good morning to you." I tried to force cheer in my voice to match hers and failed, miserably.

"Uh-oh. Talk to me. What's wrong?"

"Gran's in the hospital. She's going to be all right, but we had a big blow-up."

"Let me guess, was it about your mom?"

"Isn't it always?"

Dawna gave a gusty sigh. "Pretty much. Sorry. Why's she in the hospital?"

I told her the whole story. If the phones were being tapped, I wanted everyone listening to know that we'd stopped the a-hole and that nobody who targeted my family would survive.

"Wow! Sorry times two, girlfriend."

"Me, too. I figured I'd call and see if you had any good news to cheer me up."

"Actually, I do have some," she assured me. "First, Ron's moving out today. The movers are due here at nine o'clock and the cleaners are coming at one. I'm supposed to tell you that"—she imitated Ron at his most pompous—"he's abiding by the agreement and expects you to do the same."

I found myself letting out a knowing snicker. "Write the man a check and sign it. And don't quibble."

A chuckle was followed by the shuffling of papers. "Dom Rizzoli called. He said I'm supposed to tell you"—she paused, and I heard another rustle of papers as she dug for the right message—"He said to tell you: "'Good news. You won't have to testify against Raul.'"

That was a shock, but a good one. "Say what?" Paulo Ortega was the drug king pin whose tunnels I'd used to escape. Raul was his baby brother and right-hand man. Paulo was a violent psycho who ruled his own private army with an iron fist and practically unlimited funds. The stick, and the carrot, generally used in that order. I'd been scheduled to testify about the tunnels and the vampires in them. I wondered what had happened. Had the Mexican authorities decided—or been convinced—not to prosecute?

Dawna continued, "Rizzoli didn't say, but I actually know why. I read about this online. The border patrol found scattered remains in the desert, the morning after the full moon. There was enough to do DNA matching, and it's Paulo and Raul. It looks as if they got on the wrong side of a pack of werewolves."

Wow. What an ugly way to go. Almost as brutal and violent as some of the things I'd heard they'd ordered. I couldn't say I was sorry. I bet it was Maria's family. Paulo had learned the hard way that payback is a bitch.

Literally.

"Celia? You still there?"

"I'm here. I wouldn't wish that on anybody, but I can't say they didn't deserve it."

"That's almost exactly what the guy who wrote the online article said."

I believed it. Thinking about the Ortegas, though, reminded me of Mexico. Not good. Not the kind of memories that would improve my mood.

"Anything else?"

"Yup. When you get back, the INS and the DEA both want to meet with you and have you map out as much of the tunnels as you can remember. Oh, and the Levys are on their way to Serenity with the dresses and they are *gorgeous*. You are going to look so amazing! Bruno's finished your joint present for Adriana and King Dahlmar. Since he was working on it in the same office with Jan, he had it checked to make sure it hadn't been tampered with, and it's fine. Emma swears it's the best focus she's ever seen, even better than the mirror you had made for Vicki."

Oh! So that's what he'd been making at the college. I'd assumed the mirror was a class assignment.

Wow. That was awesome. It would be the perfect gift for

Adriana, who was a fairly powerful clairvoyant. And Dahl-mar was enough in love that pleasing her was sure to please him. Score.

"He said to let you know he'll bring it with him when he flies out to Rusland. He doesn't want to risk letting it out of his sight until then."

I didn't blame him. Major magical artifacts are big business and valuable as hell. Even the express courier companies won't insure them for full value. They're just too likely to be stolen. "He's sending you his itinerary by e-mail, so be sure to get online."

Thinking about seeing Bruno made me smile, and while Dawna couldn't see it, she knew me well enough to guess.

"I'm supposed to tell you he loves you and he's really, really sorry. Just between the two of us, I'm thinking that you're going to be able to hold that whole body bind thing over his head for quite a while."

I laughed. "Maybe." Probably not. Then again, he *really* shouldn't have done it. And I did not want him to get into the habit of pulling that kind of crap.

"Ready for the less good news?"

I groaned. "I suppose."

"Dottie came in and got Minnie the Mouser."

"What?" That was a shock. Fred and Dottie lived in government housing. No pets allowed. She'd gotten me to take in her adored cat Minnie after a friend—a cop—who'd been looking after her died in the line of duty. Since I'm gone so much, we'd made her the office cat. We all loved the silly furball. She was spoiled rotten.

"Dottie said it was only for a couple of days, that she didn't want her getting underfoot with the movers coming in."

Well, that kind of made sense. Although, come to think on it, we could've just locked her in my office for a couple of hours. I wondered if my clairvoyant friend was up to something. I wouldn't put it past her.

Dawna continued. "But she was acting all weird and sad. She wandered around the whole place, even up to the third floor."

I rolled my eyes. Of course she had. I'd told Dottie a million times not to take the stairs with that walker of hers. But did she listen? Oh hell no.

"She told me to ship all of your boxes—the ones in the storeroom—to your house. She was so insistent that I went ahead and did it. I hope you don't mind."

"Nah, it's okay. She's a seer. Who knows, maybe she saw that we'll need the space."

"Yeah, that's kind of how I looked at it." Dawna paused; in the background I heard the door open and people moving around. "Gotta go. The movers are here. Call me later."

"Right."

We hung up without saying good-bye, but that was okay. Things back at the office were in good hands. The Levys would be here soon with the dresses and Bruno had come up with the perfect wedding gift. All in all, not too shabby. Oh, there were still plenty of things to worry about: Dottie acting strange, Okalani being in danger. But I wasn't going to think about them now. I was just too damned tired. We were almost back to the compound. I wanted food and sleep, in that order. Everything else would just have to wait.

I woke to the sound of someone knocking on the door to my suite. A glance at the clock told me it was only 10:30. I'd had less than three hours of sleep, which was worse than none at all.

"*Go away*," I growled, and pulled my pillow over my head.

Baker's voice drifted through the door and the soft, feather down pillow. "Celia, Isaac and Gilda Levy are here with the dresses for the fitting. Princess Adriana has asked that you join everyone downstairs at your earliest convenience."

Oh, *hell*. Early wasn't convenient. Not at all. Damn it, anyway. I needed some rest. I was tired and depressed. The last thing I wanted was to be around people. And Gilda and Isaac were so damned perceptive, they'd know something was up the minute I walked into the room.

Still, there was nothing for it. They were here. There wasn't much time for them to do any alterations as it was. It would be rude of me to make that time any shorter.

"Tell them I'll be down in a few minutes."

"I'll tell them ten minutes."

"And get me some coffee," I added. "Please. Lots and lots of coffee."

I could almost hear Helen smile. "Yes, ma'am."

I took one of the shortest showers on record, brushed my teeth and hair, and pulled on jeans and a little yellow

T-shirt with horizontal stripes. I strapped on every weapon I'd be wearing at the weddings, from my knives on down to the Glock and ankle holster. Isaac was going to want to make sure the dress and jacket fit properly over my armament. He'd probably also renew the accuracy spells on my gear, which was never a bad thing. I practice at the range regularly and am a good shot even without the spells. But when it really matters, I want every possible edge.

When I opened the door to my suite, a scant seven minutes after my summons, Baker was waiting outside. She offered me a huge mug of coffee that smelled like everything good in the world. Taking the mug, I inhaled deeply, then took a sip, careful not to burn the roof of my mouth. It tasted fabulous. I wondered what blend it was and if I'd be able to find it back home.

Raised voices greeted my ears from downstairs. Oh, I so didn't need to get in the middle of an argument this early. Instead, I blew on the steaming liquid in the mug and decided to take my time going down. Baker didn't seem any more excited to get involved than me. Adriana's voice, crisp and commanding, cut through the quarreling voices downstairs, saying in crisp, cold, English. "That is *enough!*"

I turned to Baker. "She really wants me down there, huh? You sure?"

She nodded vigorously.

"Peachy."

I stepped past her and made my way down to the living room, where Adriana, Olga, and Natasha were gathered together with Gilda and Isaac Levy.

"Oh, Celia. I'm so glad you're here." Gilda beamed up at me. "Come with me. We need you to try on your dress and jacket so we can make any last-minute adjustments." Zipping across the room, she retrieved a garment bag from where it was draped over the bar.

I doubted there'd be any alterations. After all, they'd just seen me a few days ago. Granted, it had been a rough few days, but I doubted I'd lost enough weight to change my measurements.

Isaac gave a short wave in greeting from where he was kneeling on the floor, pinning the hem of Natasha's gown. She was standing on a raised stool, her expression one of martyred patience.

"Natasha, glad to see you're feeling better." I tried to make it sound like she'd had the flu, rather than being an instrument of near-assassination.

She turned to look at me, over Isaac's muttered protest, and her expression lightened. "Princess, I've been wanting to thank you. I am told you were the one who saved my life."

I admitted it with a shrug but added, "Not the only one. King Dahlmar's friend . . ." I had gone blank on his name.

"Igor," Adriana supplied.

"That's him. Igor. He did CPR, too. Are you feeling better? What do the doctors say?"

"They say I will be fine. The only lasting effect is the lost memories." Her face clouded with worry. "I do not like not remembering."

I could understand that. I'd had a spell worked on me

that affected my memory. It nearly drove me nuts before I was finally able to get it lifted.

She shook her head and smiled. "But Princess Adriana has been most kind. She has forgiven me, in spite of what I have done, and is still willing to have me beside her in her wedding."

I glanced over at Adriana, who was smiling. That she wasn't holding a grudge was pretty damned generous of her, all things considered—and not at all like the Adriana I'd first met. Being with Dahlmar had mellowed her. She was definitely less prickly than she'd once been. Love will do that to you.

Gilda shooed me toward the hallway that led to the nearest bathroom. "You have to try on the dress with the shoes and jewelry. I'm especially worried about the shoes. This brand seems to run narrow."

She followed me into the good-sized bathroom, shutting the door firmly behind us before giving me a quick update on what I'd missed.

"The bridesmaids are arguing. The younger one . . ."

"Olga," I said, and Gilda nodded.

"Olga is very angry and frightened. So many things have gone wrong. Nothing is going according to plan. She was counting on Natasha's fear of her father to keep her in line, keep her agreeing to whatever Olga suggested. But that's changed now that Natasha is no longer under the influence of the spell. The two of them have been arguing and sniping at each other. Olga insists that Princess Adriana is using her siren abilities to control King Dahlmar. Natasha disagrees."

"Natasha's right," I said firmly as I slipped out of my shoes and unzipped the jeans.

"You're sure?" She hooked the hanger with my dress over the hook on the back of the door, flipped the lid down on the toilet, and took a seat.

"Positive," I assured her. "First off, Adriana is way older than she looks and way, way older than Dahlmar. Sirens live a *long* time, and she's told me directly that she considers Dahlmar a younger man. She couldn't have manipulated him using siren abilities because she doesn't really have any, at least not to the level where she could control somebody as strong-willed as the king. Besides which, I made sure he had an anti-siren charm that would prevent her from doing any hanky-panky."

"Oh, I'm sure it didn't stop *that*." Gilda gave me a saucy wink. "Adriana is a beautiful woman who is accustomed to getting her own way. There are many ways to manipulate someone; you don't need to have psychic powers. And from what I've seen, most women's normal abilities are usually enough to influence most men. Now we'll just have to find a way to find a way to work that into the conversation. Because I am not letting those two little bitches ruin that girl's big day."

"I thought you said she's a manipulator."

She turned wide, innocent eyes to me. "Well, of course. But the manipulation she's doing is only the time-honored sort that all women do. I respect that."

I nearly laughed out loud, but managed to smother the burst of noise with both hands so that it came out in a muffled snort. Gilda was right, of course. We needed to intervene. But I couldn't for the life of me figure out how we were going to manage that. Still, I was game. The new Adriana was growing on me. Besides, to my mind, every bride deserves a terrific wedding day.

I stripped down to my underwear. Gilda looked me up and down. "You've lost weight again," she scolded. "You need to eat more. And that"—she pointed to the scar in the middle of my chest—"is a new scar. I thought you promised me you'd be careful."

"I am careful," I protested. She was right about the scar, though. It wasn't huge, but it was noticeable. But I'd been damned lucky not to be hurt worse when Jan had done his thing.

I wished fervently that the feds would catch him. So far though, they'd had no luck. Damn it, he was apparently as good at hiding as he was at magic.

"Hmpf." She wasn't happy, but she didn't say anything else. She also didn't suggest a "beauty enhancement spell." Silly for that remark to still sting, after everything that had happened. But it did.

I unzipped the black canvas garment bag to reveal my dress.

It was beautiful. The color was a rich, deep purple, the color of flawless amethysts. On a separate hanger, the bolero-style jacket gleamed, thanks to the black silk embroidery on the front panels and the jet beads used as trim.

My breath caught in my throat. I couldn't believe how

beautiful it was, and on such short notice. The Levys had outdone themselves, again.

At my reaction, Gilda gave me a smug little smile. I didn't mind. She deserved to be smug. It was gorgeous. "Look in the compartment in the bottom of the bag," she suggested.

I unzipped said compartment to find a black velvet jewelry case about the size of a hardback book. The velvet had browned a little with age and the brass lock was a little tarnished. With trembling fingers I twisted the little lever that locked the case and flipped open the lid.

I was speechless for the second time in a few moments.

Amethysts and diamonds, fitted in an intricate white gold necklace with matching earrings and hair combs. They were absolutely stunning.

"Oh my God! Gilda, they're . . . gorgeous. I love white gold!"

She scoffed. "With diamonds? Heavens, no. That's platinum. They're our gift to you, dear."

Holy crap! Platinum! The set must have cost a fortune! "But . . . I can't . . . I mean—"

"Nonsense." She rose to her feet so that we were standing toe-to-toe. "You can, and you will. We insist." She took my hands in hers. "You've been loyal to us in good times and bad. You, personally, have brought us as much business as we can comfortably handle what with Miller & Creede and the new Serenity Secret Service account. And now you've given us the honor of having our work displayed in a royal wedding on the world stage for millions of people to see." She reached up to pat me on the cheek with a callused but gentle hand. "You're going to look beautiful, absolutely beautiful. We're very proud of you, Isaac and I. I know that your relationship with your mother is not so good, and I am sorry for that. She is an idiot if she doesn't realize what a gem she has in you. We do. Isaac and I both love you very much."

My eyes filled with tears, making the room blurry.

"Now hurry up and get dressed." She made a tsking noise and shook her head. "It needs to be taken in more than he expects."

I was still too choked up to speak, so I just nodded and let her help me with the zipper and fasten the necklace in place so I could see it in the mirror.

It was beautiful. *I* was beautiful.

Cousin. Adriana's voice spoke clearly in my mind. *Would you mind wearing the jewels when you come out? Olga is being a nuisance, complaining about her dress. It's very tiresome. I would do much more than keep her in the wedding to please my husband, but I must admit I do not like her.*

That made two of us.

When I reentered the living room, all conversation stopped. Olga's eyes got huge and Natasha simply blinked dumbly at me.

Adriana smiled. There was pride and honest joy in her reaction, along with a certain envy, which really surprised me. "Beautiful, cousin," she said. "You look absolutely exquisite. You see, ladies, as I said before, with the right jewelry, these dresses are perfectly elegant and modest enough not to offend your countrymen." She winked at me. "I am old enough to have a bit more experience in these matters than you do, after all. I only hope Dahlmar isn't too upset about marrying a much older woman."

So, Adriana had figured out how to bring it in without any help from me. But I'd help all the same. "Luckily, the siren genes mean that you don't have wrinkles yet."

"That," she said with another conspiratorial wink, "and excellent moisturizer. Thankfully, this century has wonderful products available. Beauty mud in the nineteenth century really was *mud*."

Olga spluttered, "But you're—"

"Well beyond ancient. I'm . . . what is the American term? Ah, yes, 'robbing the cradle' by taking Dahlmar as a husband." Adriana's smile was cheerfully wicked. "Sadly, I don't have enough siren abilities to control my beloved psychically; and even if I did possess those abilities, his staff has ensured he has a protection charm. But I would like to think I am still well-kept enough to have *some* influence on him."

Okay, so now I had no doubt she'd been listening to me and Gilda Levy the whole time. I was annoyed about it, too. I gave her a stern look.

I am fighting for my honor, my life, and the man I've discovered I actually love. If you think I'm not going to use every advantage I can, you are out of your mind.

I didn't answer. I couldn't, really. I was pretty sure I'd do the same damned thing if our roles were reversed. And, hey, I had to give her props for using the information to her advantage. She'd worked it in pretty subtly, all things considered.

Olga and Natasha looked significantly at each other and Natasha gave the other woman an "I told you so" look before tipping her head down to acknowledge Isaac's slight touch on her calf.

"All right, Natasha, you're done," he announced. "Gilda will help you choose jewelry." He got to his feet and took a step back before extending his hand to help Natasha down from her perch. "Your turn, Celia." He gestured toward the stool. I climbed up with his assistance, being extra careful of the hem and the high heels.

"You've lost weight again." He scolded me exactly the way his wife had. "You need to eat more. Or drink more."

"It's been a rough few weeks." I sounded defensive. I couldn't seem to help it. Like my grandmother, the Levys know just how to make me feel guilty. But they treat me like family. And if I could add another set of grandparents to my life, Isaac and Gilda would be my first choice.

"Hmnpf." He sounded so much like Gilda it made me laugh, which made him smile. "Good. I like to see you happy. Now hold still while I pin you."

I held still.

"I understand you'll be wearing a lavalava for the ceremony here on Serenity." Isaac made it a question.

"Yes."

"What will you do about the sunlight? The procession is over two miles long."

"I'll be wearing a hat and a jacket. But I'm a little worried about my hands and feet. Sunscreen doesn't last all that long on me. Do you have any suggestions?"

He grinned impishly. "As a matter of fact, I do." He rose a little creakily to his feet. "I'm done with the pinning. Why don't you go get your outfit and we'll see if my idea is going to work for you?"

I hurried back to the bathroom, anxious to get out of a dress made scratchy by straight pins. I felt a little pang of regret taking off the jewels. They were an amazing gift, not just because of the value, although that was not inconsiderable, but because they were an honest reflection of the affection Isaac, Gilda, and I have for one another.

My family might be a source of pain and frustration for me, but my friends? My friends are *excellent*.

Adriana's voice whispered in my head. *There is a safe hidden in the floor of your bedroom. I will give you the combination so that you may keep those jewels under lock and key when you're not wearing them.*

Thanks.

You are most welcome. And I am quite pleased. The dresses you chose are lovely. You can be fully armed without drawing attention to it, and Mr. Levy has agreed to check the tailoring and hem of my gown.

That would probably piss off the designer to no end.

Perhaps it will. But it is my gown, and my wedding. And I don't want the ankle holster with the derringer to . . . show.

Wow. I guess my gun was going to be the "something borrowed." Fair enough. When this was over, I might just give it to her. Politics is a very dicey business, particularly in Rusland. She'd probably need it.

Adriana soon left for a meeting with her priest. Olga left

almost on her heels; only Natasha chose to stay while Isaac finished making adjustments to the lavalavas I'd be wearing to tonight's state dinner and the wedding the day after tomorrow.

Natasha seemed very nervous. Isaac and Gilda sensed something was up and made some excuse to run out to their rental car for something, giving us a moment alone. The minute they were out of earshot, Natasha turned to me and spoke quickly and quietly. "You must not trust Olga. She is devious and determined. She does not believe the wedding should happen." Her expression was so earnest it almost hurt to see it. I was glad that she'd come around. Adriana wasn't perfect, but she did love Dahlmar, and she truly wanted to be a good queen for his people. I hoped that his people would eventually come to appreciate that, and her. That Natasha was coming around was a good sign.

"I know," I assured her, "and I don't."

She didn't seem reassured. "I wish I knew what she was planning. I do not. If I had proof, I would go to Igor and the king. But I have no proof, only suspicion. Olga is the king's niece, a member of the royal family. Without proof I can do nothing. But I know, in my heart, she is planning something."

"I believe you." I did. Natasha's suspicions fit with what Gilda had told me and with my own observations. "I'll be keeping a close eye on her."

Natasha looked searchingly at me. After a long moment, she said, "I think, perhaps, she is planning on that, as well. Please, look where she would not expect."

25

Checking the schedule I saw that tonight was going to be a busy night for Adriana and, consequently, for me. First, in the early evening, there was the big rehearsal dinner for the Serenity portion of the ceremonies—a black-tie event for the men and "Serenity formal" for the women. Later, Adriana would attend the private bachelorette party hosted by her girlfriends. I was scheduled to be with her at both events. Since nobody was throwing a fuss about this, I suspected that one or more of the royal family's clairvoyants had seen signs of trouble. It would've been nice if somebody had warned me about the threats—the when and where—but no one had, which probably meant no one knew. There are limits to what even the best seers can do. If there wasn't, there'd be no crime. The police would head it off ahead of time.

In my business I've guarded a lot of celebrities, but until recently I hadn't done much work with political figures, so I'd never actually been to a formal state event. It was an eye opener.

The dinner itself was in a ballroom decorated in teal, sea green, gold, and tan. Round tables were covered with elegant china, silver, and crystal. Each table had its own candelabra and floral arrangement.

I was seated at the head table, which was on a raised stage, between Adriana and Igor. I had done a personal check of the security arrangements that afternoon. I could tell that irritated Special Agent Albright, but it was my job to be Adriana's last line of defense, and I wasn't going to let anyone's attitude get in the way.

Everything was perfectly normal, which made me nervous as hell, particularly since Rizzoli had e-mailed to let me know that Jan Mortensen had disappeared completely. Rizzoli's friends in the CIA had information that he appeared to be hiding out "somewhere in Europe." They also swore that he hadn't gotten there by plane, train, or boat. Which left teleportation, probably via Okalani.

Thinking about Okalani brought back the memory of Hiwahiwa's words. I prayed that she was wrong, that maybe the kid was okay, that her father was protecting her. But I didn't really believe it. Just thinking about demons and torture made me nauseous. Having been on the wrong end of that particular equation, I don't allow myself to think about it too closely. The memories were blunted, not erased, and they'd been coming closer and closer to the surface lately.

I'd need to talk about it all with Gwen, my shrink, and soon. But tonight I was working and needed to be on my game. So I forced thoughts of Mortensen and Okalani out

of my mind and kept scanning the crowd for anything untoward or unusual.

Adriana and I were passing through the anteroom, greeting the guests and schmoozing. She was a vision in emerald and gold. The queen, home at last, was sitting on the
sidelines, letting the crowd come to her. She looked lovely,
but tired, and the scars she'd mentioned to me days before
were angry red welts marring her porcelain skin.

Powerful people are just as vain and petty as the rest of
us. The women all wanted to be the most beautiful and
best dressed. This was a little trickier than usual since we
were all wearing basically the same dress. Ah, the lavalava—
equalizer of women. Of course, it really didn't work that
way. Beautiful women looked beautiful. Homely women
looked . . . really well dressed. There were dresses in every
conceivable fabric and pattern, with jewels in more colors
than the rainbow. No expense had been spared as the at-
tendees all tried to outshine one another.

All the men wore tuxedos, in a variety of classic styles
that looked good on most men. Still, some wear them better than others. I saw John Creede and felt a wash of emotions. His tux fit so flawlessly and he looked so good in it
that most people would never have guessed he was actually
working security, protecting King Dahlmar's brother, Arkady.

Greede gave me a cold nod, acknowledging me but
making it strictly business. That stung, but not as much as
I'd expected it too—probably because I was still angry with
him. There were things I missed about him, but there were
also plenty of things I didn't.

Gunnar Thorsen came up to Adriana. I hadn't seen him since he'd oh-so-nicely interrogated me. I'd found him handsome in a business suit. In a tuxedo, he was stunning. His long hair had been pulled back in a tight braid. There are men who look effete with long hair, almost girly. He wasn't one of them, not with those shoulders and those chiseled features.

"Ladies, you're looking lovely this evening." He pulled Adriana into a light embrace, then released her and said, "That's an excellent choice for you, Celia, very striking."

"Thank you." I smiled up at him. I knew I looked good. My lavalava was made of raw silk in a dramatic black and white hibiscus pattern. The dress went well with my pale skin and there was quite a lot of that skin showing. Because it was such a bold print, I'd opted for simple yet elegant jewelry: a pair of pearl earrings and a platinum chain at my wrist.

A lavalava is not made for a concealed carry, so I had been limited in my weapons choices. Had I had the option of wearing a jacket it would have been easier, but Adriana had vetoed the idea, saying that this really wasn't that type of an event. So I had a small gun in my evening bag, along with breath mints and a tube of lipstick.

"My parents are here this evening," Gunnar said.

Adriana gave him a startled look that he ignored in favor of staring directly at me. Looking at him, I saw that despite his careful grooming, his face reflected the strain of the last few days.

"My father asked for a word with you, Celia. Apparently he has a message from my grandfather."

Adriana's gulp was clearly audible over the voices of the crowd and the muted background music. Apparently I was missing something important.

"Your grandfather?"

"Yes. You should be flattered. Odin doesn't often take an interest."

Odin? Oh crap. Thorsen wasn't just Gunnar's surname. He was actually Thor's son? His father, the God of Thunder, was here at the party. Um, okay then. Wow. It was my turn to gulp. I suddenly wished I'd snagged one of the flutes of champagne that had been circulating around. I really needed a drink.

I managed to choke out a response, but it wasn't easy. "Oh, I'm flattered. I'm also alarmed."

Thorsen threw back his head and laughed.

"Shall we join my parents then?" He winked at me. "I promise they won't bite."

"Of course." Adriana looped her arm through his. I couldn't read her thoughts, but her expression was enough. She wouldn't miss this for the world. Gunnar held out his other arm for me and I took it. Not just for show, either. I needed the support.

Thor, God of Thunder, son of Odin Allfather, looked great in a tuxedo. Like his son, he was big and blond. Unlike his son, he seemed to be having a marvelous time. He was all smiles as he introduced his wife. "Father, mother, this is Princess Adriana of Serenity, the daughter of Queen Lopaka." They murmured their acknowledgment and greetings. "And this"—Gunnar gestured to me—"is Princess

Celia Graves, granddaughter of Queen Lopaka's beloved brother, Kalino."

"Ladies, it is a pleasure." Thor stepped forward. Taking Adriana's hand in his, he kissed her knuckles, bowing just the tiniest bit at the waist. "King Dahlmar is a lucky man."

"And I, a lucky woman." She smiled as he released her hand. Then he turned his attention to me; his wide blue eyes, the color of a midnight sky with flecks of starlight, took me in from head to toe.

He took my hand, as he had Adriana's, laying a gentle kiss on my fingertips. I felt a jolt of electricity pass from him to me and gasped in surprise. It made him chuckle, a low, wicked sound that earned him a poke in the ribs from his wife. "Stop playing games and give her the message," she scolded. He gave an exaggerated sigh, but released my hand and slid his arm around her waist, pulling her close to him.

"Very well. My father said to tell you these words. 'Have faith. The right weapon can overcome what will come against you.'"

That was encouraging, if vague. "I don't suppose he told you which weapon or what is coming against me?" I put a wheedling tone in my voice. It made him laugh.

"I'm sorry. No. He probably shouldn't have said anything at all, but he likes you. You remind him a bit of the Valkyries."

That was a serious compliment. I did my best to remember what little I'd been taught about the Norse pantheon back in my university days so that I could phrase my thanks properly. "My thanks to you Thor, Thunderer, and to Odin Allfather. I'll endeavor to be worthy of such high praise."

He leaned forward, close enough that his beard tickled my ear when he whispered, "You already are. Your exploits will someday be written on the walls of our great hall. So it has been foretold."

What could I say to that? I was literally speechless. Fortunately I was saved from having to reply by the ringing of the chime that signaled dinner was about to be served. Gunnar, Thor, and his lady melted into the crowd moving into the dining room without saying good-bye. Adriana, meanwhile, grabbed me by the arm and began dragging me bodily down the hallway to the back entrance.

"Come on, we're late! We were already supposed to be in there at the head table when the chimes rang." She wasn't quite running, but she was walking damned fast. At the end of the hall, the Secret Service agents standing guard came to attention. One opened the door. The other pulled a small holy water squirt gun to confirm we were who we seemed to be.

"I'm coming. Will you relax? It's not like they're going to start the party without you. You're the bride, for heaven's sake."

She glared at me over her shoulder. "Only you would say something like that." She offered her hand to be sprayed. She passed, of course, and scurried through the door and onto the dais. I was seconds behind.

The head table was long and narrow, with all seats facing the crowd. King Dahlmar and Adriana were in the center. I was seated to her right. Igor was to my right. Natasha had the last seat on our side. Dahlmar's side consisted of the king, Queen Lopaka, Dahlmar's brother Arkady, and, finally, Olga. I didn't know who'd made the seating arrangements, but I was happy with them. I was near enough to Adriana to protect her if need be, and Olga was as far away as we could decently manage.

While the tables below had only candlelight to see by, we had stage lighting. It made it difficult to see clearly out into the crowd, but put us on display nicely. Of course it also made me nervous as hell. I so didn't want to do something hideous and embarrassing in front of hundreds of people. And it would be just my luck for it to happen.

I shook my head. *Don't even think about it.*

It took a few minutes for everyone to be seated, but eventually the guests were all in their places and only the servers were on their feet, moving quietly among the tables, filling wine and water glasses.

"Ladies and gentlemen, honored guests." Dahlmar spoke without a microphone, but his voice was clearly audible throughout the room. All murmured conversations ceased as every eye turned to him. "I want to thank you all for joining me in this celebration. I am happier than I can even express at the prospect of marrying my beloved, and truly overjoyed that you have chosen to join us. We met by chance and were paired by duty, but have had the extraordinary luck to find love."

He turned to Adriana, and his smile was warm and adoring. Either he truly loved her or he was one hell of an actor.

"This morning the Princess Adriana was baptized into my faith. I did not ask this of her. It was her choice, her decision. But I am most glad to know that she shares my beliefs and the beliefs of my people." I heard gasps from several places in the room. So Adriana's actions had been a surprise to some, at least. "In honor of this, I wish to present her with a very special gift."

He gestured to Igor, who reached into the jacket of his tux to produce a jewel case, which he passed to the king. Dahlmar opened the case, laying it on the plate in front of Adriana. She stared down at it, her eyes gone wide with shock.

"The Eldritch Cross was one of the great magical artifacts of my people. Its powers are legendary. Its loss, during the sieges of the Second World War, was a devastating blow to our people. The seers among us have stated that there will be continuing strife within the ruling family so long as it remains missing."

He turned to Adriana, taking her hand in his. "Would that I had the original to give you. Alas, I do not. But this, the copy made for my mother by my father with his own hands and his own magic, is my gift to you."

He let go of her hand to take the necklace from its case. He held it up so the crowd could get a good look. It was a lovely piece, a large cross, encrusted with emeralds, pearls, and golden topaz, colors that perfectly suited Adriana's beauty. He fastened it around her delicate neck, kissed her tenderly, and turned back to the crowd.

"With your indulgence I have another bit of business

to attend to before we eat." He stood, and everyone in the room followed suit.

"There is an award given to citizens of Rusland whose actions on behalf of King and Country show such extraordinary courage and valor as to provide an example for all to aspire to. I am, perhaps, a bit tardy in bestowing this honor on its recipient, for her actions in thwarting not one, but two political coups surely earned her this honor long before now."

He turned to me, and I found myself blinking stupidly as cameras flashed blindingly. "Princess Celia Kalino Graves, I present you the Silver Eagle of Rusland with my deepest gratitude, and that of all my countrymen."

He crossed the stage to stand in front of me. He embraced me, then stepped back. Reaching into his pocket, he withdrew a loop of black ribbon with an exquisite silver bird hanging from it. He put it on me, settling the weight of it on my shoulders before turning to face the crowd. "I give you Princess Celia, hero of Rusland."

"*Huzzah!*" Male voices, scattered throughout the room, called out the honor the first time. But the second and third cries were voiced by nearly everyone, a joyous shout that echoed through the hall.

King Dahlmar hugged me again, discreetly passing me a pristine white handkerchief as he did. I wiped the tears from my eyes as Dahlmar moved back to stand behind his seat. "Now, our business is done. Let us eat."

26

The bachelorette party was scheduled for a late start, but the dinner ran long, so we didn't have time to change before dashing to the limo that would take us to the docks. Milena, Adriana's best friend, was officially hosting the party even though it was being held on Adriana's yacht. The Secret Service had derailed the original plan of renting a cruise ship and hiring caterers due to "security concerns," which I hadn't been privy to. Yet. So Adriana's own crew and staff had been pressed into service.

The limo was a little crowded, what with me, Adriana, and our security—just Helen Baker for me, but a team of four, plus the driver, for the bride.

The day I'd arrived on Serenity, the harbor had been busy but not too crowded. Now . . . my, how things had changed. Every slip was filled and more ships were anchored offshore; their passengers and crew probably used small boats to get back and forth from the island. The landward ends of the piers, this side of the security barriers, were crawling with paparazzi and crowded with onlookers hoping for a glimpse of the princess. What a freaking security nightmare!

When the car doors opened we were buffeted by a wave of sound—people calling Adriana's name, and even mine—and the flashes of dozens of cameras. We each gave a brief wave before the guards hustled us onto the yacht.

The sun was setting, bathing the low-hanging cirrus clouds in a blaze of reds, pinks, and purples that were reflected in the ocean. We were met on deck by the hostess and the other three guests. Adriana introduced me to Milena, a pretty redhead with lots of freckles and the most amazing amber-colored eyes. I'd wondered about Adriana's best friend from earliest childhood and was surprised to find that she was mostly a subdued, serious woman with an acerbic wit. She soon had all of us in stitches as she detailed how she'd been followed around all day by none-too-subtle members of the world press, many of whom had offered her obscene amounts of money for the "inside scoop" and pictures from the party.

Nani and Naneka were identical twins with honey-colored hair and blue eyes. It would have been impossible to tell them apart if Nani wasn't hugely pregnant. They were bright and cheerful, chattering away like a pair of birds. Keohi, on the other hand, was a sultry, sloe-eyed, dark-haired beauty who hung silently back, watching the others, but only rarely saying anything. When she did, it was worth listening.

Adriana noticed me watching Keohi and spoke into my mind. *You are right to be impressed; Keohi is quite brilliant.*

She works as a marine biologist, studying the effect of oil spills on ocean ecosystems and developing natural methods to contain the spills. She went on at length, talking to me about her friend while laughing at the jokes of the others. I found it fascinating that she could carry on two entirely different conversations at once. *Keohi once told me she was only able to first become published in scientific journals under a male pseudonym, because people saw too much beauty to believe she had brains.*

I'd never had that problem. In the land of the Hollywood butterflies, I'd always been a useful brown moth.

But now you are royalty, Celia. A pedigree has its own beauty.

Yeah, but that's not the sort of fame I ever wanted. Adriana looked at me curiously, truly not understanding why being royal had so little value to me.

I went back to chatting amiably by the dancing light of a string of party lanterns hung around the deck. The drinks were plentiful, the conversation excellent. It didn't take long for the atmosphere to lull me into a sense of complacency. That's why bodyguards are seldom guests at the party, but to hell with it. There were plenty of other guards there. I decided to have a little fun.

I discovered, to my delight, that the Michelin-star chef on Adriana's yacht had previously worked at the secure facility where Vicki had lived for much of her adult life. He'd once made me Belgian waffles and syrup in liquid form. Today I was treated to all the same appetizers as the other guests, liquified, in a trio of chilled martini glasses. I found that both clever and touching—someone, the hostess or the chef, had taken time to think of me.

All four of Adriana's buddies were nice, funny, intelligent women. They weren't toadies and they weren't anything remotely close to what I would have expected Adriana's friends to be like when I first met the prickly princess with a huge chip on her shoulder. They were, however, exactly the kind of people I would expect to see in the company of the Adriana I was now coming to know.

We were taken well out to sea, with our ever-present escort vessels keeping a discreet distance. Equally watchful were the helicopters that passed overhead.

Adriana, are those Secret Service choppers or press?

Both. It's the open sea, so mother couldn't legally clear the air space. I know it's annoying, but try to ignore it.

Easy for her to say. I kept remembering Mexico and the armed thugs who'd fired machine guns at us from overhead. I sat and smiled, drink in hand, but now I was on high alert, my former relaxation gone. That vigilance, and my vampire vision, let me see the diver drop from a helicopter as it swung low beside us, photographers in the cabin snapping telephoto pictures.

I sent a warning to Baker mentally. *Diver in the water. Three o'clock off the port side.* I heard her mutter something into the mic at her wrist. Almost immediately the yacht's engines roared to life. At the sound, the women all looked around, startled. It takes a couple of minutes to get a large vessel moving from a dead stop, but the captain did the best he could. In fact, the movement as the ship set sail was so abrupt and jerky that Keohi, who had been standing, had to grab onto the table to keep herself from falling.

In the distance, the escort ships started moving in.

Adriana was pulled down to the deck by the nearest guard and thought at me in alarm, *Celia, what is going on? We aren't supposed to be heading back yet.*

Stay down. A diver dropped off that last chopper. I'm pretty sure he had a PMD.

Originally developed for the military, a PMD, or Personal Movement Device, was about the size of a dinner plate and used a combination of magic and technology to allow a diver to move through the water as fast as most ships while maintaining a constant flow of oxygen. If the guy I'd seen drop off the chopper had one, he'd be here in seconds.

How could you possibly have seen . . . ?

I shrugged as I pushed Adriana's friends toward the cabin to get below decks. *Vampire night vision comes in handy now and then. Now if you would, everyone needs to get below.*

You think we're under attack. Her mental voice sounded truly shocked. Even with everything that had been happening, she hadn't expected this. Of course, as a clairvoyant she'd probably gotten used to having at least a hint of trouble before it arrived.

I don't know, but better safe than sorry. Now go.

At a word from her, the four of them darted for the stairwell, holding hands and keeping their heads below the line of the upper cabin. A pair of agents materialized from the shadows and followed them. Baker appeared at my side.

"You should go inside, too." It wasn't quite an order, more a firmly framed suggestion.

"I'm of more use out here, Helen. I'm on duty, just like you."

"We really do know what we're doing," she chided me.

"Did any of your people see him? Even those using night-vision goggles?"

She opened her mouth to answer, but remained silent when I raised my hand. I thought I'd heard the soft *whump* of an object impacting the ship's hull. There was a second thump, the sound barely audible over the noise of the engines and the slap of waves against the ship. It might be my imagination, but I didn't dare risk it.

Baker had heard it, too. We both drew guns from beneath our jackets and moved to take cover between the cabin and the built-in table. When we were concealed, she whispered into the microphone at her wrist and I saw shadows move into position around the boat.

Seconds that lasted an eternity passed as we watched and waited. A pair of wet-suited figures eased over the railing and began creeping silently forward. When they were far enough from the edge of the deck that they couldn't simply dive over and escape, a spotlight flared to life, accompanied by the voice of authority blaring through a bullhorn.

"Freeze. Move and you will be shot."

They froze and dropped their weapons.

Actually, what they dropped into the bright light were . . . cameras.

27

I **hate** the paparazzi. Just hate 'em. Some of them will do anything, risk anything, to get a picture or story. Never mind who gets hurt in the process. There are even those who, if they can't get the story, will stage a story.

Nellie Standish was evidently one of those.

She wouldn't give us her source, but admitted she'd been slipped information about tonight's party. She'd also been told that Adriana wanted "one last fling" before she and Dahlmar tied the knot and that if Standish could get a camera on board, she'd find a naked man in the princess's bedroom.

Baker and I went to check on that detail, letting others continue the questioning.

Adriana's stateroom was down the hall from the main room where the party guests were waiting. Her private cabin was spacious, beautiful, and after a thorough check, unoccupied except for a male blow-up doll propped up by pillows. The doll's staggeringly huge member was adorned by a big red bow.

I burst out laughing. I mean, seriously, a blow-up doll?

Baker gave a derisive snort. "She risked getting killed for this *toy*."

"At the right distance and angle, she might be able to make it look real. And even photos of this would be embarrassing for King Dahlmar if they got out."

"Or she could be an assassin, using this as cover."

Baker was right. Paparazzi go everywhere—it would be a great way for an assassin to hide. "When you find out, let me know. I'm going to deal with Seymour here and report to the princess."

"Seymour?" Baker asked.

"Yeah, I'm seeing more of him than I ever wanted."

She chortled and left, first handing me a device I could use to scan my cousin's "last fling." I didn't touch it, in case being tossed off the bed in disgust was a trigger. There was no bomb. But that's not the only thing that can kill.

I had no doubt I looked ridiculous hooking the scanner to the air port, which some clever soul had placed right where fluid comes out of a human male, to check out what the doll was filled with. I'd hate to find out it had been inflated with sarin gas.

I waited for the light on the device to turn green, but it remained stubbornly yellow. Not red, but there was definitely *something* more to Seymour than his obvious attributes.

I called in Baker and Griffith and managed not to blush as I told them to bag and tag the doll and get it off the boat without deflating it.

I took Adriana into a small cabin to brief her. She was rightly alarmed as what looked like a body bag was removed from her personal cabin. I explained what had happened without mentioning the contents of the doll, then she and I went back to the main room, where the other guests were sitting and staring at nothing. That likely meant they were busily talking mentally.

"Excuse me," I said out loud, startling several of them, "but which of you left a *gift* on Adriana's bed?" Nobody answered. That wasn't good. "Really, this is important, ladies. If you did, we need to know."

Finally, Nani raised her hand sheepishly. "It was poor taste on my part, I know. But the expression on it made me laugh. I'm sorry if it frightened anyone."

Adriana laughed and told the others what I'd found. They all chuckled before Adriana swatted her friend's knee. "You scamp, Nani! I'm sorry I didn't get to see it."

Ouch. I'd been hoping it hadn't been left by one of Adriana's friends. Now came the hard part. "Did you actually *fill* the doll?"

Nani, big-with-child, been-with-a-hundred men siren Nani, blushed. "Good heavens, no! Did you see where they put the nozzle?" She turned to the others. "It was right on the end of his . . . well, you know. Most of them have the place where you blow it up on the back of the head. No, I asked one of the servants to fill it."

I heard a *cheep* near the door. It was Baker's earwig. She listened intently and then nodded. "Ten-four," she said into the mic at her wrist. She stepped forward and took over the questioning. "Did you instruct the servant to place any-thing in the doll except air, your ladyship?"

Nani shook her head, confused. "No. Of course not. Why, what—" She didn't complete the sentence but her expression told me she'd figured out what was going on. Gasps from the others told me everyone else had gotten it too.

"What did you find, Agent Baker?" Adriana's voice shook, and for good reason. Everybody on board, with the exception of the reporters, was someone she trusted.

"There was THC suspended in a mixture of air and ethylene. It wouldn't kill the princess, but since she is a prophet, it would likely cause euphoria and hallucinations. We don't know what was intended beyond that. Perhaps the photographer would catch her in a compromising posi-tion or appearing drunk, which would inflame the Ruslan-dic population. Or perhaps someone hoped she would fall overboard and drown. Of course, that could never happen. The ocean wouldn't allow a siren princess to die by drown-ing. Or perhaps it was a prank. We might not ever know. But I do need to know which servant you asked to fill the doll."

Nani named the male bartender. Adriana protested that she'd known him for years. When the security team scoured the ship for him, they found him easily—he'd hung him-self in his cabin. We might never know why he'd done it or who he might have been working with.

The whole chain of events cast a pall over the party and it wasn't long before the captain turned the ship around to take the subdued group of friends back to shore.

28

The wedding had been being planned for more than a year with military precision and timing. An army of workers were laboring to take care of even the tiniest details. You would think that there wouldn't be any last-second preparations required on the final day.

You would be wrong.

That Nellie Standish had been able to get onto the princess's yacht and that a member of Adriana's own staff had been compromised had the secret service in a frothing fury. I went to the security meeting and listened as Thorsen went over the schedule for the next day minute by minute, confirming who would be in charge of what and which units where doing what where and when. Air space had been closed off over the capital city for the entire morning. Uniformed police would be stationed along the parade route at ten-foot intervals, providing a very visible presence. Less visible would be Creede, who was coordinating the work of the mages who would create an unseen magical barrier to protect the royals for the entire length of the two-mile procession. The Secret Service agents were doing continuous sweeps for bombs and snipers. Radio announcements and printed handouts asked all citizens and visitors to report anything suspicious.

The sheer size of the endeavor was staggering. And even with all of the preparation, Thorsen and everyone else in the room were fully aware that we couldn't keep Queen Lopaka, Princess Adriana, and the others completely safe. The route was too open and too long. But everything that could be done was being done by professionals who were the best in the business.

And all this was for the *casual* part of the program. The procedures in place for the big church wedding in Rusland were going to be even more elaborate.

I was proud to be a part of history in the making. I was terrified of screwing up.

On the Internet, the Guardians of the Faith denounced the upcoming ritual on Serenity, decried Adriana's baptism as a fraud, and threatened decisive action if she ever dared set foot on Ruslandic soil. They sounded hysterical and crazy. Then again, they probably were. But though the best minds in the security services of three countries tried, they were unable to trace the source of the messages. The bad guys had thoroughly covered those tracks. It was impressive and frightening—they'd spent a lot of time and effort to make themselves untraceable.

On Serenity, every trail connecting to the man who'd tried to kidnap my grandmother held a fresh corpse. Some were obviously victims of foul play. One was an apparent suicide. In the United States, the FBI had found Clarke, murdered with gruesome irony on a standing warehouse set that had been used in the James Bond movie *A Place to Die*. I was glad I had an alibi for that one, because it was common knowledge that Clarke had been harassing me and that I hated the bastard.

Jan was in the wind and there was still no sign of Okalani. Despite the words of Laka's seer, I was losing hope of anyone finding her alive.

It was hard. I would save her if I could. But first someone had to *find* her. Both the queen's people and the FBI were working with local law enforcement to search anywhere that Clarke had been known to frequent, so far to no avail. Okalani was off the grid and definitely in danger. Knowing that the mess she was in, start to finish, was her own fault didn't make it any better. Most of our problems are of our own making. Since there was nothing I could do to help her, I tried to put the whole situation from my mind.

The morning dawned bright and clear—something I knew because I watched the sun rise through the French doors of my suite. The procession was scheduled to start at 9:00 sharp and there was a lot to be done before then. And it wasn't as if I had been sleeping, anyway.

I brushed my teeth, then stumbled to the shower, hoping it would help wake me enough to keep me moving until I got some caffeine. I scrubbed and shampooed, but didn't dry or style my hair or put on makeup. Both would be taken care of later by professionals—Adriana, Olga, Natasha, and I would all be getting "done" in my big living room. The very best hair and makeup artists in the world had been hired to make sure we looked perfect. I was a little surprised they were letting me dress myself. They must figure I could be trusted to tie on a lavalava. Silly them.

I pulled the dress from its garment bag, laying it across the bed. It was a striking piece made of raw silk in a red so dark it was almost black, with a pattern of glittering silver and gold abstract flowers and contrasting black bamboo. It was dark enough to set off my pale coloring and blonde hair and looked good with the black jacket and matching picture hat I'd be wearing to protect the delicate skin of my face.

Isaac had come through with the solution for my hands and feet: handmade gloves and boots covered in illusion spells that made them look eerily like bare hands and feet— with a perfect manicure and pedicure to match my dress, no less. My skin would be covered and protected, but I'd look like everyone else. I was more grateful to him than I could say.

When I was dressed, I went downstairs to join the others. I'd accessorized with a boatload of concealed weapons as well as the ruby-and-diamond earrings and bracelet that I'd used to have Gilda spy on Olga and Natasha for me—not because I needed their special properties, but simply because they were the best match for my outfit.

I was directed to a tall stool, where an elderly woman with close-cropped curls and skin the color of café au lait whipped a black plastic cape over my shoulders and began using a wide-toothed comb to detangle my hair. It took a bit of time. I have a lot of hair.

"It's a bit windy today, and I understand you want to wear a hat, is that right?" she asked. There was no censure in her voice.

"Yes. I need to protect my skin."

"In that case, why don't I pull it over to one side, and arrange it in curls trailing over your shoulder?" She combed it into place, to give me an idea of how it would work.

"I like that." I smiled at her.

I sat still, letting her do her thing with a variety of pleasantly scented hair products, a blow dryer, and a pair of tortoiseshell combs. All the while I wished fervently for a cup of black coffee. I can function without caffeine in the morning, but I'm never happy about it.

The stylist was working with the curling iron when Hiwahiwa arrived at the head of a parade of servers pushing carts laden with food and drink—everything from capers to caviar, bagels with cream cheese to scrambled eggs, English breakfast tea to—oh joy and rapture—*coffee*. It smelled glorious. They even brought me a Sunset Smoothie that must have been made from Juan and Barbara's recipe. It was all I could do to sit still and let the hairdresser finish what she was doing instead of pouncing on the tray like some ravening beast. I'd have to brush my teeth again to get rid of the garlic and onions, but the coffee and the wonderful food were worth every second.

"All done." She turned the stool around so I could get a

look at myself in the mirror behind the bar. "What do you think?"

I looked great. Even without makeup. "Wow."

"You have great hair," she said as she whisked off the cape. "Now go eat. When you're done they'll want you down the hall for makeup."

"Thanks, so much." I wished I could tip her, but I hadn't brought down my purse. "Um . . ." I tried to think of an apology that didn't sound lame, but couldn't think of a thing.

It was as if she read my mind, or maybe just my uncomfortable expression. "Don't worry about it," she assured me. "Everything's been taken care of. Tips and everything."

I enjoyed my breakfast while my hairdresser worked on Natasha. I half expected Hiwahiwa to approach me with word about Laka or Okalani, but she didn't. Most likely, there wasn't anything to say. Still, I was glad to move to the next room and put some distance between us.

"I'm going to use a base with the heaviest sunscreen available," the makeup artist assured me as she swept another little capelet over my shoulders. This one was hot pink and marked with the logo of her company. The color was an almost exact match for her short, spiked hair and perfect manicure.

"I appreciate that."

"My name is Brenna."

"Celia."

"I know." She smiled, showing straight white teeth. "Now try to relax."

I tried, but wasn't very successful. It was weird having

somebody paint makeup on me. I didn't like it. Still, I couldn't argue with the result. When she stepped aside so I could see myself in the mirror, I was stunned.

That was me? Wow. I had a moment of pure ego—which was deflated the minute I got a look at my cousin, seated nearby.

Everybody says brides are radiant, and Adriana was. Her long red hair was held to one side by pearl-encrusted combs carved from abalone shells; it fell in a cascade of curls over one shoulder. The lavalava she wore was dark gold, cream, and yellow, and was tied in a way that showed off her dangerous curves. The cross King Dahlmar had given her the night before nestled in her ample cleavage; the colors of the dress picked up the topaz in the necklace and her topaz-and-pearl earrings.

The makeup artist hadn't needed to do much for her. Adriana had amazing skin and she was so excited and happy that cosmetics were almost redundant—almost.

Natasha and Olga were both looking lovely as well. I studied myself again in the mirror and was pleased with what I saw. Today I could hold my own with the other bridesmaids, and that was good, because even if the bride was going to be the center of attention, I'd be in lots of the wedding photos, and the event was being televised all over the world. Too, there'd be press photographers taking shots for all the international print media.

There was a light tap on the door.

It was time to go.

The drive from the guest house to the parade route was

surprisingly quiet. Nobody bothered making small talk. I didn't mind. I was enjoying staring out the window at the milling throngs of happy people waving and shouting congratulations as we drove past.

We arrived at the starting point exactly on schedule. Stepping out of the car into the bright morning sun was like stepping into a pool of thick, burning magic. It hurt. I'd known about the protective spells everywhere, but ow, ow, *ow*. Damn. And it was going to be like this for the long, long walk to the courthouse. I'd have to really fight not to wince the whole way—and wouldn't that look special on the front page of every paper in the world?

The procession probably looked casual, but of course that was an elaborate illusion. Everything had been planned to the last nuance. Adriana and Dahlmar were at the head of the group, walking hand-in-hand. The queen would be directly behind them, escorted by Gunnar Thorsen. If there were any concerns about whether she was strong enough to walk a couple of miles so soon after being released from the hospital, no one I knew had dared voice them. Truthfully, she looked good, and it wasn't the makeup, either. Being so close to the ocean and back on her home island seemed to be doing wonders for her. She was beautiful in bright turquoise, her golden hair left long and loose so that it fell past her shoulders in shining waves. We three bridesmaids were next, with our escorts. Mine was Griffiths, who looked terrific in traditional long shorts and a flowing white shirt. Igor followed—with Baker at his side, which gave her a reason to stay close to me. I noticed that she and Igor were smiling at each other in a genuinely friendly manner. Hmmm.

I settled my hat on my head, activating the little spell disk that insured it wouldn't fly off, even in a gale-force wind. Griffiths stepped forward, extending his arm. I took it and we began the stroll to the courthouse steps.

For all the expense, trouble, and elaborate planning, the actual ceremony at the courthouse would only take about fifteen minutes. It boggled my mind. I wondered what the cost added up to per minute, and decided I really didn't want to know.

We walked down a wide brick street that had been strewn with flower petals of various colors. It smelled fantastic, and probably felt wonderful for those going barefoot. Somewhere, someone on the Internet was probably decrying the waste, and someone else was totting up how many flowers had been denuded to make this happen. But it was beautiful, and I took deep breaths, enjoying the fragrance as I turned from side to side and waved at the crowd.

"You do not know, do you?" Griffiths spoke softly, keeping a smile on his face as he waved cheerfully to the people on our right.

His voice hinted at something amiss. I forced myself to keep smiling, even though I felt a chill of foreboding. "What?"

"Your business associate has not called?"

"I left my phone in my room." I'd figured it would be rude to leave it on during the morning's events, so I decided not to even carry it.

"Ah. I see."

My smile had probably gone brittle. Waving to the cheering crowds on the left, I whispered, "Is anyone dead?"

"No."

"Maimed?"

"No."

"Then just tell me." Military jets roared overhead in formation. I looked up. The crowd looked up. Despite the ooohing and ahhing of thousands of voices, vampire hearing, activated by my rising level of tension, let me hear Griffiths clearly.

"Because of all of the various threats against Adriana and the sirens, my king has had me put intelligence feelers out throughout the world. An informant brought us word of a threat to a siren in Santa Maria de Luna. He had helped plant a bio-magical bomb in the upstairs bathroom of a Victorian office building."

My stomach lurched. "Shit."

"I sent my people to check it out. The device they found involves both explosives and powerful curses and was linked to your DNA by strands of your hair. It is a particularly nasty piece of equipment. The bomb squad is on their way. But, based on the photos my colleague has sent me, your police are not going to be able to disarm it. They will insist on a controlled explosion."

My smile faltered and I gripped his arm tightly so that I wouldn't stumble. My building. Damn it. Damn, shit, hell, crap, fuck! Swearing internally helped me fight back the tears that stung my eyes. I loved that building. I'd loved it since the day I'd seen it while looking for office space, long before Vicki had left it to me. Yes, it was just a thing, but it was *my* thing. It was unique. And we'd *just* gotten Ron moved out.

This was why Dottie had taken the cat, had had my things sent away, had looked sad. She knew but, like Vicki, couldn't tell. Because if she had, we might all be dead; our searching for the bomb might have set it off.

I took a deep, shuddering, breath. I could handle this. Nobody I loved was dead. Nobody had been badly hurt. I'd rebuild if I could, or find another office. I could deal.

Griffiths waited until I had myself fully under control. "There is more."

Wave, smile, turn. Wave, smile, turn. My movements were a little mechanical, but the audience probably wouldn't notice. "Of course there is." I didn't bother to keep the bitterness out of my voice.

He gave the tiniest nod of acknowledgment. "My people have traced the magical signature and have found out who created this bomb and hired the man to plant it."

"The terrorists?"

"No. A woman. A human. Her name is—"

I didn't even have to guess. I finished the sentence for him. "Angelina Bonetti."

His eyes widened, his eyebrows rising. "You are not surprised."

Oh, I was surprised. I'd known Angelina was jealous. But a *bomb*? Really? How over the top was that? Still, in a weird way, it made sense. If she was going to kill me, now was the perfect time, and with all of the Guardian of the Faith crap going on, a bombing of my office would likely be written off as an act of terrorism. The terrorists might even lie and take credit for it, which would make the police less likely to look for any other culprits.

Beautiful and smart, she was quite the adversary. If it hadn't been for the informant, she would probably not only have succeeded in killing me, she'd most likely have gotten away with it.

The knowledge was both shocking and frightening. But it also made me mad. She'd tried to kill me. She actually tried to fucking *kill* me. So much for not being much of a threat to her.

"I'm smiling, Griffiths, but heaven knows what people are reading in my mind."

He squeezed my arm reassuringly. "That is why I am walking with you. I'm blocking your mind from outside reading or attack. Your thoughts are your own until this is over."

It was a relief to hear. "Thank you." Now I could be angry and hurt and terrified and still pretend for the public and the cameras that everything was fine. Everyone would think I was happy while in fact, I felt a level of rage that, if not held in check, was likely to bring out my inner monster. I managed to control it. But it wasn't easy.

As a consequence, the ceremony was something of a haze to me. I was there. I did my part, but I don't remember anything specific. Adriana and Dahlmar made their public declarations of love and fidelity, then kissed on the steps of the courthouse amid deafening cheers. We all made happy-happy in our lavalavas, and congratulated the beaming couple by tossing a few thousand flowers' worth of fragrant petals into the air to fall in a cloud around them. Flashbulbs went off so fast that the air turned white.

Fortunately, there were no other threats. I'm a professional, but I have my limits. Knowing that someone hated me enough to plant a bomb likely to kill not only me, but pretty much anyone within a full square block, was mind-boggling. Shock and anger washed over me in alternating waves as I struggled to wrap my head around the idea.

How the hell had Angelina Bonetti gotten a sample of my hair? After the events of the past couple of years I have become almost fanatically paranoid about preventing that sort of thing, for exactly this reason.

I could only think of one logical possibility. Well, actually two.

John Creede had lost his siren charm, which was made from my hair, in our battle with Glinda. Someone might have found it and made it available on the black market. The other choices were that it had been destroyed . . . or that it had been taken to Hell. I didn't want to think too much about the latter option. It was just too frightening.

It was much more likely that Angelina had gotten my hair from the charm I made for Bruno. Maybe that was how she knew he didn't have it—because she did.

What worried me more was that Angelina wasn't a witch, and Griffiths had said *bio-magical*. That little fact was just sinking into my head. Yeah, Mrs. DeLuca, Grand Hag of the East Coast, hates me, but I didn't think she'd actually help someone murder me. I mean, there's hate and there's *hate*. Besides which, Isabella DeLuca is smart and subtle. A bomb didn't seem like her kind of thing, particularly one that could be traced back so easily. She's more the death curse or poison sort of person.

Griffiths gave me his cell phone and helped me slip into the courthouse after the ceremony and before the wedding photos. Rather than use the women's room and risk getting interrupted, I ducked into the "family" restroom, which was a single seater and had a changing table attached to the wall.

My first call was to Alex. If the locals weren't in charge, she'd know who was.

Alex picked up on the first ring. "Detective Alexander speaking."

"It's me."

"Christ on a crutch! Where the hell have you been? Don't you ever pick up your voice mails?" She was almost snarling.

"Where have I been? Are you freaking serious? It's Adriana's wedding day."

"But you weren't supposed to be going to the ceremony on Serenity. We've been looking everywhere for you! There was word someone had predicted your kidnapping so we've been treating you as a missing person. Bruno is gone. Dawna hasn't heard from you for a couple of days. We can't reach John Creede."

Oh, crap. Of course she was worried. We deliberately hadn't made my change of plans public.

"Geez, Alex, I'm sorry. Things changed and the Serenity

Secret Service kept some details from the press for security reasons. I've been on Serenity for a few days. I just heard about the bomb in my building. Are your guys handling it?"

"Just crowd control. The feds are taking care of actually setting the damned thing off. You really need to call Rizzoli and Dawna—she's an absolute basket case."

I could believe that. "I'll call her as soon as I'm done with you." I took a deep breath, choosing my words carefully. "The guy who told me about the bomb said it wasn't the terrorists, that it was personal. He said that they traced the magical signature to a particular woman."

"Did he now? And how did he happen to get that information? "

"Off the record?"

"Oh hell," she grumbled. "Fine, off the record."

"He's Queen Lopaka's fixer. An informant told them about the bomb, and he had King Dahlmar's fixer look into it."

She swore colorfully. "*Fixers*. You mean international spies and mercenaries. Jesus, Celia. You are seriously telling me that you're in bed with international spies?"

"I'm not *in bed* with them."

"Unh-hunh." She gave a martyred sigh. "I'm hanging up now. Call Rizzoli. I'm sure he'll enjoy the hell out of hearing this."

I called. He wasn't thrilled to hear from me, but at least he wasn't surprised about where I was. His wife and kids were obsessing over the whole royal wedding thing because they actually knew somebody in the wedding party. He already knew about Angelina, too. He was going to tell me—if I ever got around to returning his call.

I winced at the none-too-subtle hint. "Sorry, it's been nuts and we're on security lockdown here."

"Your life is always nuts. Curled up in a corner yet with loaded weapons?"

Ouch. He was right, but saying so wasn't exactly tactful. Still, part of the whole friendship thing is putting up with the other person's foibles. Dom and I might have started out as business acquaintances, but we'd been through a lot the past couple of years. Somewhere along the way he'd become one of my friends.

So I ignored the verbal jab and changed the subject. "Have you picked Angelina up yet?"

My question was met with silence. A long, meaningful, silence. Unfortunately, I didn't have a clue what it meant. "Dom, are you still there?"

"Yeah, she's in custody now."

There was something weird about his inflection when he said it, a tiny bit too much emphasis on the last word. I was about to push him to try to get more information, when there was a pounding on the bathroom door.

Oh, hell. I should've known. I couldn't have five full minutes to myself. There simply wasn't room for it in the day's schedule.

"Princess, are you all right?" Baker didn't sound worried, but she wasn't happy, either. "They're looking for you for pictures."

"I gotta go, Dom—" I started to ask when it would be a good time to call him back, but he cut me off by saying "No problem" and hanging up. Hmnpf. Something was very definitely fishy.

"Princess?" Baker repeated.

"I'm fine," I assured her as I was opening the door. "I was just making a couple of calls."

"Well, I'm afraid you're needed for photos. Any other calls you wish to make"—her expression made it clear that it wasn't acceptable to do that in the middle of a royal wedding—"will have to wait."

The woman at the door sounded like Baker. She looked like Baker, complete with steel gray suit, tasteful pumps, and ear piece, but I didn't see Igor or Griffiths behind her. That was odd enough that I reached into my jacket and withdrew my One Shot with its holy water.

"Extend your hand, please."

She didn't argue, didn't even blink, just offered her hand. I sprayed. It was her. "Where's Griffiths? I need to give him back his phone."

"He has already joined the rest of the party." She said it politely but still managed to convey her urgency and frustration. "We're running behind schedule." She led me down a long marble hallway with hardwood doors spaced at intervals.

I was inconveniencing everybody and throwing off a schedule that had been timed with exquisite care. It was unprofessional of me. "I'm sorry. But Griffiths told me about the bomb in my office and I wanted an update."

She almost stumbled—apparently she hadn't known—but when she spoke, her voice was rock steady. "A bomb?"

"Your people didn't miss anything," I assured her. "It was planted after we left. It had a DNA trigger."

We took a sharp right turn down a narrow hall that led to one of the building's back exits. Bringing her wrist to her mouth, Baker spoke into her wrist mic. "I've got her. She's safe."

Now, yes. But for how long?

29

Sirens Live a very long time. They aren't all that fertile and they very seldom marry. So there aren't a lot of royal weddings or births, and when either occurs, it's a huge historic event. The photographer was making sure there was an extensive record of the events. There were pictures with Dahlmar and Adriana sitting on chairs that were vaguely thronelike, the rest of us arrayed in a semicircle behind them. There were photos of them kissing. There were group shots, individual shots, shots of the various couples. There were so many shots, in fact, that I would've been happy to do a little shooting of my own. But I tried to be a good sport about it and I smiled at the camera until my face muscles ached.

But all things end eventually, including royal photo shoots. When this one did, we piled into various limousines and drove in a motorcade back to the royal compound, through streets filled with drunken revelers.

I stayed close to Adriana and kept a close watch on Olga

during the luau that was the reception. And while the food and the free-flowing drinks looked and smelled amazing, I didn't taste them. While people ate, a steady stream of performers put on a fabulous show that included amazing dance numbers, exciting singers, and exquisite music. I paid zero attention. Only after the bride and groom left the reception to enjoy some time alone was I able to relax. I chose to do that by having Baker and Griffiths escort me back to the guest house so that I could have a little time to myself.

Getting away from the crowds was a huge relief. Now that I wasn't on duty I wanted a couple of stiff drinks, some food, and to have a good cry.

My beautiful office was probably a pile of rubble by now. I was likely to be treated to constant replays of the "controlled detonation" once I got home.

I didn't want to see it.

Baker and Griffiths walked me to the door. After checking with the guards on duty to be sure that no one had come in the building in our absence, and that all of the visitors and servants had left, I was given the all clear to enter.

Normally I get a real jolt crossing the spell barrier at the threshold of the guest house. Today, not so much. When I gave Baker a look of inquiry, she smiled. "Our mages came up with a special barrier with you in mind. Any other paranormal creature will get hit *hard*. But the perimeter is keyed to recognize you. We got the idea from the man who manufactured your weapons safe."

I found myself grinning. How very cool. Then I remembered that the safe was in my building. The grin died.

I needed a drink. More than that, I need to get stinking drunk, to the point I didn't care.

The guest house is big, and normally pulsing with life. Even when I am the only guest, the place is full of servants. Tonight, it was echoingly empty. The usual staff had been given the night off for security reasons. I moved through silent halls that led to the living room, my footfalls sounding loud in my ears. Hitting the light switch, I noted that the hair and makeup experts had cleared out, leaving the room spotless. Stepping behind the bar I reached into the minifridge and grabbed ice and some orange juice. To my delight, I found that the cooks had left me a plastic container of frozen au jus. I shook my head a little. Good thing I wasn't going to be staying on Serenity much longer. I could get used to having staff around who anticipated my every whim.

I popped the lid off of the au jus and stuck it in the microwave to cook while I mixed myself a stiff screwdriver in a tall glass. Once everything was ready, I settled into a comfortable chair with a good view of all the exits. A quick touch on the remote and the big-screen television came to life.

I flipped to CNN. I shouldn't have. Not until the second or third screwdriver. But there, in high definition, was my building, with a banner beneath it saying "filmed earlier." I watched in horrified fascination as an officer in a blue FBI windbreaker wrapped hair around a ball, taped it down, and loaded the ball into an air gun. He broke a spell disk over the gun. I couldn't see the rune on the disk, but I was betting it was for distance and accuracy. He had a straight shot, but was quite a distance from the building.

At his order, a marksman shot out the glass of the French doors of my office. Another barked command and mages were on standby, ready to raise the perimeter the instant after he fired.

Blinking back tears, I watched him raise the air gun to his shoulder and fire.

The explosion put the one back in Mexico to shame.

They played it full speed. Then they played it in slow motion. They showed it from every angle. I watched in horror, over and over, as the beautiful antique stained-glass window shattered, watched the flamingo-pink upstairs toilet soar through the air to crash in the middle of the street. The bones of the old building were rapidly devoured by flames made more powerful by the curse that had been part of the bomb. My old weapons safe, scorched but upright, smashed through the damaged floors to land intact atop the wreckage, its protection spells keeping it defiant against the worst the witch could dish out, even with the door wide open displaying staples, copy paper, and sticky notes. Damn. Jason was the man of the hour. He'd probably get a ton of new orders for safes—and more power to him.

The new safe didn't fare nearly so well. What few of my weapons and spell disks I hadn't brought with me had been utterly destroyed, because the safe that had "protected" them was nothing but scorched and twisted metal.

I downed my drink in a single, long pull and made my way back to the bar.

After my second drink, I retrieved my cell phone from my room and called Dawna. She was a wreck. I wound up trying to calm her down. After all, we were all alive. Even the cat was safe. Then she told me the real problem. Chris had given her an ultimatum. She could marry him, or she could work with me.

Oh, shit. That hurt. A lot. I mean, the man was supposed to be my friend. While I could understand him worrying about her, he was a mercenary, for God's sake. It was more than a little hypocritical of him to give that kind of an ultimatum.

But she loved him, enough to marry him. I didn't want to come between the two of them. It would be hard not having her there, cheerful and efficient, helping me get through the work day. Selfish resentment reared its ugly head, and I shoved it down, hard. Dawna deserved to be happy. Chris made her happy. I'd find someone else to work with.

"I understand."

She sniffled, blew her nose, and said, "He doesn't get to tell me what to do, Celie. I love him, and I don't want to lose him, but he doesn't get to." Her voice was thick with tears but I could tell she meant every word. "If I let him order me around now, what will it be like after we're married? If he expects me to understand that he has to go into war zones for his job, he needs to do the same for me."

Working with me was equivalent to being in a war zone. How sad was that?

"But Dawna . . ." I tried to find the right words. Chris was perfect for her. They loved each other.

She interrupted me. "I think we'll be able to work it out when he calms down. We both just need a little time. So don't call for a day or two, okay?"

I felt terrible. I knew she was right, knew *he* was right. I desperately wished I could do or say something, anything. But there really was nothing to say. This was their business, not mine. Still, she was my friend, and it hurt me to hear her sounding so wounded.

Two drinks later, I was ready to call Bruno. I had practiced everything I wanted to say . . . and got his voice mail. Typical. So I left a "We need to talk" message and settled into the recliner. No more news for me. I drank more alcohol and watched mindless television until I couldn't keep my eyes open.

I woke at 3:00 A.M. with a stiff neck and a pounding head. My vampire metabolism had let me down. Usually it keeps me from getting too drunk and prevents me from having even the tiniest bit of a hangover. Tonight, not so much. Then again, I'd drunk quite a bit more than I usually did.

I levered myself out of the chair and stumbled up to bed. Tomorrow . . . scratch that, today, was scheduled fairly loosely. Just a few gatherings after lunch and another luau tonight.

The gatherings were no big deal. Just a loose group of palace insiders mingling with the queen, Adriana, and Dahlmar. Since it was hot and sunny, nobody commented on my sitting under an umbrella and wearing dark glasses.

Lopaka tried to console me even while she was smiling and laughing at the Rusland ambassador's joke. *I am sorry for your loss, my niece. I know how places can hold memories and emotional attachments. I would be likewise devastated if the palace had been destroyed. I will make your apologies. Please feel free to go to your quarters and have a good cry. It will help.*

I nodded and took her advice. Adriana and Dahlmar watched me leave, their faces reflecting their concern. They nearly followed me, but Lopaka pulled them aside and I could see by their reactions that she was telling them the news. Then I closed the door behind me and disappeared into the cool, quiet palace.

I didn't drink any more alcohol. I had vowed long ago not to allow myself to go down the same path as my mother and crawl into a bottle. But it was a temptation. A strong one.

Instead, I went to the well-guarded beach and sat in the shade, looking at the horizon and listening to the waves and the seagulls.

By the time of the luau, I was sober and clear-eyed. Adriana kept the conversation away from me, allowing me to be visibly present yet stay at the edge of the gathering, satisfying those who noticed such things. I drank smoothies made with seasoned pig drippings instead of beef. Not bad, I suppose, but not up to La Cocina standards. At least the fruit juice was nice. Mango, pineapple, and pomegranate. Tasty.

I knew I had to overcome the loss of such a big part of my life, and fast. Or at least wall it off somehow.

Because tomorrow we were off to Rusland for round two of the wedding.

30

There are a lot of things I don't like about being connected to the royal family, but I'll give them credit, they know how to live. Everything is top of the line—the food, the wine, and the transportation. First thing in the morning, my luggage and I were shuttled by limo to the tarmac of the private royal area of the local airport. Once there, I boarded the queen's signature plane—the siren equivalent of Air Force One.

It was beyond nice. Everything was designed to be elegant, efficient, and comfortable. In addition to full access to the common spaces of the cabin, I'd been given a small room for my private use. All of the furniture was built in so that it wouldn't fly around in the event of severe turbulence and so well-designed that it seemed spacious. It was decorated as both a lounge and an office and the couch could fold out into a bed. The walls were dove gray, the carpet navy blue, and the furnishings combined those base colors with gleaming, black-painted wood and white and chrome metal accents.

I settled in at the built-in desk. The queen had offered me use of the satellite phone and I was happy to take her up on it. My goal was to get the insurance claim process rolling on my office building—not that I had a lot of hope of succeeding. If past experience was anything to judge by, the insurance company would do everything it possibly could to get out of paying the claim. I'd just bet that something in the "Force Majeure" clause would apply. Terrorist attack? Check. Act of War? Check. Sabotage? Check. Maybe I could sue Angelina Bonetti in civil court—if she had any money, that is.

It could just be that I have bad luck. But I didn't think so. Death curse? Check.

Forty-five minutes into the flight, after the fifth full cycle of elevator music on hold, I was finally transferred to a live person.

"We're Reliable, the company you can trust, Meagan speaking."

The teenage daughter of my insurance agent, Meagan was spending her summer working as her father's receptionist, as she had the two summers before. She could charm your socks off when she wanted to. Unfortunately, she almost never did. Today she was bored and angry. I could hear it clearly in the little sneer she put in her voice.

"Meagan, it's Celia Graves."

She perked up at that. "Ah, Ms. Graves. I've been expecting your call. I'm so sorry about your building. Let me put you through to my dad."

Ed Winters handles the insurance on my home, the

office, and their contents. He's in his early forties, already nearly bald, and nearly as wide around as he is tall, but that doesn't keep him from thinking he's a ladies' man. For all I know, he may be. The last time I'd visited in person he'd flirted with me shamelessly—after his daughter had left the room. It had been awkward enough that I was glad to be filing the claim over the phone. At least this way I only had to suffer through yet another repeat of the elevator version of "All You Need Is Love" until he picked up the phone.

"Celia, hi. Ed here."

"Ed, I need to make a claim on the office building and contents."

"Of course you do. Saw it on the news. Pretty scary stuff. Glad you're all right though." Lord, he sounded cheery enough to make my teeth ache. Nobody should be that chipper first thing in the morning.

"We were lucky. No one was hurt."

"That's a blessing," he agreed. Then, muting his tone to regret, he continued. "But Celia, there's something you need to know. There's an exceptions clause in the policy."

Of course there was. I waited, steeling myself for the inevitable.

"The policy isn't valid for acts of war. Since the president declared War on Terrorism . . ." He let the sentence tail off.

I silently counted to ten. A loophole. He was trying to get out of the claim on a loophole. Well, not this time. I smiled and there was steel in my voice. "The bomb wasn't planted by terrorists. Have you looked at the police report?" I didn't bother to keep the satisfaction out of my voice. I'd been a dutiful customer of the insurance industry in general, and his company for years, paying my premiums on time, every time. But let me try to make a claim and they'll find a reason to deny it.

He spluttered a little. "It wasn't? But the news . . ."

"Nope. This was personal. A jealous woman did it. Ever seen that show *Snapped*?"

He harrumphed at that. "Fine. Well, be sure to submit police reports and any proof you may have of that to us in writing with the completed claim. I'll send you the appropriate forms. What's your e-mail address?"

I was still on the phone with Ed until after we'd landed in L.A. I was going over the claim forms with him item by item. We were just wrapping it up when I heard a light tap on the door. Bruno poked his head into the room.

I remembered then that we were picking up several people while we refueled, to take to the ceremony. "Can I come in?"

I waved for him to come in as I spelled out my address for Ed for the second time. That finished, I was able to say good-bye to my agent and hello to my boyfriend.

Bruno looked so good. He was wearing new black jeans with a black dress shirt, the sleeves rolled up slightly to show muscular forearms. His belt was black leather, chased with silver runes that almost seemed to move as they caught the light. His dark hair had been recently cut, so it was a little shorter than I like, and there were traces of gray showing at the temples. He carried a duffel, black leather and suede in a patchwork pattern.

He stood in the middle of the room, looking at me, his posture uncomfortable and uncertain.

"Hi." I put the phone in its cradle and stood up to give him a hug.

He set the duffel on the floor and returned my hug with a fierce one of his own. "When you didn't call I was afraid—," he said, stumbling over the words. "You were already pissed about the body bind, and after what Angelina did . . ." I stopped his stammering with a kiss.

I looked him straight in the eyes, willing him to believe me. "The Angelina thing is not your fault. You didn't lead her on and I don't blame you." I tried to lighten his mood with a bit of a joke. "As to the binding, well, I'll just have to take my revenge for that later."

He winced but didn't argue. Actually, while I'd never have admitted it, there'd been so much going on I'd completely forgotten the whole body binding incident until Dawna had reminded me. That probably meant I'd already forgiven him. Still, she was probably right. It wouldn't hurt to let him try to make it up to me, and it might keep him from doing something stupid like that again. I gestured toward the couch. We sat, his arm wrapped around me. I turned toward him, resting my head on his shoulder, and felt the tenseness of his muscles start to ease.

He kissed the top of my head, then started talking, his words soft and filled with sadness. "I'd hoped that Angie had gotten your hair somewhere other than from my mom, but the more I thought about it, the less likely that seemed. So I called home and spoke to my mom, had her check the siren charm I'd given her. Angelina had tampered with it and several hairs were missing. Mama turned the evidence over to the feds, but I doubt they're going to use it." The bitterness in his voice was cutting.

"Why?"

He closed his eyes for a second. Then, taking a deep breath he steeled himself, opened his eyes, and told me the bad news. "Angelina is going into witness protection. She plans to testify against my brother Mike and cousin Joey."

Oh, hell and damnation. This so sucked. Yeah, Joey and Mike are bad guys. I get that. They were probably long overdue for a stretch in the slammer. But Angelina was getting off? Without so much as a slap on the wrist? That *sucked*. My office was downtown. What if the bomb had gone off during a weekday—how many innocent people would she have killed?

Joey and Mike were mobsters. They were also Bruno's family. I held him close, trying to ease the hurt I knew he was feeling, but was too proud to show.

We stayed like that until the announcement came over the intercom. "This is your captain speaking. Please stow all personal items and fasten your seatbelts. We are preparing for takeoff."

It was a long flight. I didn't mind. Bruno and I rarely got a chance to sit and talk in private, without any life-threatening crises or other interruptions. It was wonderful. I even took a nap, curled up next to Bruno, who entertained himself by reading.

He kissed me awake when the plane finally landed. We

disembarked at 10:38 P.M., later than originally scheduled, having been forced to reroute to avoid bad weather over the Atlantic. The motorcade was waiting and the road to the palace was lined with cheering spectators waving flags or holding candles or pictures of the happy couple. It was almost as if the common people were trying to make up for the actions of the terrorists by giving Adriana an even warmer welcome than they would have otherwise. Assuming Dahlmar hadn't arranged the whole thing for the reporters. I wouldn't put it past him. He's a cagey one and he's ruled long enough to know the power the press has over the minds and hearts of the people.

When we arrived, the palace was brilliantly lit and buzzing with activity. It looked just like a storybook prince's castle. There were elaborate architectural details, servants in elegant livery. Everything had been made absolutely perfect in honor of the ceremonies. For a long moment I just stood staring in wide-eyed wonder. I mean, yes, I do get to see some pretty fancy places guarding the rich and famous. But this . . . this was just . . . wow. It was the kind of memory you store away for a lifetime.

Creede was standing at the top of the castle's front steps. When he saw me with Bruno, I thought I saw a flash of anger cross his face, but it was gone so quickly that I might have imagined it, replaced by a façade of bland professionalism.

I had to admit he looked good, as he had the night of the dinner on Serenity. As always, I was drawn to his honey-colored eyes, though I noticed that his warm, light-brown hair was getting a little long, almost breaking into unmanageable and, in Creede's opinion, unmanly curls. The golden highlights in his hair seemed more prominent than usual and I realized he'd gotten a little tan during his time on the sirens' island. He was wearing a perfectly tailored charcoal gray suit, paired with a starched white shirt and striped tie.

"Bruno. Celia." He didn't smile and his tone was frigid. Still, what had I expected? We'd broken up badly and I was standing in front of him with the man who'd been his chief rival. But it hurt just the same. I couldn't just turn off my feelings for him, much as I might want to. I forced myself to put a good face on it and gave him a pleasant greeting, as did Bruno.

"Princess." Baker appeared at my elbow, saving us all from further awkwardness. I had no idea how she'd gotten here. I hadn't seen her on the plane. But here she was, and her timing was impeccable. She was calling me by title because everyone was watching. I could sense it. "If you're ready, I can escort you and your guest to your rooms."

"Our luggage?"

"Has been taken to your suite."

I nodded and took Bruno's arm while Creede watched with narrowed eyes. "Cool. Lead the way."

She led us through rooms and hallways that were, not surprisingly, palatial: polished marble floors, towering pillars leading up to intricately patterned and gilded ceilings. Original oil paintings by the great masters hung on the walls, recessed alcoves held sculptures by Michelangelo,

Rodin, and others whose work I was too unschooled to recognize. The artworks were displayed beautifully and looked completely unprotected. But looks were quite deceiving. I could feel the spells guarding the individual pieces from yards away, burning so hot against my senses that they stole the breath from my lungs.

"Celia, are you okay?" Baker stopped in her tracks, her eyes a bit wide.

"Fine," I gasped. "Let's just get away from the art gallery, okay?"

"Right." She moved forward again, picking up the pace. The pain didn't abate until the hallway finally opened up into an expansive chamber where a huge, curving staircase climbed three stories. The room was lit by three crystal chandeliers, each bigger than my car. Light sparkled from dangling crystal teardrops the size of my head, shooting rainbows over polished marble floors, walls covered in pale blue-green watered silk, and the thick Oriental rug that covered the center portion of the staircase.

I stopped in my tracks and stared like I'd just fallen off a turnip truck. "Oh, wow."

Baker grinned. "I know. Wait till you see your suite. You're a decorated hero now. The king wanted to make sure you were 'comfortable' *and* to make sure everyone knows how grateful he is for everything you've done for him and for the kingdom."

Oh, my.

We climbed the stairs to the third floor, where Baker led us to my suite. Some suite—if the three floors of my dearly departed office building had been laid out on a single level, they still would have been smaller than this place. The rooms were everything out of my wildest childhood Cinderella fantasies, including, in one bathroom, a walk-in tub that would pass for a swimming pool in some neighborhoods and had all sorts of whirlpool jets. It was so incredibly inviting that I turned to Bruno immediately and said, "Out. Now."

"Excuse me?"

"There's a bubble bath calling my name. Scoot."

"I could join you. The tub's big enough." He grinned, dark eyes sparkling, flashing the dimples I've always found so irresistible. But there was a shadow of unease beneath the seemingly confident expression. I could sense it. I didn't like that unease. I'd had enough of it in my own life.

I made sure he knew I was teasing as I pretended to hesitate. "Well . . . I suppose I *could* use someone to scrub my back."

He laughed, and for the first time all day, the haunted look left his face.

Later, clean and sated, we slid between the sheets of my almost criminally comfortable bed, and slept.

We woke to furious pounding on the door and Griffiths bellowing, "Princess Celia, you and the mage DeLuca are needed in Princess Adriana's suite at once!"

"Hang on a sec!" I shouted back as I climbed out of bed and scrambled around looking for something to wear. As Bruno slid into yesterday's jeans, I frantically opened drawers and doors until I found my underwear, jeans, blouses, and jackets.

We were dressed and out the door in a flash, following Griffiths at run down the short hall between my suite and the royal compartments.

The corridor was crowded with people, most of whom I recognized as Secret Service from one country or another. Thorsen towered above the rest, his long hair loose, expression thunderous. Even dressed only in drawstring pajama bottoms, he was imposing as hell. As we neared Adriana's rooms, I noticed that everyone left just a bit of distance between themselves and Igor, who was standing near the door. It was probably completely unconscious, but telling. It reminded me of how everyone acted around Bruno's Uncle Sal.

"Princess, Mage DeLuca." At Igor's gesture everyone stepped aside, allowing us to enter the royal chambers. Igor led us through a beautiful living area crowded with people. Queen Lopaka, dressed in an elegant peignoir, sat on a couch, her arms around her daughter, who was shaking and looking like she was about to vomit. King Dahlmar paced, his expression thunderous. His brother was at his side, quietly speaking in rapid Ruslandic, presumably in an effort to calm him down.

Igor murmured something to the man guarding the bedroom door, who stepped aside and gave me my first glimpse of what lay on the bed.

It took a minute for my mind to wrap itself around what I was seeing. It was just so unexpected and so incredibly gross. . . . I was looking at the severed arm of a young woman that appeared to have been torn from her body at the shoulder. The end had been cauterized, and even from where I stood, I could smell the overpowering sulfur scent of demon. Carved into the arm, around an elaborate curse mark that matched those of the other Guardians of the Faith we'd found, was a message, in English.

Prepare to die.

31

It was Okalani's arm. Oh, they'd run magic and DNA testing to confirm it, but I knew. There was this little mole near the wrist that I recognized.

Shit.

I managed not to throw up, but only barely. The poor kid. Someone had ripped off her arm and then forced her to teleport her own flesh through shields, all to send us a message. I wasn't the only one sickened by the thought.

Since the arm had been part of Okalani, it should have been possible to use it to track back to her. But I watched helplessly as multiple efforts by some of the best mages in the world failed. Bruno, Creede, and the best mages of Rusland and Serenity all tried, with a similar lack of results.

"Is it because she is dead?" Adriana asked in a whisper. She looked at Thorsen, but it was Creede who answered.

"No. She's not dead. The binding oath mark would have disappeared if she were."

Adriana swallowed hard, trying not to be sick again. I couldn't say I blamed her. My stomach was roiling.

"My question is, how did they manage to teleport this atrocity into the princess's very bedroom? Don't we have shields? Who is responsible for security here?" Prince Arkady was glaring at Igor.

"Okalani had learned how to teleport through shields. She was . . . is, the most powerful telepath I've ever even heard of." My voice was strained. I knew I had to hold it together and not think too hard about what Okalani was going through. If I did, I'd remember my own past, all of it, completely unfiltered. I couldn't let that happen. Not here, and not now. It would make me useless to Adriana, to anyone, probably for days.

I forced myself to think about the words my therapist had said to me again and again. The past was over. I had survived it. The only way it could harm me now was if I let it. I would not do that. I needed to think about the present and the future. I went over to the door, as far away from the arm as I could get and still be in the room. Leaning against the doorjamb, I took deep, steadying breaths. It wasn't easy, and it wasn't pretty, but I brought myself under control.

"If that is true," Arkady growled at me, "why was no one advised? This 'message' could have been a bomb instead, and have killed us all."

"I was advised," Igor said calmly, "as was the king. The palace shields have been modulated. Nothing that can do us physical harm could make it through. We decided that leaving them open for something nonlethal might lure our enemies into giving us something that could be tracked backward. As it has. My people will use this"—he gestured to the severed limb—"to perform magic to find the people behind these attacks. We took a calculated risk, and it has paid off."

"A calculated risk?" Arkady packed a lot of outrage into those three small words. He turned to his brother. There was a long, silent, staring contest between the two.

I was the one who finally broke the tense silence that had enveloped the room. "Someone told me about a vision a paid psychic had." I didn't give names, but I was fairly sure Queen Lopaka, at least, suspected who I was referring to. "In the vision I had been captured and Okalani was being tortured by a demon. The men holding her were going to feed me to the demon and livestream the whole thing over the Internet."

There were lots of loud reactions to that.

"With that in mind"—my voice was a little strangled, and probably half an octave higher in pitch than usual, but I plowed on, talking over the top of everyone else—"does anybody have any technology or magic that could track me through demonic magics?" I looked from Igor to Thorsen, then at Bruno and Creede. "Just in case they manage to capture me?"

"I can probably come up with something." Creede met my gaze, his eyes dark holding more emotions than I could count. "How much time do we have?"

"I don't know."

Bruno was speechless; he looked shocked and sick. He came up to me and pulled me into his arms in a silent embrace that was comforting for both of us.

"Get me a mirror or my bowl and I can find out." Adriana pulled away from her mother. Her demeanor had changed totally—she looked strong, confident in her abilities.

I was glad somebody felt that way. I didn't feel confident at all. I was pretty much scared shitless. I needed to know more, but I sure didn't want to. "Bruno, why don't we give Adriana her wedding gift now?"

A lot of quizzical looks greeted that comment, so I explained. "Our gift is a hand mirror, specially spelled for clairvoyant use by Princess Adriana."

"I'll get it," Bruno answered. He gave me a quick squeeze, then let me go and raced back to our rooms. The embrace, I knew, was a gesture meant to encourage me. It would've worked better if I hadn't seen the raw fear in his eyes.

Adriana and Dahlmar ordered the room cleared until only the three of us remained. Bruno came back and handed Adriana our gift, which was carefully wrapped in shiny paper in the colors of the royal houses. He would have stayed, but John called his name from the door and he left, probably to help work on Creede's ideas for tracking me.

We sat on the couch, Dahlmar and I waiting impatiently as Adriana unwrapped the package and brought out the mirror with a soft gasp of pleasure.

"Oh, Celia . . . it's *perfect*. The handle nearly melts into my hand with warmth." She beamed at me for a moment. "Thank you. And thank Mage DeLuca. He must have worked so hard on this."

Collecting herself, she said soberly, "If anything will help me cut through their shielding, this should."

Taking a deep breath, she started muttering the ritual phrases that would clear her mind and activate her talent.

I saw images start to flicker in the glass, only to be covered by thick, black smoke. Adriana conjured a wind, but the glass refused to clear. I watched her struggle, bringing all her formidable will to bear. The fingers gripping the mirror were white knuckled, her face flushed and her body shook from the effort.

Useless effort.

I had to put an end to it. "Stop. Don't hurt yourself."

She looked up and I was shocked to see tears pouring down her cheeks. A stray drop fell onto the reflective glass. The clouds cleared. The scene revealed wasn't the one she'd been seeking. Instead, the mirror revealed Adriana herself, kneeling beside Dahlmar, both in their wedding attire. They faced a huge, carved marble cross the exact shape of the Eldritch Cross Adriana was wearing at her neck, except for a single additional stone protrusion at the bottom. In the mirror, Adriana pressed her hand against the giant cross, and with the grinding of stone against stone, a secret door appeared in the wall directly in front of them.

In the room, Adriana gave a gasp of pain. With a deliberate jerk she broke off the vision. I didn't understand why until I caught a glimpse of her hands. The skin that had gripped the mirror was burned and blistered, a result of a curse that had been used to prevent her from seeing what she had wanted to see.

32

It would have been a busy morning without the arrival of Okalani's arm. As it was, it was insane. We vacated Adriana's apartments, leaving the investigators to do their thing.

Bruno and Creede had hustled off somewhere with Dahlmar's best mages to work on the tracking device that could be implanted in my body in case the worst came to pass. My hand was throbbing, and I glanced down at the curse mark on my palm to see it red and angry. Thanks to the late, unlamented Queen Stefania and her death curse, I'd had a lot of experience with worst-case scenarios.

My thoughts were dark, my mood darker. I had to do something to distract myself, so I went with Thorsen and Igor to look in on the people doing one last check of the various security measures. I had a vested interest in them. Still, if there were any weaknesses, I wasn't finding them. Then again, neither was anybody else.

Noon came. We broke for lunch. I asked a servant to have food brought to my rooms and went there to eat and clean up. I'd gone to Adriana's rooms in such a rush that I hadn't even had a chance to brush my teeth, so I felt pretty damned scruffy.

There was a final check of the wedding regalia scheduled in one of the downstairs conference rooms at 2:00. So I ate, took a shower, and generally made myself presentable. By the time I was done, it was 1:30. I stepped out of the bedroom and into the living area to find Bruno, Creede, and an elderly man in a plain brown suit waiting for me, their expressions serious. They rose when I entered the room.

"Well?" I looked from one to the other.

"We did it." Creede and Bruno both smiled. They looked tired but pleased. And well they should be. Breaking new magical territory on short notice and under pressure was something to be proud of.

"This"—Bruno gestured to the older man, who bowed—"is Dr. Ilia Bogdonavich. He's going to implant the device."

I started to roll up the sleeve of my blouse, but Creede shook his head. "Under the circumstances—" I had a sickening flash of memory of Okalani's arm laying on Adriana's bed.

"Right. Where do you suggest, Doctor?"

"The muscles of the abdomen or the gluteus maximus would be best."

Stomach or ass. Hmnnn, not much of a choice. I reached for my belt. "Leave the room, boys."

"Aw," Bruno teased, "you're no fun." Creede just smiled and led him out into the hall, giving the doctor and me some privacy.

"This is going to pinch," he said. Why do all doctors say that? And why are they always lying?

It didn't pinch, it *hurt*. I had to remind myself that I'd asked for this. People had gone to a lot of trouble to arrange it for me, and it was for my own good. But I was still pretty grumpy as I followed Baker through the maze of corridors to the conference room for the fitting. It's surprising how much you use your tail muscles to walk. I should have thought of that.

We arrived at more or less the same time as Adriana and her guards. My cousin looked much better than she had this morning. Her "wake-up call" had been shocking and sickening, but she's a tough cookie. It had frightened her, no doubt about it. But she was channeling that fear into anger and determination. I admired her for it.

She'd dressed in simple jeans and a white cotton tee. I was wearing my usual black jeans with a blouse and a black suit jacket. Technically I was the better dressed, but she somehow managed to look elegant, chic, and oh so much more attractive. It was a trick she and Dawna both had mastered and I just hadn't. I kept trying to figure out how they did it. Dawna said it was the fit—but Isaac had tailored this jacket. It fit perfectly. Whatever it was, I couldn't do it.

"Are you okay?" Adriana asked.

"As much I can be," I assured her. "You?"

"The same. Is it wrong to say I just want this over with?"

"No. I think that's pretty typical of most brides at this stage of the game, and they don't have to deal with terrorists. But hey, remember, this time tomorrow, you'll be Mrs. Dahlmar, Queen of Rusland, and off on your honeymoon."

She beamed at the thought, reaffirming my belief that this marriage wasn't about politics; it was true love on both sides.

Baker opened the door, revealing a small room filled to bursting with clothing and people. One rack held the bridesmaids' dresses; another, the exquisite cream and pearl confection that was Adriana's wedding dress. Holding court in the center of the room, it drew the eye, and I found myself gaping at it as my cousin and I crossed the threshold. Only as the door swung closed and I felt the rush of magic did I realize that something was terribly wrong.

No one was moving. Isaac, on his knees on the floor, was frozen rigid, one hand reaching up to smooth the fabric of Adriana's gown. Gilda was a statue, caught in midstep, her mouth open as if to speak.

Instinct took over. I shoved Adriana behind me and shouted for Baker. We needed out of here, now! Reaching behind me, I grabbed for the doorknob. The instant my skin touched the cold metal I felt the familiar lurch and the room and everything in it disappeared.

33

I landed in the center of a silver casting circle next to a bloody, lump of battered flesh that I could barely identify as female. She had been impaled with a lance of bone, pinned to the concrete floor like a butterfly pinned to a card.

Carved over every inch of the lance's surface were words written in burning red script. I recognized some of the names and phrases from my classes back in college. My gorge rose as I realized this was the spear of the chief demon in charge of Satan's legions. The writing seemed to flow and writhe before my eyes, making me dizzy and nauseous.

The woman made a sound, too weak to be a gasp or even a moan. I dropped to my knees, crawling across the floor to examine her. I was desperately careful to avoid the spear. I didn't know what touching it might do to me and I so didn't want to find out.

It was only when I reached her side that I realized her right arm was missing, the shoulder socket a burned, cauterized mess. I began to weep as recognition hit.

"Oh, dear God, no." The moment I uttered what amounted to a prayer, a gong sounded, loud enough that my ears bled. Reality shuddered and wavered as the substance of our dimension began to part. The spear began radiating soaring heat. I smelled burning flesh, like meat cooking on the grill, and Okalani's body arched. Her mouth opened, but only a raw whisper of sound came out.

My stomach heaved and I lost everything I'd ever even thought about eating, turning away so I wouldn't spew on Okalani. Despite the surge of power, the demon didn't arrive. He couldn't until a human summoner called him.

When I recovered, I checked on Okalani. Under most circumstances, she would be dead—no human or siren body was capable of withstanding the damage that had been inflicted on her. But the demon's spear pinned her soul to her body just as tightly as it held her body to the ground. She would live until the demon removed the weapon and allowed her to die. They had wanted her alive to use her talent to bring Adriana and me here. They wanted her suffering, both alive and dead at the same time. Pain, suffering, and despair are what they feed on. If her soul was tainted enough, she'd be theirs in Hell. If not, she'd be free.

I stood, steeling myself to touch that foul thing and pull it from her. Human strength wouldn't be enough to remove it. Vampire and siren strength might.

My movement didn't go unnoticed. I had been so focused on Okalani I hadn't realized anyone else was in the room, but now I spun around as Jan Mortensen stepped close to the circle, close enough to get a good look at me, but careful not to cross the line.

"*You!*" he spat. "Where is your cousin? Olga promised she'd deliver you both. Stupid, incompetent bitch."

So Olga was the traitor. I wasn't surprised. Here's hoping I'd live to accuse her, though it wasn't looking likely.

"Still"—Jan smiled, and it was pure evil that lit his face with delight—"of the two of you, you're the one I wanted most, after what you did to my brother. I will enjoy every minute of what happens to you even more than I've enjoyed punishing your little friend."

He turned and walked out of the room through an open door. I could hear him giving orders to people I couldn't see. "The sacrifice has arrived. Make sure the cameras and the computer are ready. We want to make sure this goes out live."

I didn't just hear heavy footfalls then, I felt them. The ground shuddered beneath my knees with each invisible step. The smell of sulfur filled the air, thick enough to choke on, searing my lungs each time I drew breath.

I've faced greater demons before. But I'd always been outside the safety of a protection ring. Now I was *inside*. I tried to think, tried to plan, but my mind refused.

I could sense something huge and hideous waiting, poised to pounce. All that stood between it and me was a tissue-paper-thin film of reality. He could not cross that last barrier without human invitation. Even having come so far, and having been here so often, he could not cross. Even with his greatest tool on this side of the veil, the demon could not appear until someone uttered the words to bring him forth.

Jan stepped back into the room, wearing a black robe of thick velvet. He pulled up a hood, obscuring his face, then drew a hooked silver knife from a pocket hidden in the thick folds of ebony cloth. He rolled back his left sleeve, exposing a pale length of heavily scarred flesh. With a triumphant cry, he drew a long, deep cut down the length of his forearm. Then he shook the blade, sending splatters of blood onto the silver casting ring as he began chanting the summoning.

I fought to control my terror, tried to think clearly enough to do something, anything to buy the time it would take for a rescue.

The casting had to have blood. But it also needed the words. If I could stop Jan from speaking, I could stop the demon.

Reaching beneath my jacket, I drew my gun. Dropping to one knee, I steadied myself, then fired twice, aiming at the center mass of his body. But the bullets were caught in the spell barrier, frozen in midair as if suspended in clear gelatin. He was almost finished. Just a few more seconds . . . I had an idea, a desperate, crazy idea. I grabbed one of my One Shot squirt guns filled with holy water. I raised the tiny water pistol with my left hand and my Colt with my right. I squeezed the trigger with my left index finger. I actually saw the water hit, burning away the shield for a few seconds, barely long enough for me to aim the Colt and fire.

Jan's body jerked backward as the bullet hit him square in the chest; blood and cloth sprayed the wall behind him, more blood bubbled from his lips. He dropped to his knees and I knew I'd killed him. But it didn't matter, because with his last whisper of breath, he finished the summoning. The way was clear.

I closed my eyes. If I looked, if I saw him, I would panic and wouldn't be able to think. I needed to think. Odin Allfather had said I could defeat this. I struggled, trying to remember his words even as hideous, obscene laughter made my skin try to crawl off my body while at the same time my loins tightened with desire.

The message: what was it? The words came to me then. *Have faith. The right weapon can overcome what will come against you.*

I had holy water, but only another One Shot, certainly not enough to harm something like this.

The demon laughed again and began moving toward me. I found myself weeping, praying for the courage and strength; praying to the god my grandmother had taught me of, who I'd wanted to believe in and never could. But as I knelt on the hot concrete, the words of the first prayer she ever taught me came to my mind, remembered from back when I was small enough to be afraid of the dark, before my sister had even been born.

Angel of God, my guardian dear.

The demon let out a basso bellow that shattered my eardrums, deafening me more thoroughly than a gunshot at close range.

To whom God's love commits me here.

I opened my eyes to see a huge, black dragon, like a living shadow, towering at least forty feet above me, razor-sharp claws raised to strike. When I didn't stop praying, he turned toward Okalani.

I screamed, "No," and threw myself down on top of her, protecting her body with mine. I wrapped myself around the spear that bound her to this world. I closed my eyes and waited for the blow that would end my life.

Fire flared around me, I could smell it, feel it. But it did not burn. The dragon shrieked in impotent rage. I couldn't hear it, but I could feel it, an actual physical pressure beating against me. I opened my eyes wondering what could possibly be stopping him and saw light, bright searing light, illuminating everything, making the demonic monster hold back. Words echoed in my mind, and though they were in a language I did not know, I knew full well what they were saying.

They are mine. The demon's voice, filled with honey and putrefaction.

The other voice held power and love stronger than anything I'd ever felt. *Were that so, I could not be here, and well we both know it. Begone.*

A dark laugh bubbling with evil pleasure filled my ears and made me cringe. I wanted to look again but that was the way to madness. True evil would corrupt my eyes, blind me. *One is a traitor, the other a tainted thing. They are mine!*

The sound of steel on steel filled the air, like a blade being unsheathed. *No. The betrayer has repented and is forgiven.*

And while the other has yet to choose her final path, it is she who called me forth. Again I say, begone.

I felt the power surging and risked a peek. The dragon shimmered, changing shape, becoming something more humanlike, but huge, and somehow both hideous and soul-searingly beautiful. He reached forward and grabbed the spear that I was wrapped around. I relaxed fractionally just in time as he pulled it free with no visible effort. Blood and flesh sprayed across me. But still I protected Okalani's ravaged body.

A flurry of sound and motion outside the circle drew my attention. Through a wall of flames I saw Bruno, Creede, Igor, and a priest in full regalia pouring through the doorway into the room.

I couldn't hear the priest speak, but I saw his lips move. He was performing the ritual banishment. He looked so terrified—they all did—and I realized with a shock that they thought I was alone and unprotected.

As I should have been.

My faith, while real, is shaky at best. And the demon had been right about my being tainted. It wasn't just that I was part vampire; I'd been marked by a demon once before.

The voice in my mind was patient, kind, and loud. *No one is perfect. But you do have faith. You hold truth dear. You hold loyalty sacred. And some days, that is enough.*

The demon snarled and paced around the parts of the circle he could reach, eyes blazing with hate every time he reached the invisible boundary line created by the light. I began to think I might survive.

As I watched, the priest dipped the sprinkler into the bucket of holy water and flung a spray of liquid into the air above the circle. The drops passed through the barrier as if it weren't there. The demon howled his defiance even while he dodged frantically, trying to avoid being hit. Drops splattered to the ground. When the water hit the being of white fire, the flames soared, turning it whole and perfect. Nearly too perfect to look at.

Again and again the priest repeated his actions, until the floor of the casting circle was covered in water and there was nowhere left for the minion of hell to hide.

As the priest raised the sprinkler one last time, the fallen angel called out. Jan's corpse levitated up from the floor and flew into his clawed hand.

He turned to me with a chilling smile. *I will see you in your dreams, dear one. We are linked, you and I. For all eternity.*

Then he was gone.

34

WOULD like a private word with the princess." Igor stood just inside the door to my private hospital room. It was 4:00 A.M. but he looked as fresh as if it was the beginning of his day. He'd showered and changed clothes in the hours since I'd last seen him. Looking at him now, you'd have no clue that he'd been up all night dealing with the fallout of everything that had happened in the last twenty-four hours. His black suit was immaculate, the crease in his pants sharp enough to shave with. The white dress shirt he wore almost gleamed under the fluorescent lights.

Bruno, on the other hand, was a wreck. Slumped in the chair at my bedside, he wore the same clothes he'd thrown on in a hurry yesterday morning; his hair was rumpled and he had more than a shadow of a beard. Still, he was alert and wary as he sat up straighter in his seat. The look he gave me said as clearly as words that he didn't think I was up to this.

He might have been right.

I am a fairly tough cookie, but everybody has a limit,

and I was coming perilously close to mine. It wasn't the violence, or even the demon—although I wondered if I'd ever relax enough to sleep soundly again. No, it was the memories. The things I'd seen in Mexico had cracked the protective magical shield that had blunted my memories of Ivy's death and my torture. Seeing what had happened to Okalani had shattered that barrier entirely.

I remembered every cigarette burn, every cut, the threats and the terror. But most of all, I remembered my sheer helplessness as I watched my sister die a hideously gruesome death because she couldn't control the ghouls her talent had raised. Each memory was as vivid, as raw, as the day it had happened.

I looked at Igor, who was standing silent and patient, then took a deep breath and shoved the memories into a box in my mind. I slammed down the lid and hoped it would hold. "I'll be fine," I said to Bruno. "Let us talk."

Bruno didn't argue, he just stood. He bent down to give me a tender kiss. Still leaning close, he whispered, "Whatever he wants, say no. You've done enough—more than enough."

I didn't answer. It wasn't Bruno's decision to make. It was mine. But I had to admit that I was leaning toward having the doctors give me enough sedatives to knock out an elephant, in hopes that I would be too deeply unconscious to dream.

Bruno straightened and shook his head. Walking past Igor, he gave the older man a very unfriendly look, but didn't say a word. Only after the door was fully closed and we were alone did Igor come over to stand beside the bed.

"You are stronger than he knows," Igor observed.

And more fragile than you think, I thought. What I said was, "What do you need?"

He looked down at me, his expression so utterly bland that it was at odds with his words. "We interrogated Princess Olga thoroughly." I winced. He didn't say *torture,* but I couldn't help thinking it. "While the man you knew as Jan Mortensen was one of their top men, he was not the head of the organization. That man is still in place. So long as he lives, the movement will continue."

I didn't speak, just waited. There was more. I could tell.

"They have one final plan in place for during the wedding tomorrow." He sighed, sounding weary. Either the strain of the last few days was showing, or he was a superlative actor. I couldn't tell. But the regret in his voice when he spoke next sounded sincere. "Unfortunately, the oath she had taken killed her before she could give us any details. But we have a plan."

Of course they did, and judging by his presence here, it involved me. "Tell me."

"We do not believe that the enemy knows that we discovered Princess Olga was the traitor. Her arrest was handled discreetly, as was her questioning. We have a spawn on staff who is capable of being Princess Olga for the duration of the wedding. He is one of our best agents. Having him in place in the wedding party will assure the safety of the king and offer us the opportunity to surprise the enemy, and possibly lead him into an indiscretion that will reveal the identity of their leader."

It was possible. I wouldn't have thought it was likely, but I wasn't a spy. Igor was, and was good enough at his job to have risen to the top of the Ruslandic intelligence agency during a time of serious political turmoil. Too, the fact that it was the best chance didn't mean it was a good one. I gave Igor a searching look and asked the million-dollar question. "Who do you think it is?"

"We don't know," he admitted. "But it has to be someone highly placed and close enough to the royal family for Olga to have been able to contact him or her freely and without notice. We have had her under close surveillance for the past several weeks."

It made sense. And while Igor hadn't said that Olga's father, Prince Arkady, was a prime suspect, he had to be. Poor Dahlmar. He had already had to deal with the betrayal of his sons and his niece. Now his brother was a suspect, too. "So, what do you want from me?"

"Just do what you have been. Be the maid of honor. Guard the princess until the wedding is over."

"That's it?"

"We will handle the rest."

He sounded awfully confident, but was he really? If he was that confident, why even tell me the plan? I could have just guarded her without needing to know all of this. I was emotionally battered and utterly weary. I wanted to crawl in a hole and not come out for at least a month, and they knew it. So why tell me?

Because Adriana needed me. If I quit now, and something happened to her, I would never forgive myself.

Igor watched while I worked it out in my head. "So telling me the plan will keep me in the wedding party, huh? Sadly, you're right. But hey, how bad can it be?" I asked with a forced smile, even though I knew how stupid a question it was.

Igor smiled with me. His baring of teeth was as cynical as mine. What a pair we were.

Igor pulled strings so that I was released from the hospital immediately and with minimal fuss. Bruno didn't say a word in argument, just glowered menacingly at all and sundry. I found this equally annoying and endearing. I was glad that he loved me and was worried about me. At the same time, I was irritated that he was trying to protect me, for the same reason I'd objected to protection in the first place. I knew that didn't make sense, but emotions frequently don't.

The doctor met alone with me one last time before letting me go.

Dr. Shablinski was an older woman, probably in her sixties. She wore her hair in a short, spiky style that suited her harsh features. She was striking but not pretty. And right now, she was annoyed and wasn't bothering to hide it. I could hear it all too clearly in her heavily accented mental voice when she spoke to me mind-to-mind.

I am not pleased that you are leaving the hospital. It is too soon. Your ears will not be fully healed, and there is posttraumatic stress that needs to be dealt with. You must rest in order to heal, and I am certain you will not if you leave. So while I cannot stop you, you are doing this against medical advice.

I shrugged. What was there to say? *I understand and, actually, I agree with you. Once the wedding is over, I intend to take a nice, long vacation.*

A . . . vacation. Her voice sounded dry in my head. *How do you plan to do that if you can't sleep?*

Ouch. She was evidently as observant as she was efficient. *I don't know. I keep remembering . . .* I let the sentence drag off unfinished, not wanting to repeat the demon's parting words to me.

She sighed. *I am going to order a sedative for you—but only enough pills for one week. It will allow you dreamless slumber, but it is not a permanent solution. You will need to work something out with your cleric, and I would strongly suggest therapy. If you don't have a therapist—*

I have one back home on the mainland.

She nodded and started writing on a pad. *Good. If you give me her number and sign a release, I can update her as to what has happened. You are going to need to address tonight's events.*

No kidding. Tonight's events. Last week's. Last month's. Last year's. Sheesh. I could foresee paying for Gwen's future mansion with the therapy bills. But she was the best. And it would absolutely be worth the price if she could help me pull myself back together. Because, while I had been trying to put up a good front in front of Bruno and Igor, I was faking it big-time.

At the same time, I was worried. Gwen had once told me that if anything happened to my protections, she wouldn't be able to reestablish them—doing so might destroy all my memories.

I signed the appropriate paperwork, took the proffered prescription, and we were on our way.

Creede was waiting at the car. Like Bruno, he didn't say a word. But it wasn't the first time he'd seen me throw myself into danger right after a demon encounter. He just shook his head and got into the front passenger seat while Bruno got in next to me in the back.

Even early as it was, there was an electric excitement in the air. It was as if the whole country was a small child and it was finally, *finally* Christmas morning. Today was the wedding day.

The limo drove through the streets leading to the castle in the thin, watery light of dawn. I watched through the window as the vendors bustled and tourists stumbled sleepily up to the police barriers, clutching steaming mugs or Styrofoam cups as they shivered slightly in the early-morning chill. Later in the day it was supposed to be sunny and in the seventies, but at the moment it was quite cool.

Had it really only been days since I'd made a similar pre-wedding drive through the streets of Serenity? It felt like years. Bad, dark years filled with pain.

Enough with the depressing thoughts, I admonished myself. *It's Adriana's wedding day.* I wished I could be as excited about it as the bystanders I saw outside the car windows. I just wasn't. I tried giving myself a little internal pep talk, but the results were less than stellar.

Just get through the day. You can do this.

We reached the compound at 6:30. I sped to my rooms to relieve myself, have a quick shower, and retrieve my weapons and jewelry before heading down to the dressing room. At my request, the servants agreed to bring my breakfast there.

We were getting dressed in a different small room, not the one used for the fittings the previous day. I was glad. I don't exactly believe in bad luck, but I wouldn't have wanted to start this day in that room.

As before, the dresses were hung on racks, with the bridesmaids' dresses shoved down to one end and Adriana's wedding gown taking the rest of the space. I'd gotten only a peek at it before I was teleported away; now I took a closer look.

It was gorgeous, a simple, elegant design in ivory silk with embroidery and pearl beads and a long train trimmed in lace. I knew she would look absolutely stunning in it.

On the east wall were the hair and makeup areas. Neither were manned at the moment, but all the equipment was laid out at the ready. On another wall, a television played. The British announcers were filling the time before the actual event translating local background stories about everything from the designers of Adriana's dress and veil to Rusland's wedding traditions. A clock in one bottom corner of the screen showed a countdown until the wedding.

When she saw me at the door, Adriana ran to greet me with a glad cry and a huge hug. She was wearing a full-length housecoat, her hair loose and uncombed. Even so, she was gorgeous. She was radiant with joy and quivering with nerves. Her embrace was gentle and warm, and I could feel her delight as she released me.

Natasha hugged me next. She was a little shy and awkward about it, but that just made it feel more sincere.

"You are all right?" Natasha asked as I followed her over to the corner to examine my dress.

"My ears still hurt," I admitted. I was having some problems with my balance as well. It wasn't anything too serious, a touch of vertigo. Dr. Shablinski had said both problems would probably fade in a few days. The ear damage had been extensive enough that a regular human would have been permanently deaf. Of course, I didn't go into that with Natasha. "Other than that, I'm okay."

"You were fortunate." She shuddered visibly. "A *demon*. You are very fortunate."

"You got that right."

"*Celia!*" I whirled at the sound of Gilda's joyous shout. "You're all right? I wanted so badly to warn you, but I could not move or speak. What a hideous, terrible spell." Gilda burst into the room like a little tornado, with Isaac following in her wake. The two of them swept me into yet another hug. Apparently this was the day for it. While I'm not normally all that huggy, today it felt good, reassuring.

Gilda drew me away from the others, leading me behind the screens that had been set up to give us a private dressing area, and whispered, "Are you truly all right? You look . . . strained."

"It was rough, but I'll be okay."

She pursed her lips, giving me a narrow-eyed look of pure skepticism. "If you say so."

"I do."

As she was helping me out of my shirt, she whispered near my ear, "We haven't told your grandmother about what happened, darling. It wouldn't help her heal. But she's doing much better. She plans to watch you on television, so we'll make you look extra special." I thanked her for visiting my gran and wondered what the three of them—I assumed Isaac had gone, too; the Levys were rarely parted—had talked about.

It took a few minutes to slip out of my clothes. I was sort of sore. Sue me. Then I donned my best frilly underthings and armed myself. Next came the dress and jacket. I smoothed my hands along the fabric of the dress as I stepped out from behind the screen to give Isaac and Gilda a chance to examine their work.

The two of them circled me like sharks, examining me from every angle for long moments before finally expressing their satisfaction. I was happy with the result. The dress and jacket fit like a dream, and, thanks to Isaac's magic, I could be well armed without looking like it. I had all my usual gear and then some—Isaac had tucked things I wasn't sure even how to use into hidden pockets, murmuring, "If all else fails, throw them."

Released, I sat on the edge of a chair and pulled on my

thigh-high hose. Gone were the days when my legs would
tan enough for me not to need stockings. These were black
silk and as sheer as cobwebs. They perfectly matched my
brand-new black lace bra and panties, so I felt very sexy
pulling them on. I didn't put on the shoes yet. The heels
were high and because of the ear injury I figured I wouldn't
be entirely steady on them. I'd have switched shoes, but
there was no time to rehem the dress. So I just said a quick
prayer that I wouldn't fall on my ass and make a fool of
myself in front of the entire world.

Now that I was dressed, it was time to accessorize. I
opened the jewel case sitting on the table beside me. Diamonds and amethysts sparkled in the bright overhead lights.
I felt tears welling in my eyes as I looked at them. Isaac and
Gilda were wonderful, wonderful friends. I loved them. But
at this moment, I wished very much that I had family here.
I missed my gran so much; missed Ivy's ghost. I wanted to
hear Gran say I looked pretty, have Ivy draw a heart in ice
crystals on the mirror like she used to. I slipped on the earrings, controlling my expression, trying hard not to show
anyone what I was feeling.

As if in response to my wish the temperature in the
room dropped like a stone. The lights flickered overhead as
Gilda fastened the necklace around my neck.

"Ivy?" I whispered. The lights flashed once in response.
Our old code had been once for yes, twice for no. "I'm so
glad you're here." I felt myself smiling. "I've missed you."

As I watched, ice crystals formed on the full-length mirror in front of me, taking the shape of a heart.

Is that my cousin Ivy? Adriana came over to stand beside me, her voice perfectly clear inside my mind.

Yep. I think she knew I missed my family today.

Adriana opened her arms and let the cool air flow around her. *Welcome, beloved cousin. I am most glad to have you at my wedding.*

The lights flickered on and off joyfully. Few people ever spoke to Ivy directly except me. I could tell she was pleased by the way the air danced cool and then warm. *But Celia, you should know that we are your family, too; my mother and I, and now Dahlmar as well. In fact, if you will come with me for a moment, I have a special gift for you.*

Natasha was being quiet as a mouse, standing in the background, looking . . . sad. It was an odd reaction, out of place. Then again, she'd had a day like this not too long ago and had lost her husband shortly after. Maybe this brought back painful memories.

"Natasha, are you all right?" I asked.

She smiled at me in response. "I'm fine. Just remembering."

Adriana spoke out loud for Natasha's sake. "Ladies, before things get started, I'd like to give you each a thank-you gift."

Adriana picked up a jeweler's box from the top of her dressing table and passed it to Natasha. Inside was a necklace with an amethyst the size of my thumb, set in gold with accents of diamond. "I hope you like it."

Natasha beamed and babbled something in Ruslandic that I assumed was thanks. Adriana answered her slowly, also in Ruslandic, then turned to me.

"My gift to you," she said aloud as well as in my mind as she slid a pearl ring off of her finger and offered it to me. *It's not as valuable as the many gifts you've given to me, but it's been in our family for a very long time. I hope you'll wear it as a token of the affection I have come to feel for you.*

I slid the ring onto the middle finger of my left hand. It fit perfectly. I felt a gentle thrum of magic as it slid into place and for an instant I could've sworn I heard the rush of waves tumbling into the sand. What in the world? I turned to Adriana, my eyes wide with surprise and pleasure. "Thank you."

"No, thank you." *I am most grateful for the help you've given me and mine. I'm sorry for how I treated you when we first met. I was jealous.*

I felt cool air on my tongue as my jaw dropped. *Of me? Why? You had no reason to be.*

But I thought I did. You look so much like the woman in my vision, the one who will follow my mother on the throne. It hurt. So, take this with my apology. The ring is a family heirloom. Its sole purpose is to strengthen and focus the telepathic abilities of the wearer. My mother gave it to me to encourage my siren abilities.

Wow. I knew Adriana's siren abilities weren't strong because her talent as a clairvoyant kind of cancelled them out. If she gave me this ring, would she have any siren powers at all? *Are you sure you want to part with it? Won't you need it?*

No. I will be ruling Rusland. It is a land-locked country. Too, my abilities tell me that you will need it more. Not today, but someday. This is best.

It was such an unexpected gesture that I found myself sniffling.

Don't you dare cry. If you do, I'll start, and I don't want red eyes and a chapped nose at my wedding.

I'm not crying. Well, not much. I gave her a bright smile and then spoke out loud. "It's beautiful. I don't know how to thank you."

"Celia, you've saved my life *how* many times now? I think that's more than thanks enough. I just wish there was more I could do." She reached forward and held both of my hands in hers, squeezing lightly but with warmth.

We were interrupted by a light tap on the door.

Adriana glanced around, making sure everybody was decent, withdrew her hands, then called, "Come in." The door opened, revealing Queen Lopaka, a vision of loveliness in a coral-colored skirt suit with pearl buttons, her blond hair swept into a perfect chignon. She stepped into the room and closed the door behind her. Crossing the room to the privacy screen, she disappeared. In less than a minute the queen's suit was hanging over the top of the screen. I felt magic in the air, and a moment later, a deep male voice asked, "Could someone please pass me Princess Olga's dress?"

I plucked it from the clothes rack and brought it over, inadvertently catching a glimpse of a hairy man with bushy eyebrows wearing a pair of Wile E. Coyote boxers. I managed to hide my smirk. I hoped.

"Hi. I'm Celia Graves," I said as I passed him the hanger.

"Lars Balakan. It is an honor to serve my king and his

queen." Despite his appearance, Lars bowed with immense dignity.

I turned, letting him do his thing in private.

As he was changing, there was another knock. This time it was the hairdresser and makeup artist, who hurried to their stations. I recognized them both from the ceremony on Serenity.

"Princess Celia," Brenna called. "I'll start with you."

As I walked across the room toward her, I felt the surge of magic. Moments later, Lars emerged from behind the screen as Olga.

"You there. I'll start with makeup," Lars called in Olga's exact voice as he swished his way over to us, wiggling his hips. Wow. He even had her snarkiness down pat.

That was just . . . disturbing.

Are either of you as bothered by that as I am? I thought to Adriana and Natasha, but apparently Ivy overheard, too, since overhead, the lights blinked once. Hmm. I hadn't known she could hear thoughts. Across the room, Natasha shuddered and gave me a small nod.

Adriana didn't respond. She was too busy getting into her gown and veil.

I waited until Lars was finished before taking my place at the makeup station. The stylist began with a layer of sunblock as I sat utterly still, watching the clock on the television counting relentlessly down to the moment when we would leave. With each tick, I felt the tension in the room ratchet up another notch. Each of us tried to pretend we weren't nervous and failed miserably.

Once again I went over the arrangements in my mind. The men had gone ahead and would be meeting us at the church. Gunnar would escort Adriana up the stairs to Dahlmar and the priests. Yes, priests, plural. The king's confessor had been given a small part to play in the ceremony as a courtesy, while Adriana's father, Feliks, would be the primary officiant. As best man, Igor would escort me. Prince Arkady was next with "Olga," and Sergei, a distant cousin who was so reserved I'd barely noticed him (and had yet to hear speak), would follow with Natasha.

We'd pose at the top of the steps, then go into the church's vestibule for the betrothal ceremony that would take place before we entered the nave, where the dignitaries of the world awaited.

Two minutes to go. Adriana slipped the fine, lace-trimmed veil onto her head, pinning it in place. In the vestibule, a crown would be placed over the veil and an elaborate ritual would take place, including both Dahlmar and Adriana being given communion. I put on my heels and took a couple of experimental steps, telling myself that I would be fine. My balance still wasn't good, but I could do heels. I hoped.

The door opened. It was time. Surrounded by a phalanx of Secret Service, we made our way outside, to the waiting pair of horse-drawn carriages. Adriana rode alone in the first carriage. Natasha, Lars, and I rode in the second.

The procession only lasted a couple of miles, but it seemed endless. The crowd roared as the two coaches drove past. I waved, the silly, little royal wave it seemed I had figured out how to do. I still felt ridiculous. But at the same time it was a huge rush, seeing the crowds waving and cheering, hearing them scream our names. I could see how it could get addictive.

Ahead, Adriana's carriage pulled to a stop at the foot of the long staircase that led up to the cathedral. As planned, our male escorts waited for us in a row near the stairs. Dahlmar cut quite a figure at the top, in his traditional Ruslandic uniform, which was black with silver buttons and a silver sash. Not that it was easy to see the fabric of the sash, because it was so heavily medaled and beribboned. It must have weighed a ton. He wore the charm that offered him immunity from siren magic out in plain sight for everyone—and the cameras—to see. But his real, unenchanted joy in his bride was obvious the minute he caught sight of her.

It was as if the sun rose at her arrival, and when she smiled back, you could see the love between them. Next to Dahlmar stood Anton, Dahlmar's old confessor, and beside him, Feliks. Both clergymen wore full regalia, their robes glittering with elaborate embroidery and sparkling gold thread.

"Awwww," Lars cooed in Olga's voice as our carriage pulled to a stop behind Adriana's. "Isn't that sweet?"

Natasha looked at him, blinked, shook her head, and looked away, obviously disconcerted. I couldn't say I blamed her. It was more than a little disturbing to me, and this wasn't the first time I'd worked with a spawn. I was worried about whether or not he'd be able to go into the church. Surely he'd have told someone if that was a problem? On the other hand, I really couldn't imagine the almighty being okay with a half-demon entering the cathedral.

"Showtime," Lars said as the footman opened the carriage door.

I watched as Gunnar Thorsen stepped up to Adriana's carriage. Holding her hand, he helped her down from the step stool the footman had provided, then began escorting her up the stairs to join her future husband.

I waited, as I'd been told, until the bride and her escort were ten steps ahead. Igor stepped up, his actions a perfect echo of Gunnar's, and the two of us began to make stately progress up the steps. Ten steps behind us were Lars and Dahlmar's brother, Prince Arkady. Natasha and Sergei took their first steps just as Gunnar and Adriana reached the top.

On cue, the entire group turned and waved. The crowd went wild.

Gunnar stepped aside as Adriana took Dahlmar's arm. The cathedral doors opened of their own accord, thanks to a little magic. We entered the cathedral in pairs. As Natasha and her escort crossed the threshold, the doors swung closed behind them, muffling the crowd noise; a moment later, the privacy spells clicked into place, cutting the sound off completely as the church became isolated.

Dahlmar and Adriana had chosen to keep the betrothal portion of the ceremony small and private. Even Queen Lopaka wasn't present; she was seated in the nave, in the front pew. That might have seemed odd to outsiders, but in her eyes, her daughter was already married. The ceremony on Serenity had been the one that mattered to the queen.

It took a moment for my eyes to adjust to the dim lighting, but it was a pleasure to be inside the church vestibule and out of the burning sunlight.

I'd seen photos of the church but they hadn't done it justice. White marble walls soared nearly forty feet upward, the silver-veined stone elaborately sculpted where it framed huge stained-glass windows. The glass depicted the patriarchs of the church, each with their right hands raised in blessing, each image laden with symbols. Sunlight streamed through the windows, painting rainbow patterns on the polished black marble floor.

Once we moved into the main chapel, the eyes of the world would be on us. But not now. For the moment we were a small, quiet group of friends and family in a peaceful, intimate, and beautiful setting. I glanced around, taking it all in at the same time as I automatically checked for threats.

To my right, on the wall opposite where the ceremony was to take place, was a long stand filled with candleholders of bright red glass. Each burning votive represented a petition being placed before God.

Dahlmar and Adriana moved to take their place on a matched pair of wooden kneelers, elaborately carved and stained black, polished to shine as brightly as the floor. Each had an embroidered and tassled cushion to kneel on and a crown resting atop. They faced a cross carved directly into the wall; its exquisite detail mimicked the stones set into the cross Adriana wore around her neck.

Anton, the aged priest who had served as Dahlmar's confessor from childhood, shuffled slowly into the space between the kneelers. He had asked to give a blessing to the pair before the official ceremony began, and King Dahlmar had gladly agreed. No one suspected anything was wrong when Anton raised his right hand and began murmuring softly. I certainly didn't—until I felt the swirl of powerful magic building and caught a glimpse of a spell ball clutched in his hand.

"No!" I shouted, lunging toward him. Time seemed to slow. I saw a blur of motion out of the corner of my eye and Arkady body-checked me, slamming me to the floor and knocking the wind from my lungs. My head banged against the marble and I saw stars. I tried to draw my gun, but Arkady grabbed my arm, forcing it away until he pinned both of my wrists to the floor with more strength than any mere human could manage. I'm not human anymore and I still couldn't break his grip. I shouted in rage, calling for help until Arkady began to strangle me.

Lars, still the image of Olga, moved to help me, but Sergei intercepted "her," apparently intending to protect her from the violence. His mistake. Lars flung the other man aside as if he were made of feathers. Igor grabbed Arkady, probably intending to do the same to him. But the prince felled Igor with a single blow. Still, in the moment it took him to do that, Lars was upon him. Evenly matched, the two began fighting in earnest, moving away from me. I rolled to my knees as I drew a weapon, knowing even as I aimed that I was too late. Dahlmar and Igor were both in motion, but everyone was moving so slowly. . . .

With a triumphant cry, Anton prepared to throw the spell ball onto the floor to break it.

He hadn't counted on Adriana. No one had. Despite all the turmoil around her, she had remained calm. She had pulled my derringer from the holster at her ankle; now, even as Anton laughed, she flicked off the safety and fired.

She hadn't taken time to aim and she was unfamiliar with the gun, but the bullet hit the old priest squarely in the center of his mass. Anton shrieked in agony as blood blossomed like a hideous flower in the middle of his torso, spreading in a rapid stain over the white and gold of his ceremonial robes.

It was a shot that would kill, but not instantly. With the last vestiges of his strength, the old man tried to fling the spell ball to the floor. Dahlmar grabbed his arm, wrenching the little ball from his hand. Anton fell, dying, onto the cold marble floor that was already slick with his blood.

I turned away. That part of the fight was over. Drawing a One Shot from its slot in my jacket, I watched Lars and Arkady's struggle and waited for my chance. When I saw an opening, I aimed a stream of holy water directly at Arkady's face.

He shrieked in shock, pain, and rage, the illusion magic of a demon spawn ripped away by the impact of holy water.

Lars was splashed as well and his true form suddenly shredded Olga's bridesmaid's dress.

Dropping the One Shot, I drew my Colt. From the corner of my eye I saw Igor draw a weapon from beneath his jacket. Adriana was also taking aim with my derringer. A tiny part of my mind was free to be amused, imagining the picture we made. "Freeze or die."

They froze. With my mind I sought, and found, John Creede's thoughts, not far away. *John, it's Celia. Is Prince Arkady with you? I've got a spawn here in the church.*

He sounded surprised at the clarity of my mental voice and confused, like I should know what was going on. *Sure, he's here. He suggested using an imposter, said he didn't trust security with so many people in the church. He told me he was going to tell you and the other bodyguards.*

Yeah, right. His spawn just attacked me as part of an attempt on Dahlmar and Adriana. The scene is secure but the bride and groom will need to clean up a little before the public ceremony.

The language Creede used in my mind wasn't polite, but it was certainly colorful. The real Arkady was going to have some explaining to do. *Are you all right?*

It hurt to swallow and my head was swimming a bit, but by God I was alive, so I wasn't about to complain. *I will be. Don't let Arkady go anywhere, okay? I want to have a little chat with him, and I know King Dahlmar will, too.*

John's voice in my head was filled with dangerous outrage. *Don't worry. He'll be right here.*

While I'd been talking with John, Natasha's father had moved away from where he had been shielding her with his body. Feliks knelt beside his fellow priest and began muttering prayers in Ruslandic. I realized that some of the pounding in my head was pounding on the church doors; Lars opened one just wide enough to admit Gunnar Thorsen. Igor smiled at me as the door opened and said, "No one outside will see anything."

Igor bound the fake Arkady, using fetters handed to him by Thorsen, though where Gunnar been carrying them inside his well-fitted suit, I had no idea.

Dahlmar and Adriana simply stood, holding each other, as Natasha and a red-faced, embarrassed Sergei looked on. Now what? We had a captive, a corpse, and the world waiting for a wedding. If the public found out what had happened, there'd be outrage at the violation of the sanctity of the church. We had a few minutes, at best, to figure out some way to salvage this debacle. I thought furiously, trying to come up with some sort of solution.

King Dahlmar's face was lined with worry, probably for his rotten brother. I could at least reassure him about that. "Your brother is fine. He's with John Creede. John will keep him safe and close by so we can question him and see if he's involved." Honestly, I was thinking he was. He was Olga's father and she'd been in this up to her eyeballs. Yes, she could've done it without him. But putting a spawn in his place without advising the king looked awfully fishy, and not just to me. I could tell from Igor's expression that he was looking forward to spending some quality time with the prince.

Dahlmar's reaction, however, was relief so pure that his body sagged with it. He loved his family. A lot of them hadn't deserved it, but he loved them. I felt his pain.

"What do we do about the wedding?" Natasha asked. "It must proceed . . . but this—" She gestured at the mess we'd made of the vestibule.

She had a point. Suddenly I remembered Adriana's vision. This was the room. Now was the time.

"Adriana, Dahlmar, kneel back down on the kneelers."

They looked at me as if I were insane. And not just for breaking protocol by not using the king's title.

"Please?"

"What are you thinking, cousin?" Adriana asked suspiciously.

"This is the place we saw in your vision in the mirror. If that vision was accurate, there's a secret room somewhere close at hand. We can hide the evidence until after you're safely married."

She gave me a doubtful look before meeting Dahlmar's eyes. Face set with grim determination, he strode back to the kneeler and took his place. Seconds later, she joined him. She took a breath and her eyes unfocused for a moment; I guessed she was recalling the details of the vision. Then, as she had in that vision, Adriana reached out to press the small protuberance at the base of the kneeler.

With the grinding of stone upon stone, a door appeared in the far wall, behind the display of votive candles.

Everyone turned to stare at me in wide-eyed wonder. Even Igor looked impressed. Wow. Alrighty then. Trying not to act too startled that my shot in the dark had worked, I poked my head into the secret room. "Gunnar," Adriana ordered, "go with her. Let nothing harm her."

I waited for Thorsen to join me and we went through the door, which was marked with an ornate cross that matched the one Adriana wore.

It was a small room, not much larger than a walk-in closet. The walls were the same white marble of the church foyer; three of them were lined with shelves. At the sight of what rested on those shelves, all I could think was *whoa*.

"Impressive," Thorsen whispered. Whispering seemed proper, for the shelves were filled with treasures. There were paintings, many wrapped in cloth, others left bare; jewel boxes and caskets; crowns; gold and silver altar implements— all crowded together without any kind of order.

Dahlmar started to rise, and I heard the faint creak of stone. "Um, please don't. I don't want to get trapped in here."

He growled in frustration but didn't move. "I want to see!"

Remembering my quick history lessons about Rusland, I answered, "It's the missing state treasures, Your Highness. The ones that disappeared during the war. I'm guessing that all of them are here."

We stepped back out of the room. The minute we did, King Dahlmar rose. Smooth as silk, the cross slid back into place, concealing the door so perfectly I would never have guessed there was anything unusual about the wall. The craftsmanship was amazing. So was the concealing magic.

As a paranormal creature, I can usually sense all kinds of magic, but I'd never have twigged onto this. Wow. Just, wow.

From the look on his face, King Dahlmar was about to order someone to kneel so he could get a look inside the closet. Before he could say anything, though, I spoke up.

"Okay," I said briskly. "I suggest we put the corpse and Arkad . . . whoever the spawn is, in the room until after the wedding. Um, Lars . . . would you mind watching over them? We can't risk him getting away."

Lars gave a brisk nod of agreement. With Thorsen present, I really wasn't sure who was in charge, but everybody was still looking at me, so I kept talking, making up a plan as I went along. I said to Feliks, "If you will go ahead with the betrothal, I'll use some of the cloths they wrapped the paintings in to clean up the mess as best I can."

I took a good look at the bride and groom and realized that they'd both been spattered with blood when Adriana had shot Anton. On Dahlmar, it was mostly invisible—in a few spots the glitter of his medals was dimmed—but on Adriana's lovely gown even a tiny scattering of red seemed screamingly bright and obvious. "Oh, there's blood on Adriana's dress. . . ."

"I have a beauty enhancement charm left," Natasha said.

I blinked at her somewhat stupidly. She was gorgeous, why on earth would she need—

Sensing my confusion, she explained as she rummaged in the hidden pocket of her jacket. "You are both sirens. I am not. I thought I might need some help in such company."

Sergei shook his head, his dark eyes bright. "You are perfect as you are, Princess. Then again, you always are."

I raised an eyebrow at that one, but it certainly made a favorable impression on Natasha, judging by her blush. Then again, maybe he'd known her for years and was just now speaking up. How would I know?

"Thank you, Sergei." Natasha shot him a smile as she handed the charm disk to Adriana, who wasted no time cracking it open. Immediately the stains on her wedding dress disappeared, as did the small wrinkles from where she had been kneeling. The lines of strain around her eyes disappeared as well. She looked *perfect*. It might be an illusion, but it was a damned good one.

What is taking so long, niece? Queen Lopaka's imperious voice intruded on my thoughts. Normally she's gentle, but now she was worried and irritated.

We've had a bit of a . . . complication. Everything is fine. But we need another minute or two, and Arkady and Olga won't be attending.

There was a pause but then she answered smoothly. *I will warn the musical director. You are sure Adriana is all right? Her voice in my head is very faint.*

I looked at my hand. No wonder the queen had been able to reach me through the privacy shields. *She gave me her ring.*

Oh. The queen's mental voice didn't sound any too pleased about that. I hoped I hadn't gotten Adriana in trouble with her mother. But I didn't have time to worry about that now. As she'd so aptly pointed out, we were running late.

"Let's go, folks. The queen just told me the natives are getting restless."

King Dahlmar and Adriana knelt. The priest crowned them, wrapped their hands together with ribbon, and spoke his part very quickly before unwrapping their hands and moving out of the way.

Adriana hit the secret button again. When the door appeared, Lars and Thorsen dragged Anton's corpse and the struggling spawn into the secret room.

Sergei, Natasha, and I set to work grabbing rags and cleaning blood from the foyer floor and furnishings.

The results weren't perfect, but when we threw the bloodied rags into the treasure closet and closed the entrance, I looked around carefully. If you hadn't known what had happened, you probably wouldn't notice, particularly with the crowds of people that would be soon passing through.

"It will do," Adriana assured me. "Now, everyone take your places."

Igor came up beside me, taking my arm. "Do I look okay?" I asked.

"You look lovely," he assured me. "No blood anywhere."

"Oh good."

35

The rest of the ceremony went off without a hitch. Of course there were questions raised about where Olga and Arkady had gone, but Igor lied beautifully, telling everyone that the prince and his daughter had insisted on standing guard over the newly discovered treasures. We'd actually left Gunnar Thorsen outside the secret room; Igor had cast an illusion on him to make him look like Prince Arkady.

It seemed like a thin excuse to me; after all, the treasures had been safely hidden for many years without anyone guarding them. But if anyone doubted Igor, they didn't say anything. Probably because there were too many other things going on.

It was finally done. King Dahlmar and Queen Adriana were now fully wed in the eyes of the church and by the laws of both of their countries. I was out of a job and I couldn't have been more elated.

Dahlmar and Adriana had left the reception early. By the smiles of some of the guests as the newlyweds departed, people thought they were getting an early start on their honeymoon, but I knew they were going to take care of questioning Arkady and to finish tidying up what had happened earlier. I expected Thorsen, Igor, and Creede's people had already cleaned out the treasure closet and conveyed the hidden riches, the corpse, and the prisoner to their appropriate destinations. I wasn't in the loop anymore and, God help me, I didn't want to be.

I was done to the point of being crispy. I'd put on a good show during the church service and danced a couple of dances at the party, and I was more than ready to go back to my room, take the pretty pink pills Dr. Shablinski had given me, and try to sleep.

"You look like you need a drink, and you're walking like your feet hurt," Bruno observed as he led me off the dance floor.

"I do and they do."

"Then sit. I'll be right back."

It sounded like such a wonderful idea I did just that. Hoping no one would notice, I reached down to slip off my offending footwear. The relief was immediate and intense enough that I closed my eyes and gave a deep, pleasurable sigh. A soft cough, and I opened my eyes to find Queen Lopaka and Gunnar Thorsen had joined me. Lopaka sank gracefully into the seat across from me. Gunnar stood over her protectively, making sure we could speak without interruption.

"I wanted to thank you in person," the queen said, speaking softly enough that no one passing by could hear. I was honored by the fact that she spoke aloud, knowing that I preferred audible speech to voices in my head. Adriana's gift to me hadn't changed that—yet.

"It was my pleasure." I smiled at her.

"I appreciate it more than you can know. My prophet tells me that Adriana and Dahlmar will be very happy and that he will live a long and prosperous life; when he dies, he will know that their grown son will safely ascend to the throne." She smiled. "I am looking forward to being a grandmother, and I am delighted to see my daughter so joyful."

"So am I."

"Tell me, what can I do to repay you? Surely there is something."

I thought about it for a moment. What did I want from the queen of the sirens?

The answer came to me. Something had been bothering me, nagging at the back of my mind since the interrogation of the man who'd tried to kidnap my grandmother. I was, at least in part, responsible for the hatred that had caused the Guardians of the Faith to be formed. My actions had been a catalyst. I couldn't change the past. But I might be able to make amends for my part of what had happened. I at least needed to try.

"I need to know something."

"Yes?"

"When a mind is broken by siren power, can it be fixed? Can they ever be normal again?"

The light left Lopaka's face. I felt her mind focus on mine. *Why do you ask this, niece?*

Oh, she was not happy. She didn't want to show it, not in the middle of the reception, so she'd switched to mental speech. I felt bad. This was a party, a celebration, and I was ruining it for her. *Never mind. I'm sorry. This isn't the time. We can talk about it later.*

No. Something is weighing on your mind and conscience. I want to help you with this burden if I can. Tell me.

So I did, mind to mind. I told her how my battle with Eirene had destroyed the minds of the men we were fighting over, turning them into drooling idiots. I confessed that I'd been too ashamed, too afraid, to check on them, and that my actions and Eirene's had been part of the root cause of the terrorist movement against the sirens.

I felt tears burn at my eyes as I confessed to her. *I didn't mean to harm those men. I want to fix it, to help them if I can. But I don't know how. I don't even know if it is possible.*

She let out a slow breath and looked around the room as if seeking an answer. *Celia, there were good reasons why we sirens retreated to our islands. It wasn't just to protect ourselves. We were protecting humanity as well. Our powers can be very terrible. It is a great burden to try to use them wisely.*

I was afraid of that. *But if I could find those men, is there anything I can do for them?*

I do not know. But if you wish it, we can try.

I do. Very much.

Then we will speak of this again. In a few weeks, after you've had a chance to recover.

Thank you.

You're very welcome. She smiled. *I see the mage DeLuca*

coming with your drinks. I believe I'll leave you to his tender care.

Bruno was coming all right, and he wasn't alone. Sergei and Natasha were behind him, holding hands. Gilda and Isaac Levy, along with Lars, brought up the rear of the little procession. Bruno toted a pitcher filled with what looked suspiciously like margaritas, and the rest were carrying plates of food, some of which it appeared they'd imposed on the kitchen to run through a blender.

Adriana's ring pulsed on my finger and I knew without being told that they were all coming to cheer me up and to distract me from my troubles. It was very nice of them and I was sure they'd be terribly disappointed if it didn't work.

Well, I couldn't let that happen.

So I drank . . . a little. I had liquified roast and vegetables. Later, Lars even enticed me out onto the dance floor.

Tomorrow I'd have to face my problems. But that was tomorrow. Tonight I let my friends help me relax and live in the moment, and if it wasn't perfect, it was still pretty damned good.